UNDER AN INDIGO MOON

A HOLCOMB SPRINGS SMALL TOWN ROMANTIC SUSPENSE BOOK 2

JL CROSSWHITE

Tandem Services Press
SOUTHERN CALIFORNIA

PRAISE FOR JL CROSSWHITE

"This is a very suspenseful story and I'm looking forward to the next book in this series."—Ginny, Amazon reviewer

"I was impressed with the suspense in this book as well as the romance. Great storyline. Morality issues were great. An overall great read."—Kindle customer

"Absolutely loved it. Fast paced and kept me guessing concerning the outcome. I highly recommend it to all who like a good mystery or suspense."—Linda Reville

"Very well written, with interwoven stories and well developed characters"—Mary L. Sarrault

OTHER BOOKS BY JL CROSSWHITE

Hometown Heroes series
Promise Me, prequel novella
Protective Custody, book 1
Flash Point, book 2
Special Assignment, book 3

In the Shadow series
Off the Map, book 1
Out of Range, book 2
Over Her Head, book 3

The Route Home series, writing as Jennifer Crosswhite
Be Mine, prequel novella
Coming Home, book 1
The Road Home, book 2
Finally Home, book 3

Contemporary romance, writing as Jennifer Crosswhite
The Inn at Cherry Blossom Lane

Eat the Elephant: How to Write (and Finish!) Your Book One Bite at a Time, writing as Jen Crosswhite

Devotional, writing as Jennifer Crosswhite
Worthy to Write: Blank pages tying your stomach in knots? 30 prayers to tackle that fear!

© 2022 by JL Crosswhite

Published by Tandem Services Press

Post Office Box 220

Yucaipa, California

www.TandemServicesInk.com

Ebook ISBN 978-1-954986-05-3

Print ISBN 978-1-954986-06-0

Library of Congress Control Number: 2022923119

Scripture quotations are from the New International Version. THE HOLY BIBLE, NEW INTERNATIONAL VERSION®, NIV® Copyright © 1973, 1978, 1984, 2011 by Biblica, Inc.® Used by permission. All rights reserved worldwide.

This book is a work of fiction. Names, characters, places, and incidents are either products of the author's imagination or used fictitiously. Any similarity to actual people, organizations, and/ or events is purely coincidental.

Cover design credit: Alexander von Ness of Nessgraphica

To all parents of special needs children

When I consider your heavens,
  the work of your fingers,
the moon and the stars,
  which you have set in place,
what is mankind that you are mindful of them,
  human beings that you care for them?

Psalm 8:3-4 (NIV)

PROLOGUE

FOUR YEARS EARLIER

After tonight, everything would change. Kayla glanced at the astronomy fans clustered around their telescopes. If she ever came back to one of these star-gazing events, it would be different. She would be different. Kayla loved how close the stars seemed this high up in the mountains—especially tonight when the moon faded for the lunar eclipse. There was a great sense of peace that wrapped around her when she viewed the stars.

Which was probably why she joined the Holcomb Springs High School astronomy club. Tonight was a lunar eclipse. Last month was national Astronomy Day and a great opportunity to view Saturn. There was always something to see in the night sky. But this was the last time their club would meet before graduation.

Their astronomy teacher and club sponsor, Mr. Lancaster, had them all gather in the parking lot of the marina. The over six-thousand-foot elevation reduced atmospheric distortion and made for great viewing. The lake gave them a wider vista of the night sky.

The beauty of it made her shiver, and she shrugged deeper into her coat as the moon grew full again.

Tyler nudged her shoulder, his aftershave a little too overpowering. "Why aren't you wearing my letterman jacket? It'd keep you warm." His voice turned low and for her ears only. "Unless you had something else in mind?"

She stepped away at his chuckle. This had to end. Tonight.

Her best friend, Madison, and Anthony wandered over. "Let's get outta here. The eclipse is mostly over. We can head to the Delamar Place. My dad said someone was interested in buying it, asked him for a quote to rehab it. So this might be our last chance."

"We'd better make sure to take any of our stuff with us," Madison said, reaching for Anthony's hand.

After they'd checked in with Mr. Lancaster and completed their observations, they were free to go. It was time. She gave the stars one last look, taking comfort in the fact they'd look the same in Chicago, where she was headed to college in the fall.

"Ride with me," Tyler said. "We can get your car later."

"Uh, no thanks." She slipped away and hurried into her car. Tyler's letterman jacket sat on the passenger seat. She steered her car through the dark mountain roads, ones she knew by heart, until she turned onto Gold Mine Street. She shut her lights off as she glided to the side of the road. She wasn't pulling around to the side of the house. She wouldn't be long and didn't want to be trapped.

Anthony's car and flickering lights from the windows told her Madison and Anthony were already here. There was another car she didn't recognize, an older Ford Escape. Maybe someone was borrowing their parent's car. Tyler would be along soon.

She snatched his jacket from the passenger seat, pocketed her keys, and using her phone flashlight, headed around to the back of the house where the rear porch door had been jimmied open a long time ago. Through the mudroom and then the kitchen, she wandered through the house. One last time.

It was a beautiful Victorian. She hoped whoever bought it would see the beauty and bring it back to its former glory. She trailed her fingers along the carved newel post and, avoiding Madison and Anthony in the parlor, headed upstairs for a final look around. Broken furniture and a few extra doors and stair railings littered the various rooms, like someone had started a rehab and had given up. But she could picture what it would look like fully restored.

She peered out one of the bedroom windows, the one with the view of the lake. The eclipsed moon tonight made for a good observation of stars, but the lake was just an inky-black spot beyond the trees. She unhooked Tyler's class ring from where it hung on a chain around her neck.

A hand landed on her shoulder, and she jerked, spinning, her phone light skittering around the room. The ring clinked across the floor.

Tyler. Of course. He carried a pillar candle; their shadows danced across the cracked plaster walls.

He grinned and set the candle on the wide windowsill. "Nice of you to find a spot up here away from the others." He touched his jacket still in her grip. "How come you're not wearing this?"

She dropped her gaze, willing him to be understanding. "Tyler, we're graduating, going to separate colleges across the country from each other. I think it's best if we end things now so we can enjoy the rest of our senior year without sadness hanging over us." She shone her light on the floor, searching for the ring.

His face darkened. "What? You can't be serious? We've been together our whole senior year. You can't leave me now. I know you don't want that." He pulled her roughly to him, planting hard kisses along her neck.

"Stop." She struggled to break free, dropping his jacket. She pushed at him, but he didn't relent.

He knocked her hand away, loosening her hold on her phone, which clattered to the wooden floorboards. "Come on.

You brought us up here alone for a reason. You want this." He grabbed at the front of her shirt through her open jacket.

She pulled away, the *tink* of buttons hitting the floor as they gave way under his unrelenting grasp. "I just wanted to give us privacy for our talk, to not embarrass you." She spun, but he grabbed her jacket, pulling her back.

"You've been holding out on me all year. Now I'm going to get what I deserve." He reached for the waistband of her jeans.

Panic surged through her. He was too big and strong for her. Yelling would probably only bring laughter from the other house occupants. She spotted a broken spindle on the ground. She gave a lunge, and her fingers closed around it as he yanked at her pants, pulling her to him.

She swung and connected with the side of his head. Immediately she fell back. But she was free.

"Ow! What'd you do that for?"

Kayla scrambled to get her feet under her, plucking up her phone from where it had fallen. She flew out of the room, down the hall, and finally reached the stairs.

Heavy footsteps pounded after her. "Where are you going? You can't do this!"

As she headed down the stairs, Eli passed her going up. She hadn't known he was here. Maybe he'd calm Tyler down and distract him from coming after her.

In the downstairs parlor, Madison called after her. Anthony laughed, said something. There was cussing and a heavy clattering upstairs, but she wasn't waiting around to find out what Tyler was doing. She ran through the kitchen and out the back, not stopping until she was in her car and driving toward home.

Toward safety.

CHAPTER
ONE

The metal key warmed in Carissa Carver's hand, the teeth cutting into her palm as she cradled it. Odd how the future could be held in such a small item.

The real estate agent and notary public had left the Sleepy Bear Lodge's one meeting room. Leaving her alone with the folder holding the paperwork, proof that she'd mortgaged—or as the French said, pledged until death—her future. She shot up a prayer, again, hoping that she was doing the right thing.

It wasn't a huge lodge, but it had a pool and a small day spa. According to Yelp reviews, it was the best in the area. The *area* vaguely included their new town in Wildernessville, California. Real name, Holcomb Springs. But it could have been the other side of the moon as foreign as it felt to them being from Arizona.

She gathered her sons—Brandon and Jayden—from their room, dropping the packet of paperwork on the room's desk but hanging on to the key, and ushered them toward the pool. She'd gotten a massage at the spa earlier. It was a treat after two days on the road, to celebrate this new stage of their lives.

She, Carissa Carver, *was* an architect, and now she was doing something risky. Her friends and family didn't equate her with risky. They didn't expect her to pull up her roots and move four hundred miles away either. Then again, she didn't expect her husband to, well, never mind. A lot of *nevers* became *had tos.*

The boys ran on ahead, down the hall to the indoor pool. The tang of chlorine and dampness made her eyes sting. The boys plunged in without hesitation, their laughter echoing.

Squeezing her hand into a fist—the metal pinching her skin —she lifted it to her nose. The smell of cucumber lotion on her hand merged with the metal, creating a new scent: their future. She had just bought a house. Sight unseen. Well, almost. She'd been on a video tour. It had a new roof, a remodeled kitchen, and new appliances.

She shoved the key into her pocket and lowered herself into a pool chair.

Brandon and Jayden splashed with abandon, shedding days of confinement in a moving truck cab. Waves sloshed over the curled concrete edge; wet footsteps dotted the deck.

"Watch, Mom, watch me!" Six-year-old Jayden scrambled over the pool's edge, the water tugging his too-big swim trunks back over his small hips while he grabbed at them. With a burst, he was out of the pool, tucked in a ball, and hurling back into the water.

Brandon whooped as his brother surfaced and then waded in her direction. At ten, he shouldn't have dark rings under his eyes. The responsibility of having a little brother on the autism spectrum was aging him too quickly. Jayden had no sense of danger; it fell to Brandon to be Carissa's extra set of eyes. "Wait. Did we get the house?" He swiped water from his face.

She reached into her pocket and showed him the key.

"Cool! Let's go see it!" He hauled himself out of the water. "Come on, Jayden. We're going to go see our house."

"Hang on." She touched his clammy shoulder. "We need to get dinner, and it's going to be dark soon. We'll look at it tomorrow."

Brandon's shoulders seemed to fall to his hips.

Jayden ran up, arms clutched to his chest, jumping up and down. She gave him a straight arm like the Heisman football trophy to keep him from throwing his wet body on her. She was in jeans and a stretchy cotton tee. No more business casual for her, but she didn't want to go for the wet T-shirt look either. Satisfied he would stay if she removed her hand, she took three steps back to the towel rack and grabbed two fluffy bits of terry cloth and tossed them to her boys.

The look on Brandon's face hurt. So many disappointments, this didn't have to be one. "Dry off and change, and we'll go."

Deputy Sergeant Jonas McCann lifted his radio to respond to the dispatcher's call about a suspicious person at the Sleepy Bear Lodge. He suppressed a groan. "Who called it in?"

"Selena."

His shoulders relaxed. Not Mariah. Good. Mariah was using every opportunity to put herself in Jonas's path and hadn't taken any of his hints that he wasn't interested in her. Or any woman. He never would be. He'd had his one great love and lost her. He told the dispatcher his ETA and in a few minutes wheeled his department SUV under the porte cochere of the Sleepy Bear Lodge and headed inside.

Selena was indeed at the desk. "Hi, Deputy." The high schooler worked here and as a hostess at Bella Sorgenti and still managed to be active in school activities. The advantage of living and working in a small town was he knew the locals well. She glanced off to the side, back toward the office, biting her lip.

"Where's the suspicious person?"

"Um…"

Mariah appeared out of the back, swinging her long, dark hair over her shoulder and smiling. She was in her early thirties and positioned herself as a savvy businesswoman, though she only owned this small lodge. "Jonas! Thank you for coming so quickly. I always feel safe knowing you're keeping our town secure."

He did not have time for this. "Did you see a suspicious person?"

She came around the desk. "There was this man in the parking lot I didn't recognize. I don't see him now. But I'd feel better if you had a look around."

He was a professional, so he bit back what he wanted to say. "You run a lodge in a tourist town. There are going to be a lot of people you don't recognize."

She gave him a bright smile as she sidled up next to him. "Let's look around."

The public lobby didn't take more than a cursory glance to see no one occupied its rustic, oversized leather furniture or sat in front of the two-story stone fireplace. He strode down the hall, passing the vending machine alcove and laundry room. The spa area and pool were next. Through the glass door to the pool, he spotted a woman and two school-aged boys.

He peered in, the sharp bite of chlorine wafting around him. The woman was tall with dark-blonde hair. Her back was to him as she helped the younger boy dry off. Memories of summers spent splashing in the pool with his brother, Jon, flooded him. The best times were when Dad came in after work and joined them via a giant cannonball that washed out half the water.

Frozen in time, he let the long-forgotten memories spill over him until the older boy spotted him, tapping his mom's side, and pointed.

Mom turned and frowned a moment before giving him a tight smile then turned back to the boys.

"Everything okay?" Mariah stood just behind him, her perfume fighting with the chlorine for dominance.

He'd forgotten she was there. Time to get this over with. "Do you want me to look in the spa area? I don't want to disturb anything you might have going on." The idea of walking in on a massage or facial wasn't one he wanted to contemplate if he didn't have to. He couldn't imagine anyone lurking back there unnoticed. If there even was a lurker—which there wasn't. He headed back down the hall.

She shook her head. "No, we don't have any clients, and it's closed for the day." She reached for the knob as they came to the door. "Locked. Just as it should be. Perhaps just a look around outside?" Her questioning tone was much less certain than it had been in the lobby. She used her card to swipe them out the service entrance.

One lap around the building proved that this had been a useless trip. "Mariah, you remember the fable about the boy who cried wolf?"

She at least had the grace to look abashed. "I really did think I saw something. I'll be more certain next time."

He gave a stiff nod and headed to his SUV, memories of summers with his brother coming back. He hadn't seen Jon in a while. It had been too painful after the deaths of Autumn and Ava, his wife and daughter. Too hard to see Jon's happy family when his had been brutally taken from him by a drunk driver.

He glanced at his watch. He usually liked working the three-to-eleven shift, but it made it inconvenient at times to get in touch with friends and family.

Climbing into the SUV, he pushed the painful memories away. He would call Jon. Soon.

THE GPS WAS USELESS. HER iPHONE'S SERVICE CUT IN AND out, leaving the device guessing as to their true location. She finally figured out—the old-fashioned way by looking at the addresses she could see—she needed to be going in the opposite direction. By the light of the moon, she squinted at the infrequent reflective numbers on the side of the road. They seemed to be getting closer. Old sturdy trees grew over the road, and she slowed, peering through gaps in branches and leaves.

A bit of moonlight peaked through thick pine boughs to shine on a small section of white picket fence. She stopped the moving truck that had been their home on wheels for the last two days and contained all their earthly goods. The house sign was missing a number, but the ones there matched her paperwork.

This was their new home. On Gold Mine Street. She hoped it was one.

"Look boys! A picket fence!" She'd always wanted one, but they weren't much in vogue in southwest-inspired Arizona where rocks took the place of grass. Not much grass here either. Instead, a layer of pine needles coated the ground between the bushes.

"Cool! A fortress for my Lego mini-figs," Jayden commented.

Carissa was pretty sure that meant it was a good thing.

She turned as Brandon leaned over Jayden in an attempt to get a clearer look. "That'll keep the ball from rolling into the street when we play catch. Sweet."

Okay, this was good. The boys seemed happy with her choice.

Black lumps squatted around the yard, but she'd expected the landscaping would need some trimming. She scrunched in her seat to maneuver her line of sight around the pine's arms to see the house. It was an old farmhouse-style, late Victorian, but it looked solid. She let her foot off the brake and inched forward. A glint of something from the backyard. The pond. If she could keep Jayden from drowning in it, the boys would love it.

It had taken her entire 401k to fund this next segment of life. A benefit from her very nice architectural firm in her very nice city with her very nice house. If she could rehab this place and sell it for enough money, she was hoping it would adequately provide for the kids and her while she figured out the other parts of the equation. Yeah, she'd have to pay the piper—

in this case the IRS—but what choice did she have? Life required money. This was the only gamble she'd ever made in her life, and she hoped it would pay off.

It just had to.

"Mom, look, there's sparks in the sky."

She smiled at Jayden's view of the stars. They were so much more visible up here in the mountains than they'd been in Arizona. No city lights.

Stars, a picket fence, and moonlight. All it needed was a porch swing. She envisioned her boys running around the backyard, laughing while she lounged in the porch swing set in motion with her toe, a cold glass of iced tea dripping down her hand.

For once, she'd made a good decision.

CHAPTER
TWO

Carissa rolled down the moving truck's windows and marveled at how many shades of green there were on these mountain roads. So different from the desert browns. The air smelled sweet with the tail end of spring. As she turned down their new street, she slowed, looking for the house.

Then she came to a dead stop.

This could not be the same house. No way. Like an aging movie star, bright sunlight was not kind to the old Victorian. Carissa double-checked the paperwork, but the house sign was still missing the same number, the picket fence and the oak were in the same place as last night. Without the moonlight, the paint on both the fence and the house peeled more than a redhead in Arizona.

She pulled into the cracked-concrete driveway—which was long enough to accommodate both the moving truck and the tow dolly pulling the Explorer—and got out. The boys made a beeline for the backyard.

"Not yet. Stick with me." She didn't want Jayden near that pond until she had a better idea of what was going on.

Pushing past the bushes arching over the pathway, she gingerly tested the front steps to the wide front porch. Seemed solid. She tried to spring up and down on the porch boards, but they didn't give. Whew. She felt a bit safer, though she expected the house to need work. This was supposed to be a rehab after all. She needed room for sweat equity.

Jayden thought she had started a game and jumped up and down the stairs, top to bottom. She hoped he didn't fall and scrape or break something. She had no idea where the nearest emergency room was.

At least he wore shoes. And clothes. As usual, his shirt was inside out and backwards. He hated tags and seams. Most of the time he considered clothing optional. Which was a problem for a six-year-old. Luckily, he liked his Lego pajama pants, so he could be convinced to change into those the minute he got home from school and stripped off his clothes.

Knocking away a few stray cobwebs, she slid the key into the door. It didn't turn. She used two hands—one to wiggle the key, one to jiggle the knob. The key finally moved, but she had to put her shoulder to the door to force it open. Her first purchases would be some WD-40 and a wood plane. If she could find the nearest hardware store.

The house was cool inside and a bit musty. The paint was yellowed, the floors stained and scratched, but they were solid hardwood. At least the windows—the ones she could see—were new, as advertised.

Footsteps bolted towards the stairs.

"Stay here." Carissa pulled her gaze from examining the room and to her boys poised on the bottom steps of the staircase.

"I wanna see upstairs." Jayden was bouncing up and down. "I wanna see my room."

"Not till I check it out."

He pulled Lego bricks out of his pocket and started zooming around the empty room, giggling at the echo his sound effects made.

Brandon folded his already-turning-spindly legs and plopped down with his Nintendo Switch.

Through the next doorway, she spotted the kitchen she recognized from the pictures, though not the grand scale it looked on the internet. New Corian countertops and new stainless-steel appliances. The laundry area was just past the kitchen in what looked to be a large mudroom. The floor under her Sketchers didn't seem quite as solid here as before. She shifted her weight. Yep, definitely a bit springy. But the stacked washer and dryer she'd salivated over were there. Cherry red and brand new.

And not hooked up. And no sign of any place to hook them up.

She dragged her fingers through her hair in frustration. She needed to check this whole place out so she could get the full picture of what she was getting into.

And so she could find the trouble spots before Jayden did.

Off the mudroom was a door to the back deck, which overlooked the small—algae-filled, she now noticed—pond and a huge old red maple. There was a nice sunny patch that would be great for a garden, which she wouldn't have time for since she'd be fixing up the house, and this time next year they wouldn't be there. She hoped. But maybe the boys would enjoy planting a few things they could watch grow and then eat.

As she headed down the deck stairs and made a note to fix the wobbly railing, she heard what sounded like a storm door slamming next door.

"George! You put that down right now. Mabel Mae left that out for her daughter-in-law. She don't want you to have it or she'd given it to you."

"I's just lookin' at it, Gladys. No harm in that."

Carissa rounded the edge of the deck, curious, and peered through the trees.

An older lady, apparently a neighbor, stood in her front yard talking to an older man. Gray hair pulled up in a bun, she had nice skin for an older woman. Which Carissa knew because Older Lady was wearing a tube top.

The older man looked like Grandpa Walton from that old TV show, his gray hair a bit too long and overalls about to fall off. He was rummaging around some trash cans and a pile of stuff stacked in front of the neighbor lady's house.

Carissa's movement must have caught the lady's eye. She turned and beckoned vigorously, the wings under her arms flapping like birds trying to take flight. "Well, hi, dear. You must be the new owner. I'm Gladys. Let me tell you something."

Carissa took a tentative step toward her new neighbors, not sure what she was getting in the middle of. "I'm Carissa. I have two boys, Brandon and Jayden." She gestured toward the house.

Gladys nodded then leaned closer. "Don't leave anything outside your fence you might want to keep. George here is a klepto." That last part was stage whispered as she pointed at the older man. "Welcome to the neighborhood."

Indeed.

George shuffled on down the road, pulling a two-wheeled cart behind him past Gladys's house and disappeared among the trees. Gladys gave Carissa a finger wave and headed inside a small cabin.

And here Carissa had thought the house's poor shape was the reason for the auction. Now she wondered if it might not have been its location. Somehow, she had managed to plunk her kids down near two odd neighbors, another example of her brilliant judgment. Why had she thought this small mountain town was going to be less crazy than down in Laguna Vista, California, where the rest of her family lived?

There was a three-day cooling-off period, wasn't there? She could get out of this deal and find something else while she still had time. Perhaps the escrow company hadn't cashed her check yet. The excuses sounded as weak as wet paper and as easy to poke holes through. But they'd gotten out of one bad set of circumstances, and she wanted the boys to have a chance to heal before they landed in another one. She had so hoped this place would be an answer to her prayers: close to the office that specialized in the therapy Jayden needed, and something that would be a good return on her money.

The back door barreled open, both boys piling out. She grabbed Jayden's shirt as he tried to jet past.

"Can we see the pond now?" Brandon asked, right behind Jayden.

She started to say no. She didn't want the boys getting attached to this place if there was any chance she could get out of it. But a big part of their trip out here was to make it seem like an adventure. They'd taken a very long way around to see things like the Grand Canyon, the London Bridge in Lake Havasu, the Palm Springs Tram, and the giant dinosaurs that lived off the I-10. Fun, quirky things that made America so great. She hoped that if her boys experienced their leaving Arizona as an adventure, it would be easier to put behind them the trauma they'd escaped.

So this house, and the pond, could be seen as just one more quirky stop on our adventure to ultimately finding home. If she ever discovered where that was.

"Go ahead, but be careful near the edge. It might be marshy or muddy."

A chorus of yays! greeted her decision. It must have been the right one. Only if all of them were that easy. "Brandon, watch your brother, please. Jayden, stay out of the water." Hands planted on hips, she was torn between joining the boys at the pond or pulling out her file of phone numbers to see what she could do about ridding herself of this money pit in Kookyville.

Jayden dipping his sneakered toe into the pond decided for her. She jogged toward the pond where the boys were picking up rocks and throwing them into the water. Staying clear of the splash zone, she peered into the algae-covered surface. A loaf-sized boulder or two resided on the leaf-coated bottom, which seemed to be only about eight to twelve inches away.

She felt the vibration through her feet first before she heard the pounding, then what sounded like air being chuffed through bellows. Looking for the source, she spotted a giant black dog tearing around the side yard—tongue hanging out, ears flapping —heading straight for them. Adrenaline made her movements jerky, as she wasn't sure if the dog was a threat she needed to respond to. She took a step forward as Brandon turned.

The dog didn't even slow, trying to leap into Brandon's arms. The problem was the dog probably weighed twice what Brandon did. He went down on his butt into the squishy mud. The dog pranced around licking Brandon's face.

"Are you okay?" She shoved the dog's muzzle away from her son, a little late at trying to protect him.

Brandon ignored her, pushing to a sitting position. "Hey, boy." He ruffled the dog's ears. "Wanna play fetch?" He turned to her. "Mom, he doesn't have a collar. Can we keep him?"

The dog sat, cocked his head, and aimed his melted-chocolate eyes at hers. Did that tongue ever go back in? She turned to check on Jayden, making sure in all the commotion he hadn't decided to wade in. He was squatting by the edge, balancing a Lego mini-figure on a leaf.

"I'm sure he belongs to someone. In small towns, people often let their dogs roam." Not a practice she approved of, but she was pretty sure her opinion wouldn't make anyone change their behavior.

Gladys came over to the fence and clutched the pickets. "I see you've met Charlie."

Carissa turned. "Is that his name? Who does he belong to? He seems friendly." How could she get this dog back to his owner?

"Well, I guess he's yours now. He comes with the house."

What? Dogs didn't just come with houses. After the revelations about klepto George, Carissa wasn't too sure about Gladys's perspective. "His owner used to live here?"

"I don't recall old Mason ever having a dog. Besides nobody's really lived in that house for about five years, and I suppose Charlie's just a couple years old. He's just always hung around your house there. Like I said, he comes with the house. Us neighbors, we feed him and such, make sure he has water, but he sticks around that house pretty close there."

So he was a stray. She should probably call the humane society, but that was one more thing on her ever-growing list. Right now, a home for her boys was a higher priority, not a stray dog. She turned from Gladys, trying to figure out what to do.

Jayden had left the edge of the pond and was on his knees burying his face in Charlie's ears. When he looked up, he was smiling.

Smiling. The word met the emotion in her heart.

Few things caused Jayden to smile. Even when he enjoyed things, his demeanor was stoic.

Brandon rescued a stick from the pond and tossed it. "Go get it, boy!"

Charlie took off after it but lost it in the bushes.

Jayden giggled.

Tears pressed up in her eyes. Looks like they'd found a dog.

And a home.

CHAPTER
THREE

Jonas strode into the community center, glad that it was warm enough to show up in basketball shorts and a T-shirt instead of having to change in the locker room first. He didn't have a ton of time before his shift, and he still needed to meet with his boss, Sheriff Shannon McIntyre. But he needed a quick game of basketball to throw off the dregs of tiredness that had been dogging him the last few days... Weeks, if he was honest.

The usual group of guys was already in the gym. Reese Vega, who would be busy soon between teaching at the community center on their new climbing wall and leading outdoor excursions as tourist season picked up, was talking with Marco Valdez, one of their local firefighter-paramedics and part of the search-and-rescue team.

Pastor Tony and Ryan, their church's worship leader, were tossing the ball around with Zach Lang, Sheriff McIntyre's son, who was out of school with the other seniors not required to take final exams if their grades were good enough. Graduation was Friday.

Jonas swallowed. He remembered Zach as a gangly freshman. And, as always, his mind did the calculations. Ava would have been entering high school in the fall. The loss of his daughter never failed to punch him in the gut.

He shook it off. "Hey, you guys want to play or just stand around and talk?"

Ryan passed the ball to him. "Bring it, old man."

"Old man?" Jonas caught it and dribbled. "I see how it is. Pastor, what say we show these guys—" he pointed at Ryan and Zach, who was laughing— "what a little experience can do?"

"I'm in. Reese, Marco, you two can pick sides. Young or old?"

Reese joined Jonas and Pastor Tony, while Marco chose Ryan and Zach. The game was fast-paced and mostly good natured. Jonas felt vindicated when the old guys won, twenty-one to twenty. He checked his watch. He had to hurry if he wanted to talk with the sheriff before his shift. He grabbed a towel out of his duffel bag and wiped his face as the good-natured ribbing and threats of a rematch reverberated through the gym. But the game had done its job. His blood was pumping, and he was ready to get to work.

He waved at the guys as he pushed through the gym doors and into the part of the town center that housed the public and safety services. A quick stop at the showers, and he was soon in his uniform and headed toward the sheriff's office.

Her admin and de facto bodyguard, Donna Littrel, sat at the desk outside the sheriff's office.

"Afternoon, Donna. Is the sheriff in?" Jonas glanced through the glass windows next to the door.

The sheriff spotted him and waved.

Donna nodded. "Go on in."

Jonas headed inside, closing the door behind him.

The sheriff motioned him to a seat. "You're early for your shift."

"I played basketball with the guys. Zach is becoming quite a force on the court."

She smiled at that. "It's going to be strange come fall when he heads off to college at UC Irvine."

"It's not too far from Laguna Vista. We both know plenty of people who can keep an eye on him. He'll be fine."

She nodded. "I know. But I can't help but worry, given what we see in this job."

Yeah. He knew that only all too well. "I wanted to see if you had an update on Beckett Lorde and to go over assignments for traffic control and security for graduation Friday."

There was nothing new on Lorde, which wasn't surprising. That man was made of Teflon. Nothing stuck to him—nothing they could prove. But their staff couldn't shake the feeling he was behind a number of unlawful happenings in the area, including illegal pot farms and possibly drug trafficking. The rest of their meeting was routine.

"Anything else?" The sheriff's gaze pinned him. They'd worked together too closely for too long for him to hide anything from her. He wouldn't have sought her out for a routine update.

He told her about the encounter with Mariah. "I can't help but feel her interest in me is more than professional. I was hoping—" His face heated. It was rare he couldn't keep his reactions under control. "With tourist season picking up, I won't have time to run over for nuisance calls. Maybe you could talk to her. You being a woman, she might take it better." He finished lamely. Why was this so difficult?

Shannon's gaze narrowed thoughtfully. "Perhaps Mariah's not the problem."

"What? I mean, what do you mean?" How could Mariah not be the problem?

She leaned back in her chair. "I can talk to her." She looked at him a moment. "I'm going to take off my boss hat right now and put on my friend hat."

Okay. What was this about?

"I've been thinking about this a lot in regard to my own life, so in some respects, I'm saying this as much to myself as to you. But when people like us have been hurt, we tend to withdraw. You lost your wife and daughter tragically. I've been a single mom for more years than I can count. It's very hard to open up and let other people in. They might let us down or hurt us. In a small town like this one, that could be awkward."

Jonas resisted the urge to frown. What was the sheriff getting at? He had seen a growing relationship between her and Pastor Tony. He wasn't sure how far it went beyond friendship, and it wasn't his place to ask. But what did this have to do with him?

She continued. "I'm not saying you should be interested in Mariah. Not at all." She gave a small shake of her head. "But I do think she treads on a sore spot with you. When Wally Cosgrove calls because a bear has knocked over his trash or Stan Marley complains about the raccoon in his attic, you gladly go help them, even though it's not your job."

Jonas opened his mouth to protest and then shut it again. She was right. Mariah was different.

A small smile crossed the sheriff's face. "All I'm saying is to be aware of those tender places and be open to seeing what God might have for you in the future." She put her hands on the desk. "Okay, friend hat off, sheriff hat back on. Have a good shift, and be safe out there."

He nodded and exited her office. At his desk, he grabbed his keys and noticed the framed picture of his wife and daughter. It was such a part of his cubicle, he hardly noticed it. But the sheriff's words rang in his head. He picked up the photo. Autumn had taken Ava to get her nails done for her birthday. At ten, he thought she was far too young for that, but what did he know? If it were up to him, his little girl would never grow up. In a twisted way, he'd gotten his wish. Their faces were squished together, smiles lighting them up. So happy. He'd gotten home late from work that night and left early the next morning, so he hadn't seen Ava's nails until the next day.

How many other moments of joy had he missed because of

his job? It was why he'd moved up here after their deaths. He needed a slower pace than Laguna Vista.

If the sheriff was right, perhaps he needed something else as well.

He put the frame down and headed out to his unit. He would swing by the Jitter Bug Too just before it closed. He needed a jolt of caffeine and something to go with it. After the calories he'd burned playing basketball, he could afford it.

The bell above the door jingled as he entered the coffee shop. Cassie Chang—the sheriff's sister and newly married to fellow deputy Brett Chang—smiled at him from behind the counter. "Hey, Jonas. There's one blueberry muffin left."

"I'll take it. Along with a large, black coffee."

"You got it."

As she moved around getting his order together, he scanned the space. Wally and Stan were long gone, their usual booth in the back empty. A group of high school seniors sat in another booth, likely enjoying the fact they didn't have to be in class on a school day. He lifted a hand, and they waved back. "You guys looking forward to Friday?"

A chorus of *oh, yeahs* answered him.

He grinned. "There's nothing like your high school graduation. You'll remember it forever."

The students gave him some nods and smiles. He always wanted to be seen as approachable to these kids as he saw them around town and in church. He wanted them to think about coming to him with a problem first.

Cassie handed him his order. "Be safe."

"Always." He pushed out the door with full hands.

Parked next to his unit was a silver Ford Explorer. A woman was peering in the driver's side while two elementary-aged boys stood next to her. "Brandon, go see if one of the other doors on the other side is unlocked." The woman tugged on the door handle while the older boy ran around to the other side.

"Nope. They're locked too."

"Ugh." She dug in her purse. "I hope I can get Triple A up here. I can't believe I did that."

Jonas set his coffee and muffin bag on the hood of his SUV and stepped over. "Can I help?"

She jumped and spun around. "Oh, sorry, Officer." She glanced at his uniform. "I mean, Deputy. I didn't see you come up. I locked my keys in my car. I can't believe it, but there they are, sitting on the seat." She sighed.

She was the blonde woman and boys from the Sleepy Bear Lodge pool. It wasn't unusual to help tourists with things like lockouts from their cars or rental units. He peered in the window. Yep, a set of keys sat on the car seat.

"I think I can help."

"Really? I was just going to call Triple A. I don't want to take you away from anything important."

He smiled. "As long as I get to drink my coffee while it's still hot, which doesn't always happen, I think I'll be fine."

She smiled back, a slow smile that looked a bit rusty and mostly polite. "We were headed into Bella Sorgenti for dinner. I must have had too many things on my mind and lost track of my keys."

Wrangling two boys on vacation couldn't be easy. The younger one kept hopping up and down off the running board and pulling on the door handle. The other one stood by the hood of the SUV watching everything.

"I've got tools in the back of my unit." He slid past her and popped the back of his SUV, which was almost the same model as hers.

She moved to the front of her car and put her hands on the older boy's shoulders.

"You guys want to see how this works?" Jonas motioned them over. "What are your names?"

The older one stepped over. "I'm Brandon, and that's my little brother Jayden." The younger one stopped bouncing on the running boards and stared up at him. A lot of kids were shy around him. He always tried to make them as comfortable as possible.

"I'm Jonas." He leaned down to Jayden in a low whisper. "What's Mom's name?"

Jayden just bounced up and down and pulled out a Lego guy from his pocket. His shirt was on backward.

The woman smiled again and took a small step forward. "I'm Carissa Carver. These are my sons."

Jonas took his tools and manipulated them in the window. Brandon peered over at him and took a step closer to see. Jayden was too busy running his Lego guy around the car. Jonas explained what he was doing, and soon the door popped open. "See? It's all about having the right tools." He reached inside, grabbed the keys off the seat, and handed them to her.

"Thank you so much. I really appreciate it."

"No problem. I just need to get some info from you for my report. ID?"

"Sure." She dug in her purse, pulled out a wallet and handed over her driver's license.

Arizona. The weather here was a lot more comfortable than there this time of year. He ran the info while she corralled the boys. Jayden was now bouncing on and off the curb. Oh to have that kind of energy.

He finished up and handed her back her ID. "Have a good rest of your day."

"You too. Thank you so much. Enjoy your coffee." She put a hand on each boy's shoulder and steered them to the door of Bella Sorgenti. Then she looked back and gave him one more smile before they disappeared inside.

He hoped the rest of his shift was as easy. After Memorial Day next week, tourist season would officially begin, and things would get busy. He grabbed his coffee and muffin and pulled onto Holcomb Springs Road.

The sheriff's words chased him all the way around his patrol route. She was wrong. Yes, Mariah irritated him because she was perfectly capable. Stan and Wally were older guys who needed a hand, though they didn't want to admit it. Just because the sheriff was thinking of a future relationship with Pastor Tony didn't mean he needed to. She was projecting in that annoying way people did when they had found happiness or success in some area and suddenly felt everyone around them needed it too. Like the latest multilevel marketing deal.

No thanks. Not for him. Even in a slower-paced department like Holcomb Springs, being a deputy was at odds with being a husband and father. He wouldn't want anyone else to suffer for his choices.

Not ever again.

CARISSA SLID INTO THE BOOTH AT BELLA SORGENTI AFTER Brandon and Jayden, finally letting out her breath. When they had pulled up in front of the restaurant, she was trying to keep Jayden from climbing across the console of the Explorer from the back seat. Which was likely how she lost track of her keys.

The town had been good to her so far. Who knew a deputy would be right there when she needed him? A good-looking one at that. Not that she'd really noticed. Men were so far down on her priority list that she'd likely never get around to them again. And that suited her just fine. While her boys were the most precious things in her life, their father had caused all of them a great deal of pain.

A waitress named Miranda came to take their pizza order, and Carissa let the boys each get a root beer. They had been good helpers today, and the pizza was their bribe. The cashier at the hardware store had mentioned that Bella Sorgenti had the best around.

Jayden got out his Lego men and started using the salt, pepper, and cheese shakers as props. Brandon played on his Nintendo Switch.

Carissa leaned back and rested against the booth. Yesterday she'd unhooked the Explorer from the moving truck dolly, and they'd taken a trip into town to discover the hardware store and the Belleville Flats diner. Both had been delightful.

The hardware store was about what she'd expect from a small town. Lots of dusty bins with a little bit of everything. Two older guys sat at a pot-bellied stove toward the back under a second-story loft. An old barrel nearby had a checkerboard painted on top. And glass jars filled with old-fashioned penny candy delighted her boys. She'd picked up a few emergency supplies like WD-40 and a wood plane. Mostly she wandered the aisles, seeing what was available that she might need.

The Belleville Flats diner played up the Old West gold rush theme with faux cowhide-covered booths, farming and mining implements hung on the wall, and even straw embedded in the plaster. It served amazing burgers with giant onion rings. So far, the boys had been enchanted with their move and their new town. It had been more than she'd hoped for.

But Carissa kept seeing dollar signs attached to everything, draining her bank account. Today she'd toured the house and made a complete punch list of everything that needed to be done. It had made her stomach drop. There was so much more work than she'd planned, even considering the unexpected she'd factored in. There was just so much more of it.

In the morning, they would check out of Sleepy Bear Lodge and go grocery shopping. She could stock the fridge, and they'd sleep on air mattresses. They had the moving truck until next week because she had been uncertain what would need to be unloaded when. She hadn't gotten around to checking out the garage yet. That would have to wait until tomorrow.

Her mind started whirling with plans when Miranda delivered the pizza and set it on a stand on the table. It smelled fabulous. She hadn't eaten much for lunch.

Carissa dished up slices of the melty, cheesy pieces to the boys. "Be careful. It's hot." But the smell was tantalizing. She bit into a piece. Chewy, tangy, creamy heaven. Too bad they couldn't eat here every night. She'd taken a peek at the menu, and her mouth had watered from the dishes listed. With all the work she had to do on the house, they'd be eating a lot of sandwiches and cereal. But it was worth it to be close to a place that had specialized therapy for Jayden.

Somehow, they'd make this place work as a home for them. She just had to.

CHAPTER
FOUR

arissa opened her creaky wooden garage door, the mid-morning sun lighting up dust motes. The cool space smelled of grime and motor oil. She looked for a light switch and found one near the door... Surrounded by spider webs. Ugh. Grabbing a stick off the ground, she knocked the webs away, looking carefully where she was reaching as she flicked the switch on. One bare bulb in the center of the garage barely lit it up. Sturdy wooden shelves lined one side, but the floor was filthy and oil stained, and the bare stud walls were only covered with tar paper. It was a big enough space that once finished would be a great asset to the house. But it wasn't a priority. For now, she could stack her boxes on those shelves and try to keep everything off the floor.

Charlie, their apparently adopted black lab, sniffed his way inside. Jayden tried to follow him, but Carissa held him back. "Wait until we do something about those oil puddles. Charlie, get back here."

The dog looked up and obeyed, wagging his tail. Someone had trained him at some point.

Had it only been three days since she'd first laid eyes on this house? The mounting problems every time she turned around made it seem longer. She unlocked the cargo area of the moving van she had backed close to the garage and lifted the door. She'd done a good job of marking the boxes. Or so she thought. Toward the end, everything was a blur.

With a little cleaning, the garage could store some items that would just be in the way inside the house. She mentally added a bag of kitty litter to her list to absorb the oil. And a push broom.

What she was looking for was one of the boxes of kitchen things. Her coffeemaker in particular. They'd checked out of the lodge this morning and hit the grocery store for the essentials. Eventually, she'd need to hire some help to unload the heavier items out of the moving truck. But she had to decide what needed to go where. She had to make a priority list. And coffee would help with that.

"Can I help?" Brandon stood on the driveway at the bottom of the ramp. He had such a sweet heart. Jayden was tossing a stick to Charlie, who was bringing it back with his endless energy. The two were a good match.

"Sure." She pulled her essential toolbox out first and removed a box cutter. She handed him the toolbox. "Can you put this in the mudroom?"

He frowned. "What's a mudroom?"

Jayden's head popped up. "I want to see a room with mud."

Carissa laughed. "It's not a room with mud. Well, maybe it is if you come in with muddy shoes. When you go in the back door of the house, it's that room where the washer and dryer are."

"Okay." He took off, and she scanned the area for Jayden. He was building a fort out of twigs next to the fence. Perfect.

She opened a few more boxes, trotting them down the ramp to the shelves. They were bigger kitchen items she didn't need yet, like her KitchenAid stand mixer. But the Instant Pot would come in handy. Brandon carried things inside, and finally, she found the coffeemaker. Success!

Finally, she spotted the air mattresses and the box with the bedding. She'd put them toward the back of the truck for easy access. After dragging those boxes inside the mudroom, which she had determined would be their staging area, she closed and locked the garage and moving truck.

After making herself a cup of coffee, she grabbed her legal pad and sat on the back porch steps, watching the boys play in the yard. Brandon was helping Jayden build a bigger fort with thicker branches. Charlie kept bringing sticks over. This would be good for them, letting them use their imaginations and get dirty.

A soft breeze blew the earthy scent of the sun warming up the soil. Tension slipped from her shoulders. The day was beautiful, warm sun and cool air, so different from the oven-like temperatures of Arizona, even this early in June. She took this cherished moment of peace to pour out her heart to her heavenly Father. She wasn't even sure what she was asking for. Mostly that she wouldn't mess this up. Her boys didn't deserve any more hurt.

She didn't know how much time had passed, but eventually she picked up her pad and pen, tapping it against the page like it was a magic wand, hoping it would reveal to her the best way to tackle the list. Flipping through it, she starred items that needed to be done first. Like hooking up the washer and dryer. That was at the top. They'd be out of clean clothes soon. On a new page, she arranged the starred items in priority order and put an estimated cost next to them. She had to be smart about this. There was no margin for error.

A shadow fell over her paper, and she looked up, expecting to see one of the boys. Instead, it was Gladys carrying a foil-covered plate. "I thought you and the boys would like some chocolate-chip cookies. A little welcome-to-the-neighborhood gift."

"That's so kind of you. Thank you." Carissa got to her feet and took the plate. "Would you like a cup of coffee? It's about all I've got right now, but it's freshly made."

"No, thank you. I just wanted to bring these over and see how you were doing."

Carissa scanned the area. "It's a bit more than I was expecting. But I'll make it work."

Gladys studied the house. "She's got good bones, this Delamar Place. Even if the roof was leaking last year."

A leaking roof? She'd have to check the attic to see if it had been repaired. She hadn't seen any signs of that. Heaviness draped like a lead blanket over her shoulders. She didn't have the money to fix a leaky roof.

"It's nice to see someone finally living in it. It used to be a hangout for the high school kids before the last owner tried to renovate it. Do you think you'll change the name?" Gladys asked.

"What do you mean?" Carissa was lost, and a little distracted by today's hot-pink tube top.

"The house's name. It's been known as the Delamar Place, well, probably since it was built. I bet Anne Cartwright down at the library has information on your house. She's also our historian. Our town used to be quite a wild place back in the gold rush days. Money does funny things to people."

"I'd love to know more about the house's history. Guess I'll have to head over there." Cell service was spotty at the house, and she couldn't get internet installed for two weeks, so the library computers would help with a few things she needed to check out. The boys could use some books too. She glanced at them playing with Charlie. "Are you sure the dog doesn't belong to anyone? He knows basic commands and is pretty obedient."

Gladys shook her head. "I think he got abandoned here by one of the construction workers on the house. I think that's why he hangs around, waiting for the guy to come pick him back up. So sad. But it looks like he loves your boys."

"He does. And they love him." And vet bills for a dog weren't in her budget. But if he'd been abandoned, he likely wasn't up to date on his shots. She suppressed another sigh.

"Then it looks like it was meant to be. Where did you folks move from? Down the hill?"

Carissa wasn't sure what Gladys meant by "down the hill." "Uh, Mesa, Arizona."

"That's a fair piece from here. Quite a different environment. How did you come by this place?" Gladys tapped the porch railing.

Carissa told her about finding it via an online auction. Then she eased into Jayden's autism and his need for special therapy that was available in Big Bear. There was something about Gladys that made her easy to talk to. Perhaps it was because Carissa had only had two young boys for conversation for the past week. But she found herself spilling more than she'd told anyone.

"This might sound silly, but there was just something about this house that made me think we could make a home here. I do plan to sell it after I fix it up, but if there is one house like this, then maybe there would be another that we could settle in permanently. So far, we really like the town. I just hope I can do this old girl justice and Jayden will benefit from the social program."

Gladys glanced up and scanned the house. "She's not in too bad shape for an old house." She laughed. "Better than me on some days. One old woman knows another."

Carissa smiled at her. She seemed pretty spry. And then there was the tube top fashion choice, making it hard to guess what Gladys's real age was. "Well, I hope so. This list seems to get longer by the minute."

Gladys patted Carissa's arm. "Just trust in God. He's got a bigger plan than you can see."

For some reason, Gladys's words didn't come off as trite drivel but instead as sweet assurance. Carissa smiled. "He's definitely gotten us through some rough spots before."

"And he'll do it again. Now, I need to get home, but enjoy the cookies and holler if you need anything." Gladys hustled down the steps and picked her way across the yard, more spryly than Carissa would have expected for the woman's age. She was touched by the Gladys's kindness. Perhaps they hadn't landed in Kookyville after all.

But a quick glance at her list—and Gladys's revelation about the roof—caused panic, her all-too-frequent companion—to push at her chest. She trusted God. She was out here, wasn't she? They'd left the familiar for the unknown.

She stood and picked up the plate Gladys had left and took it inside, wishing she could leave all her problems on the back deck.

CHAPTER
FIVE

Shannon McIntyre walked across the football field and behind the stage set up for graduation, careful to keep her heels from sinking into the grass. She'd debated wearing her dress uniform, as she'd be speaking to the graduates as a representative of the town. But today she was a mom first, so she wore a dress and heels. Not something she often got the opportunity to do.

Other officials milled around before the ceremony began: the mayor, the principal. Tony. Her heart did a little flip. He was wearing a suit, something he rarely did. But it showed off his former-construction-worker build, and the dark color made his eyes look like melted chocolate. For a moment, she remembered what it was like to be in those arms as he moved her around the dance floor at her sister Cassie's wedding to Brett. Since then, they'd had regular "official" coffee dates where they discussed how they could work together for the good of the town. The personal had become professional.

Given both of their jobs, maybe that's all it could ever be.

Tony spotted her and walked over, a grin spreading across his face. "Congratulations, Mom. You did it."

She smiled back. "Zach did most of the work. But I have to admit, there were times I wasn't sure I'd see this day. I about lost it when I dropped him off to line up with the other graduates in his cap and gown."

Tony's gaze on her softened. That was not what she needed. She swallowed and grabbed for her professional demeanor. "Do you know if Samuel got here okay?" Samuel Kinsey was a foster care runaway who had been squatting in the old Victorian Alex and Claire Wilder were renovating for a B-and-B. Tony had been instrumental in getting Samuel a good foster home with one of the church families, and the church had rallied around him, giving him jobs to help him prepare for aging out of the system.

Tony nodded. "He did. The Markeys brought him earlier. The church donated for his cap and gown from our benevolence fund. He's even got a line on some work with a landscaping and snow removal company after graduation."

"That's good to hear. It's been so great seeing the town come together to help someone. I want us to do more of that."

"Me too." Tony looked like he was about to say something else, but Cassie popped over and squeezed Shannon's shoulders.

"It's Zach's big day. Are you going to make it through your speech?" Cassie gave her a mischievous little-sister grin.

"Yes, I'll be fine. Especially if people stop asking me if I'm fine."

"Okay, I can take a hint. Mom and Dad are already in their seats. I just wanted to say hi. And good luck." Cassie scooted off.

Shannon rolled her eyes, and Tony laughed.

"She's better behaved when Brett is around. But he's working traffic control with Jonas. However, my folks should keep her in check." They were out here from Texas and would stay the weekend. Out of habit, she scanned the area around them, looking for potential problems. Then her stomach tightened. Dan. She knew he'd be here. Though, as unreliable as he was, there was a chance he'd miss his own son's graduation. For Zach's sake, she was glad he was here.

Unfortunately, he had spotted her and was headed their way.

"Something wrong?" Tony asked.

She gave a short laugh. "Looks like you'll get to meet Zach's dad."

Dan closed within earshot. "Hey, Shannon. Did Zach get to where he needed to be?"

"Yep." As always, no thanks to him. "Dan, this is Pastor Tony Stafford. Tony, Zach's dad, Dan Lang."

The men shook hands.

Dan stuffed his hands in his expensive, tailored suit pockets. "A pastor, huh? In a resort town like this, it must be a great job, not a ton of drama. I've always seen why Shannon preferred to stay up here. Better pace of life."

Tony shifted his weight closer to Shannon. "We keep busy. People bring their troubles with them on vacation."

Dan tilted his head a bit, the way he did when he didn't agree but was going to let you continue with your misinformed opinion.

Shannon wanted to roll her eyes again. Instead, she opted for diplomacy. "There's still plenty of seats left. Zach and the other kids are leaving after graduation for Grad Night, but we'll get a few minutes with him before they head off."

"Sure. I want to make sure he gets my graduation gift. I'm offering him a trip anywhere he wants this summer."

She shouldn't have been surprised. Dan was all about grand gestures, even if the follow-through was lacking. "They can't take anything with them, so you might want to save it for his graduation party later this month. I'll just end up taking it home with me."

Tony touched her arm. "We'd better check in with the principal. Looks like he's getting everyone ready to get on stage shortly."

She saw the escape he was offering and took it. "Yes, we'd better make sure we know what's going on and when we're supposed to speak. I'll see you later, Dan."

Tony lifted a hand. "Nice to meet you."

Dan nodded. "You too," he threw over his shoulder as he turned to find a seat.

Tony took her elbow as they took a few steps in the direction of the principal. "So that's Zach's dad. He's not what I expected."

"What did you expect?"

"Not sure, honestly. I just can't picture you with him."

She nodded. "He's changed a lot. Or maybe who he really is came out when I graduated the academy. He confessed at one point he didn't think I'd make it through, so he never took it seriously. Then when I got pregnant with Zach, he thought I'd quit. I think his threat of divorce was actually a bluff to make me."

"Some people get so wrapped up in the way they want reality to be that they can't see it for what it is."

"That's Dan exactly."

The principal and his admin waved them over. He ran down the order of events and pointed to where they'd each be sitting. "Five minutes, then we'll head up to the stage."

The others who would be on the stage gathered around, including teachers and school and town officials. Shannon took her place on the stage, down a few chairs from Tony. They were sitting in the order they would speak, and he was giving the convocation. She scanned the crowd and spotted her parents and Cassie. She recognized nearly everyone in the audience, the advantage of living in a small town. Dan was seated toward the back. He always made it clear how provincial and quaint he thought Holcomb Springs was.

But when the graduates lined up in the back, tears sprang to her eyes. She homed in on Zach, looking so grown up in his cap and gown.

Tony leaned forward to catch her gaze. He winked at her. "You did it, Mama," he mouthed.

Her heart about broke open, and she turned away, blinking furiously. He understood. And in that moment, she realized with the force of a punch that she wanted more from Tony than just a business relationship.

CHAPTER
SIX

Jonas folded the last of his laundry. The house was clean, the fridge was stocked, and he was officially out of things to do on his Saturday off. The restlessness that had been haunting him was back in full force.

He'd gone running this morning with Tony, Reese, and Marco. Sometimes the sheriff joined them, but not today. The high school graduates returned from Grad Night early this morning. It had been uneventful, just the way they liked it. They'd discussed the upcoming tourist season. This might be the last easy weekend before things ramped up for the summer.

But even the running hadn't taken away his restlessness. He grabbed his keys and phone. Maybe he'd take a walk down to Holcomb Springs Road. The ice cream shop was still open. Could be he just needed a shot of milk fat and sugar. Outside, he headed down the street, grateful he was able to live and work in a small town. He lived just a few blocks from the main drag, though his long driveway and the slope of the mountain hid his cabin from the view of his neighbors. Hopefully the walk would clear his head.

He turned the corner and spotted the library. That would be a good first stop. Maybe he could find a classic movie to rent. Or

Anne might have a good recommendation. She seemed to read his mind and always have just the book for him.

He pulled open the door, headed through the brick entryway, and then into the main library. A surprising number of people milled around the library for a Saturday evening. Did Anne have a special program going on since it was Memorial Day weekend? She was great with coming up with ideas to engage the community.

Anne strode across the room, her hands full of papers. She spotted him and changed direction. "Jonas! Good to see you." She sorted through the papers in her hand, peeled off a round, blue sticker, and pasted it to his T-shirt. "You're a thriller/mystery/crime guy."

He frowned. "What's this for?"

"It's tonight's program. Meet someone based on their taste in books. Just look for someone who has a sticker like yours. Pink is for romance and women's fiction, green is for historical, purple is for fantasy, black is for sci-fi. There's a cheat sheet on the wall." She pointed to a poster across from the check-out desk. "You can have more than one interest too."

"I'm just here to pick out a book or a movie." He started to peel the sticker off, but Anne stopped him.

"That's okay. Could you just leave the sticker on so it looks like you're participating? It will make the others feel more comfortable."

He wasn't sure he believed her, but Anne was persuasive. And what could it hurt? "Fine, but you owe me a good book recommendation."

She smiled and pulled her long, blonde curls over her shoulder as she glanced at the new releases display. He always thought she was the most unlikely looking librarian. "Hmm. The latest Aggie Gilchrist is back."

He shook his head. "Too tame for me."

Her face dropped for just a second. "Not a cozy mystery fan, are we? You like the harder stuff."

Gladys Marley walked up behind Anne, followed by her husband, Stan. Pink and green stickers adorned her shirt. Stan didn't have any stickers. "Can you help us settle an argument, dear?"

Anne pasted on a smile. "If I can."

"I'll let you get to it." Jonas started to move off.

"I'll find you in a bit. I think I have something you'll like, but it hasn't been shelved yet."

He nodded and headed toward the movie section, knowing any disagreement Stan had would likely take hours to resolve. He and Wally liked to argue for the sport of it. Jonas didn't think they even believed half of what they said. How their wives put up with them, he didn't know. Maybe it was because they spent most of their days at either the Jitter Bug Too or the hardware store.

Jonas scanned the movie selections, looking for anything to catch his eye. He didn't even know what he wanted, but maybe something would jump out at him.

"So you're into thrillers and crime. Any favorite authors?"

He turned to find Mariah smiling at him, standing a little too close for comfort. Shannon obviously hadn't talked to her. Then again, this was a community space, not a crime call. Still, at some point he was going to have to tell her he wasn't interested. He just didn't know how to do that without making things awkward, always a problem with small towns.

Lord, if this is your idea of a distraction, it's not funny.

AFTER A CRAZY FEW DAYS OF GOING THROUGH THE HOUSE, creating a massive punch list, and identifying the trouble spots and Jayden-proofing them, Carissa was exhausted. They were living out of suitcases, sleeping bags, and air mattresses. She'd need to see about hiring some help to unload the truck. What she wouldn't give for her Tempur-pedic mattress. She'd spent the day cleaning the garage so items could be safely moved into it.

But she'd promised the boys ice cream for helping out around the house and staying out of trouble the last few days. A trip to the library was a fun break and within their budget. Plus, she needed to find an electrician and plumber to get the washer and dryer hooked up. The previous owners had it installed in the downstairs bathroom in a janky and unsafe way. Then someone had just moved it into the mudroom, which was a great place for it if she could get it hooked up properly. They didn't have internet at the house yet, and the cell service was spotty, so she was hoping the library computers—and possibly the librarian— would help her find some service providers who wouldn't break her budget.

They pulled into the library parking lot. It looked like it shared a building with the historical society. That would be fun to explore. The town had an Old West vibe. Someday it would be fun to know the story behind that.

They piled out of the car—Carissa double checking she had her keys before getting out—and the boys headed into the library. There was a brick-floored foyer with benches and hooks, probably for winter gear, before another set of doors opened into the library proper. The smell of paper and ink was like coming home.

Brandon immediately spotted the sign for the kids' area and led Jayden that direction. Carissa followed behind, amazed at how busy the library was on a Saturday evening. Probably not a lot to do in this town.

Just past the kids' area was the historical society. Glass doors separated the two, but a cute transition space had a mural on the wall depicting the town during the gold rush. There was an old wooden phone with the separate pieces for talking and listening and a crank on the side. It had privacy panels on it with a small sign, a collection of slips of paper, small pencils, and a wooden box with a slot on the top.

"Boys, come look at this." She motioned them over. "This is an old-fashioned phone." She showed them how to lift the bell-shaped receiver off the hook to listen and then speak into the funnel-like mouthpiece. The sign explained how operators used to connect callers before there were even phone numbers. Then at the bottom was another section that explained how many people felt like they could tell their secrets into this phone, and if they wanted to, they could leave notes for loved ones in the wooden box.

The boys took turns calling various friends and relatives and cartoon characters. But Carissa wondered about the secrets in the box. Who read them? Were they just thrown out? It was a curious thing in a small town, one she was discovering had more than a few quirks.

"Okay, let's go find some books." She shooed them out of the wooden booth, creaks and all, and toward the shelves. The corner of the children's area had a replica of a mountain the kids could climb up on the back and slide down on the front. There was a "gold mine" entrance underneath it with shelves of books and a reading area. How perfect for a town with a foot still in the Old West.

The boys took turns climbing the mountain and sliding down. She found a section on dinosaurs for Jayden, then turned to Brandon. "Can you keep an eye on him? I need to go use the computers right over there." She pointed back the way they came toward the circulation desk. "You can pick out some books, and we'll get our library cards."

"Can I get my own library card?" A hopeful look lit up Brandon's face.

"Sure, if they allow it."

He grinned. "Cool."

She seated herself at a computer where she could still keep an eye on the boys. Then she began searching for local electricians and plumbers, jotting their info down on a small notebook from her purse. Not like there was a lot to choose from. She checked her email and her bank account while she was at it. Both were depressing. Most of her emails were newsletters and ads for retailers. Nothing from any friends. They'd be more likely to text her though. She hadn't had many of those either. Heaviness draped over her shoulders. Usually, she could keep it at bay, but right now she was feeling a lot like she was out of sight, out of mind. Still, she'd make new friends here. She needed to focus on that.

But one email jumped out at her and made her stomach drop. She glanced around, not certain if she wanted to read what was sure to be an emotional email in a public place. But if she didn't read it, the unknown contents would haunt her. It was from Greg, and the subject was child and spousal support.

She clicked on it and scanned it quickly, then read it closer. What a jerk. But was she even surprised? The gist of it was that he'd decided he'd been too generous in her settlement. She'd had a good paying job, and it wasn't his fault she wanted to leave it for some harebrained idea. He shouldn't have to pay for her impulsivity.

She laughed out loud at that, then glanced around. No one seemed to have noticed. She was the least impulsive person she knew. And he knew it too.

No, he was simply trying to justify abandoning his family because a child with autism wasn't in his life plan. So he was taking her back to court for an adjustment. In Arizona. Unless she agreed to his terms now.

She closed her email and erased the browsing history before getting up from the computer. She did not need this. She didn't need the expense of paying her attorney to represent her or going back to Arizona to represent herself. But if she didn't show up, who knew what would happen? He didn't even ask about the boys. She had gotten all the parental rights, and he hadn't even put up a fight, other than when it came to money. Was his new wife complaining about the amount of money he had to pay each month? He'd probably lied to her too.

Checking to see that Brandon and Jayden were reading in bean-bag chairs, she slipped into the fiction section. She needed something to take her mind off things. And a good book would always do that.

Jonas looked past Mariah to the shelf in front of him. "Just looking to see what might be good. I think Anne has some recommendations for me. She's good at that."

Mariah smiled. "She is. This whole event to meet someone based on their taste in books was her idea. I think it's great, don't you? Books make for a good discussion over dinner."

He made a noncommittal sound. It was time he laid things out plainly for her, since she couldn't take a hint. "Uh, Mariah, look." He blew out a breath. Why was this so hard? *Lord, some help here.*

Someone entered the aisle. He'd have to wait for them to leave before he continued. But when he took a closer look, he saw it was the same blonde woman who'd locked her keys in her car the other day. They must still be in town. She was a tourist, so he'd likely never see her again if he made a fool out of himself. He didn't know if this was God's answer to his prayer, but he jumped at it.

"Sorry, Mariah. I see someone I need to talk to. Hope you find a good book." He moved down the aisle to intercept the woman. "Hi, have any more trouble with your car keys?" He smiled at her.

She glanced over from the shelf, confusion crossing her face for a moment until recognition dawned in her sky-blue eyes. "Oh, Deputy. I didn't recognize you. We've been fine, thanks."

"Good." He glanced back over his shoulder. Mariah hadn't moved. She was studying them, a crease in her brow. Okay. He'd noticed the woman was pretty when he helped her with her lockout, but up close something vanilla and floral from her wrapped around him, making him a little heady. This might be the stupidest thing he'd ever done, but she was a tourist he'd never see again. And if it solved the Mariah problem…

He lowered his voice. "This might sound strange, but would you play along with me, act like we know each other?"

Wariness crossed her face. She glanced around, and he could see her making the calculations. She'd never see him again, so what could it hurt? And she knew he was a deputy, and they were in a public place. It was all right there on her face.

She smiled and gave a small nod.

"Thanks," he whispered. Then louder, "Good to see you again. How are the boys?"

"Great. They're actually over in the kids' section. In fact, I should probably check on them."

"Yeah, let's head over there. I'd love to talk to them again." He followed her out of the aisle, taking a quick glance back at Mariah as they rounded the endcap.

Her gaze was still on them, and her frown deepened.

Carissa leaned close to him as they approached the kids' section. "Avoiding that woman back there? She runs the Sleepy Bear Lodge, right?"

"Right on both accounts. Thanks for playing along."

"No problem. Never hurts to be on the good side of law enforcement. Plus, I do have you to thank for getting my keys out of my car. I'm Carissa Carver, by the way. I don't expect that you remembered my name, as busy as you must be."

He did but he didn't let on. "Jonas McCann." He spotted the boys absorbed in their books ensconced in bean-bag chairs.

But before he could say anything, Anne came up. "Here's the book I was thinking of." She handed him a hardback with a dramatic cover. She looked over at Carissa. "You don't have a sticker. But I do see you have an Elin Hildebrand in your hands. Women's fiction lover?"

Carissa raised an eyebrow. "Sticker? And yes, Elin Hildebrand is like a beach vacation."

"We're having an event where you meet people based on their taste in books." Anne pointed to Jonas. "His blue sticker says he likes thrillers and crime novels. I'm Anne Cartwright, by the way. I'm the librarian."

Carissa's face lit up. "I wanted to talk to you. I bought the Delamar Place and was told you might have some information on the history of the house."

Wait. What? Jonas digested that information. She wasn't a tourist? Had he just made the biggest fool out of himself in front of someone he'd have to see on a regular basis? He was never this foolish and had rarely misjudged a situation so badly.

Carissa and Anne continued to talk, paying him little mind. Perhaps he could just slip away without them noticing.

But Mariah walked up just then.

Could the situation get any worse? That was likely the wrong question to ask.

CHAPTER
SEVEN

C arissa took the pink sticker Anne handed her and attached it to her shirt. This had been a good trip. Anne knew about the Delamar Place and was sure she had some information on it.

"I've got to get back to tonight's event, but let me do a little digging and I'll get you the info on your house later this week," Anne said, a warm smile lighting her face.

"That would be great. Thanks." Carissa noticed Mariah had joined them, standing just behind Jonas. And shooting daggers at her. This could be interesting.

Anne turned to go. "Hi, Mariah. Need help finding anything?"

Mariah swung her long, dark hair behind her shoulder. "Nope, I think I have everything I need."

Anne nodded. "Okay, let me know if you need help," she said and moved off.

Carissa, Jonas, and Mariah stood in an awkward tableau. But her boys came up to save the day.

"Dinosaurs! *Rawr!*" Jayden zoomed his book in front of her.

"Can we get ice cream now?" Brandon balanced a stack of several books as he looked up at her with pleading eyes.

She'd gotten what she needed. And then some. But she didn't want to abandon Jonas, who looked more awkward and at sea than she imagined he was used to. "Sure. Jonas, you're still coming with us for ice cream, right?"

His eyes widened, and then he caught on. "Sure. Yeah. Can't let the boys down." He grinned at them.

Brandon frowned. "Who—"

"Let's get these books checked out and head for ice cream before it gets to be too late." Carissa put a hand on each boy's shoulder and propelled them toward the circulation desk before one of them said something inopportune.

"Jonas, can I talk to you?" Mariah said.

Carissa glanced over her shoulder at Jonas. "Could you help the boys with their books while I fill out the library card info?" She gave Mariah a sweet smile.

Mariah just looked confused. Carissa wasn't sure if Mariah remembered they had stayed in her lodge. The boys were pretty memorable. She didn't want to make an enemy when she'd just moved into town, but perhaps by giving Jonas a little space, he'd figure out how to deal with Mariah on his own terms.

Another woman was behind the circulation desk when they reached it.

"We'd like to get some library cards. We just moved into town."

The boys put their books on the counter.

"Certainly." The woman pushed across a form. "We just need your ID and proof of residency."

Carissa pulled out her license, which was still from Arizona. "Like I said, we just moved here. I haven't received any utility bills yet."

The woman frowned. "Do you have a lease?"

"I bought the old Delamar Place."

"Oh." An odd look crossed the woman's face, and she took a step back. "Um, do you have anything related to the sale?"

"Not with me." Carissa pulled out her phone. Maybe she

had some confirmation of something on there. "I wasn't thinking, I guess. It's been a crazy week."

The woman pulled the books closer to her. "I can hold these until you come back with some proof of residency."

Jayden reached for his book, but the woman tugged it farther out of reach. "I want my dinosaur book." He jumped up, trying to grab it from her.

Brandon looked at her, shoulders slumped. "Mom? Why can't we have the books?"

Carissa grabbed Jayden and slung an arm across his shoulders, pulling him to her, slowing him.

Jonas stepped up. "Hey, Meredith. I can vouch for them. She's not lying about buying the Delamar Place. A piece of paper isn't going to change anything. Can we just give them the cards?"

The woman pursed her lips. "Deputy, you know we like to do things by the rules around here. Anne runs a tight ship."

"I'll talk to Anne. I'm sure she won't mind. The whole point of the proof of residency is to prove someone lives here. And Carissa and her boys do."

Jayden sprung up and down behind Carissa's confining arm, landing on her foot. She bent down to speak softly in his ear. "Just a minute." Jonas's action flooded her with warmth. If he could save Jayden from a meltdown because he didn't get his book, she'd be indebted to Jonas.

Meredith pushed the paper to Carissa. "Sign here. And then fill out this one for the junior library card."

Carissa did, and Meredith handed them a couple of plastic cards with barcodes on them and finished checking out their books. "They're due back in three weeks."

"Thank you." Relief washing over her, Carissa handed Jayden his dinosaur book. "I'm sure we'll be back in before then." She herded the boys out the doors. In the foyer, she turned to Jonas. "Thank you so much for that. Jayden was about to lose it. I wasn't looking forward to telling him he couldn't borrow the book."

Jonas grabbed the outer door and held it for her. "Happy to help. It's a small town; we like to be neighborly."

"I'm beginning to see that. So is that gift shop-slash-candy store-slash-ice cream shop the place to go for ice cream or is there a hidden gem I haven't discovered yet? Because I definitely owe you ice cream after that save."

He laughed. "It's the place to go. And it's walkable."

"Great. Anything to burn off their excess energy." She turned to the boys. "Want to leave your books in the car while we walk to get ice cream?"

Brandon nodded, but Jayden just hugged his closer. Carissa put Brandon's books in the Explorer.

The library door opened, and Mariah came out and stared at them, hands on hips. Carissa pretended not to notice, but Jonas gave her a small wave then seemed to become interested in what Carissa was doing.

They headed down the sidewalk toward the heart of their little town, the boys walking ahead. Carissa glanced back. Mariah was no longer there.

"So, is this going to create problems for you?" She tilted her head back toward the library.

"Nah. Well, no more than I had already created for myself. Thanks for the rescue. As soon as we get around the corner I can head out."

"What? No, I owe you ice cream. I meant it when I said anything that prevents Jayden from a meltdown is worth rewarding."

He chuckled. "Seems like we've been rescuing each other. And I was headed to get ice cream after a stop by the library." He paused. "So you bought the Delamar Place?"

"Yeah. It needs some work. To say the least. But I'm hoping to flip it to earn some income."

"Have you done that before?"

She nodded. "I'm an architect, and I flipped a couple of houses in Mesa, Arizona, where we used to live." She raised her voice. "Brandon, we're crossing here. Look both ways, please."

The boys did; the traffic was non-existent. A blessing since Jayden often didn't look before darting into the street. But it would likely pick up once the summer tourist season was in full swing. She and Jonas followed them.

"Anything I should know about the Delamar Place?" She glanced over at Jonas.

He shoved his hands in the front pockets of his jeans. "Well, it's been vacant awhile, but you knew that."

"Yep."

"A few different people have tried to make a go of it over the years. Kids used to use it as a hang out until…" He grimaced slightly, like he said more than he intended.

"Until?" she prodded.

"About four years ago, one of the kids went missing. No one's really sure what happened to him. After that, the kids stopped hanging out there and a local contractor bought it and started fixing it up. He sold it to someone who never actually moved in. That's probably who you bought it from."

She nodded. "Some work has been done on it. Some definitely hasn't." She thought of the washer and dryer hookups and pulled her little notebook out. "Hey, do you know anything about these guys?" She read the names she'd gotten off the internet. "I need the washer and dryer hooked up properly."

His eyes narrowed as he scanned her list. Then he seemed to choose his words carefully. "I don't know them personally. But you'd be better off talking to Claire and Alex Wilder. They're rehabbing a Victorian just around the corner from yours and turning it into a B-and-B. They're almost done. Alex is a contractor. And actually, so was Pastor Tony. I'd trust whatever they recommend."

"Pastor Tony. What church? Or is there more than one in town?" She grinned.

"There is. But he's the pastor at Holcomb Springs Community Church."

"I'll have to check it out. We'll be looking for a church." One more thing off her to-do list.

"Services are at ten on Sunday."

He spoke like he was familiar with the church more than just as a community member.

They had reached the ice cream-candy-gift shop, and Jonas held the door for them. The boys ran to the glass ice cream display case in the back. Carissa hadn't brought them in here yet, knowing it would be difficult to pry them out. It had the feel of an old-fashioned candy store, with wooden racks and display cases of candy and gift items highlighting the local area. The smell of sugar and cream permeated the air.

"I think you're more than earning your ice cream." Carissa smiled at him and then helped the boys relay their selections to the kid behind the counter. She got mint chip, and Jonas ordered rocky road. "That's my second favorite." She slipped Jayden's library book from him in exchange for a cone.

"Hard to beat chocolate, nuts, and marshmallows."

"Very true." Carissa managed to get her debit card to the kid before Jonas could get his wallet out. "I said it was my treat."

He shook his head and frowned as he put his wallet back. Carissa grabbed a handful of napkins and hustled them outside to some small, old-fashioned soda fountain tables. The daylight was fading fast, but it was still pleasant out. She wasn't eager to return home.

"What all have you seen of our town, or have you been mostly in work mode?" Jonas studied her over his scoop.

"Mostly in work mode. But I've bribed the boys a few times." She told him about the places they had discovered. She hesitated a moment. "Anything I should know about my neighbors?"

He took a bite of his ice cream before answering. "Gladys is as sweet as they come. But she's definitely her own person."

Carissa laughed. "Oh, yeah. I figured that."

"George is harmless, but he does seem to have sticky fingers. I don't think he means anything by it. He just has a loose sense of what personal property means. No one wants to get him in trouble, so we all just look out for him. He doesn't have any family that we have been able to ascertain. Gladys lets us know if he needs anything."

Carissa finished off her cone and wiped her hands, then handed napkins to the boys. This had been a surprising day. So maybe Gladys and George were just the town characters. Every town had some, didn't they?

And Jonas, he was a pleasant surprise for sure. The library trip had definitely been a good idea, and the town was growing on her every day. Perhaps once she flipped the Victorian she'd be able to find another, smaller place for them to live here. Hope kindled a small ember in her chest, and for the first time in a long while, she felt like she could fully breathe.

THAT WAS UNEXPECTED. JONAS PLOPPED ON HIS COUCH, the silence of his cabin a contrast to the background chatter of Carissa's boys—Jayden and Brandon. They were good kids, but she had her hands full—with them and the Delamar Place.

He winced at the recollection. He certainly didn't believe the rumors about the indigo moon and the missing kids. As an astronomy buff himself, he knew the high school astronomy teacher, Brian Lancaster. The elevation and lack of distortion from the cool mountain air made Holcomb Springs a great place for stargazing.

The disappearance of Tyler Cohen after an astronomy club meeting studying a lunar eclipse was one of Jonas's first cases here in Holcomb Springs. And because the Delamar Place had been a local teen hangout, all sorts of rumors and legends sprung up around it. Nothing he gave any credence to. It was human nature to fill in the missing pieces with whatever their minds made up.

And he didn't think telling Carissa about it would be helpful to her. Though, she should be aware that some people believed the rumors. She'd likely hear them at some point. But right now, it would just add to her load. And her plate was full.

Hopefully she'd show up at church Sunday. He could make sure she met the right people, people who would help her. Because that's what they did in this town. They helped each other.

He was only being neighborly.

Plus, he'd never let a woman buy him a meal, even if it was just ice cream. So he owed her.

But he still needed to talk to Mariah.

CHAPTER
EIGHT

Carissa repressed a sigh. She should have known better by now. They were running late, but Jayden needed time to be coaxed into a new situation. In this case, church. Gladys had come over last night to invite them to Holcomb Springs Community Church. Given that it was their second invitation, Carissa figured God was pointing her in that direction. She was looking forward to meeting more people, some adult conversation, and community worship. When they'd left Arizona, she'd been heartbroken at the way many people in her church had treated her as a result of her ex-husband's "disinformation campaign." Shooting the wounded, she'd heard it called.

Perhaps here it would be different. But she wouldn't find out if they couldn't get a move on. Unfortunately, rushing and pushing Jayden just made him dig in his heels more. Unfortunately, she had no choice.

There was a knock on the back door. Probably Gladys. She'd offered to go with them to introduce them to folks.

"Just a sec!" Carissa dropped the wet comb into the sink, giving up trying to wrestle Jayden's hair into some semblance of order. He hated having his hair touched, let alone cut, so most of the time it resembled a bush birds had nested in.

She started for the front door then realized the knocking was coming from the back door. She pulled it open. "Sorry, we're running a bit late."

Gladys wasn't wearing a tube top today. She had on a flowered-print camp shirt and coordinating polyester pants. But on second glance… Yep, there was a tube top under the shirt.

Carissa hadn't been sure what the dress code was like up here, so she'd opted for business casual—dress pants and a wrap-front blouse that didn't need ironing—and collared shirts and jeans for the boys.

"I noticed you still have the moving truck out there." Gladys jerked a thumb over her shoulder. "Does it need to be unloaded yet?"

Jayden had escaped from the bathroom and was plopped down among the boxes in the living room. Two Lego guys were engaged in combat while Jayden provided the sound effects.

"It does. I need to hire some strong guys to unload the heavy pieces. I've figured out what needs to be in the house and what can go in the garage." The newly cleaned garage. Her shoulders still protested yesterday's work. She made one last attempt to smooth down Jayden's hair while calling upstairs for Brandon.

He clattered down to the bottom before she'd finished. "I can't find my Bible."

"It's in a box somewhere, I'm sure. We'll just have to go without this morning."

He cocked his head, and Carissa could see him considering arguing with her before thinking better of it. That boy could never play poker. She wasn't going to complain, though. Having one child whose emotions and thoughts she could read was a blessing.

"Okay, boys, let's go. Is Charlie in the house?"

"I'll get him." Brandon ran for the back porch calling Charlie's name.

They'd discovered the hard way—after he'd chewed two shoes from different pairs and part of a book—that he couldn't be left to wander the house freely when they were gone. And she didn't feel right leaving him outside, even though that's where he'd been when they found him. Luckily the mudroom had a door to it, and it was now Charlie proof.

"We'll be in the car." Carissa herded Jayden out the front door and held it for Gladys.

Ten minutes later, they were in the church foyer and Gladys had already introduced them to a number of people. Carissa couldn't help but scan the crowd for Jonas, but she was acutely aware she needed to get Jayden to his Sunday school class. He would need time to acclimate. He was already stoic, head down, ignoring all the people who were trying to talk to him.

By the time they were down the hallway to the classrooms, he was shuffling his feet and leaning against her. She had her arm around his shoulders, rubbing them.

They dropped Brandon off at his classroom first. He waved and went in. He was looking forward to meeting some kids his age. She desperately hoped he did.

A few more doors down the hall, Gladys stopped in front of a door pasted with cartoon Noah's ark cardboard cutouts. "Here's the little guy's classroom. This is Miss Rebecca."

A lady who appeared to be about retirement age— her dark bobbed hair was streaked with iron gray—tried to grab Jayden from Carissa.

With a whimper, he turned his face into her leg.

Carissa knelt, taking up most of the narrow hallway, and he threw his arms around her. "Jayden, don't you want to go inside and listen to some music and hear a Bible story?"

His face didn't move from her shoulder.

"Want to sit in big church with me? You can draw."

He lifted his face, eyes pooled with tears, and nodded.

Carissa never knew if she was doing the right thing. Did she push him to be uncomfortable and risk a huge meltdown, or make him even more afraid of trying anything new because he couldn't trust her to keep him safe? Or did she give in? Though in this case he would have preferred to stay home, so even being here among all these strangers was a victory.

"Okay." She took his hand and straightened. "Let's go get a seat."

Gladys and Miss Rebecca looked at Carissa like she had two heads.

"Are you sure he wouldn't be more comfortable here?" Miss Rebecca's voice climbed higher the longer her sentence went.

Carissa didn't want to explain about the autism now. Though she'd have to at some point if they continued going here. "He'll be fine with me."

"Well, I never heard the like." Miss Rebecca gave a small shake of her head.

Carissa gave her a tight smile and followed Gladys back down the narrow hallway that was considerably emptier now. Music poured from the sanctuary. Church had started.

As they entered the sanctuary, Carissa scanned for seats near the back. They were all full. Plus Gladys moved resolutely toward the front, greeting people all along the way. Carissa was grateful the first song had started, which kept Gladys from introducing her to everyone. The worship leader appeared to be about her age and good looking, with a strong resemblance to Chris Hemsworth. The front rows had an overabundance of young women enthusiastically singing along.

She spotted Klepto George in his overalls behind them.

They ended up on the second row from the right. Luckily—though they had to squeeze in front of a few people—she was able to put Jayden next to the wall. He stood quietly through the rest of the music. Music had always calmed him.

She ruffled his hair and kept her hand on his shoulder during the meet and greet. A few people attempted to shake Jayden's hand, but he pulled away with a growl and flopped in the chair with his arms crossed. Carissa was sure they thought he was rude. Wouldn't be the first time.

About ten minutes into the sermon, she decided it was surprisingly good. She hadn't known what to expect. But it was sound biblical teaching. And Pastor Tony was an engaging preacher, though he looked like he should be a football player. A refreshing pool after a journey through a desert of betrayal, lies, and pain.

A rustle and a thump pulled her eyes from her Bible. Jayden was laying sideways in the pew, his feet on the wall, leaving footprints. She grabbed his pant legs and yanked his legs down. "Sit. Up," she hissed into his ear.

He complied, mostly, slouching and swinging his legs. The next thumps were going to be against the back of the occupied chair in front of them.

She handed Jayden the bulletin and rummaged through her purse until she found a pen and a piece of gum. Handing them to him, she whispered in his ear, "You can't flail around in church. You have to be calm. In Sunday school you can do more things. Here you have to be still." Yeah, it sounded lame to her too. "Hang on and we'll go get lunch after this, okay?"

"Ice cream?" His voice was too loud. Volume control was not his strength. Maybe not even within his ability.

"Whisper! No, that's not lunch. Let's go get hamburgers." She didn't want Jayden to melt down in the middle of the sermon either. One she had now missed a good chunk of. Sigh. She managed to catch a few more snatches of the message between drawing funny pictures for Jayden and shushing and bribing him.

As soon as they were dismissed, he jumped up. "Come on, Mom. Let's go." He pulled on her arm, making her lose her Bible and drop her purse.

"Jayden, stop."

"Have you met my new neighbor?" Gladys's voice interrupted Carissa's attempt to put things back in order.

"Actually, I have."

Carissa turned at the distinctly male voice.

Jonas stood in the aisle. "Glad you made it." He waved and winked at Jayden, who lifted up one of his dinosaur pictures.

"Did you draw that?" Jonas asked.

Jayden shook his head and pointed at Carissa.

"Ah, Mom's good at drawing dinosaurs." The corners of his eyes crinkled with mirth.

"Lots of practice." Carissa said.

Jonas waved a couple over. "Here's who I wanted you to meet. Carissa, this is Alex and Claire Wilder, the ones rehabbing a Victorian as well. I figured you all could share resources."

A woman about Carissa's age with straight, shoulder-length light-brown hair and blue eyes reached for Carissa's hand. "It's so nice to meet you. I'd love to show you what we've done and what we'd wished we done." She smiled and glanced over to the broad-shouldered man next to her—Alex.

Before Carissa could respond, Brandon squeezed in next to her. A girl a little older than him nudged Claire.

Claire smiled. "Sunday school must be out. Were you two in the same class?"

The girl and Brandon nodded.

"Even better. Our kids can be friends too. This is my daughter, Lizzie." Claire handed over her phone to Carissa. "Put your info in there, and we'll connect."

"Great." Carissa tapped in her details and handed Claire's phone back. Carissa's phone dinged with a text containing Claire's info. She turned to check on Jayden, but he and Brandon were talking with Jonas about the last weird thing Charlie ate. Amazed and grateful for the moment to carry on a conversation, she knew her time was running out. She was about to wrangle the boys when Gladys reappeared with the pastor.

He reached out his hand. It was massive, much like the rest of him. She would have never guessed he was a pastor—though, what did pastors look like anyway? "Thanks for coming. I'm Tony Stafford."

"Carissa Carver and my boys Brandon and Jayden." She placed a hand on each of their shoulders.

"Good to meet you all. Gladys says you need a moving truck unloaded. We can get a group of folks over there this afternoon. Even though it's Memorial Day weekend, we've got a lot of people around. Will that work for you?"

It took a moment for the words to penetrate. Were they offering help? Unexpected tears sprang to her eyes, and she blinked them away, embarrassed, and acutely aware of Jonas's gaze on her. "Um, yeah—" her voice broke. This was so humiliating. What a great first impression she was making. "That would be wonderful. Thank you so much." She swallowed. "Uh, just let me get these two guys fed, and then any time would be great."

Jayden jumped next to her. "Can we go now? I'm hungry."

"Sure." She touched his shoulder, relieved he'd been as patient as he had been.

"See you in a bit." Pastor Tony moved off to talk to someone standing nearby.

Jonas winked at her. "I expect the full tour."

Carissa laughed, grateful for the chance to switch emotional gears. "You got it."

Gladys touched her shoulder. "I'm headed over to the Wilders' for lunch, so I don't need a ride home. Claire's grandma, Erma, and I have become friends. And it looks like you've got all the help you need for this afternoon. Not that these old bones can do much lifting."

"Thank you so much for making that happen." Carissa covered the bony hand with her own. "I really appreciate it."

"We take care of our own up here." She squeezed Carissa's hand and moved off.

Carissa hustled the boys out to the car, her mind already

spinning with the change in plans. Burgers to-go at the Belleville Diner. Checking whatever mess Charlie had made at the house. Making sure nothing embarrassing was laying out in the bathroom or her bedroom, like the underwear she'd been handwashing.

She was not someone who liked to change her plans on a dime. But in this moment, she recognized the gift from God when she saw it. And she was grateful.

JONAS PULLED HIS TRUCK UP IN FRONT OF THE DELAMAR Place. He'd have to start thinking of it as Carissa's house. It was odd to imagine anyone living here. No one had as long as he'd been a resident. And all he could think of was associating it with the kids who went missing when he first arrived in Holcomb Springs. Carissa was doing a good thing in making this a livable home. Even if she planned on selling it.

Tony's truck pulled in behind his, and before he could even get to the front porch, Shannon and Zach had arrived, along with Ryan… And Amanda, Ella's co-teacher? Interesting.

As Jonas knocked on the front door, Marco Valdez and Vince Smithton pulled up. Huh. Tony must have grabbed everyone he could. With this crew, they'd be done in no time.

Carissa came to the door with a smile. She'd changed into shorts, tennis shoes, and a T-shirt. "Thank you all so much. Let me unlock the truck and the garage, and I can show you where things go." Her gaze met his for a second before taking in the folks gathered in the front yard. "Gosh, I don't think I met everyone."

Tony made the introductions. Carissa appeared to be a bit overwhelmed. Which was understandable. She seemed to be the take-charge type, so it probably surprised her when someone else did that for her.

Jonas followed her to the truck, the rest of the crowd trailing behind like some odd version of the Pied Piper. After she unlocked the door, he lifted it. "Why don't you just point where you want things to go, and we'll do the rest?"

"Great. Some things will go in the garage for now. But it will be wonderful to have the beds and a dining room table." She unclasped the garage lock and started to wrestle up the old wooden door before Jonas grabbed it and shoved it up.

She turned to him. "You know, I'd better show you which rooms are which. I know you wanted the grand tour, but we should start with the short version." She headed toward the back deck, her long legs eating up the ground. Nice looking long legs.

As he pulled his gaze away, he noticed the boys playing by the pond. "Hey, guys."

Brandon waved, but Jayden kept playing with his Lego guys.

Inside, Carissa grabbed a Post-it pad and pen from the kitchen counter.

"Wow, they fixed up the kitchen. It looks nice." Jonas took in the new appliances and renovated space.

She glanced around. "Yeah, it's the only room that does."

"A working kitchen and bath are pretty important."

"True. And I'm grateful for it."

They passed through to the next room with a beautiful built-in buffet. "It's amazing this is still here."

"I know. The woodwork is beautiful. And it's never been painted. That's a miracle. This is the dining room. We can put the table and chairs in here. I guess that's pretty obvious."

Square pillars embedded into the wall at the opposite end of the room led to the living room. He examined them. Sure enough, they hid pocket doors. He tugged them open a bit. "Cool feature."

"Yeah, and they still work. I dreaded having to take the wall apart if they needed to be fixed." She pointed to the space beyond. "This will serve as the living room. We don't have much, but it can go in here."

They crossed to the front of the house to the foyer and the

great wooden staircase. Across the way was another large room. He peeked in.

"That's the grand parlor, but it has some damage. Plus, I don't have anything to put in there. Beyond it, down the hall, is the downstairs bath." She put her hand on the newel post. "You'll probably need all the guys to get my adjustable Tempur-Pedic bed up here." She scribbled on the notepad while she climbed the stairs.

Jonas roved his gaze over the plaster walls and woodwork to keep it off the woman in front of him.

At the top of the stairs, she continued down the central hall to the door on the left. "This will be the boys' room. They'll share for now." She stuck a Post-it to the door with *Boys* written on it then gestured down the hall. "There's a bath and another bedroom, but it has a bunch of junk in it left over from previous renovations."

She turned to the door behind her. "This is my room." She pasted another sticky note on her door. "On this side of the stairs there's another bedroom. It's not in too bad of shape, but these two were the best. Plus, mine has a master bath. Someone had taken a bedroom and made a master suite, which I'm grateful for."

He scanned the area, the vision of the last time he'd been here overlaying the present. Different, but similar. "Great. That will help. We only have two rooms to put things in."

She nodded and headed downstairs. "Yeah. That was the plan."

Back outside, the truck was being unloaded, and the yard was littered with boxes and furniture.

And Vince had shown up. Great. Jonas wasn't sure why the guy always rubbed him the wrong way. Perhaps because his happy-go-lucky nature seemed a little too good to be true. But there was no concrete reason, just a personality clash.

The moment Vince spotted Carissa he was all smiles. He

strode over, extending his hand. "Hi, I'm Vince Smithton. Welcome to Holcomb Springs."

"Thanks. I appreciate your coming to help. It's a little overwhelming, but so appreciated."

"Not a problem. We like to take care of our own. You need anything, you just let me know." Vince grinned at her.

Jonas's gut churned. The guy really knew how to lay it on. In the distance, Amanda and Ryan were play fighting over a box and laughing. What was going on with those two? He shot a look at Carissa, who had spotted it as well, giving them a wry grin.

They needed to get moving. Jonas clapped his hands together. "Okay, everyone. We only have the dining room downstairs and the two bedrooms upstairs. Carissa, you want to make sure anything we grab should actually go in the house?"

"Sure." She checked the labels on the boxes nearest her and began directing where things went. Folks hopped into action, and soon boxes and furniture were moving across the yard and into the house or garage.

Jonas had lifted a box when he felt a hand on his shoulder. He turned.

Shannon's voice was low. "Way to take charge." She winked and moved off.

What did she mean by that? He shook it off, but when he came back out from dropping off his box, Vince was talking with Carissa, asking her how she had come by the house.

"So the blue moon legend didn't scare you off?" Vince was taking his time picking up a box, clearly lingering to talk to Carissa.

Why did he have to mention that stupid rumor? Carissa didn't need any more stress, but it was out there and there was no way, even if he dragged Vince away, to get the words back.

"What legend?" Carissa propped a hand on her hip.

"Some kids in the high school astronomy club used to hang

out here when it was vacant. After one of their excursions watching a lunar eclipse, they came back here. To do whatever high school kids do." Vince grinned. "One of them disappeared that night. The legend has it that his ghost comes back whenever there's anything to do with the moon—a lunar eclipse, a blue moon."

Carissa scoffed. "Well, maybe his ghost can get some work done around here."

Vince shook his head and hefted the box. "You laugh, but ask Jonas here. He worked on the investigation of the missing kid."

Jonas caught sight of Brandon watching them intently. Great, they were going to give the kid nightmares about ghosts. He had to nip this in the bud. "There's a reasonable explanation. He'd told his friends he wanted to take a road trip and see the sights before college. He just left without telling them." He took in Carissa's frown. They needed a change of subject. "Anyhow, that was four years ago. It's ancient history. It has nothing to do with the house now."

Vince started to say something but stopped at Jonas's scowl.

Another car pulled into the driveway behind the moving truck. Gladys climbed out of the passenger side, a square plastic container in her hands. Erma VanKirk got out of the driver's side and reached into the back seat of her sedan.

"We come bearing refreshments!" Gladys lifted her canister higher. "Cookies and iced tea and lemonade. Vince, be a dear and help Erma with those jugs."

Vince jogged over to the car while Gladys continued into the house via the back porch.

Carissa shook her head and smiled, meeting Jonas's gaze. "That woman is a wonder."

It wasn't too much longer before all the furniture and boxes were out of the moving truck and in their proper places. Everyone gathered in the kitchen to demolish the cookies and drinks.

"Thank you all so much. I literally couldn't have done it without you." Carissa lifted her plastic cup in salute.

"Tell us your plans for this place." Shannon leaned against the counter, Tony rather close next to her. "The kitchen looks great."

Carissa gave a wry grin. "Yeah, it's about the only thing. It needs a lot of cosmetic work. There's something wrong with the mudroom floor. And the washer and dryer need to be hooked up. And a long list of other things. But it all seems doable."

Vince disappeared into the mudroom and returned a moment later. "Have you been down in the basement yet?"

"I've only gotten as far as the utility panels. It's not finished down there, and it's pretty creepy." Carissa gave a small shudder. "I found a dead bat in one of the cripple studs."

"I'm happy to take a look, to see what's going on with the supports. Even though I'm a landscaper, my brother's a contractor, and I worked a lot of summers with him."

"I'd appreciate that."

The rest of the group dispersed with many thanks by Carissa. Vince headed for the basement door. "Let's see what we've got."

No way was Jonas going to let him go down there with Carissa alone. He followed.

Vince flipped on the light, illuminating a single bare bulb over rickety wooden stairs. The walls were unfinished studs and tar paper, with plaster seeping in between the lath on the areas that abutted the finished spaces upstairs. He headed down, Carissa following, and Jonas bringing up the rear. The air was dank and musty. He could see why she didn't want to come down here.

"Watch your step. There's no handrail," Jonas cautioned. He pulled out his phone and turned on the flashlight. The bulb in the ceiling cast more shadows than light. At the bottom, the basement walls had been whitewashed, and a thin layer of concrete covered part of the floor. The part under the mudroom was still dirt with sheets of plywood laid over it.

Vince scanned the floor joists with his own phone light. "Looks like you need another Lally column here to support the floor's weight."

Carissa nodded. "Yep. Too big of a span for the size of those joists. And since we don't care about obstructing traffic flow, a Lally column will be a cheaper solution than an engineered beam. And I can concrete over this dirt. Ugh."

A commotion at the top of the stairs caught Jonas's attention. Brandon and Jayden peered down.

"Mom? Are you down there?" Brandon's voice had a hint of a waver.

"Yes, we'll be up in just a second. Don't come down."

But another clatter, and "Charlie!" shouted by Brandon followed by the pounding of paws down the stairs. Charlie trotted over to them.

"It's okay, I've got him." Jonas got a hold of Charlie's collar and rubbed his head.

He licked Jonas's leg and then whined, pulling against him.

"Easy, boy. I don't think there's anything down here for you."

He kept whining and tugging. A chill ran down Jonas's spine. "We done down here?"

Carissa shivered. "Yes, let's get out of this place. It's giving me the creeps." She headed up the stairs.

Jonas followed close behind, making sure Charlie didn't jump ahead and take her out. Once they were all out, he closed the door firmly behind them. "Nobody should go down there by themselves. It would be too easy to fall and get hurt." He specifically looked at the boys.

Brandon nodded, eyes wide, but Jayden just petted Charlie.

Vince handed Carissa one of her Post-its. "This is my number. Call me and we'll see about getting that washer and dryer hooked up too." He nodded to the red appliances in the corner of the mudroom.

Carissa took it. "Thanks, I appreciate that." She glanced around. "You all were a huge help. I so appreciate it. Now I just need to get the moving truck returned over in Big Bear. I think I can get it back just before they close and save a day's rental fee if I hurry."

"I can go with you to bring you back," Vince volunteered.

Jonas supressed a huff, not very successfully. "You don't have space for her and the boys in your truck. My truck has an extended cab, so I can bring you home."

The look that crossed Vince's face proved he'd forgotten about her boys. He held Jonas's gaze a touch too long. Marking his territory, no doubt. Jonas refrained from shaking his head, but Vince was so predictable.

After a moment, Vince tapped the sticky note. "I'll expect your call."

"Thanks for your help." Carissa gave a small wave as Vince left, then searched the kitchen until she came up with her purse and truck keys. She turned to Jonas. "Let's get everything locked up, and we can head over there."

"Let's go."

In a moment, they had Charlie and the house secured, the garage locked up, and the moving truck ready to return.

"Can I ride with Jonas?" Brandon asked, looking between the two of them.

Surprised, Jonas managed to respond, "It's fine with me if it's okay with your mom."

Carissa met Jonas's gaze. "Sure, it's fine." She helped Jayden into his booster seat in the truck, and soon they were on their way, Jonas following behind.

As they drove the twisty mountain roads, Jonas replayed the day in his head. He'd never been Vince's biggest fan. But why had he gotten under Jonas's skin today more than ever?

With a blinding flash that almost made him catch his breath, he realized something. He glanced in the rearview mirror to see if Brandon had noticed anything, but he was staring out the window.

Jonas was attracted to Carissa.

And he'd sworn that he'd never again let his heart get involved.

CHAPTER
NINE

Carissa woke up in her bed and smiled. Her first night in her actual bed instead of an air mattress. It was glorious. Once again, she was grateful for the lovely people who helped get everything inside and saved her from hiring folks to do it. Which meant she could now afford to take Charlie to the vet.

She got up and peeked in on the boys. Both were still asleep in their beds, but they wouldn't be for long.

Downstairs, she started the coffee and let Charlie out. The morning air was cool, but the sun promised warmth. Charlie inspected the yard, his nose leading him on some sort of journey. As he wandered around the pond, it reminded her she needed to get it cleaned out before Jayden ended up in it. And before it got too hot.

She called Charlie in. He glanced up at her but went back to whatever had his attention. Usually he was good at obeying, which made her think he had a home at some point. He sniffed all around the garage and then the far side of the house. He was on the trail of something. She was still in her pajama pants and T-shirt, so she wasn't going to chase him. He'd come when he was hungry.

Back inside, her coffee had finished brewing. She got the boys up and fed. Charlie still hadn't come in yet.

"Brandon, will you feed Charlie and see if you can get him to come in. He was chasing some squirrel or rabbit earlier."

Brandon jumped up, and a moment later kibble tinkled in the metal dog bowl. The back door opened. "Charlie! Here, boy! I've got your breakfast."

Carissa had just finished her coffee when the sounds of boy and dog entered the mudroom, then there was slurping of dog food.

Brandon came into the kitchen with a grin on his face. "He sure likes to eat."

"He sure does. Where'd you find him?"

"All the way on the other side of the house in all those bushes. Something was interesting to him over there."

"Hmm."

He looked up at her. "Do you think it was the ghost?"

She shook her head. "There's no such thing as ghosts. Vince was just being funny. Some people like to tease other people by trying to scare them." She wanted to wring Vince's neck for saying something that might scare the boys. Clearly he hadn't been around kids much. But Brandon seemed to take her explanation in stride.

Today she wanted to get the pond mucked out since Jayden had such an interest in it. Once she got it cleaned, would it be good to put some fish in it? She'd have to research that as well.

Outside, she glanced around for the shovel. It had been leaning up against the garage wall yesterday. She hadn't wanted it to get buried behind the boxes in the garage. But it wasn't there now. Weird. Maybe someone had moved it.

She rounded the corner. There was her shovel leaning against the house. The dirt behind the bushes around the foundation looked disturbed. Charlie had been over here this morning chasing some animal. Had he dug around trying to get it?

Or had someone used her shovel?

But that didn't make any sense. Most likely George had borrowed it and hadn't returned it properly. Checking the ground one more time and not finding anything to be concerned about, she grabbed the shovel and headed to the pond.

Last fall's decomposing leaves lined the bottom. It was only about a foot and a half deep, which only made it a little less nasty job. It smelled vaguely of an old barn. She wasn't sure if the common scent was manure or rotting plant material.

The pond wasn't the most pressing need of the house, though it was a forgone conclusion that Jayden would end up in it, and she wanted to have a less-disgusting mess to clean up. And having something to do with her hands was good therapy. It was an easy project to cross off her to-do list.

Plus, it'd be likely that Gladys would show up to chat. Carissa was curious about her take on the rumors, given that she lived next door to the offending house. Gladys was outside a lot. That was probably how she kept tabs on George and their little neighborhood. It was different. Back in Arizona, she and her neighbors just hit the remote on the garage door and pulled in, not stopping to visit often.

She lifted a shovelful of muck and dumped it in the green waste can. If they were going to be here longer, she'd start a compost pile with all these leaves. Her mind went back to Vince's offer yesterday. It was kind—and tempting since she needed a lot of help and had a small budget—but she was hesitant. It felt like there was something more than neighborliness attached to it. And the last thing she wanted was to start owing a man something.

She'd be better off connecting with Claire first and using her resources. Maybe Vince was one of them. Or maybe not.

The squeak of her neighbor's storm door alerted Carissa as she tossed another icky pile into the can.

Gladys came out wearing a yellow tube top, her hair in a

bun. Spotting Carissa, she waved and came over to the picket fence. "Great day for yard work, isn't it?"

"It is. Thank you again for the cookies and drinks yesterday. Everyone was so kind and helpful. It was great to be able to give them some treats." Carissa rested a minute on the shovel handle. As much as time seemed to press down on her, she was learning to take a minute to visit with people in the stores and coffee shop. Small town life took a bit of an adjustment, but she didn't want to be seen as rude. Plus, nearly everyone had been nice.

Gladys waved it off. "We take care of each other here. And since we couldn't tote boxes, Erma and I figured we could bake."

"I actually wanted to ask you about something." Carissa walked closer to the fence so the boys wouldn't overhear. "Vince mentioned something about rumors regarding my house and some missing high school kid. Do you know anything about that?"

Her lips curled down. "That stupid rumor. Vince should know better than to shoot his mouth off. I oughta talk to him. There's no truth to it. Yes, those kids would hang out here sometimes at night. I was almost always in bed, and they were good about not being too loud. My biggest fear was that they'd be careless with candles or try to light a fire and burn the place down and the neighborhood with it. Once or twice the deputies would come by and ask them to leave. But overall, they were good kids."

A little bit of the load slipped off her shoulders. She was surprised that it had been there, given that she'd pretty much dismissed the rumor too. Jonas wouldn't lie to her, and he didn't seem to think there was much stock in it. "What about the teenager who disappeared? Did you know him?"

"Tyler? Just the way I know all the young people. Barely, by sight. They grow so fast, I can hardly recognize them. I knew his parents better."

"Knew?" Carissa had caught the past tense.

"They moved out of the area about six months after he disappeared. I don't know what happened to them."

"Do you think Jonas is right that he just went on a road trip?"

Gladys looked off into the distance. "That's what they say. I didn't know him well enough."

That topic seemed to be drawing to a close. Carissa bounced the shovel up and down in the dirt. "Have you seen George lately? My shovel was misplaced, and I wondered if he'd borrowed it."

Gladys's eyes narrowed. "That doesn't sound like George."

Carissa was surprised. She thought it sounded exactly like George and his loose definition of personal property.

"If you found it again, it likely wasn't him. Unless you found it on eBay." Gladys gave a rough chuckle. "But he also doesn't go into fenced yards. He recognizes that boundary. Probably just one of your boys playing with it."

"Yeah." But she wasn't convinced. The shovel was too big for Jayden, and Brandon would have no purpose for it. He would have told her. "Well, I'd better get back to cleaning out this pond."

Gladys waved and moved off, pulling on a pair of gardening gloves and setting to work around some bushes in her yard.

Carissa scooped the last of the plant matter off the bottom. Once the sediment settled, the water should look pretty clear. She'd be glad when the internet was installed and she could put in a few Wi-Fi cameras so she could see what was going on. Who'd have thought she'd need that up here?

TONY LOCKED UP HIS HOUSE AND HEADED FOR THE JITTER Bug Too. It was his day off and the day for his coffee date with Shannon. He would walk. It wasn't too far, and he needed the time to clear his head. It was a beautiful day, and the tourists hadn't descended on them yet, but they would—starting with Art Fest, the unofficial kickoff of the summer season.

He pocketed his keys, checked for his phone, and started out down the street, the sun peeking in between the pine boughs lining his way. He and Shannon had developed a deep friendship over the past six months. They'd bonded over their love for and service to this town and its people. But there had always been an undercurrent of something more. They'd moved toward it last March and then backed off. But at last Friday's graduation, there was a real moment of vulnerability with her. He wanted more of that.

Of course, that meant he'd need to be vulnerable too. And he had finally worked up enough courage and trust in their relationship to tell her about his dyslexia. He was fully conscious of the fact that his delay in telling her made it seem a bigger deal than it was. But of all the people in this town, her opinion of him meant the most. His head told him her opinion of him wouldn't change. But his heart remembered all too well the painful teasing he'd received in the past.

Janelle, his deceased wife, had been his best supporter and never made him feel defective or less than for how the words scrambled in his brain. If he was honest with himself, Shannon was far more like Janelle than anyone else who had been hurtful. It was time to make the leap.

He took a deep breath of the clean, piney air. The timing needed to be right. She would be busy until Art Fest was over. And they'd need to get out of town. Maybe he could convince her to take a day trip somewhere. A place where they could both be off duty completely, something that wasn't possible in this town. Something that was definitely a date. Something that let her know he was serious about changing the tone of their relationship.

He wouldn't mention the idea today. He'd think on it a bit, come up with some options, and then talk to her about it.

The smell of coffee and fresh-baked scones greeted him as he neared the Jitter Bug Too and pulled the door open, the small bell tinkling above the door.

Ryan and Amanda stood at the counter. Ryan turned. As the worship pastor, today was his day off too. He'd been spending a lot of time with the schoolteacher lately. Something was going on there. Amanda was a great woman. Ryan still had some growing up to do, though he'd made good strides in the six months he'd been up here. Tony just hoped he'd grown up enough to not hurt Amanda.

Ryan lifted a hand. "Hey, Tony. Guess we don't see enough of each other at work, huh?"

Tony chuckled. "When this place has the best baked goods and coffee, odds are good I'll show up here at some point."

Amanda turned and smiled. "Hey, Pastor. We're headed out on the lake with Ella and Reese. Just picking up some coffee and goodies to go."

"Sounds like a great plan." It would be a busy day at the lake, since it was a popular destination on Memorial Day. He moved to the counter as Ryan and Amanda took their order and left. He placed his order with Cassie, exchanging a grin with her as her gaze drifted past him to where Ryan and Amanda had exited.

"Seems like those two are spending a lot of time together," she said, pulling his coffee.

Tony shrugged. He never commented on people to others unless it was positive. Gossip—or even the hint of it—would gut a church faster than a fire in the building. He took his order from Cassie and slid into his usual booth and thought about his decision again.

A smile creased his face. It was a good plan.

JONAS HEADED INTO HIS MONDAY MEETING WITH THE sheriff to recap the graduation event and make any tweaks for next year and plan for this week. With Art Fest starting soon, they had to plan for that as well.

He grabbed onto the routine to stabilize him. His realization yesterday that he was attracted to Carissa had thrown him off-balance. He'd gotten her and the boys home from returning the rental truck with minimal polite conversation and then quickly extricated himself and headed home.

He told himself that attraction was a natural thing. And it didn't mean anything. It was simply an attraction. Carissa was a beautiful woman, strong, doing an amazing job raising two boys by herself. There was a lot to admire. It didn't mean he had feelings for her beyond being a friendly neighbor.

But sleep eluded him. And even a vigorous basketball game before his shift hadn't shaken the dregs off.

He settled himself across from the sheriff's desk. "You did a great job with your graduation speech." Though Friday seemed a lot more than three days ago.

"Thanks. I was happy I got through it without tears. I couldn't look at Zach until I was finished." She let out a deep breath, and they recapped the event before moving on to Art Fest plans. He would work the weekend, which was what happened during big events. They needed all hands on deck and even brought in temporary help from other departments. But he'd have Sunday off. He and the sheriff made sure everyone had a chance to enjoy the fun if they wanted to.

At the end of their meeting, he stood to leave, but the sheriff stopped him. "One more thing. I heard Vince blab about the missing kids to Carissa yesterday. Do you think she's concerned about it?"

"Didn't seem to be. I told her what we had turned up, which was that Tyler Cohen had taken off on a road trip. There was nothing to indicate any kind of foul play, especially not at her house. But people like to make up stories about old, vacant houses, and since the kids used to hang out there, the rumors started. Though I don't think Vince should have said anything. Brandon overheard and looked scared."

"Vince doesn't always engage his brain before opening his mouth." She tapped her pen on her desk then gave him a thoughtful look. "That was nice of you to organize all the help yesterday."

He raised his hands. "Wasn't me. That was Pastor Tony."

"He recruited all of us, but you ran the show once we got there. You appear to know her better than anyone else. She seems like a nice lady." Her eyebrows rose.

"She is. I helped her get her keys when she locked them in her car. I thought she was a tourist then. Later, I saw her at the library. Anne was doing some sort of matchmaking event, and Mariah was there." He felt his face heat. This shouldn't be so uncomfortable. "Carissa bailed me out by pretending we knew each other and were going to take the boys for ice cream. I told her about the church and about Alex and Claire. Just being a good neighbor." He squeezed the back of the chair.

"Uh huh. Good."

"By the way, you might mention to Mariah that calling dispatch as a way to get me to swing by the Sleepy Bear Lodge isn't a good use of our resources." His voice had taken on an edge.

"Did you tell her that?"

"I did, but I thought she might take it better coming from another woman. That you could, you know..." This was ridiculous. He always had an easy rapport with Shannon, so why couldn't he just spell it out for her?

"I'm not going to be your go between. I'll talk to her about police business, but if you're not interested in her, you need to tell her." She paused a moment. "Or maybe that won't be necessary if it's obvious you're interested in someone else."

"I'm not," he said a bit too hotly.

She raised her hands. "Not my business, and I'm not trying to cross any lines here. As your friend, I just wanted to say I really like Carissa and thought you were doing a great thing by helping her." She paused. "And here I will cross a line, but as your friend. It's okay to get back out there, Jonas."

"And as a *friend*, I'd say the same to you about Pastor Tony."

She sighed and looked away. "Touché." She pushed to her feet. "I'm on my way to see him now."

CHAPTER
TEN

With yesterday being Memorial Day, Carissa had taken Jonas's advice and stuck close to home, avoiding the tourist traffic in town. Which was fine. They had plenty to do unpacking boxes and getting their lives in order, as much as they could. And she'd gotten the pond cleaned out, which was satisfying, given how much the boys enjoyed playing around it.

But first thing today, they needed to make a trip to the library. She had a few things to look up, and it had been closed yesterday.

The boys were excited about visiting the library again. They headed out to the SUV in the driveway. By the time winter got here, she hoped she could get the car in the garage. She didn't relish the idea of shoveling snow and chipping ice off her windshield. As beautiful as today was, it was hard to believe snow would blanket this area come winter.

Theoretically, the library was within walking distance, but that would take longer than she had time for. She paused. The boys needed to burn off the energy, and she needed to do something other than work on the house for five minutes.

"Boys, let's walk." They started down the street. The slower pace gave her a chance to peek at her neighbors' houses nestled between the pine trees. The curving road made some of them difficult to spot.

George was walking down the street pulling his cart. He waved when he spotted them. "Nice day, isn't it?"

"It is." Carissa wasn't sure what else to say, but apparently she didn't need to make more than pleasantries with him. He nodded as he passed, and she noted his cart was full of cans, bottles, and other scraps.

"Just doing my part to keep our town clean. Those tourists have no problem throwing their trash around. Always get a good haul after a holiday."

"That's great."

"If you ever have any cans or bottles, I'm happy to take 'em off your hands."

"I'll keep that in mind."

He tipped his nonexistent hat as he passed by and whistled a tune.

Carissa thought about what Gladys had said. She was right; George didn't seem the type to take her shovel. It likely had gotten moved when the truck was being unloaded, and she just hadn't noticed.

When they arrived at the library, the boys made a beeline for the kids' section. They loved the mountain and the "gold mine" reading area underneath it.

Anne waved to her from the circulation desk. "How goes the remodeling?"

Carissa gave a tired laugh. "The church folks helped unload the moving truck Sunday. That was a real blessing. And I've been sleeping in a real bed. That makes a huge difference in my perspective on things."

"There's nothing like a good night's sleep, for sure. I found some things out about your house. Be right back." She disappeared into the back and then returned with books in her arms. "I had pulled some of these for the Wilders, and interestingly enough, your houses had the same architect and builder. Have you met Alex and Claire yet?"

"Just at church. I'm looking forward to seeing what they've done."

Anne leaned forward. "It's really amazing. They're nearly finished. We've got our big Art Fest coming up at the end of June, and they plan on having their grand opening then."

"Well, I can't wait to look through these. I have an unrelated question. Is there a good vet up here? We found a dog—or rather, he found us. I want to make sure he doesn't belong to anyone and get him a checkup before my boys get even more attached to him." Though, she was pretty sure that was a lost cause. She hoped he didn't belong to anyone else. The boys couldn't handle any more loss.

"There is." Anne typed something on the computer then reached over for a scratch piece of paper, wrote something down, and passed it over to Carissa. "Dr. Green. He's great. And not very expensive. All the locals use him."

"Thank you." Carissa tucked the paper into her purse. "I figured you really were the source of information."

Anne gave her a sassy smile and tossed her blonde waves over her shoulder. "I like to think so. Anything else I can help you with?"

Carissa considered asking her about the rumors around the missing kids that Vince mentioned, but Brandon came up just then with another stack of books. She didn't want him over-hearing anything that could upset him. Jonas had done a good job of downplaying it all.

"I'm sure I'll come up with something else, but for now I just need to use the computer before we head out."

"Great. And I can help this young man check out his books." Anne took Brandon's books and library card.

His grin was so wide Carissa couldn't help but smile. "I'll just be a sec." She glanced around the end of the aisle to make sure Jayden was still in the kids' section, and he was. "Five minutes, bud, okay?"

He didn't look up.

Carissa went over and touched his shoulder. "Five minutes, then we need to leave."

He gave a short nod but didn't look up from the book that captured his attention.

She went to the computer and responded to a few emails that were easier to do than from her phone and its few bars. The email from Greg about the court date sat there. She hadn't had much time to think about what to do.

Instead, she searched for "missing kids" and "Holcomb Springs." There were a few newspaper articles about the missing high school senior. She scanned them quickly and then printed them out to read later. Back at the search results page, she found a few blogs and social media posts that referenced the missing teenager and hit on the rumors Vince had mentioned about the moon. The most concerning site seemed to keep a running list of the happenings at the Delamar Place. And it forecast the next blue moon at the end of June, speculating that the ghost would return then.

It all seemed pretty far-fetched to her, but she jotted down the sites to revisit when she had more time. Rumors of any kind could scare off potential buyers. But by the time she'd revamped the house from top to bottom, she'd be able to erase any trace of mysteries. And though the end of June was a month away and the house wouldn't be completed by then, she was sure they could put any talk of ghosts to rest.

She just had to make sure the boys didn't hear about any of this.

CHAPTER
ELEVEN

Carissa's stomach growled as she toed off her soggy old sneakers in the mudroom. She'd need to find a place to put them out of Charlie's reach tonight, but for now, flip-flops would do. She'd picked up a small, solar-powered fountain at the hardware store to add to their pond to keep the algae down. Unfortunately, that required wading into it.

She needed to eat, but she hadn't had a chance to read the articles she'd printed off at the library yesterday. When she went upstairs to grab her flip-flops, she picked up the articles from her dresser and flipped through them, reading more carefully, resting on her bed a moment.

There was nothing too much beyond what Jonas had told her. As far as the facts went. But one of the teens interviewed, an Anthony Smithton, had been Tyler's friend. Why did that name sound familiar? It was a small town, so… Oh, that was Vince's last name. What was the relationship there? Maybe he was an uncle or some other relative?

And then the rumors about the ghosts and the moon. Most of it was ridiculous. Still, if she could have something concrete to refute it, it would help her sell this place. Or she'd have to make it so fabulous buyers couldn't resist it.

Her mind drifted to Jonas. She kind of wished she could talk to him about this, see if there was anything else. He'd been so calm and matter of fact about all of it on Sunday. Of course, he'd noticed that Brandon was listening. So what would he tell her if Brandon wasn't around?

It didn't matter. She wasn't going to bother him. Maybe she'd see him next Sunday at church and could ask him then if the boys weren't around. And she was definitely looking forward to seeing him again. He was easy on the eyes and a great guy to boot. A rare package.

She levered herself up off the bed, slipped on her flip-flops, and returned the articles to her dresser. Time to make dinner.

At the grocery store, she'd picked up simple but comforting things that would make her look forward to whipping something up rather than grabbing food out. And tomato soup with grilled cheese sounded good.

The boys had been unpacking their room. She was sure it would look like a hurricane hit it, but it would keep them busy.

She crossed the hall to the boys' room. Yep, hurricane city. Boxes were partially opened and clothing and toys were strewn about. Brandon sat in the middle of it reading a book from the library.

"Where's your brother?"

He looked up then scanned the room. "Oh, I think he was doing something with his Legos."

Of course. The question was, where was he? It wasn't fair to make Brandon his keeper. But she also had a lot to do. She would be grateful when school—and Jayden's special therapy program—started in the fall. Unfortunately, she couldn't wait until then to start work on the house.

"How are you liking your room?"

Brandon studied the space around him, nodding. "I like it. We can see across to the lake from our window. Can we go to the lake sometime?"

"Yes, we can. We'll definitely have to check that out. In the meantime, maybe some of these clothes could get into the dresser?" She swirled her finger around the room. "And I'm making grilled cheese and tomato soup. You can come help, if you want."

"'Kay. Just let me finish this chapter."

Carissa smiled. He was a bookworm after her own heart.

At the top of the stairs, the railing ran across the opening that looked down to the entryway on both sides of the staircase. It was a beautiful feature that made for a dramatic entry to the house.

It scared her a bit too. The spindles were too close together —thank goodness—for Jayden to climb through. But would he try to climb over? She shuddered. As she skimmed her fingers along, they snagged on a rough spot. She looked more closely. There was another one. Hmm. This railing had been damaged at some point and repaired. There were two breaks a few feet apart repaired with wood filler. And not very expertly done. The stain didn't quite match, and the area hadn't been sanded well. Probably the same crew that redid the kitchen. Yet one more thing for the list. But, hey, she could cross the pond off.

She headed downstairs, lucky the stairs were pretty solid with just a squeaky spot or two. It added to the charm. She could even sell it as a feature. "Folks, you'll know if your kids are trying to sneak out or raid the refrigerator at night."

Running her hand over the banister, she was amazed at the craftsmanship. This was what she loved about old houses. Someone took the time to make something functional beautiful.

Rounding the corner into the living room and then the dining room, she spotted Jayden. He had set up his Legos on the dining room table into an intricate tableau. He must have dragged his tote bin down the stairs. If she'd been inside, she certainly would have heard that.

"Wow, that's a lot of stuff you've got going on there." She bent to examine the buildings with various figures perched on them. "I'm making dinner, so you'll need to move this some-where else so we can eat."

"I can't move it. It's my ninja city."

"Okay, well, we need to eat. I'm not sure we can eat in the ninja city. Maybe move it over to the sideboard." She touched the wooden built-in. "No one will bother it over here."

He kept building.

"Jayden, we need to eat in a few minutes. Go ahead and move your stuff while I'm finishing up." Carissa left the dining room and went into the kitchen. Sometimes he'd do things if she wasn't standing over him. This would give him some time to figure out how he could make it work his way.

She started the soup—canned, but who cared—and got out the pan for the grilled cheese. She sliced up some pickles and tomatoes.

Brandon's footsteps thumped down the stairs, and a minute later he appeared in the kitchen. "Smells good. I'm hungry."

"It's almost ready. Will you see if your brother moved his Legos off the table yet?"

Brandon disappeared while she dished up the soup. Shouting between the two of them floated into the kitchen.

"Mom said!"

"No! That's mine."

With a sigh, she dropped the ladle and peered in the dining room. Brandon was trying to move Jayden's Legos, and he was moving them back just as fast. "Brandon, that's fine. I'll take care of it. Jayden, I told you we need to eat. We can move everything without messing up any of it." She shifted a few of his buildings to the sideboard. "See? It's fine. Now you do the rest, and I'll bring in the food."

Back in the kitchen she grabbed the bowls, balancing the three of them on her arm like she had done when she waitressed in college.

In the dining room, Jayden had moved everything back onto the table.

She scooted a tower over so she could set the bowls down. "Jayden, come on." She picked up the buildings again, and a piece fell off one.

Jayden screamed and threw himself after it. "You ruined it!"

"It's fine. We can put the piece back on."

"No!" He threw his arms around the rest of his city.

"Jayden. We'll find a place for you to build your ninja city. But we need the table to eat." She put her hands on his shoulders and kept her voice low and even.

"No!"

"Either you can move your city, or I can."

"No!" He threw an elbow, which she barely caught before it slammed into her midsection.

"Hitting is not okay." Carissa looked to the ceiling, wishing some guidance was written there. This was not going well. She didn't want to reward a temper tantrum. She understood this creation was important to him. But he was also part of the family that needed the table. She wondered if UN peace negotiators had such a difficult task. Her stomach growled.

Brandon was chewing on a grilled cheese sandwich, watching. Guess he'd gotten hungry.

"Jayden. Last time. Either you move your city, or I will.

He crossed his arms with a huff and scowled.

She picked up his city and carried it over to the sideboard.

He howled. He threw his arms around her legs in an attempt to stop her.

She wobbled a moment but regained her balance. Luckily the table was close enough to the built-in that she only had to manage a few steps with him clinging to her legs. She got everything relocated, but Jayden hadn't stopped screaming.

His howls turned to sobs. You'd think she'd said they had to toss out his Legos, not just move them.

She knelt next to him. "Jayden—"

He picked up a bowl of soup and threw it against the wall before wrenching out of her grasp.

She gasped. "Jayden!" Red dripped down the plaster wall; the broken bowl lay on the floor.

He flew out of the room, and the pounding of his feet on the stairs said he was headed for his room.

JONAS POINTED HIS WORK SUV THROUGH TOWN, HIS headlights illuminating the twisting roads he knew by heart. The Memorial Day traffic was mostly gone now, several days past. They'd established some new traffic patterns to keep bottlenecks at a minimum. It was a test to see how it would work for Art Fest and Gold Rush Days in August.

They'd written enough tickets to augment their budget for the quarter, and George had made a nice chunk of change picking up cans and bottles the tourists left behind. So far, so good. Jonas owed the sheriff a report on it.

But instead of sitting at his desk writing, he was heading out to Little Bear Lookout. Ostensibly to make sure everything was okay after a holiday weekend, though he knew Brett and Roberto had covered it. The moon was nearly full—would be full tomorrow. He thought watching it rise above the treetops and create a moonbeam across the lake might just clear his head.

He turned onto the two-track. The chain was across the road and locked. He opened it; he should have the place to himself, unless some kids had hiked back in there.

His SUV rocked down the rutted lane until it opened up to a clearing where he parked. No bonfire lit the firepit. He switched on his Maglite. The wood benches were empty. A few steps down the paths in either direction told him that no one was lurking about. Didn't appear to be any graffiti or trash. This was pretty much a locals-only hangout. You had to be a resident to have a key to the lock across the road. But a few others had spotted it on occasion and hiked back here. Perched on the cliff above the lake, it had the most spectacular view at sunset. Nighttime viewing wasn't too bad either.

He switched off his light and let his eyes adjust to the growing darkness as his thoughts wandered.

He'd talked to his brother, Jonathan, earlier today before work. They didn't talk about anything in particular, but Jon had promised to bring his family up for Art Fest. Jonas would be working for most of it, but he'd have some time off. It'd been too long since they'd seen each other.

Carissa and her boys would enjoy ArtFest. What kid wouldn't? Then he thought about Jayden. Maybe the festival would overstimulate him. There would be carnival games and rides, food booths, bands, as well as art booths of all kinds, including some hands-on projects for kids. His thoughts ran in that direction for a moment, and he eased down onto a bench.

Then again, why was he thinking about this? It wasn't his concern. Yes, Carissa was attractive. All the more reason he should keep his distance. She and her boys needed to get settled into their new life here. Folks like Alex and Claire would help her.

And someone like Vince needed to stay away. He nearly growled at the thought of Vince shooting his mouth off about ghosts in front of Brandon. The guy was an idiot. Carissa was too smart to fall for him.

Jonas tilted his head. The gibbous moon skimmed the top of the trees, casting its glow on the lake. The sight had always brought him peace before. But now...

He thought of Shannon's words about getting back out there. He shook his head. Nope. Not for him.

He rose from the bench and flipped on his light. The moon wasn't working its magic tonight. Better head back and write some reports.

CHAPTER
TWELVE

Carissa and the boys headed out to the Explorer the next day. For a town that was walkable, she was sure driving a lot. She was going to need to get some paint and didn't relish hauling a five-gallon bucket home from the hardware store, their planned stop after visiting with the Wilders.

Claire had texted and invited them over. And told Carissa to bring her laundry with her. She jumped at the chance. They were running out of clothes, and the nearest laundromat was in Big Bear. And she needed some adult company today. Along with clean laundry.

She'd cleaned up Jayden's mess last night, digging out a bucket, rubber gloves, and TSP to clean and prep the walls. She had the dull ache between her shoulder blades as a memento. He'd cried himself to sleep fully clothed and without dinner.

Gladys's storm door squealed, and she appeared shortly, leaning over the picket fence. It was like she knew the moment Carissa was trying to leave. While Gladys caught Carissa up on the local gossip, which Carissa half listened to, the boys inspected the pond. By the time she'd extricated herself with the comment that Claire was waiting on them, Jayden had already splashed his shirt and shorts with the fountain.

When they climbed into the car, she buckled Jayden into his booster and handed him hand sanitizer and a napkin. It would have to do. There wasn't time to go inside and change. Claire had a daughter; hopefully she'd understand.

On the drive over, Carissa's mind spun with the questions she wanted to ask. Until she spoke to Claire and Alex about subcontractors and the squishy floor was fixed, she was hesitant to do much else. Shifting could make plaster crack. And there was plenty of that that needed to be repaired.

This week she'd been washing down the woodwork; there was a ton of wax on the windowsills. Someone had been burning candles. The teens, she supposed. She could clean out the junk from the upstairs rooms, but she was hoping one of the contractors she would need to hire would rent a Dumpster or a Bagster she could use, saving her that expense.

But the dining room had been the one room that didn't need work. Now it did. Carissa had started creating paint schemes for the house in Arizona when she'd first seen it and dreamed about its potential. Now that she was living in the house, she'd finalized them. She could get the paint and fix the dining room. Then she'd be ready to move around the house painting rooms as they were ready. She liked painting. You could see immediate results. And right now, she needed to see some immediate, positive results.

She pulled up in front of a gorgeous Victorian. She could see the resemblance to her house in the placement of the front porch, the gables, and the windows. But this one was much bigger. And in much better condition. She climbed out of the SUV, studying the house as she went, getting ideas for landscaping. She could see a sweet gazebo peeking out from the back. This was already a lovely space.

Claire stepped onto the wide front porch decorated with a cozy seating area and a porch swing at the far end. "Welcome to the Cope House B-and-B! So glad you could make it."

"This is beautiful. I can't wait to see what else you've done."

Carissa climbed the painted porch steps, dragging her laundry basket, the boys trailing her.

Lizzie, Claire's daughter, came outside. "Hi, Brandon." She was twelve, almost two years older than Brandon, but she didn't seem to mind hanging out with the younger boys. Of course, Brandon was old for his age, given the amount of responsibility he'd always had on his slim shoulders.

"Hey." Brandon had his hands shoved in his shorts pockets.

"Want to see my room?" Lizzie looked like a miniature version of her mom—straight, light-brown hair and a sprinkling of freckles across her nose.

"Sure." The kids headed inside.

"Jayden, you want to go with them?" Carissa asked.

He nodded and trailed after them.

"Brandon," Carissa called. "Jayden's coming too."

"'Kay," came the reply from inside the house.

Claire laughed. "I think they'll be fine. Let's get your laundry started, then I'll show you around."

Their laundry room was tucked into the mudroom, in a similar spot to where Carissa wanted hers. But Claire had multiple industrial-sized machines to handle all the bedding a B-and-B would require. Carissa started her laundry then Claire showed her around the house, which had the same basic layout as hers, but the rooms were much bigger. And upstairs had more bedrooms.

Claire took her into one. "Have you discovered any hidden rooms in your house?"

Carissa's eyebrows shot up. "Hidden rooms? No. I suppose there could be, if they were well hidden. I haven't gotten to any demo yet."

Claire walked through a bedroom and to the far wall. She pushed on a panel that just looked like part of the wainscoting. It popped open, revealing a narrow closet that ran behind the wall. There was a small window in it, up near the ceiling.

"That's amazing. I wonder if I have something similar.

There's something up high in one of the gables that I thought was an attic vent. But perhaps it's a window to the secret closet."

"We think they might have used it to store booze during Prohibition. Or maybe gold from the local mines. We had a secret room in our last B-and-B in Michigan. It led to some interesting things." Claire gave a wry smile. "But that's a story for another time. Still, it brought Alex and me together."

"I'm going to have to look for this when I get home." Carissa could hardly wait. How fun. Houses always had secrets; old ones had more. But this was the best kind of secret.

"We only found it because Samuel—he's helping Alex outside—was living in the house when we toured it. It was vacant, and he was a runaway from a foster home. Pastor Tony and Deputy Brett Chang—he's Cassie's husband, who owns the Jitter Bug Too—worked to find him a new foster home. The town has adopted him. He graduated last week, and he's got a job with the landscaping company in town. Have you met Vince Smithton yet?"

"Yes, he came to help me move on Sunday." Carissa wondered if Claire would know how Vince was related to Anthony Smithton, but they hadn't lived here then.

Claire nodded. "Samuel works for him and helps around here. Alex has trained him well with basic handyman skills. He'd probably be able to help you as well."

"That sounds fantastic. I have a small budget and will need some affordable muscle."

"He's quiet, but he's a hard worker."

They peeked in on the kids in Lizzy's room. She and Brandon were playing some computer game while Jayden had found some blocks and dinosaurs and was lost in his imagination. It was nice to see Brandon have fun with a friend closer to his age.

They headed back downstairs. The faint smell of fresh plaster and paint wafted throughout. "The finishing touches always seem to take the longest. But I think we'll be ready to open in a month—not that I'm counting—for Art Fest. We're already fully booked." Her face lit with excitement.

Carissa jotted notes on her phone. "This is fantastic. And so helpful." Her head was full of ideas—the fun kind like finishes and furnishing, not saggy floors and stained plaster.

Out back, Claire pointed out the gazebo and the sweet garden her husband Alex and the kid who must be Samuel were working on, digging holes for the gallon containers of plants scattered around the yard.

Alex leaned on his shovel and waved. "So what do you think?"

Carissa looked around. "You guys have done an amazing job. I have so many ideas." She slipped her phone into her pocket. "But first, I need to get a Lally column installed in my basement to shore up a saggy floor. And my washer and dryer need to be hooked up properly. Do you have some recommended contractors I can contact?"

Alex waved his hand. "I'll come take a look. Should be something Samuel and I can knock out with no problem."

Carissa shook her head. "No, you guys are busy with the final preparations to open on time. I know how pressed for time you must be."

"It's not a problem. I actually have an extra Lally column here that we didn't end up using. Why don't I come over tomorrow and take a look? I'm sure Samuel will be ready for a break from digging." He glanced over at the young adult, who nodded. "Carissa bought the old Delamar house."

Samuel took a step back and paled, glancing from her to Alex, then down at his shovel.

Great. There was someone else who believed the ghost rumors. But she smiled and acted like she didn't notice. "After here, I've got to pick up some paint at the hardware store, then I'll be home all day tomorrow painting."

Alex nodded. "I'll text you before we head over."

"Thanks." Carissa followed Claire back into the house,

switched her laundry to the dryer, and then they headed into the fully appointed chef's kitchen. This was definitely bigger than hers.

The older lady who had come over with Gladys and brought cookies for Sunday was in the kitchen. She smiled at them. "Fresh-baked ginger cookies."

"Smells wonderful." Claire smiled. "Carissa, have you met my grandma Erma? We call her GiGi Ma. For being Lizzie's great grandma."

"Yes, she and my neighbor Gladys brought cookies over Sunday for everyone who helped move. Thank you so much. That was very sweet. I don't know if I got to thank you personally."

Erma waved it away. "My pleasure. You have a lot on your plate." She pushed the platter of cookies across the marble island in their direction. "Would you like some coffee? Claire, do you want tea?"

Carissa nodded while Claire said, "Tea sounds great." But she made a face as she turned to Carissa. "I still can't stand the taste of coffee." She paused. "Alex and I are expecting. Due this fall."

"Congratulations! That's fantastic news. I don't know how you do it all, renovations and being pregnant. I was so tired with my two." Carissa took the mug Erma gave her, along with the small creamer, and dosed her cup.

"I couldn't have done it without Alex." While they sipped their drinks and nibbled on cookies, Claire told her about the Inn at Cherry Blossom Lane, the B-and-B they owned in Michigan, how Alex had made some friends in Laguna Vista on one of his trips out here for work during the winter, and how they decided to move out here for warmer weather. "We can have a strong book of business all year round here. And it's easier on GiGi Ma."

Erma smiled. "I can't complain about the weather here. There'll be snow, but it doesn't last six months out of the year.

And if I don't like it, I can just get down the hill into the warm sunshine."

Carissa's phone buzzed. Her clothes were done in the dryer. Claire's industrial machines were fast. She noted the time. "Wow, I'd better get going. Thank you so much for the tour and the cookies. I've been revived enough to head to the hardware store." She laughed then retrieved her clothes from the dryer, laying them in the laundry basket. Hopefully the wrinkles would stay to a minimum, but so what? At least they'd be clean.

They headed out to the foyer and called upstairs for the kids. A clatter of footsteps brought all three of them down. With goodbyes and promises to visit, Carissa and the boys left.

But to mitigate their downcast faces, she decided to tell them what she'd discovered. "Guess what? I think our house might have a secret room."

THEY COULDN'T GET HOME FAST ENOUGH. LUCKILY, THE hardware store wasn't busy, and she got her paint mixed quickly and then lugged it out to the SUV. As she pulled into the driveway, she looked for the gable vent. It wasn't on this side of the house. She walked around to the far side. Sure enough, now that she studied it more closely, it was a very dirty window.

The boys couldn't get upstairs fast enough. She thought she knew which room it was in. The room with all the discarded junk from previous renos. No wonder she hadn't found it. She hadn't done more than a cursory look around this room.

It had the same wooden wainscoting that Claire's B-and-B, the Cope House, had. Carissa ran her hands along the panels, examining them for any clue. And there it was. A slight gap between the groove of two panels. You wouldn't even see it if you weren't looking for it. She pressed on it. There was a slight give, but nothing happened. She tried again. It was likely old and stuck. Figuring there was no harm in really leaning into it—

because if it didn't open now, she'd have to cut into the wall anyway—she gave it a strong shove, and it popped open just a bit.

"Hand me a scrap piece of wood, something I can wedge in here."

Brandon handed her an old staircase spindle. She wedged it into the opening. "Now give me something I can use as a fulcrum, like that block of wood there."

Brandon complied, and with the wood crammed under the spindle, Carissa leaned her weight against it. Wood popped and groaned, but the compartment flew open without anything breaking. Whew!

The boys ran over and peered inside.

"Be careful." Little light shown in through the window. Carissa popped on her phone's flashlight and shone it around. Just like Claire's, a narrow closet ran behind the wall. It was full of dust and cobwebs. No secret treasures.

"Can this be my room?" Brandon looked hopeful. "A secret hiding place would be so cool."

"We'll see. It's a mess right now. I'll need to make sure it's safe and that you can't get yourself locked in there." She studied the mechanism. It had a latch on the inside of the panel, too, but as rusty as it was, it would be easy to get locked inside and not be able to get out. "Don't play around with this. I don't want anyone getting locked in. It's not safe yet. Okay?"

When both boys nodded, she let out a breath. "All right. Time to paint. You guys can put a movie on my computer down in the living room." They'd be occupied, but she'd be able to keep an eye on them.

She exchanged her Sketchers for flip-flops. Her grubby shoes were still wet from the pond, and she didn't want to get paint on her only good sneakers.

The stepladder, bucket, and rubber gloves sat where she had left them from last night when she had washed down the walls with TSP. It was the last thing she'd wanted to do, but she knew she'd regret it if she didn't. Preparation was the key to pretty much everything. Sloppy preparation led to sloppy results. And with the kids occupied, she had fewer potential hazards. She could get this room painted without any more disasters and move on.

She touched the walls. Dry. Good. Or at least it meant she could start slapping on a coat of paint. She couldn't afford to get behind on this house, and right now that was as reasonable a definition of "good" as any. Alex's help tomorrow would be a godsend. She just hoped his professional eye didn't uncover problems she hadn't seen.

But that was tomorrow's problem. Popping a playlist open on her phone, she chose an '80s station, setting her phone on top of the ladder. She dragged the dining room table and chairs into the living room and out of the way. Last night, she'd brought in her box of painting supplies, and it sat in the corner. In the toolbox, she found her box cutter and slit the tape, setting the knife up on the ladder, out of Jayden's way if he happened to wander in here.

Grabbing a screwdriver, she pried around the lid of the five-gallon plastic drum of stain-blocking paint. A buttery cream greeted her from the bucket, along with the tang of latex.

Paintbrush in hand, she considered the red-spattered dining room wall. She dipped a brush in the bucket, disturbing the surface, then stroked it over the remaining pinkish stain. Nice. The pale color covered the stain. She stepped back, squinting to see if it truly was the right color.

It was. Now time to cut in. She grabbed a rag, a straight edge, and knelt on the drop cloth, skimming the tip of her brush along the edge of the wall, careful not to touch the unpainted wood baseboards. This part took the most time and concentration.

Time she didn't really have, if she was honest. Painting the dining room had been way down on her to-do list. If truth be told, she was running close to tired and cranky. Jayden had been through a lot of change, and he'd coped remarkably well. A meltdown was inevitable at some point. But why did it have to be in here? She'd guessed it'd be around the pond, thus why she'd cleaned it. But he was continually surprising her.

Some people considered Jayden's high-functioning form of autism a disability. She considered it an invitation to look at the world in an Alice-in-Wonderland kind of way. Fascinating and entertaining, but at some point trying to view the world through the looking glass of autism was tiring too. Especially when she was trying to do it all on her own.

The burden of being a single parent to a special-needs child sometimes felt like too much to bear. She knew this was supposed to draw her closer to God, to encourage her to lean on him and his strength. And he had taken care of them and provided for them in amazing ways. But sometimes the day-to-day was overwhelming.

She sat back on her haunches, the bottom cut-in complete. The color was perfect against the warm wood. It gave her a bit of inspiration to keep going to see what the whole wall would look like filled in. It was definitely a better color choice than the original. She just hadn't planned on repainting so soon. But there was no way to pass off the tomato-stained splotch as some sort of Tuscan-inspired design statement.

After a quick check on the boys to see they were fully absorbed in the movie—they were, Charlie too—and a run to the fridge to grab the last icy Diet Coke, she got lost putting tongues of creamy paint on the wall. The cutting in went fast after the baseboards, and she switched to using the roller on the extension pole.

She backed up a few steps... And into the stepladder. It wobbled a bit. She reached out a hand to steady it but only succeed in knocking it with the tail of the extension pole. Which fell off the roller. Her Diet Coke sloshed on the top ledge like a drunken sailor before splatting on the drop cloth, but she couldn't save it in time without dropping the paint roller. At least Diet Coke was easier to clean up than paint.

She set the roller in the paint tray then grabbed a bunch of paper towels and sopped up her caffeine fix. The box cutter had fallen and pierced the can, making the soda spill out with greater force. She stuck it back up on top of the ladder. Her energy leaked out, and she knew she should take a break and get something to eat. She was tired, but she wanted to be finished already. And that was the last of the Diet Coke.

Picking up the pole, she examined it. Maybe it had just come unscrewed. But no, the head had broken clean off—the screw was stripped—leaving no way for her to attach the roller. Great. Without the extension pole, she'd have to use the roller and move the ladder around. Constantly. Ugh. Her thighs screamed at the thought of climbing up and down the ladder a million times. But if she didn't finish it, or find a good stopping point, she'd end up with drying lines.

She wanted to flop on the ground and throw a temper tantrum like Jayden.

Studying the wall, searching for a solution that didn't involve cleaning up, packing up the boys and heading to the hardware store for a new pole, she saw a spot she'd missed. She went after it with the brush, slapping the brush on the wall for emphasis, liking the spattering sound.

Six months ago, she'd been a successful architect. She slapped more paint on the wall, harder this time, splattering herself. She didn't care. Latex would wash off, and these were her paint clothes. It wouldn't hurt to cut lose a little, vent some of her frustration.

She dunked the brush. *Who am I?* Huh. She scrawled it on the wall. Better yet, *who did you make me to be?* Big splat at the end of that one. Anger fueled by fatigue gave her a bigger rush than a double shot of espresso. She started writing on the walls, the fat brush giving her letters a calligraphic effect.

Artist.

That surprised her. She didn't usually think of herself as an artist. She remembered her sister's taunt from their adolescent years. "Hey, Carissa, you know what your problem is?"

She would roll her eyes and ignore Christina. Or come back with some remark about her being a know-it-all. But the punch line was always the same.

"You think too much."

Maybe she did. *Don't think, just write.*

Designer, mom, sister, friend, drawer. She laughed at that. Draw-er, not a drawer. Maybe a draftsman was a better word, but not really. Draw-er was what they'd said as kids. "Aren't I a good draw-er?" as they held up their crayoned papers. Weird there wasn't a better word for that in English.

She kept going.

Lover, beautiful. Dare she put sexy? Why not? No one would see it. It should be good therapy, and some day she'd feel all that again. Right?

Magical, dream, creator, mover and shaker, dancer, life-giver, homemaker, safe-haven giver, protector, do anything for my kids.

But what about her? Who took care of her? What did she want?

The house of my dreams, a fireplace that works, a big claw foot tub full of bubbles, good chocolate, a classically designed herb garden, good wine, a room of my own, an old drafting table, bike rides with the kids, pressing fall leaves in a book, hot cocoa with marshmallows and whipped cream after a snowball fight, making an igloo, a snow fort, going sledding, making snow sculptures.

I want to design dream houses for other people, not just commercial buildings. I want to help other people's dreams come true. I want mine to come true.

She stood back. Sloppy calligraphy covered three walls. Her dreams in buttery cream. Not a trace of tomato.

CHAPTER
THIRTEEN

Jonas sat in front of his computer at his desk. It was a slow night, just the way they liked it. He didn't want to think about it too much and jinx it though. Not that he believed in that kind of thing. But ever since last Sunday when Vince had mentioned the rumors around Carissa's house, Jonas had been thinking about the missing kid. He pulled up the case file to refresh his memory of what had happened. Maybe the next time he ran into Carissa he could set her mind at ease.

Tyler Cohen was reported missing in May four years ago by his parents when he hadn't come home the next morning after the final astronomy club outing of their senior year. It was the first big case Jonas had covered after moving up here. He had been grateful for the distraction, since his pain from the death of his wife and daughter months earlier was still raw.

Jonas had interviewed the astronomy teacher, Brian Lancaster. He said Tyler had been at the event, along with the kids he normally hung out with: his girlfriend, Kayla Mills; best friend, Anthony Smithton; and Anthony's girlfriend and Kayla's friend, Madison Gonzales. They had all seemed to leave around the same time.

The kids all admitted to going back to the Delamar Place

and that Kayla had broken up with Tyler because they were going in different directions after high school. She left first, and Tyler went after her. Anthony later said that he'd talked to Tyler, and he'd been upset but decided to take that road trip he'd been talking about. He didn't seem to care if he missed graduation.

Jonas leaned back in his chair, studying the screen for anything they'd missed. Tyler's car hadn't been found. There was no reason to believe he hadn't done just what he'd said and gotten into some trouble somewhere. No one had ever heard from him again. But Jonas had found it odd that he hadn't returned home to at least pack a bag or call his folks. His personal conclusion was that Tyler was upset, perhaps had been driving recklessly, and had gone off the road somewhere. It was an explanation that fit the facts.

It wasn't until later that summer that rumors started about the moon and Tyler's ghost. Jonas thought it was just silly, small-town lore with no basis in fact and had dismissed it. But now…

He typed in a few terms into the search bar and came up with several sites that listed rumors and other ridiculous fabrications about the ghost and the blue moon. Where did people come up with this stuff? And why did people believe them? Given that Carissa didn't have internet at her house, he hoped she hadn't seen them. But if there was some rumor of ghosts, the weirdos were likely to come out of the woodwork. He'd talk to Shannon about making sure they did a few drive-bys each shift, especially as it got closer to the blue moon in June.

And why had Vince brought them up? His nephew, Anthony, had been Tyler's best friend. Maybe he was one of those guys who wanted a woman to need him and depend on him. Scaring Carissa would be a good way to do that.

Though she didn't strike Jonas as the type of woman to scare easily, given what she'd taken on.

He read through the report again. He didn't think they'd missed anything. It was always hard when a case like this went cold with no resolution for the family. They had moved out of the area about a year after Tyler's disappearance. His mom had developed early-onset dementia and they had moved to a care facility. As far as he knew, they'd never heard from their son.

But the logical explanation said that if he took off down the mountain roads in the dark, perhaps angry or upset over his girlfriend breaking up with him, he easily could have taken a turn too fast, gone over the edge, and hadn't been discovered. The trees and the chaparral could be quite dense. It wasn't that uncommon for a forest fire—or occasionally some hikers—to uncover a wrecked car. One time they'd even found a plane.

He got up and walked over to the vending machine. Then he changed his mind. He'd hop in his unit and drive around. Something about this case was bothering him, but he didn't know what. Maybe a change of scenery would reveal it.

CARISSA STUDIED THE DINING ROOM. AT LEAST ALL THE "calligraphy" on the walls would keep there from being any obvious drying lines when she painted over it. It was a mess, but it was late, and they needed dinner. Maybe food would improve her mood. She poured the paint from the tray back into the bucket, sealed it, then wrapped up the paint roller and brush in plastic. The ladder needed to be put away before Jayden got any ideas. She flipped up the latches holding it open and shoved it shut.

Something sharp rapped against her big toe, then instantaneous, searing pain. It froze her brain, and she couldn't even think, much less yelp. Blood flooded over her foot and shocked her into movement. She scanned for the paper towels. Blood didn't clean up easy either, and this house didn't need any blood-stained floors to add to its rumors.

She hopped over to the roll, grabbed a wad, and shoved them on the geyser. It stung, and she sucked in a breath. She pressed hard for a few seconds then lifted. The glimpse of dull pearl she saw before the blood flowed back in, along with the dull throb, confirmed her fear. The box cutter that hit her foot had cut to the bone. Fear began swirling like a tub drain in her stomach and threatened to weaken her completely.

Come on. She'd had worse than this. Much worse than this. *It's just a flesh wound.* She didn't do Monty Python very well. But the dark humor helped cut through the pain so she could think about what to do next.

Huey Lewis and the News were singing about how it was hip to be square from her phone, which gave her a clue as to where it was. Under the ladder. Out of reach.

She glanced in the living room. The boys were still absorbed in their movie. Jayden was laying across Charlie. If Charlie were a German shepherd, perhaps he'd be in here already to rescue her. But if it didn't involve food or a stick, Charlie tended to stay glued to the boys. She could ask Brandon to get her phone, but the sight of blood might panic him.

Gripping her toe tightly, she scooted over to the phone. She definitely needed stitches, but driving while holding her toe presented a bit of a challenge, even for someone as flexible as she was. But Gladys should be home. She rarely went anywhere. Though it would be just Carissa's luck if Gladys was out grocery shopping or visiting Erma or something.

She punched Gladys's number on the phone. The blood was seeping through the paper towels, and she grabbed another one. Hopefully Gladys wasn't too talkative and Carissa could cut to the chase.

Gladys picked up on the first ring.

"Gladys, it's Carissa."

"Oh, hello, dear—"

"I need a favor. I need to go to the emergency room. I've sliced open my foot, and I need stitches."

"Oh my. I'll be right over."

The phone went dead.

Huh. Those must have been the magic words.

CHAPTER
FOURTEEN

Jonas pulled to an abrupt stop in front of Carissa's house and jumped out. Gladys met him at the door. She'd called him and said Carissa needed to go to the emergency room, but Gladys didn't drive at night.

"Come in, come in." Gladys waved him past her. "She's in the dining room."

Carissa sat on the floor, fingers wrapped around her foot. Paint flecked her arms, legs, and clothes. She glanced up at him and then around the room, her cheeks turning red.

There was some kind of writing on the wall in paint. Maybe it was a new decor technique. He wasn't up on those things. He knelt next to her. "What happened?"

"The box cutter nose-dived off the ladder and stabbed my toe. Not very nice." She briefly lifted the red-soaked paper towel to reveal a deep cut.

The tension eased from his shoulders a bit. He pulled out his phone and dialed Dr. Tia. The urgent care family clinic was closed, but if she didn't mind coming in, they wouldn't have to go over to the hospital in Big Bear. While he was explaining the situation to her, he scanned the area. The boys were huddled in the living room, a computer open in front of them, but they alternated between studying him and their mom. He winked at them.

Tia agreed to come in. He'd deliver a box of goodies from Jitter Bug Too to her office tomorrow as a thank you. He hung up and turned to the boys.

"Hey, guys. What are you watching?"

"*Lego Batman*," Brandon offered.

Jayden's lip quivered.

Jonas squatted down next to them. "Your mom's going to be okay. I'm going to take her to the doctor's to get stitches, and then I'll bring her right back. Okay?"

Jayden nodded, eyes wide.

He turned to Gladys. "Can you stay with the boys while we're gone?"

"Absolutely."

"Thank you both," Carissa said. "Brandon, can you get my purse from my bedroom?"

He jumped up and ran upstairs.

"Have the boys eaten yet?" Gladys asked.

Carissa shook her head. "I was just cleaning up to do that. I think there's a pizza in the freezer."

Gladys patted Carissa's shoulder. "Don't worry about us; we'll be just fine."

A slight frown and a shadow of worry crossed Carissa's face, and she glanced at Jayden. "Jayden, Miss Gladys is going to stay with you and make you guys pizza for dinner. You be a helper to her, okay?"

He nodded, but his eyes filled with tears.

"Oh, honey. Come here. Give me a hug." Carissa awkwardly opened her one arm not holding the paper towel on her toe.

Jayden flew into her, flinging his arms around her neck.

"It's going to be okay. It's just a cut that needs stitches. It's happened before." She partially rocked him from her awkward position.

Brandon clattered back down the stairs dragging a purse.

Carissa gave Jayden one last squeeze then set him to the side. "Okay, now to figure out how to get up while keeping pressure on my foot."

"Not a problem." Jonas stepped over and slid his arms under her knees and around her back, lifting her up.

"Oh, you don't have to do that."

"Don't be ridiculous. Brandon, slip your mom's purse over her shoulder. There you go. Now, can you get the door for me? And the door to my unit?" Giving someone something to do in an emergency immediately made them feel like they were helping. He had a feeling Brandon needed that.

Brandon ran ahead and opened both doors.

Jonas tried not to think about the feel of Carissa pressed against his chest, that floral vanilla smell of her tickling his nose. He set her in the front seat and belted her in. "Thanks, bud. Go inside and lock the door behind you, okay? We'll be back soon."

Brandon nodded and ran back in. Jonas rounded his unit, climbed in, and headed them toward the urgent care.

Carissa glanced over. "Thanks so much for doing this. I didn't expect you. But I didn't think about Gladys not being able to drive at night. Are you sure I'm not taking you away from your duties?"

"This is one of my duties. And there's nothing more pressing right now." It beat looking at old case files about missing kids and rumors about her house. But he should keep her talking to get her mind off the pain. "So, you were painting the dining room?"

She let out a sigh, and her face reddened again. What was that all about? "Yeah. And usually I wear tennis shoes, but I'd been mucking out the pond and installing a fountain, so they were gross. And the extension pole had just broken. I should have quit sooner. But I did make it over to Alex and Claire's house today. And I discovered we both have secret rooms in our houses."

She continued to explain about the visit, but his ears had

perked up at the secret room comment. They'd not found that during their search of the house after Tyler's disappearance. Perhaps there was something there that could be helpful to the case. Likely not, but it would be worth exploring if Carissa was open to it.

He was still thinking of how to approach her about that when they pulled up to the clinic.

Dr. Tia unlocked the doors when she saw them and pushed out a gurney to his unit.

He lifted Carissa out of the SUV and onto the gurney. Dr. Tia asked how it happened, took a peek under the paper towel, then placed an icepack on the toe. "I'll make you earn your keep tonight, Deputy." Dr. Tia smiled. "You can push the gurney into treatment one, that first curtained area. I'll be right with you."

"Yes, ma'am." Jonas did as he was told, maneuvering the gurney back to the partitioned area. He got it situated then straightened. "Okay, just have Dr. Tia come get me when you're done. I'll give you your privacy."

Carissa reached out and touched his arm. Unexpected heat shot through him. "You don't have to leave, unless you have something more important to do. Having stitches on my toe isn't exactly a private matter. With the fact that I'll have to wear flip-flops and the stitches will be quite evident, I think everyone will know about it." She grinned.

"If you're sure you want the company." It sounded lame to his ears, but he was inexplicably grateful that she wanted him to stay.

"I'm sure. Unless this kind of thing makes you faint." She gave him a bit of a sassy look.

"I'm good." He keyed his mic and updated dispatch on his location and status.

She shook her head. "I should have known better than to wear flip-flops during a reno. I never do. If I'd been wearing tennis shoes, I might have a bruise, but I wouldn't need stitches. And, dang, I won't be able to get them wet for ten days. Which means I've got to figure out if the tub in the hall bath works. It's pretty grimy, and the boys and I have been using the master shower, which Jayden hates. He's not a fan of getting his face wet." She flopped her head back against the pillow. "Lately it seems like it's one step forward, two steps back."

"You could wrap your foot in a trash bag and seal it with duct tape to shower." The ridiculous image was a lot safer than picturing her in either the tub or a shower.

She laughed. "That's not a bad idea. Getting the duct tape off won't be a picnic though."

He turned his gaze to her toe to keep his mind off other things. Blood was seeping around the icepack. Where was Tia?

As if his thoughts had summoned her, she pushed the curtain all the way open, guiding a computer on a portable stand in front of her. "All right. Let's get you in the system, and then we can do the real work."

Carissa rummaged in her purse and handed over her ID and insurance card.

Dr. Tia entered the information, asking a few questions. "Bear with me. My medical assistant usually does this. I'm not as fast as she is." When she was done, she handed Carissa the cards back and pushed the computer stand out of the way. She snapped on a pair of gloves and dragged over a stainless-steel tray with a syringe and a packet of instruments. Sitting on a stool, she scooted over to the edge of the gurney. She lifted the icepack and poked around as the blood began to ooze. As she cleaned the area, Carissa sucked in a breath.

"So, it's a lot quieter in here than a typical ER." Carissa gave a casual look at Dr. Tia then turned her attention deliberately to Jonas. "Last time I needed stitches there was this poor old lady screaming obscenities and demanding her clothes and cane back. Poor thing. I felt sorry for her. She was probably alone and confused."

Dr. Tia pricked the area with the syringe, and Carissa winced, her voice faltering.

"We don't see as much of that here," Dr. Tia said, focusing on her work. "We get a lot of injured tourists, the injuries vary with the seasons. Keeps things interesting."

Carissa peeked over as Dr. Tia began stitching. "I guess I'll have to put off updating my pedicure. My chick-flick cherry has grown out."

Dr. Tia laughed. "I'll hook you up when you come back to get your stitches out."

Jonas was lost, but as long as it kept up Carissa's spirits, he was all for whatever the women wanted to chat about.

Dr. Tia straightened. "All done. And let me tell you, the black caterpillar look? It's all the rage. Toe rings are so basic."

Carissa laughed. "Great job, doc. I don't think it'll even leave a scar. I've had enough stitches to be a good judge of technique."

"Always happy to please a connoisseur of emergency medicine. Now, I hear you're renovating the Delamar Place, so I don't need any repeat business." She handed Carissa a sheet. "Aftercare instructions, not that you need them. Come back in ten days so we can get your pedicure hooked up. Oh, and the stitches out." She stripped off her gloves. "Let me grab you an icepack for the road. Ice will be your best friend for the next two days." She winked at Carissa. "But you knew that already."

"I did. But it never hurts to be reminded."

Dr. Tia left, and Carissa scanned the gurney. "Oh, I only have one flip-flop."

"The other was soaked in blood." Jonas reminded her. "I'll carry you back to the unit."

"You don't have to do that."

"Yes, I do. You're not walking barefoot out there, especially on a foot that just had stitches and you can't get wet."

"Good point."

Dr. Tia came back in with a chemical icepack, crushing it to activate it, then handed it to Carissa. "You are free to go."

"Thanks, Doc," Jonas said. "I appreciate not having to get her over to the hospital in Big Bear."

"Not a problem. We take care of our own."

Jonas scooped up Carissa, who clutched her purse, the instruction sheet, and the icepack to her chest. Dr. Tia opened the doors for them and soon he had her strapped into the SUV and on their way back to her house.

"Thanks so much, Jonas." Carissa glanced at him. "I really appreciate it. That was sweet of Dr. Tia. I really like her. And I think she'd be good with Jayden. He's terrified of going to the doctor."

"We're lucky to have her. And I'm happy to help. But I do have one question for you."

"What's that?"

"Can you show me that secret room?"

CHAPTER
FIFTEEN

Clarissa opened her eyes, sunlight streaming through her bedroom window. She was stiff and sore, and it was later than she thought, based on the brightness. Her toe, elevated on a pillow, peeked out from under an old blanket. She'd been too tired last night to figure out how to get all the paint off her, so she'd scrubbed the worst of it with a damp washcloth and laid an old beach towel on top of her bed with a ratty blanket covering her. Her toe wouldn't appreciate getting caught in the sheets anyway, and icepacks were notorious for leaking.

Her toe throbbed, and she needed to get some food in her so she could take ibuprofen, but she needed to get clean first. Running up and down the stairs wasn't going to be easy, so she'd need to think ahead to minimize her trips and get the boys to grab things for her.

With a sink full of warm water, she was able to do a better job of cleaning up than she had last night. She found another pair of flip-flops, since shoes would be off-limits for a while. Luckily, being from Arizona, she had a good selection of them.

Jonas had been so sweet last night. He was just doing his job, but being held against his strong chest sent a wave of feelings crashing over her that she had long thought forgotten. They hadn't known each other long enough for her to ask him a personal question, such as why he wasn't married. And having been the subject of gossip and hating it, she wasn't going to ask anyone else about him. Maybe he had a girlfriend. Perhaps one day they'd be good enough friends for her to ask him about his story.

But it wouldn't be today. He was coming over to see the secret room. He told her how it related to their previous investigation and that she didn't have to agree to it. He was just surprised his team hadn't found it when they searched the house. She explained why they missed it.

Somewhat to her relief, he didn't mention the dining room walls. If he'd seen what she'd painted, he hadn't said. Maybe he hadn't really noticed. Maybe she'd actually dodged one embarrassing thing. She had to take Charlie to the vet today, but as soon as she could get an extension pole from the hardware store, she was painting over it. What had she been thinking anyway to be so silly? Just went to show how tired she'd actually been. It was amazing she hadn't hurt herself worse than a couple of stitches.

Grabbing the melted icepack, she checked on the boys. Jayden was up, playing with a Lego guy in his bed. They had done well with Gladys last night, which had been a huge relief. Both boys were curious about her stitches but not freaked out by them.

"Hey, bud. I'm about to make breakfast. Do you want waffles?" Though only toaster waffles, they were whole grain, so that counted for something, didn't it? And they had fresh strawberries for the top.

"Yeah!"

"Okay, wake up your brother. But nicely. I'll see you downstairs." She gingerly picked her way down the treads, tossed the icepack in the sink, and started coffee. Taking a deep breath, she headed into the dining room. Maybe it wasn't as bad as she remembered.

The morning sun snuck through the windows and exposed her dreams. Or that's what it felt like. The paint glowed and shimmered on the walls in a way she hadn't remembered last night. Paint changed color in different light, but still…

She was torn between forbidding the kids to enter the room and taking a picture. Before she overthought it, she pulled her phone from her pocket and snapped a photo. She read the words one more time. Maybe she needed to take some of this to heart. If she didn't believe in herself, who would?

The clatter of boy footsteps down the stairs put a stop to her musings. She got busy getting them fed and drinking coffee and thought through her day. She should have no problem getting Charlie to the vet as long as he didn't step on her foot. She didn't know how he felt about car rides, but he loved being with the boys, so she figured he'd get in the car if they were there.

Jayden squatted at her feet, examining her stitches. He reached out a finger, poking them like they were some sort of bug. "Does it hurt?"

"Not too much. Looks funny, though, doesn't it?"

He nodded then clambered in his chair for waffles.

A knock at the front door interrupted her planning. It was probably Gladys. Except she always came around to the back door. Had Alex decided to come over early?

She peeked out the sidelight flanking the front door. Jonas stood on her front porch. Surprised, she opened the door. "Hey, Jonas. Come on in. Want some coffee?"

"Sure. I hope it's not too early." He stepped inside then looked at her foot. "Doing okay today?"

"Not too bad. Just waiting for the ibuprofen to kick in." She headed toward the kitchen. "We even have toaster waffles with strawberries if you want breakfast."

He laughed. "Sounds tempting, but I already ate." He

entered the kitchen. "Hey, guys. How was your time with Miss Gladys last night?"

"Good." Brandon said around a mouthful of waffle.

Jayden nodded.

Carissa poured a mug of coffee. "Take anything in it?"

"Just black." He took it from her. "Thanks."

There was a knock at the back door. "That must be Gladys. Man, we're popular this morning." Carissa set her coffee cup down.

Jonas laughed. "Life in a small town. We check up on each other."

Carissa went to let Gladys in, asking her if she wanted coffee.

But she saw the moment Gladys spotted Jonas. Her eyebrows rose. "Good morning, Jonas. I didn't expect to see you here."

Carissa's face heated. She wasn't sure what Gladys thought.

But Jonas seemed to take it in stride. "Morning, Gladys." He raised his mug to her.

So he didn't say why he was here. Carissa wasn't sure she wanted to mention the hidden room yet either. It was something she needed to talk over with him. The three of them stood in the kitchen for a long moment while the boys finished their breakfast.

"I just stopped over to see how you were faring and if you needed anything. But I see you've got Jonas here, so I'll just head on out. Don't want to interrupt." Her voice lilted at the end as she turned and headed for the mudroom and back door.

Carissa followed her. "Oh, you're not interrupting anything. Thank you again for helping with the boys last night. That was a real blessing to not have to take them to the clinic with us."

"Happy to help. That's what neighbors are for." Gladys gave a little wave as she exited the house and headed across the yard.

Carissa stood there a moment, thinking about what she

could do to thank the woman. Maybe some treats from Jitter Bug Too.

Back inside, Jonas wasn't in the kitchen. Had he already gone upstairs to find the secret room? He hadn't—

She stepped into the dining room, a sinking feeling filling her gut.

He had.

Jonas stood in the dining room, coffee mug in hand, reading what she had painted on the wall.

Could the floor open up and swallow her? No, that'd be one more thing she'd have to fix.

———

Jonas had read the words on the wall and the embarrassed look on Carissa's face. She clearly hadn't planned on anyone reading what she'd painted. Which made him wonder why she'd done it in the first place. The words were interesting. It gave him a unique peek inside her mind. Kind of like reading someone's diary.

Still, he needed to put her at ease. "I wanted a closer look. I couldn't tell what technique you were using from my vantage point last night. It's different."

"Um, thanks. It was… I was… I'm going to paint over it. As soon as I get a new pole."

He nodded. "Sure. Well, you've got things to do today. Why don't you show me that secret room?"

She led the way upstairs, babying her stitched foot.

He resisted the urge to sweep her into his arms and carry her up. As much as he'd enjoyed it last night, he didn't think she'd appreciate it. And he didn't need the smell and feel of her messing with his head.

She entered the first room, one littered with old house parts and construction debris. They'd combed through here after Tyler had gone missing but hadn't found anything, though they were mostly looking for blood or signs of foul play.

Over on the far wall, part of the wainscoting was peeled away from the wall. She ran her hands over the panels. "There's a seam here. You wouldn't know unless you knew what to look for. Even then, it's not easy to find. The latch is old and stuck. I had to pry it open." She swung the panel open, and he peered in.

The space was dim, so he pulled the Maglite out of his back pocket and switched it on, running it around the room. "No wonder we never found this. There really is no clue that it's here." The room was dusty, and he had little hope that they'd find anything,

"Wait, go back." Carissa stopped him with a touch to his wrist.

He froze, focusing on her touch and taking a second for her words to register.

"I thought I saw something glint in the light. Over by where the wall and door open into the room."

He got his thoughts back on track and swung the light back closer to them. It took a few passes, but he saw the flash, like the light hitting something small and metal. Kneeling down, he examined it, then pulled out a pair of latex gloves. He took a few pictures of the area then picked it up.

"It's a class ring." He shone the light on it. "I want to look at it in better light. But let's make sure we haven't missed anything." From his vantage squatting, he played the light across the floor from a nearly horizontal level. Lots of shadows lifted up, mostly of dust bunnies. But a few other interesting items emerged. Several, small, pale-colored buttons lay scattered on the floor. Not sure if they were related or not, he took pictures of them from different angles before picking them up.

Rising, he moved toward the window and better light, tilting the ring. It was a Holcomb Springs High School ring, and it had the initials TC engraved on the inside.

"This could be Tyler's. It seems to have his initials inside.

And it's not that big of a school. It's not completely surprising, because we knew he had been in this house. And, I suppose, it's not even that unusual for a kid to lose his class ring under innocent circumstances. I have no idea if these buttons have any relevance either, but if you don't mind, I'll take them in as well."

"I don't mind. I'm glad you found something. I hope it'll be helpful in making some resolution on the case. The sooner we get it resolved, the better info I'll have to give to prospective buyers."

"It's something to check out. I'll have to try to get in touch with Tyler's parents. They moved out of the area." He ran the flashlight beam around the corners of the room and the baseboards; nothing but dust revealed itself. "Thanks for letting me take a look."

Carissa nodded. "If I happen across anything else, I'll let you know. Renos reveal the most interesting things."

He thought of the words on the dining room wall.

That they did.

ON THEIR WAY BACK FROM THE VET, CARISSA GOT ALEX'S text asking if now was a good time to come over. She sent a quick voice text to say sure. Charlie had been a good sport, eager to get in the car—wanting to sit between the boys in the back seat—then charming all the vet clinic staff with his sweet disposition and desire for attention. Dr. Green had pronounced him healthy and couldn't find a chip on him, so after he got all his shots, he was officially theirs.

Another burden slipped off Carissa's shoulders. She couldn't imagine the disappointment that would crush her boys if they had to give up Charlie. They just couldn't weather losing one more thing. To be honest, she had delayed the vet visit and had dreaded it out of that fear.

And Jonas's discovery of the class ring seemed to overshadow his discovery of the words she'd written on the dining room wall. The newly purchased extension pole was in the back of the Explorer, but she wouldn't have time to do any work before Alex got there. She just hoped he wouldn't need to go in the dining room. Once again, she wondered what she had been thinking.

She hoped Alex could resolve the washer and dryer situation fairly easily. Claire had been sweet to let them use her machines, but Carissa hated to bother her again.

She pulled into the driveway, and the boys and Charlie piled out. She hadn't even gotten into the house before Alex drove up in his white construction truck, Lally pole hanging out of the bed. Definitely not enough time to get started on any painting.

Alex and Samuel exited the truck, and she waved to both of them. "Thanks for coming over."

"Sure. Let's take a look at the washer and dryer situation first." Alex waited for her to lead the way.

Samuel headed off toward the back of the house before pausing and looking around.

She thought about what Claire had told her about his home-lessness. He'd probably stayed here when it was vacant too. He was a shy kid, but if the timing was right, maybe she'd be able to ask him. Not that she was upset about it, merely curious.

She led the way around the back and into the mudroom, limping slightly. It hurt to take a full step and flex her injured toe.

Alex noticed and asked about it. She explained last night's trip to the ER.

"I've had a few on-the-job ER trips myself. Never a good thing." Alex entered the mudroom and laughed when he saw the mock setup. "It'd look good in pictures, but it wouldn't do much for actual use."

"Right."

They discussed the best position for the machines and how to hook up water, electric, gas, and venting. After poking around in the bathroom and kitchen, Alex said, "This isn't going to be that hard. It's close enough to both the kitchen and bathroom that we can access everything we need."

"That's a relief. I'd hoped that'd be the case based on what I could see, but I've had a number of unpleasant surprises with this house."

Alex grinned and nodded. "Gotta love old houses. Always surprising you."

"Unfortunately." Carissa pulled out her phone, accessing her notes app with the names of the contractors. "So who do you recommend I call to do the work? I've got a few names."

"Don't worry about it. I think Samuel and I can knock it out this weekend."

Samuel stood with his hands in his pockets, shoulders hunched, looking at whatever Alex pointed out, but not making eye contact with Carissa. He was definitely a shy kid.

"Oh no. You've got to finish your place before your grand opening. I know you must have a ton to do."

He waved a hand at her. "It's not that big of a deal. I'll get it started and a couple of guys can do most of the heavy lifting, then I'll come back and check their work. Let's go check out that basement."

"Changing the subject, huh?" Carissa smiled. "Is that how you win your arguments with Claire?"

He chuckled. "Of course. It's the secret to a happy marriage."

She shook her head and followed him down to the basement. "It's funny how similar this is to your house."

"Yeah, basically just a smaller version. Have you talked to Anne at the library about the history of this place? She's got some interesting documents." At the bottom, Alex shone his light up to the floor above.

Samuel followed behind Carissa, slowly making his way down.

"She gave me some info, but I haven't had a chance to look at any of it yet."

Alex's flashlight found the saggy part of the floor above.

"Yep, this joist definitely needs a bit more support." He studied the rest then came back. "But the good news is, it's the only one. Once we get the Lally column in here, it'll support the floor just fine." He scuffed his toe on the plywood floor. "What's under this, do you know?"

Carissa shivered. "I've barely come down here. It's too creepy. I'm certainly not lifting any plywood."

"Samuel, come give me a hand." Alex bent down and found the edge of the wood.

With slow steps, Samuel moved around Carissa. He bent down next to Alex, and the two of them lifted the wood sheet up on its end without much resistance.

"Just what I thought. Dirt," Alex said.

Carissa moved around to take a look. Hard-packed dirt greeted her. "Surprisingly, not too many bugs either."

"Should make our job easier. We'll dig a footing, slide in the Lally, get it all jacked up and level, then concrete it in place. Might as well take care of the floor with concrete too." Alex slid the plywood against the basement wall. "Let's get to work."

"That is good news. And if you don't need me, I've got some painting to do in the dining room." Carissa started up the stairs.

"Nope. We've got this."

Good. Maybe she'd get the painting done while they worked. The internet was supposed to be installed tomorrow, so she really needed to get it done before anyone else got a peek at her innermost thoughts. Ugh.

She checked on the boys in the living room watching a movie. She was going to have some bad habits to break with them when this reno was over, but she didn't want them getting in Alex and Samuel's way, so the living room was the safest place for them right now. Satisfied, she retrieved the pole from the Explorer and got to work setting up her paint zone.

Alex and Samuel headed up and down the basement stairs with their equipment, their footsteps clattering on the worn boards. She'd have to get some better light down there at some point. And redo the stairs. But that was at the bottom of her list.

She'd poured her paint and put a few stripes on the wall when she heard a shout.

"Carissa! Get down here!"

She dropped her pole. Had someone gotten hurt? Had he uncovered another problem? Was this house cursed? Heart in her throat, she hurried to the basement door and down the steps. "What? Is everything okay?"

Samuel sat on the bottom step. When he glanced up at her, she'd swear he was pale. It was hard to tell in the basement light, even though Alex had several work lights set up on stands.

Alex had his back to her, staring into the hole he'd started in her basement floor. He turned. "There's a body down here."

CHAPTER
SIXTEEN

For the second time today, and for the third time in less than twenty-four hours, Jonas found himself heading to Carissa's house. The sheriff would meet him there. She'd called in crime scene techs from the county since this would likely be a bigger job than Holcomb Springs normally handled.

He pulled his unit in behind Carissa's Explorer. Alex's truck was parked in front of the house. He was the one who'd called it in.

The front door opened, and Carissa stood in the doorway, pale and shaken.

He took the front porch steps two at a time. "Are you okay?"

She nodded and rubbed her arms. "Yes. Alex found it. I didn't see it. But the idea…" She shook. "Do you think it's the missing boy, Tyler?"

"We'll have to wait until the crime scene techs get here and the coroner does his examination." He hoped it was Tyler for the closure it would bring to his family. If it wasn't Tyler, that meant there was another murder they hadn't known about. One missing kid associated with this house was bad enough, but the idea that another crime had been committed here would be a terrible burden for Carissa.

She nodded. "If no one needs me, I'd like to get back to painting."

"That's fine. I've got to talk to Alex. I'll come find you when I'm done."

She nodded distractedly and headed toward the dining room.

He continued on to the basement. Alex and Samuel stood around the top of the stairs. Jonas spent the next part of his day taking their statements, directing the techs, and conferring with Shannon. When the coroner's van finally removed the body, he went in search of Carissa.

He'd have to break the news to her. Her house was now a crime scene, and they'd need to stay somewhere else until it had been fully processed.

Faint music came from the dining room, and he entered from the back hall. She was methodically stroking paint on a wall, but she had two more to go. She hadn't spotted him, and he didn't want to startle her. He studied her a moment longer, watching her fluid, practiced motions. When she went to reload her roller, she must have caught a glimpse of him because her head whipped around.

"Jonas! I didn't see you." She dropped the roller in the pan. "What?"

All he really wanted to do was take her in his arms and hold her while he broke the bad news to her. The thought and the intensity of the desire surprised and frightened him. He pushed all of it away.

"I can help you and the boys, but you'll need to pack up and move out for a few days while they process your house. It's a crime scene."

Her face crumpled, and she covered it with her hands. Her shoulders heaved.

He fought the urge to reach out to her. This was work, not personal. He had to maintain a distance.

She shook her head, grabbed a paper towel, and wiped her

eyes. "I'm so sorry. I don't know why I'm so emotional. I'm sure it's the thought of some poor boy and all the work I have to do." She dropped her hands to her sides and looked up to the ceiling. "I'll have to reschedule the internet installation. And the cost. And what are we going to do with Charlie? It's just so much."

Glancing around the room, panic came over her face. "Jonas, I have to finish painting this room. I can't have people walking through here with the walls... looking like this." She gave a helpless gesture then turned her big blue eyes on him. "Please. I'll figure everything else out, I just need to finish this."

He studied the walls. There was no point in making her the talk of the town any more than she already was. He could help preserve her dignity. "Do you have another roller?"

She pointed to the box.

"Between the two of us, we can get this done. Then I'll get you settled back over at the Sleepy Bear Lodge."

Relief washed over her face, and a split second later, her arms were around his neck, her body pressed against his.

He'd barely had time to move before she was gone. The loss was palpable.

"Sorry." She tucked a strand of straight, blonde hair behind her ear. "I'm... I'm just... Well, thank you. I appreciate your help." She scanned him up and down. "Uh, you're in uniform. You'll get paint on it."

"I have some extra clothes in my unit. I'll change."

She retrieved her roller and started back on the wall.

He hurried out to his unit, updating the sheriff on what his plan was as he grabbed his duffel from the back.

The sheriff eyed him then nodded and went back to her conversation with Brett Chang. He was happy to not have to defend his decision to her or why Carissa's dining room suddenly needed to be painted before she left.

After changing clothes in the bathroom, Jonas entered the dining room. Carissa glanced at him before going back to painting. He studied her a long moment, took a deep breath, and grabbed the extra roller from the box. A moment later, he was rolling paint on the wall perpendicular to hers. As the lines of paint covered over the words, he felt a twinge of sadness as they disappeared.

Carissa needed to believe these words about herself. For a moment, he figured she had when she'd slapped them up there. He only hoped she could keep them alive in her heart and mind even when they were no longer visible on her dining room walls.

CARISSA SURVEYED THE DINING ROOM, HANDS ON HER hips. The freshly painted, buttery-cream walls shimmered in the light. It was the perfect complement to the stained wood. Finally, one room was the way it should be.

She turned to Jonas, who was sealing the paint container shut. "Thank you. For letting me stay and finish this. For helping." She paused and swallowed. "For understanding."

He met her gaze for a moment and nodded. "Happy to help. I'll clean up the rollers and brushes. You can go get yourself and the boys packed up."

It didn't take too long to throw what was left of their clean clothes in a suitcase, grab the toiletries and Charlie's food, and haul everything out to the car. She let Jayden take his bin of Legos, and she grabbed the laundry hamper. She'd find out if the Sleepy Bear Lodge had laundry facilities.

She had broken the news to the boys about having to move out for a few days by saying that there were some problems in the basement and they couldn't stay here while they were fixed. Which was true. She didn't mention the body. That might give them nightmares. She hoped no one else would mention it either. She'd sold the boys on the trip by pointing out that they could go swimming again. But the resigned look in their eyes made her hope they could finally move beyond this and get settled.

Of course, the little voice in her head told her that this wasn't exactly their permanent home either. Just a flip to earn enough money to pay for Jayden's therapy and buy something smaller. There were a lot of cozy little cabins in Holcomb Springs.

She was making the final trip downstairs, everything taking longer because of her sore toe, when her gaze caught on the poorly repaired railing. It might be nothing. But Jonas should at least be aware of it.

"Jonas, there's something I want to show you."

A moment later his form appeared in the entryway. "What's that?"

She pointed to the railing on the second floor. "I noticed something about this railing earlier. I don't know if it has any relevance, but you might find it interesting."

He mounted the stairs and examined where she was pointing. She showed him the breaks and the shoddy repair. He studied them then scanned the area all around and finally peered over, down to the entryway. Frowning, he took the stairs back down to the ground level.

Carissa followed him. He examined the floorboards in the entryway. She saw it as soon as he did. Some of the boards were shorter, like they had been patched. Common enough with an old house.

But they were directly under the spot where the railing was broken. Carissa bit her lip. "So if someone—say Tyler—had somehow fallen through the railing up there, he would have landed down here. Possibly breaking or at least damaging the floor. Or, if there had been enough blood, the floor would have been stained and would need to be replaced."

"Don't jump to any conclusions. There are a number of possibilities, and until we get the cause of death from the coroner, we have to keep all of the options open."

But Carissa could see it. Tyler had either gotten in a fight with someone or was drunk and had fallen through the railing to the floor below. Then, someone had buried him in the basement and said he'd gone on a road trip. Seemed pretty obvious to her. However, she needed to let Jonas do his job. Though she found it interesting that if she hadn't needed work done in the basement, Tyler's body would likely have never been found. That brought up a whole other cascade of questions, ones that weren't hers to answer.

She had enough on her plate as it was.

She headed out to the Explorer. The boys were in the yard playing with Charlie. Gladys was hanging over the fence talking to the sheriff.

Sheriff McIntyre turned, compassion in her eyes. "I'm sorry to have to do this to you. Hopefully it'll only be a few days."

Carissa nodded. "I understand. I hope it will resolve well and give closure to someone's family." Whatever happened, it'd have to be disclosed when she sold the house. So it would benefit her as well if they could close the case neatly. She gestured to the dog. "Is there someplace I can board Charlie? The Sleepy Bear Lodge doesn't allow pets."

"Have you talked to the vet, Dr. Green, yet? He might do some boarding. Otherwise, the only place I can think of is over in Big Bear."

"I'll call Dr. Green's office and ask. Thanks." She didn't want to make the twenty-minute drive into Big Bear multiple times a day so the boys could visit their dog. And she wasn't keen on another bill either. And since they'd be eating out again and paying for a room... The numbers started *cha-chinging* in her head like an old-fashioned adding machine.

In the meantime, time was ticking away to get work done on the house. There was nothing to be done about it, but Carissa wanted to climb in a shower and let the tears fall unrestrained. She blinked. She was not going to fall apart in front of her sweet-but-gossipy neighbor and the strongest woman she'd ever met, the sheriff.

"Boys, let's get in the car. Brandon, get Charlie's leash on him." Carissa opened the back door to the SUV.

The sheriff handed her a card. "Let me know if you need anything. I mean it."

Carissa started to say that she could just call Jonas—he'd given her his cell phone number last night—but caught herself in time. "Thank you."

Jonas jogged down the front steps, back in his khaki uniform. His gaze took in the three women, all staring at him. He focused on Carissa. "Have everything you need?"

"I think so."

"If you forget anything, I can come by and get it for you. There'll be a deputy present the whole time the techs are here."

She nodded. She really wasn't worried about anyone stealing their stuff. Not that they had much. She glanced at the back seat. The boys were strapped in, Charlie between them, tongue hanging out. "Okay, well, we'd best get going. I need to get us checked in and then feed the boys." She held Jonas's gaze. "Thank you so much for your help. I really appreciate it."

"Happy to." He gave her a short nod.

She climbed in the driver's side and waved at Gladys, the sheriff, and Jonas and drove away from her house.

A few minutes later she pulled in front of the Sleepy Bear Lodge. Back where they'd started eight days ago.

Their progress was so slow they were going backwards. She wanted to bang her head on the steering wheel.

SHANNON WATCHED CARISSA'S SUV PULL AWAY. SHE FELT bad for the single mom trying to make a life for her boys. She knew from personal experience exactly how hard that was. She had some thoughts about what they could do, but she and Jonas needed to get out of earshot of Gladys. The woman was sweet, but she'd never met a tidbit of gossip she couldn't elaborate on and spread.

She wanted a more thorough tour of the crime scene and to get a better read on what was going on with Jonas. There was a spark there between him and Carissa. She'd never seen him act this way toward anyone. He was polite and helpful, but never to this extent. And she was glad. Jonas needed some light in his life. He needed to have more than just work. And he needed to stop blaming himself for the past.

Unfortunately, there wasn't too much she could do to help him with that. But she had an idea.

Jonas gestured with his head toward the inside. "Sheriff, I need to show you something."

She lifted a hand to Gladys and followed him in the house.

He pointed out the replaced boards in the entryway floor and the repaired railing on the second floor. "It looks like someone fell through this railing and hit the floor below." Jonas made an arc between the two spots. "Was it Tyler? Assuming that was his body in the basement, it's a good guess."

"You've looked at the reports recently," Shannon pointed out. "What do you think?"

"The body was partly decomposed, so dental records will be required for a positive ID. But what was left of the clothing is consistent with what Tyler was wearing the night he disappeared."

Shannon nodded. "Let's assume it was Tyler in the basement and he also broke the railing." She started up the stairs. "The question is, why did Tyler fall? Was it some kind of accident? Or was he pushed? Kayla wasn't big enough to push Tyler over without him being incapacitated in some way. She's a likely suspect because she broke up with him. This looks more like what happens when two guys brawl. But Anthony was his friend. Unless someone else was here."

Jonas nodded. "We clearly don't have the whole story. Someone lied to us about what happened that night."

"The question is, who?" Shannon clasped his shoulder. "Guess you'll be making some calls. Now show me this secret room."

Jonas led the way while Shannon let her eyes take in everything about the hall and the rooms.

"You know how there are rumors about this place and the moon?" Jonas glanced back at Shannon as they headed upstairs.

"Yeah, you've mentioned it."

"Last night was a full moon."

"And how could anyone predict when the body would be discovered?" Shannon followed Jonas into a room off the hall.

"They couldn't. Just find it interesting. That, and there's another full moon at the end of the month. A blue moon. If someone is planning something around lunar events, it's something we need to be aware of."

"Noted."

There was a lot of junk in the room that contained the secret space. "Anything in here could be used as a weapon. If these things were here at the time. Hard to tell with the number of renos that have been attempted. Let's see what we inventoried after the original crime and have the techs spend some time up here."

The secret room door had been propped open with a piece of wood. Jonas swung it open and flicked on his light, stepping back to let Shannon take a look.

"This is where you found the ring and buttons?" she peered in at the dust-covered floors.

"Yes."

"Either of them could have come off during a struggle." She stepped back and considered Jonas a moment. He maintained a professional demeanor, but she'd known him long enough to see the desire to squirm under her gaze. Interesting. "It's a good thing Carissa felt comfortable enough with you to tell you about this room."

"Yep."

It was clear he wasn't going to say anymore. And she'd pried as much as she dared. Bottom line, Jonas's private life was just that. Private. If he chose to keep it that way.

She thought a moment. There was another way. A better way, even. "Brett's got watch until Roberto takes over. You can start figuring out who you want to contact first." She headed out of the room and then turned back. "You know, your place would be great for a dog. You've got a fenced yard."

And with that she headed downstairs, punching up Tony's number.

CHAPTER
SEVENTEEN

Tony paced outside Bella Sorgenti. He was early, but he couldn't help himself. He hadn't expected Shannon to call and ask to meet him for an early dinner. They normally met for coffee, so what did dinner mean? Early meant they'd have fewer witnesses to their meal.

Maybe she was just hungry. Maybe he was overthinking it.

Shannon pulled up in her unit, still in her uniform. So she hadn't been home to change yet. Was this more work than social?

But her face lit up when she spotted him, and she smiled as she got out and walked over. "Thanks for meeting me on such short notice."

He pulled her into a quick hug. He was not going to overthink this.

She responded with warmth and a tight squeeze before pulling back.

Good. So that wasn't a mistake. "I was about ready to call it a day anyhow. And I can't resist Bella Sorgenti." He held the door to the restaurant open for her.

"Hey, Selena." Shannon nodded to the high schooler standing behind the hostess podium. "Just the two of us."

"Right this way." Selena led them to a back booth. Smart girl.

Once they were settled with drinks, orders placed, and a basket of breadsticks in front of them, Tony met Shannon's gaze. "So, what do you need to talk about?"

"That transparent, huh?" Shannon reached for a breadstick.

As much as he'd love it if she called him to have dinner just because, that wasn't where their relationship was. Yet. He considered saying as much but figured it'd be best to let her say what was on her mind. "Anytime you want to have dinner with me, I won't say no. Doesn't matter the reason."

Her face softened, and she opened her mouth and then closed it. Whatever she was going to say, she changed her mind. Instead she leaned forward and lowered her voice. "They found a body at the Delamar Place—Carissa Carver's house—today in the basement. It'll be all over town soon." She gave him the basic details. "The bottom line is, Carissa and her boys had to move out until the techs are done. It'll be at least a couple of days. I know how hard it is to be a single mom. I want us—the town—to help her."

Tony nodded. "Of course. Did you have something in mind?"

"She was going to head over to the Sleepy Bear Lodge. But there's a couple of problems with that. One, it costs money, and I have a feeling she's on a tight budget. House renos aren't cheap. Two, there's no place there for the boys to run around. There's a pool and that's it. She'll have to get meals out and all that. Plus, what do they do with the dog, Charlie, that adopted them? Finally—"

Their server arrived with their food. Both got lasagna. The hot tomato-y, cheesy smell made his stomach rumble. The steam coming off the dish told him he'd burn his tongue if he didn't wait. He blessed their food then waited for Shannon to continue.

"Just between the two of us..." She chewed on the corner of her lip and scanned the restaurant. "I'm probably way out of line here, but I care about Jonas."

Tony raised his eyebrow but didn't say anything.

"Mariah at the Sleepy Bear Lodge has a thing for him. He does not reciprocate it in the least. I don't think Mariah would be vindictive against Carissa, but..."

Tony poked at his lasagna. Still too hot. "I'm not following." Then he grinned. "I'm a guy. If there's some subtle relationship thing going on, there's a good chance I'm too dense to pick it up. You've gotta spell it out for me."

Shannon's cheeks got faintly pink, and she shifted in her seat. "Okay, it's none of my business, but Jonas acts differently around Carissa. He's always done his job well and professionally. But he goes the extra mile for her. If there's something between the two of them, I'd rather encourage it than discourage it. I know, I'm meddling." She picked up her fork and stabbed a slice of lasagna, blowing on it before taking a bite.

"Ah, okay." He took his own bite. Still hot, but amazing. "So what did you have in mind?"

"I just think it'd be better to have her stay somewhere else. Preferably for low or no cost."

"And did you already come up with an idea?" He enjoyed watching her work through problems. Actually, he enjoyed watching her period.

"What do you think about this? I know the Wilders aren't done with their renovation yet, but they're close. They're opening in a few weeks. Perhaps they wouldn't mind putting up Carissa and the boys early. The families already know each other. I don't know how they would work meals, but I would imagine Claire would be fine with them using the kitchen. The biggest problem is the dog, but I have something cooking on that front too." Shannon worked on her dinner a bit more.

Tony leaned back. She'd worked this out in her head. He

wasn't sure why she needed him, but he was glad she'd called him, even if just for the company. "I think that sounds like a good idea. Erma loves to mother people. Lizzie and Brandon are close in age. There's a yard, and the library and downtown are within walking distance."

Shannon nodded. "That was my thought too. Do you mind if I call Claire now?"

"Not at all. And then after you talk to her, I'm curious what you did about the dog."

She gave a wry grin as she pulled up Claire's number and explained the situation to her. From what he could hear, Claire had already heard about the body from Alex and they had the same idea themselves. Their only concern was what to do with Charlie. Shannon assured her she had that covered, so Claire was going to reach out to Carissa now.

Shannon hung up the phone and smiled at Tony before eating again. If she wasn't careful, her food would get cold.

"So what's the Charlie solution?" Tony pushed his empty plate away.

"Jonas has a fenced-in yard." She gave him a sassy grin around a bite of lasagna.

Tony laughed. He talked her into splitting a piece of tiramisu with him, and they lingered over coffee. The restaurant was starting to get busy with the dinner rush, and he caught some speculative glances. But Shannon being in her uniform gave off the vibe that this wasn't a date.

Though it sure felt like one. Over Shannon's objection, he picked up the tab. Once they were outside, he walked her to her unit, slipping in another great hug before wishing her good night.

"Thanks for everything, Tony."

"My pleasure." He waved and headed toward home, glad he had walked, since they'd gotten the tiramisu. Plus he needed time to sort out his thoughts. She really hadn't needed his help to solve any of her problems.

Which made him extra glad she'd called him just for the company. He needed to talk to her about getting away. Tonight hadn't seemed the right time to bring it up. And he knew she'd be busy with Art Fest soon and all the tourists and complications that brought. He would be too, for that matter. He didn't think they'd be able to go anywhere before that.

But after tonight, he thought she'd be open to discussing the idea and getting something marked out on the calendar. He just needed to bring it up.

———

As soon as Carissa pulled up in front of the Sleepy Bear Lodge, Jayden announced he was hungry. Brandon was too. So after thinking through their options, Carissa put the car in gear and headed toward the Belleville Diner. She'd pick up some burgers to go, and they could eat in the park. Then Charlie and the boys could run around and get all of their energy out so they'd be able to stay cooped up in a hotel room. And she could make some calls and figure out what to do with Charlie.

It was a good plan. And less than an hour later, they were seated at a picnic table with burgers. She'd looped Charlie's leash through the leg of the table and given him some food of his own. There was about another hour until sunset, and the air was cooling off. Still, it was the peaceful antidote to what had been a stressful day. She'd have to make sure their room had a tub in it so she could finally get properly clean.

"Can we go play?" Brandon asked.

Jayden bounced on the bench.

She eyed their wrappers with mostly eaten burgers. "Are you done eating?"

They both nodded.

"Okay. Charlie has to stay on the leash, though." That should be entertaining to watch. Who would walk whom? She undid the leash and handed it to Brandon. The park was mostly a giant grassy area with sports fields, a small picnic area, and a playground. No one else was around.

Before she could stop him, Jayden tossed the rest of his burger to Charlie, who inhaled it in one gulp.

They scampered off, and she shook her head as she pulled out her phone. Dr. Green's was closed for the day. Figured. She scrolled through Google looking for pet boarding places. There were only two, both in Big Bear. She called first one, then the other, just to discover no one was answering, even though their listings said they should still be open. Great.

Maybe Gladys wouldn't mind if Charlie stayed with her. No. She could just imagine the big lug knocking the old lady over and breaking her hip or something. There was probably no way to sneak him into the Sleepy Bear Lodge. Bad idea, anyhow. Not a good example for the boys. If worse came to worse, Charlie could just sleep in the Explorer. Hopefully he wouldn't do too much damage overnight.

A quick glance at her email since she had a few bars of service reveal Greg's email still sitting there. And what was she going to do about that? Could she drive back to Arizona for the court date? The logistics of that—assuming she even had the time and money to do it—were overwhelming. She had to deal with the problem in front of her first.

Carissa plopped her head in her hands. She needed a moment to recalibrate. She was good at solving problems. She could solve this one.

A truck pulled into the parking lot. She scanned for the boys. They were tossing Charlie a stick, and he was dragging them along like skiers on a tow rope. Their laughter made the day that much better.

A man climbed out of the truck and headed her direction. It was someone from church who'd helped her move. Vince. That was his name.

He shoved his hands in his pockets and grinned, heading

directly for her. "Hey there. Taking a break from the reno-vations?"

She let out a breath. "Something like that." It was a small town, so she was sure the news would soon be circulating, but she didn't want to contribute to it. Plus, she was just too drained to talk about it. She didn't want to be rude, but she was hoping for some peace to get her thoughts in order.

He gestured to the wrappers on the table. "Good choice. Belleville Diner makes the best burgers and onion rings."

"They really do. The boys like them quite a bit." She gave him a polite smile.

He laughed, glancing past her. "Looks like your dog is walking the boys instead of the other way around."

"Yep. They have fun together. I'll have to round them up soon since it'll be getting dark."

"Yeah. It's still nice out though. In a couple of weeks when we have Art Fest, this place will be wall-to-wall booths and food trucks and carnival rides. The kids will love it."

"Something to look forward to." She began gathering up their wrappers and shoving them in the bag.

"Well, I saw you sitting here and just thought I'd stop by and see how things are going. I heard about the discovery of the body. And last night was a full moon. Looks like those rumors are coming true."

She didn't need this. "I'm sure it was just a coincidence."

Vince shrugged. "Like I said, let me know if you need any help with anything. You still have my number?"

Her phone rang. Claire's name popped up. "I should prob-ably take this. Have a good evening." She gave him a little wave while she swiped across her phone. "Hey, Claire."

Vince lingered a minute.

Carissa gave him a tight smile then got up from the bench, headed in the boys' direction. She didn't want him eavesdropping, even though she likely didn't have anything gossip worthy to say.

"You haven't checked into the Sleepy Bear Lodge yet, have you?" Claire asked.

"No, the boys and I had dinner in the park. I was just headed back over there."

"Don't. I want you guys to stay with us."

Tears sprang to Carissa's eyes. "Oh, Claire. That's so sweet of you. But you're still getting things ready for your grand opening. We'd be in the way."

"No, you won't. Our family suite is all ready. You'd be doing us a favor by testing it out. I'm not convinced the pull-out sleeper sofa is the best choice, so I'd love the boys' feedback on it. Lizzie's complaining about being bored since school's over and wants someone to hang out with. And Grandma wants to try some recipes for our guests. So say you'll come and be our guinea pigs." Her laughter floated over the line.

Relief about made Carissa's knees weak. "Alex told you what happened."

"Yes. It's horrible. I'm so sorry that happened to you."

Carissa waved the boys over and then turned around. Vince was gone. Good. She let out a breath. "Thank you. That means a lot. We'll be right over. I just need to see if I can find someplace for Charlie. Otherwise, he can sleep in the car. It won't be a big deal."

Claire laughed again, which Carissa found odd. "I don't think that will be necessary, Carissa. I think it's all been worked out. Just come on over. See you in a few."

Carissa called the internet provider and canceled the service call for tomorrow. When they asked if she wanted to reschedule, she said yes. Unfortunately, it meant another two-week wait. She wanted to cry.

She wrangled the boys and dog back into the SUV. They made the short trek over to the Cope House, pulling in behind Jonas's unit. What was he doing here?

She'd soon find out because he exited the front door and

headed toward them, Lizzie with him. The boys opened their doors and spilled out, running toward Lizzie. Carissa grabbed Charlie's leash as she got out so he wouldn't take off.

"Need some help?" Jonas met her around the front of her car and reached for Charlie's leash.

"Feels like you've been helping me a lot lately." For a moment, Carissa thought she could get lost in those deep gray eyes of his. She was overly tired and emotional. That explained her reaction. Jonas was a lifeline that she was jumping for. But she was too tired to care.

"I told you that's what we do around here. Charlie can stay with me while you guys stay here. I have a fenced-in yard. It'll be a good experience." He gave her a grin that must make all the women go weak in the knees. "Who knows? Maybe it'll convince me to get a dog." He rubbed Charlie's ears. "Hey, boy. Want to spend a few nights with me?"

Charlie licked him.

She laughed. "I somehow doubt that. But I'll gladly take you up on the offer."

"As soon as you get unloaded here, you can follow me to my place and get Charlie set up. I was thinking it might help if the boys could see where he was staying."

Carissa wanted to melt with his thoughtfulness, but Alex and Claire came out at that moment.

Claire gave Carissa a hug. "I'm so glad you guys are staying with us. And Gigi Ma made cookies for the kids, so I'm sure that's where they headed off to. She loves the idea of having more people to cook for."

Alex started grabbing bags out of her car.

The kids came running out of the front door and down the steps with cookies in their hands.

"Hey, boys. Charlie is staying with Jonas for a few days while we stay here. We're going to follow Jonas over to his house and help get Charlie settled."

"Is Charlie going to be a police dog?" Jayden asked as he held his cookie out of Charlie's reach.

Carissa laughed at that. Maybe he'd subdue the bad guys with his tongue and endlessly wagging tail.

The boys and dog got wrangled back into the SUV with Jonas's help. Would this day ever end?

CHAPTER
EIGHTEEN

Jonas pulled his unit into his driveway. He informed dispatch that he was unavailable for the next thirty minutes.

Carissa pulled in behind him, the boys and dog exiting her SUV.

Jonas came around to grab Charlie's food and bowls. The pines that crowded his place made dark come early, and his exterior lights had already turned on. But the nearly full moon cast deep shadows. "Come on in."

Carissa climbed the front porch steps, and for a moment, he wondered what his cabin looked like through her eyes. "It's pretty out here. You can't even see it from the road."

He held the door for her. "Yeah, that's why I picked it. From inside my house, I can't see anyone else's place."

The boys trailed in after them. "Boys, you can take Charlie to the back and let him sniff around. Maybe he'll burn off some of that energy." He turned to Carissa. "Though I think it's unlimited."

Carissa laughed. "Kind of like the boys. Probably why they get along so well."

The boys darted through the house and out the back sliding door that led to a deck and then down to the yard.

Jonas led the way to the kitchen. "Want some coffee? I have decaf."

"Sure."

He plugged a pod into the Keurig. "Take anything in it?"

"Cream, if you have it. Otherwise, black is fine."

"I do have it." He pulled a carton out of the fridge. There was an odd tension between them, made worse by the small talk. Like a dance between familiarity and politeness. He handed her the mug.

"Thank you. For this," she lifted her mug, "and for taking Charlie and being so kind to the boys." She wandered over to the slider to look out. The outside lights illuminated the deck and part of the yard. Charlie had his nose to the ground and the boys trailed him.

Jonas followed her. He didn't have people over. But it didn't feel strange to have Carissa and the boys here. It felt... natural.

She turned back to him. "Thank you, also, for not giving me grief about the dining room walls." Her cheeks turned pink, giving her a vulnerable look.

He waited until she met his gaze. "They're all true, you know. The words. Or at least the ones I know about." He gave her a wry smile.

"Oh." Her face flushed deeper, but she didn't break her gaze with him.

He stepped closer. The urge to take her in his arms, to show her how true those words really were was overwhelming. It wasn't a good idea—not at all. But he didn't really want to think about what was a good idea.

He reached up and tucked a strand of her honey-blonde hair behind her ear, his hand lingering on her neck.

She shifted her weight closer to him, her gaze soft, dipping to his lips and back up.

A clatter of footsteps on the back deck had her taking a step back and him dealing with a mix of emotions—regret, relief?

The boys came in. "Do you have a shovel or a pooper scooper? Mom said we had to clean up after Charlie." Brandon's cheeks were pink with exertion, and he was almost panting.

Jonas grinned. "Yeah, I think we can manage that. Let's go out back to the shed." He brushed his fingers over Carissa's as he walked by, giving them a squeeze.

Out back, he showed the boys where the shovel was and what to do with Charlie's droppings. When he came back in, Carissa was standing by the fireplace, looking at the photos on the mantel.

"That's my brother, Jonathan, and his wife and two kids. I don't spend as much time with them as I should." It was a picture of the four of them at the Grand Canyon from their vacation last summer. If Jonathan's wife, Marita, hadn't sent him the photo already framed, it would have been stuck on his fridge under a magnet.

He took another photo down and pointed at the faces. "This was my wife, Autumn, and my daughter, Ava. They were killed by a drunk driver over four years ago. Ava was ten at the time." The photo was taken at the beach. It was his favorite picture of them, sun-kissed and happy.

"Oh my gosh, Jonas. That's terrible. I can't even imagine how devastated you were."

He nodded and put the photo back then gestured to the couch. She moved over to it and sat, her gaze on him. He joined her.

"I was working at the Laguna Vista PD at the time." He gestured to that photo. "That was our last family day together. We were at the beach. Just a perfect day." He let out a sigh. "But I worked long hours. I missed some of Ava's school events and family time. Autumn probably felt like a single parent often. I have a lot of regrets." He ran a hand through his hair. He hadn't vocalized much of this to anyone other than Tony, and only just recently on one of their runs.

He stared through the back window. "Autumn and I had been struggling. She didn't like all the hours I worked. I can't blame her. But we were on a big case that needed my attention. We had been fighting that day when I left for work. She had texted me a few times, and I ignored her. Then my lieutenant called me in with the news that the fire department had responded to a crash. A drunk driver had hit our car with my wife and daughter in it. Both were fatalities."

He laid his head back on the couch, hating reliving that moment, yet needing to get it all out there. Maybe Carissa would understand why she shouldn't get involved with him, why he was no good at relationships and should never be in one. Maybe it would quench the attraction brewing between them.

Her gaze was on him, silent, but full of compassion.

"After that, I needed to get out of there, to start over. There was an opening up here, just what I needed. A slower pace and a change of scenery. And that's what I got."

She reached over and took his hand. "I'm so sorry you went through all of that."

He finally glanced at her, enjoying the feel of her hand in his. She gave him a squeeze then moved her hand away. His felt strangely empty.

"Thanks." He was glad she knew. He had wanted to tell her, but there hadn't been a good time before now. But his chest felt funny, a feeling he didn't like. Time to change the subject. "So tell me what brought you guys up here. I know it wasn't for the thrill of rehabbing an old house." He gave her a grin he hoped would lighten the mood.

She tilted her head. "Yeah, well, that was part of it. The boys' dad left us several years ago. He traveled a lot, so he was hardly there anyway. And though he never said it, he didn't want the responsibility of a kid with autism. It wasn't what he'd bargained for. He got angry, frustrated with Jayden. When he got physical with him…" Her jaw tightened, and he could see bad memories flash across her eyes. "I gave him an ultimatum to get out and get help. He responded with divorce papers."

She swirled the coffee in her mug. It had to be cold by now. "He sees them occasionally. But he's remarried and mostly can't be bothered. I found a great therapy program for Jayden in Big Bear and started thinking about starting over. My folks live only a few hours away. But I needed money to fund our new life and his therapy. So I began looking for houses to flip. And that's how we ended up here."

He couldn't imagine how a parent lucky enough to still have their child would reject them the way the boys' dad had. Carissa was better off without him. She deserved better, she and the boys.

But Jonas wasn't it. He really had no business feeling comfortable with her here in his house, thinking about kissing her. He wasn't cut out for relationships. He was married to his job. He would just end up hurting Carissa and her boys. They'd had too much of that already. He didn't want to make it any worse.

No, he'd be a good neighbor, but he needed to untangle himself from their lives. The sooner the better.

He stood. "It's late. I've got to get back on duty and you need to get settled in. It's been a long day."

She rose and nodded. She moved to the slider and called the boys in. "Time to go."

Charlie followed, walking into Jonas's house like it was his own.

Jayden threw his arms around Charlie's neck while Brandon patted the dog's head. They were sure attached to that dog. Which made Jonas even more glad that he'd volunteered to keep Charlie.

Jonas squatted down next to Jayden. "I'll take good care of him, and you guys can come over in the morning to feed him, take him for a walk if you want."

Jayden looked up with wide eyes. "Promise?"

"I do. And I always keep my promises." Jonas stuck out his hand. "Let's shake on it."

Jayden put his much smaller hand in Jonas's and gave it a firm squeeze.

He met Carissa's gaze. "Come over any time after nine."

She nodded. "Just hide your shoes. He has a thing for them."

"Noted."

A moment later, she and boys were driving away. Charlie whined at the door, then followed Jonas as he made sure the dog had food and water and closed his bedroom door. Hopefully there was nothing he'd destroy in the house, but Jonas would be back in several hours.

He was glad he had work to go back to. Because for once, the silence of his house felt wrong.

CARISSA PULLED IN FRONT OF THE COPE HOUSE, GRATEFUL Alex had taken their bags inside. She didn't think she could get herself up the stairs, let alone anything else.

Claire met her on the front porch, a speculative look in her eye as the boys headed inside. "Jonas is good with them. I've never noticed that about him before."

"Yeah." It was a lame response, but Carissa was out of words. It'd been a long day.

Claire looped her arm through Carissa's. "Let me show you your room. It has the most delicious claw-foot tub. I think you're going to love it. I can pop in a movie for the kids, and you can go soak."

Carissa thought that sounded like heaven.

Fifteen minutes later, she was soaking in warm water and a haven of lavender-scented bubbles. *Thank you, God.* She really didn't know what else to say. The spout was actually on the right side for her to lean back and hang her stitched foot out. The rolled edge even made it somewhat comfortable.

Now that she had a minute to herself, her emotions were all over the place. Exhaustion was the overriding theme. But also sadness for Tyler, or whoever it was in her basement, and the family. She hoped the discovery would bring healing.

And Jonas. She didn't have words. Gorgeous, kind, considerate of her boys. In the short time he'd known them, he had been more sensitive to their needs than their own dad had been.

He hadn't given her any grief about those words she'd written impulsively on the dining room wall. He'd gone out of his way to spare her embarrassment. If she was ever interested in sharing her life with another man—and she wasn't—he'd be the kind of man she'd want.

But they'd almost kissed. She hadn't imagined that, had she? But then he'd told her about his wife and daughter and the whole vibe changed. He grew distant, cooler, like he was ready for them to leave. She wasn't sure what to make of it, but she rounded up the boys and left. Probably for the best, to be honest. She was emotionally drained. He had to be too, sharing about his loss. That didn't make for good decisions.

Right now she had more pressing issues to deal with—her house for one. It had been one problem after another. She'd tried to fix several of them only to find a few more. Was it even worth it? Maybe she should just sell it as is and move on. Who knew what other problems were going to turn up? She just might have gotten them all in over their heads. Perhaps it was time to cut her losses and not throw good money after bad.

And if the boys found out about the body in the basement, would it traumatize them too much to stay in the house? Would they hear rumors about ghosts? They'd been through so much already.

But she'd sunk a big chunk of money into this house. It wouldn't leave her much to find something else, something that would still need some work to be affordable. She wouldn't be able to build the equity she was counting on with this house.

But if this one bankrupted her, she wouldn't have any equity either. Where was a crystal ball when she needed one?

She studied the bathroom. A Victorian chandelier hung from the ten-foot ceiling over the tub. The pale blue-gray walls shimmered with crystal-refracted light. The floor was tiled with white hexagons and black grout with a border tile around the walls. The twin pedestal sinks were topped with etched mirrors and sweet sconces. It was the perfect mix of luxury and days gone by.

And it was exactly what she wanted to create. Alex and Claire had shown her the path forward. The town had been welcoming and helpful.

Besides, she'd put all of her eggs in the Delamar Place basket. She'd known the risk when she'd done it. She just hoped it would pay off. For her and the boys.

CHAPTER
NINETEEN

Carissa helped with the breakfast dishes at Cope House. The bed had been comfortable for her, especially after the wonderful bath last night, and the boys enjoyed the novelty of the pullout sofa bed. Seeing Charlie settled at Jonas's house last night had helped the boys, especially Jayden. It was hard to tell what went through his head, how he interpreted the world. The last thing she wanted him to think was that they were giving Charlie away.

And she'd seen a different side of Jonas in his house last night. They'd almost kissed; he'd told her about his wife and daughter. And then… It was like he withdrew into himself. Something had shifted between them.

Maybe she'd just misread all of it. But she wouldn't have too much time to dwell on it. Today she was going to help Claire with the finishing touches on their place and hope the sheriff's department released her house soon.

Alex was finishing up work on the landscaping. She hadn't put much thought into that for her house. It would be done with whatever she had leftover in her budget, if anything. The bushes and trees definitely needed to be trimmed up, and there were some plants that needed some TLC. But it wouldn't hurt to get some ideas from Alex, see what she could translate into her much-smaller budget.

She headed outside toward the back. Alex, Samuel, and Vince were working back there laying paving stones and mulch. Working on the weekend to get everything in place for the grand opening in less than a month. And Claire had told her they were hosting a graduation party for Zach, Isaiah, and Samuel before that as a way to show off the place to the townsfolk. She didn't know how Claire wasn't a bundle of nerves. Then again, this wasn't her first B-and-B.

Vince spotted her first. "Hey, Carissa. Good to see you."

"Hey, Vince. I came back to see what ideas I might be able to steal before I started helping Claire."

"Well, I can show you the landscaping plans, and then I could draw something up for your place."

"Oh, I don't want to interrupt." She looked at Alex—who lifted a hand in greeting—but Samuel kept shoveling mulch from the wheelbarrow, acting as if she wasn't there.

Alex waved them off. "Go ahead. Vince has some good ideas."

Vince laid his shovel down and nodded toward his truck. "Let me show you."

She followed him slowly, trying not to limp with her sore toe.

He noticed. "Hey, what happened? Are those stitches?"

"Yeah. I was attacked by a box cutter that jumped off the ladder. Dr. Tia did a great job, however."

"Yikes. Glad you're okay." He opened a compartment in the back of his work truck and pulled out a set of rolled-up plans. He spread them across the lowered tailgate.

"Alex and Claire wanted a traditional-slash-luxurious feel to their property. So we used local versions of what you might find in an English country manor. We focused on symmetry and elegance with some hidden surprises, like the labyrinth."

Carissa laughed. "Really? I haven't seen that yet. I'll have to check it out."

"I'll show it to you. It's small because the plants will grow into it. But it's there with a sweet fountain and bench in the center." He pointed to where it was on the plans, in the far back corner of the property nestled under pine trees.

"I don't think I'll need anything that elaborate. Something much more simple. I like the idea of using native plants but paying homage to Victorian design with an English country garden. Much more relaxed and less formal." Her brain began ramping up with ideas, and she knew she had to rein herself in. "However, it's at the bottom of the budget list. I've got to get the house in sellable shape before I can begin to think about landscaping."

"Sure. I get that. But you'd be surprised what you can do with a small budget. You don't have to worry about it looking spectacular from day one like Alex and Claire do. You can buy smaller plants at the end of the season when they're on sale. You can do a little at a time. But if you have a good plan, nothing will go to waste."

"That's exactly my thought." She smiled. "I love a good plan." A car driving by caused her to look up. One of the sheriff department's SUVs. As it drew closer, she saw it was Jonas. She waved.

He lifted a hand, but didn't smile, his dark glasses hiding his expression as he drove away.

When she turned back to the plans, Vince was watching her. "I heard Jonas is keeping your dog. That was nice. Not much like him."

She frowned. "What do you mean? He's been super helpful to me and the boys."

Vince shrugged. "I've known him ever since he moved up here. You know his wife and daughter died, right?"

"Yes. He told me." Just last evening, but she wasn't going to mention that part.

"He's always kept to himself."

"Huh." She'd noticed a bit of tension between the men

during moving day, so perhaps there was a history there. Still, she was not a fan of gossip, so she changed the subject.

"Thanks for showing me these. It's definitely given me something to think about."

"Sure. When they release your house, I can come over and we can walk through some ideas. Just one neighbor helping out another." He gave her a friendly smile.

"I appreciate that." She glanced at the house. "I'd better get inside and help Claire—and make sure the kids haven't gotten into any trouble."

Once inside, she and Claire started down a punch list of items: touching up paint, installing shoe molding with the finish nailer, noting which rooms still were missing items. It was fun working with someone who had done this before.

"I think the finishing touches take up about eighty percent of the project time." Carissa straightened from touching up baseboard paint. Claire hadn't let her use the nail gun since she was wearing flip-flops—a smart move.

"I agree." Claire scanned the room. "And this one is actually finished. Ta da! I think we deserve a treat. Let's see what Gigi Ma's cooked up." She touched her stomach. "Now that I'm past the nausea of the first trimester, I'm always hungry."

Downstairs, Carissa checked on the kids. They were in the backyard playing with scraps Alex had given them. They had built a fort for Jayden's Lego mini-figs. It warmed her heart to see another child, in this case Lizzie, accommodating Jayden and taking some of the burden off Brandon.

Warm oatmeal cookies scented the kitchen. Erma smiled at them. "Just cooled off enough. Why don't you take some to the kids? And those hard-working men."

After Claire and Carissa delivered the goodies, Carissa turned to Claire. "Vince said you had a labyrinth here. Could I see it?"

Claire's face lit up. "It was the one thing I told Alex we had to figure out how to put in. Yes, let's take our cookies and drinks and go sit by the fountain."

They picked their way around the unfinished landscaping and across some pine-needle scattered dirt to an area of boxwood. It looked like a low hedge until Claire pointed out the arch. "This way." She led the way into the maze. The plants were only about knee high and there was space between them, but once inside, the pathway was obvious.

"Do you know the secret to finding your way out of any maze?" Claire asked.

Carissa shook her head. "What's that?"

"Put one hand on the wall or plants and don't let go. Follow it wherever it goes, and eventually it will lead you out. It's not always the fastest way, and you'll do some backtracking, but it's a sure-fire solution. Also," she pointed to the second-story of the house behind them. "If you look from one particular bedroom window, you can see the whole maze laid out and the exit is pretty evident."

Carissa laughed. "But the fun part is the experience, not the exit. It's like that saying, 'the joy is in the journey.'"

"Exactly."

The sound of a burbling fountain drew them to the center, and after a few wrong turns, they found their way to a sweet, multi-tiered fountain surrounded by teak benches. Carissa turned in circles, admiring the private space. "This is gorgeous. You'll get fabulous Yelp reviews just for this alone."

Claire laughed. "I hope so. But Alex really did it just for me."

Carissa sat. "He seems like such a great guy. So generous. I hate that he and Samuel were the ones who found the body."

"He was just glad it wasn't you." Claire took a bite of her cookie. "Mmm, so good. I don't know what I'd do without Gigi Ma." She gave Carissa a speculative glance. "Jonas has been pretty helpful to you."

Carissa nodded, taking a bite of her own cookie. She hadn't realized how hungry she was. "Yeah. Jonas seems pretty sensitive to the boys' needs." Thinking back to how their visit with Jonas ended and the conversation with Vince, she said, "I just wonder if we've worn out our welcome. Vince said Jonas usually keeps to himself."

Claire considered for a moment. "We've only been here since February, but Jonas is usually helping behind the scenes somewhere at church or town events. He and the sheriff make a good team. I don't think it's a bad thing. I just think Vince and Jonas are very different men." She studied Carissa a moment. "Did he tell you about his wife?"

Carissa nodded. "He did. Last night. Is it something everyone in town knows?"

Claire shrugged. "Probably. I don't think it's a secret, but he obviously doesn't talk much about his personal life. It came up at church one time because Lizzie is just a little older than his daughter was when she died. He'd asked me about her and then told me his story." She leaned back against the bench and studied the pine trees forming a partial canopy above them. "I was married before. I don't think you know that. Alex isn't Lizzie's dad."

"Ah, so we have one more thing in common." Carissa lifted a cookie in salute.

"We do. Alex and I grew up together, were high school sweethearts, and then drifted apart. When I moved in with Gigi Ma to start over, Alex and I reconnected." She gestured around them. "And the rest is history."

She smiled a moment before growing serious. "I don't know what it's like to lose a spouse and a child to death. That has to be earth shattering. But I do know that I was cautious about Alex, even though I'd known him forever. Jonas might be feeling a bit lost. I've watched him around you. He's always been a helpful person, but never with the deep interest he shows in you and your boys." She met Carissa's gaze. "Give him a chance. He's an honorable man. He just needs to find his footing."

Carissa shook her head. "I don't doubt that. I just am not

sure he has those kinds of feelings for me. Or if a relationship between the two of us is a good idea. With the boys... I just can't take the risk that they'll get attached and then rejected again. Their dad doesn't want to deal with Jayden's autism and his meltdowns, so he just stays away. It's hard on the boys. I don't want more of that for them." She got to her feet. "Anyhow, it's all speculation. What isn't speculation is that we have work to do inside that needs to be finished. And mooning out here in your gorgeous labyrinth isn't getting it done."

Claire laughed and headed out of the maze. "But it sure is fun. I'm glad you're here, Carissa."

JONAS EYED CHARLIE AS HE CONSIDERED WHAT TO MAKE for dinner. He had skipped running with Tony this morning. It was what they normally did on Saturdays. But for some reason, a reason he didn't want to examine too closely, he hadn't been up for company today. He felt a small twinge of regret. The rest of the guys who usually ran with Tony were out on SAR training this weekend, training he should have been on but wasn't because of Tyler Cohen's reappearance. In fact, he'd spent today in the office on his day off working that case.

Maybe the sheriff had run with Tony. That would be good for the both of them. Maybe get her off his back, though he knew her intentions were good.

Now that he was back home, Charlie was following him around the house and looking up at him with his big, brown eyes. Did he miss the boys? Probably, and since the dog had been in the house all day, Jonas should probably burn off some of his energy. He grabbed his running shoes and the leash and soon they were out the door, though Jonas was careful to stick to the streets around his neighborhood and not head downtown or toward the park. It had just gotten dark, and the trees deepened the shadows. He was glad he'd popped on his headlamp.

Charlie seemed to love their run. Though Jonas hadn't found anything the dog didn't love. Luckily, Carissa had warned him about the dog's fetish for shoes. So with closet doors securely closed, Charlie had spent the night on the rug next to Jonas's bed.

It was different running with a dog, but nice to have the company. Something he'd never thought he'd say. The dog noticed critters and smells and kept Jonas's mind on what they were doing and where they were going. Which was a good thing. Because it constantly wanted to drift back to Carissa and their almost kiss.

She seemed such a natural fit in his house, like she'd been having coffee on his couch with him forever. And other than his brother and Pastor Tony, he'd not talked to anyone about Autumn's and Ava's deaths that way before.

Tony had been encouraging him to let his guilt go, to embrace God's forgiveness. But something felt wrong about that, like he was dismissing Autumn's and Ava's lives. Or perhaps it was just comfortable, giving him a reason to keep others at a distance.

What had he been thinking? That Carissa was sweet and kind and every once in a while a bit of vulnerability peeked out from her capable exterior, making him want to help her in whatever way he could. His heart was drawn to her in a way he thought was long dead. It put him off balance, and he didn't know what to do with that.

He knew one thing: He didn't want to hurt her or the boys. And getting tangled up with them would lead to exactly that. He needed to create some space between him and Carissa. So he'd do what he always did. Bury himself in work. With the added benefit that it could get Carissa back in her house that much sooner. Then she wouldn't need his help, and they could settle in to becoming small-town neighbors.

Either way, she was a distraction. As he headed toward his cabin, he made a decision. He'd feed the dog and run with him.

And he'd text Carissa not to worry, that he'd take care of Charlie for the next day or two until she got her house back. The boys would be disappointed. Jayden's face flashed through his mind and tugged at his heart.

But there was only one way to deal with this, and that was cold turkey.

Back home, he typed out the text before even hopping in the shower. He paused, his thumb over the send button. Should he call Jon, ask for some advice? He was more distant from everything going on up here than Pastor Tony was. He could use a good excuse to talk to his brother.

Then he glanced at the time. It was late. He didn't want to interrupt family time.

He hit send. He'd call Jonathan later.

BEFORE THEY HEADED OFF TO CHURCH, CARISSA WAS washing her coffee mug out at Claire's kitchen sink, staring out the window. Her mind kept replaying Jonas's text from last night.

> You don't need to come over to feed Charlie.
> I'll take care of him until your house is
> released back to you in a day or two.

She'd texted back a quick thanks, but the message had kept her from falling asleep last night, even after a day of hard work. She'd thought they were becoming... at least friends. Was it because he'd shared about his wife and daughter? Was it because they'd almost kissed? Or was that her imagination? Possibilities and replays had chased themselves around her mind, preventing sleep until she'd given up trying to make sense of it.

Bottom line, she couldn't afford things to be awkward between Jonas and her in this small town, so she'd play it off like everything was normal. Maybe it was, and she was overreacting.

"I think that cup's clean by now." Claire peered over Carissa's shoulder. "Something on your mind?"

Carissa turned. "Huh?" She'd forgotten about the mug in her hand. "Oh. Yeah." She rinsed it and set it on the drainboard. "Just the house and everything."

"Well, church will give us all a break from working and worrying for a bit."

"It's been wonderful being here. You all have been so kind. Jonas said our house should be released in a day or two." Her voice sounded tight even to her own ears.

"So you've heard from him?" Claire raised her eyebrows.

Carissa shrugged. "Just about that and the dog."

Compassion crossed Claire's face. "Give him time. He probably never expected to be attracted to anyone. I'm sure he needs to make some mental and emotional adjustments."

"He can have all the time he needs. We're just friendly neighbors in a small town. That's all." She wiped her hands on a dishtowel and leaned against the counter.

Claire wasn't very successful at trying to hide her smile. "Okay, sure."

At church, Brandon and Lizzie ran off to their class. In the small church, a number of the grades were combined together. Jayden still didn't want to go to Sunday school, so she didn't push him. He sat with her and Alex and Claire.

She waved to a few people. It was nice to know that she knew more folks now than she had a short time before. But the one person she was looking for and dreading to see—Jonas—wasn't there.

When they stood to sing the first song, she saw him slip into one of the back rows. A mixture of emotions ran through her. Did he see her? Would he come over after the service?

Feeling ridiculous at her own thoughts, she forced her mind back to the words of the song. Words she'd need to sink into her soul and provide her strength and comfort throughout the week.

When the service was over, Carissa tried to catch a glimpse

of Jonas. She was trapped behind Alex and Claire and the other folks who were visiting around them. After a minute, she was able to maneuver around everyone and could see where he had been sitting.

But his spot in the row was empty.

CHAPTER
TWENTY

A faint mist hung in the trees as Jonas clipped Charlie's leash on him. The dog's tail wagged like an uncontrolled water hose. He loved walks or runs or pretty much anything. Jonas had been enjoying Charlie's company; he'd miss the dog when he was gone. But every time he looked at him, he saw Brandon and Jayden.

Jonas took off down the street, Charlie keeping pace with him. He hadn't slept well last night, or the last several nights, but he hoped this Monday run would reset his world. After a miserable weekend, he had to get out of his head and hoped Tony could help him start the week off better.

As he headed toward the park, he spotted a lone figure. Large enough build that it could only be Pastor Tony. Maybe he'd get lucky and get some time with him before anyone else showed up. Weekdays didn't generate the same group of runners the weekends did.

The figure grew larger, and Jonas waved.

Tony approached them and held out a hand for Charlie to sniff. "Nice running buddy. He's probably got better endurance."

"Better than any of us." Jonas headed off at a jog, Tony next to him until they found a good pace.

After a moment, Tony broke the silence. "Busy weekend? I noticed you didn't stick around church yesterday."

"I was working on the Cohen case, hoping to get Carissa's house released back to her sooner. I discovered that both of Tyler's parents are dead. The mom's death wasn't surprising. She had early onset Alzheimer's, but his dad died soon after from cancer."

"That's sad. So no one to give any closure to."

Jonas nodded. "I'm looking for other relatives." They ran on in silence again.

Tony gave him a look. "Something else on your mind?"

Jonas wasn't sure how to answer the question. The great thing about Tony was that he didn't push. He let you come to your own words in your own time.

"I think I'm getting too attached to Carissa and her boys. It started out with just being a good neighbor and helping out. But, I have to admit, I'm attracted to her." He wasn't going to admit he'd almost kissed her.

Tony ran for a bit without saying anything. "Why is that a problem for you?"

"Because I was already married once. And I blew it. I don't want to go through that again."

"We could debate what that means that you blew it. But let's say you did. What makes you think that would happen again? You're a smart guy. You learn from your lessons."

Charlie darted off to the side, and Jonas tugged him back. "At some level, it feels disloyal to Autumn. Like I'm just erasing her, like she didn't matter."

"Autumn's always going to be part of your life. Carissa doesn't strike me as the type of woman who would want you to erase all traces of her existence or expect you to act like she didn't exist. In fact, I'm sure she'd be open to hearing about your wife and daughter."

Yeah, he was pretty sure she would be too, based on their previous conversations.

But could he avoid hurting her the way he'd hurt Autumn? He might have hurt her already.

CARISSA AND CLAIRE SAT AT THE KITCHEN ISLAND WITH tall glasses of iced tea and Claire's punch list of things still to be done between them. "What's next?" Carissa tapped the paper.

Claire studied the list. They discussed order and priorities of the last few rooms. Decorating them and staging them was the fun part. But it never failed that they found something that needed to be fixed as well. Scuffed paint, a ding in the wall, a missing switch cover.

Claire covered a yawn. "I seem to run out of steam a lot earlier than I run out of things to do."

"I thought I'd take the kids over to the library today and get them signed up for the summer reading program. I could take Lizzie, and you could lay down for a nap." Which actually sounded pretty great to Carissa, too, but Claire needed it more.

Claire touched Carissa's arm. "Would you? That would be wonderful. I feel bad that all the kids have had so much screen time while we've been rehabbing."

"I know. But they've been a lot better about it when the three of them are together. They manage to come up with things to do."

Claire nodded. "It's been really great having you here. I don't think I could have made as much progress on the rooms without your help. We'll return the favor on your house."

"I think Alex already has. Though he got more than he bargained for." Carissa thought about Tyler's body in her basement and suppressed a shudder.

Claire squeezed her shoulder. "He was just glad it wasn't you that found him." She yawned again.

Carissa slid off the stool and laughed. "Go lay down. I'll round up the kids."

CARISSA TRIED TO STRETCH DISCREETLY AGAINST THE circulation desk at the library. Her back ached from walking funny because of her stitches and the work she'd been doing. The kids were at the sign-up table for the summer reading program, Adventure Under the Stars. The kids' area was decorated in a wilderness camping theme, complete with log stools and a fake campfire. Pup tents created reading nooks, and each kid got a Ranger Reader card to track their books when they signed up. A lot of great prizes awaited the winners. Each book read garnered an entry for the prizes.

The boys and Lizzie were excited and occupied while Carissa waited for Anne to come back with a stack of research she'd printed out. Carissa and Claire had gone over the books Anne had previously discovered that mentioned both of their houses and the previous owners in the founding of Holcomb Springs and the gold rush that led to its population explosion in the 1860s.

But today Anne had more recent information about the missing kids and the stories surrounding that.

Anne appeared from the back. Today she was wearing skinny jeans tucked into hiking boots and a faux-fur vest over a tailored plaid shirt. It looked cute and trendy on her. Carissa figured she'd just look like she'd gotten lost in the woods if she attempted the outfit.

Anne placed the printouts on the counter. "These are some of the reports from when Tyler went missing and the original investigation. *The Sun* newspaper is our big, official paper for the county, and it has the most professional reporting. We also have a smaller, local paper, *The Mountain Monitor*, that covers the mountain towns. It interviewed some of the high school kids and also printed some of the rumors. Because Tyler was part of the astronomy club and disappeared during a lunar eclipse, they have tied him to all sorts of lunar events."

She pushed over some more papers. "These are printouts of discussions from various forums. You can find them yourself here." She pointed to the URLs printed at the top of the page. "They are places for people who are into ghosts and haunted houses, as well as some treasure hunter sites. But Tyler's disappearance has made news on a few of them. Especially since his body was found after a full moon."

Carissa scanned the pages and noticed references to the Delamar Place and speculation that Tyler had been killed for money. She scoffed. "There's no money in that house. It's a money pit. Maybe I should charge admission to the place."

Anne tapped the desk. "Just be careful. Most of this is just nonsense talk online. But some of those treasure seeker folks have created problems other places. They've been convinced there was money and were very persistent. I think Claire and Alex had some trouble with that back at their place in Michigan."

"I'll have to ask her about it. I had to reschedule the internet installation because of the body discovery. But I can't put up any Wi-Fi cameras without it. And the other kind are way too expensive or not practical."

"At least you have an excuse to visit the library." Anne grinned.

"Not that I need one."

"I've put up a search alert on some of these terms, so I'll let you know if anything else turns up. I imagine Jonas has already discovered this himself, but I made copies for him as well. Just in case." Her sly grin made Carissa think Anne had uncovered a few things the sheriff's department hadn't in the past. Well, librarians were trained in research.

"Thank you." She gathered up the pages and stuck them in her bag. While the kids were occupied, Carissa slipped into the anteroom, pulled out her phone, and tried to call the courthouse in Arizona to see what she could do about Greg's threatened lawsuit. After running through what seemed like an endless warren of automated messages, she finally got a voicemail of a court clerk. Frustrated, she left a message and hoped that helped.

Back inside, she grabbed a Jennifer Lynn Cary novel off the shelf to read before bed—she needed to time travel back to the 1970s—and helped the kids get checked out after oohing and aahing appropriately at the prizes they had their eyes on.

Maybe if they got home quickly, she could sneak in a quick nap too. But all she could think about was what she had read on one of the threads.

Tyler had disappeared during a lunar eclipse, and the thread was predicting that his ghost would return on the next blue moon, which was at the end of this month.

What kind of craziness would descend on her house then?

JONAS STOOD FROM HIS DESK AND HEADED TO THE sheriff's private office. He'd spent the day reviewing the case file, talking to the coroner, and finding contact information for the original kids he'd interviewed. He'd also noticed an uptick in the number of discussions and rumors about the Delamar Place, since the discovery of a body there had been leaked.

One rumor in particular was disturbing. It said that Tyler's ghost would return on the next blue moon—the end of June. A rumor made all the more certain, the poster said, because Tyler's body had been found the night after a full moon.

Which was just great. All he—and Carissa—needed was a bunch of ghost hunters poking around her house. What was wrong with people?

What was wrong with him? He'd buried himself in work to keep his mind off Carissa. He had plenty of work to keep him busy.

The sheriff's admin, Donna, waved him in. He entered and lowered himself into the chair in front of the sheriff's desk.

"What have you discovered?" She pulled out a bag of peanut M&Ms and offered him some.

He waved them away. "The coroner hasn't gotten to him yet. It's not a priority since it's a cold case. He estimated a few days. I've located contact information for Kayla Mills, Madison Gonzales, and Anthony Smithton and have left messages with all of them to contact me." He then told her about the rumors he uncovered. "I'd like to make sure we have patrols going by the house regularly. We don't know what kind of ghost hunters will come out of the woodwork."

"Check with the techs to see if there's any evidence of money anywhere around the scene. It's hard to believe a teenager would be killed for money, especially up here, but stranger things have happened. I agree about the patrols. If people wouldn't believe everything they read on the internet, our job would be so much easier."

He gave her a wry grin. "And what would be the fun in that?"

She batted his comment away. "Let me know as soon as you hear anything back from the coroner or if any of the interviews turn up anything. I find it interesting that all of these kids moved out of the area. Yes, they were the age to go off to college, but why did their parents leave too? Tyler's folks had a good reason. His mom went into a special memory care facility. Anthony is the only one with family here still, but I've never seen him visit."

"There's definitely a cover up. The question is, who is lying? Or are all of them? Someone buried Tyler's body. It's a stretch to imagine he left like the kids said, then somehow ended up back at the house, dead and buried. The two things are connected somehow."

"Let me know if you need me to facilitate some interagency cooperation to get those interviews done."

"Will do."

He left her office and headed for his unit, catching himself automatically heading for the Wilders' B-and-B. But he couldn't just drop in over there. It wasn't like Carissa's house where he had an excuse to check on her. She was fine with the Wilders, didn't need his help.

Instead he headed to her house to talk with the techs. Brett was at the scene, sitting in his unit writing a report. Jonas leaned in the window. "Anything happen?"

Brett shook his head. "It's been quiet."

Jonas updated him on the rumors on the ghost finding sites.

"I'll keep an extra eye out. I was just getting ready to do a perimeter check. Need to stretch my legs." Brett exited his SUV and followed Jonas around to the back of the house.

Jonas headed inside and stopped at the top of the stairs to the basement. A glow came from below. He called out and one of the techs came up the steps. It was a woman in a bunny suit —what they called the full coveralls, shoe and hair coverings the techs wore so they wouldn't contaminate the scene. She had a spiderweb tattoo peeking up her neck and dark eye makeup. He could hear footsteps upstairs as well.

"Any updates? Particularly, have you found any money?" Jonas asked.

The tech looked surprised. "Not yet. Do you think there is some we should look for?"

He updated her on the rumor that Tyler had been killed for money and the speculation that it was hidden around the house. He'd asked the county IT folks to see if they could identify who posted that.

The tech didn't have any further updates, said they hadn't discovered much else of note and expected to release the scene in the next day or two.

Jonas left and drove around, not quite ready to head back to his office yet. Carissa and the boys flashed through his mind with annoying frequency. He thought about Tony's words. He didn't know what to do.

But before he could make a decision, his phone rang. The sheriff.

She cut to the chase. "The SAR guys found a car registered to Tyler Cohen."

SHANNON GATHERED EVERYONE IN THE CONFERENCE ROOM. Roberto, Reese, and Marco were dirty and tired. She'd make this as quick a debrief as possible so they could get showered and head home.

They'd trained on the backside of the mountain, where the landscape turned into more desert terrain. The area wasn't frequented, especially since the fire road that provided access had washed out a few years ago. They'd scoped out an area that would be typical for an over-the-side technical rescue, a place on a curve where a car might go over. And at the bottom, they'd found a Jeep buried deep in the brush.

Pictures of the vehicle, the surrounding area, and the inside were flashed on the screen.

As lead of the SAR team, Marco shared what they'd found. "Nothing too surprising in the contents. Typical fast-food wrappers and soda cans. But what is surprising is that there were no bloodstains, no signs of trauma. No way anyone was in that car when it went over. No one could survive that fall and escape. And if they were inside, there would definitely be signs of trauma."

Shannon nodded. "Which makes sense because Tyler's body is in the morgue, and there's never been any reason to believe that anyone else would have been in his car. No one else is missing."

The SAR team had winched the Jeep off the side of the mountain and hauled it to where a tow truck could access it. "The techs will start on the Jeep as soon as they finish up at

Carissa Carver's house. I expect that to be today." Shannon looked to Jonas for confirmation.

He nodded. "The latest rumors about there potentially being money on the property has them doing an extra thorough check for that, but it doesn't seem likely."

Shannon made sure the SAR team didn't have anything else to add, then dismissed them.

What had seemed a tragic but simple case four years ago was spiraling into something much bigger. She hated to see Carissa and her boys caught up in it. She stopped Jonas as the room emptied. "What's your gut on all of this? Is it going to be safe for Carissa and her boys to go back in that house?"

A variety of emotions played across his normally stoic face. That told her more than anything he could say.

"Whatever it takes, I'll make sure it is."

CHAPTER
TWENTY-ONE

On his morning run, Jonas couldn't get yesterday's conversation with the sheriff out of his head. He'd promised he'd keep Carissa and the boys safe. The strength of his feelings and conviction around that surprised him. But it was there, rooted in who he was and not just his duty as part of his uniform.

He would keep them safe.

Anne had emailed him some research she'd pulled up the other day. Mostly things he'd already discovered. But the depth of her digging always impressed and surprised him. But it reminded him again of how much they still didn't know. He didn't like that. And he didn't like that his lack of knowledge could put Carissa and the boys in danger.

Today, he'd either get in touch with those who had been dodging his calls or he'd get the LEOs to pay a call on them.

One thing he could do to help Carissa and the boys would be to bring Charlie to visit them before he started second shift. Maybe they'd all go to the park.

He'd been dumb and selfish. Just because he was struggling with seeing Carissa and his feelings for her didn't mean the boys should suffer.

He reached down to ruffle Charlie's fur. "Want to go see your kids?"

The dog wagged his tail. Then again, he wagged his tail at the slightest attention. Jonas had gotten used to having the company. He used to think that he liked the solitude of his cabin, of not being able to see any other houses. It was an oasis for him.

And if he was honest, it was a place to hide. So perhaps God was telling him it was time to come out of hiding, to engage with life again.

As soon as they got home and he'd showered, he texted Carissa.

> Okay if I swing by with Charlie and take him and the kids to the park?

Minutes dragged without a response. She was likely busy helping Claire. But was she mad at him? He wouldn't blame her if she was. He would need to apologize for sure. Hopefully, he could get her alone.

> That would be great.

"Hear that Charlie? She's okay with us coming over. Let's head out." He grabbed the leash off the hook and snapped it on Charlie's collar, always a challenge because the dog wiggled so much when he saw the leash come out. But in short order they were out the door, in the truck, and were pulling up in front of Cope House.

Jonas had barely shut the engine off when the boys ran outside, and if the window had been down, Charlie would have jumped out it. He whined and pranced around on the seat.

The moment Jonas let him out, he dashed across the lawn and just about bowled Jayden over. A mass of dog and boys formed a wriggly pile on the lawn. He chuckled. Oh to have something that brought him as much joy.

Lizzie came out of the door, followed by Carissa, her expression guarded.

He shoved his hands into his front pockets. "I guess they were kind of excited to see each other."

She smiled at that. "Just a little." She crossed the lawn closer to him. "Mind if Lizzie and I tag along? That way Claire can lie down for a bit. The house is so close to being ready. We're just staging the rooms at this point. But she has more energy in the afternoon if she's able to take a nap."

"Sounds great. The more the merrier."

Carissa nodded. "Okay, Brandon, take Charlie's leash. Jayden, we're heading to the park, so stay close and watch for cars when we cross the street."

Brandon grabbed the dog's leash, and the three kids trotted down the sidewalk toward town.

Carissa started after them, Jonas next to her. She turned to him. "Thanks so much. They really missed him."

And that was his opening. He let the kids get a few more paces in front of them. "I need to apologize. I shouldn't have changed our arrangement. I'm used to being alone." He gave a short chuckle. "It's actually been nice having Charlie around. I've enjoyed the company. But I know your boys missed him."

The kids all took turns with the leash and sprinting past each other with the dog.

After a quiet moment, Carissa spoke. "They did miss him. But life has been a bit chaotic lately." She also laughed. "I think it's our new normal. Anyhow, apology accepted." She gave him a warm smile.

Once they reached the park, he and Carissa headed toward a bench while the kids ran between the playground and the field, playing some game they'd made up. Now was the time. It wasn't going to be easy, but it was going to be necessary.

He stretched his arm on the back of the bench. Without

much effort, he could reach her shoulder. Instead, he kept his hand to himself. "Lizzie reminds me a lot of Ava. Can I tell you about her?"

Carissa's gaze on him was soft, full of compassion. "I'd like that a lot."

"She would have been starting high school this fall. I know Lizzie's only twelve and Ava was ten when she was killed, but they both have that open-hearted joy. Ava always looked out for the kids at school who didn't have anyone sitting with them at lunch. She loved animals. She was a chatterbox and a bundle of energy." His heart felt like it was going to pound out of his chest. A swirl of emotions surged through him, and he wasn't sure what to do with them.

"You must miss her a lot."

He nodded, unable to speak for a moment. "The first time I saw you and the boys was at the Sleepy Bear Lodge." He noted her surprised look but kept going. "Mariah had called about a suspicious person, so I was checking the place out. Your boys had just gotten out of the pool. And for a moment—I think it's the smell of chlorine that does it—I remembered playing with my brother Jonathan in the pool, waiting for our dad to get home from work and join us. The one thing I had insisted on when Autumn and I bought our house was that it had to have a pool. I wanted to swim with our kids after work the way Jon and I had done with our dad."

"So did you have a pool?"

He smiled at the memory. "Yeah, we had a great pool with a slide. I'd always wanted one as a kid. Ava and I would swim when I got off work in time. And we lived close enough to go to the beach. I suppose it wouldn't matter if we'd done it every day, but looking back, I wished there'd been more times, more opportunities."

He pulled himself out of the memories and looked at her.

She reached over to his hand lying on the back of the bench and covered it with her own. "Life never works out the way we want. But we do have our memories to hang on to. Ava was lucky to have you as a dad."

Tears sprang to his eyes and he stood, squeezing her hand quickly before pacing away, staring out over the fields, watching the kids throw a stick to Charlie. He worked his jaw, trying to get his emotions under control.

He felt more than heard Carissa stand next to him. "Thanks for sharing that with me. I hope you know you can always talk about Ava and Autumn. They're a part of you. And I'm honored that you trust me with those memories."

Without a second thought, he pulled her into his arms. Her arms went around his waist, her head on his shoulder, and the warmth of her pressed against him felt right. Instead of being alone with his thoughts, memories, and regrets, she was sharing them with him, giving him exactly what he needed when he didn't even know what that was.

After a moment, he kissed the top of her head and pulled back. "Thank you."

She gazed up at him, hope, trust, and something else shining in her eyes. "I'm here for you, Jonas. I hope you know that."

And he thought he might begin to believe that.

JONAS CARRIED HIS LAPTOP INTO THE SHERIFF'S OFFICE. The coroner's report had come in, and after a few phone calls, he felt better about this case than he had up until now. Plus, Carissa was getting her house back today. After his meeting with the sheriff, he was heading over to Cope House to deliver the news in person.

There was a lot he didn't know, but they were making some progress.

The sheriff waved him into a seat. "What did you find out?"

"No surprise, the body was Tyler Cohen's. The dental records provided a positive ID. Cause of death was massive trauma.

There was also a skull fracture that wasn't fatal but was significant, likely prior to the other trauma. The rest of his body had trauma consistent with a significant fall. Given what we know about the railing and floor at Carissa's house, somehow Tyler probably fell from the second floor to the first."

"Possibly the result of the skull fracture? He stumbles and falls over? Or is pushed?"

He nodded. "That's what I'm thinking." He clicked to another document. "The preliminary report from the techs was that they found a spindle with a trace of blood and hair on it matching Tyler's."

"So someone hits him on the back of the head, and he stumbles or is pushed over the railing." The sheriff tapped on her desk.

"That's my working theory. The question is, who? I talked to Anthony Smithton today. He's sticking to the same story. Kayla Mills broke up with Tyler, and he left, determined to hit the road and put it all behind him. He has no idea how Tyler's body got in the basement or his car in the national forest. But Anthony was pretty eager to get off the phone. Madison Gonzales had pretty much the same reaction, though she seemed more shaken up on hearing that Tyler was dead."

"You haven't talked to Kayla Mills yet?"

"No. She's living in Chicago, I discovered. I'd kind of like to get her on a video call. She's the one with motive here. Perhaps Tyler didn't like the idea of her breaking up with him. They were all alone in the room upstairs. We found blouse buttons, but we don't have Kayla's prints on file to know if they're her buttons. Perhaps he tried to force her to do something she didn't want, and she whacked him with the spindle, not hard enough to kill him, but enough so she could get away. He stumbles around and falls and dies. After that, somehow Tyler gets buried in the basement."

The sheriff leaned back in her chair. "Burying a body in the basement doesn't strike me as something a teenage girl would do.

Not ruling it out, just not seeing it as my first choice. I can see it all as an accident and the kids panicking and making bad decisions."

"It's a working theory, but we have a lot of gaps to fill. There's one other thing that showed up. Eli Schiller's prints."

The sheriff sat up straighter. "Isaiah's older brother." Isaiah was her son, Zach's, best friend. She nodded pensively. "Yeah, I forgot he was in the system for some petty theft. His parents had their hands full with him for a while, but he just graduated college. I think he's back working for Vince for the summer."

"It doesn't necessarily mean anything. There were a lot of prints. A lot of kids were in and out of that house, plus workers. Eli was in Tyler's class, so it was likely he was there at some point. It'll be worth talking with him about what he might know."

"None of the kids mentioned he was there?"

"No. Could be he wasn't there that night."

She nodded. "Alumni Day is coming up the first night of Art Fest. Might be a good time to talk to kids from that class and see if there were any rumors or anything they remember now that we can officially announce Tyler's death. Keep at it and keep me in the loop." She grinned. "Now go tell Carissa she can have her house back."

CHAPTER
TWENTY-TWO

Carissa pulled up in front of her house. It felt so good to be back, especially after seeing the potential at the Cope House. Jonas had delivered the news yesterday afternoon, but Alex had wanted to fill in the basement hole, install the Lally column, and concrete over the whole thing. He and Samuel had headed over yesterday to get it started.

And sure enough, a cement truck rumbled down the street, coming to a squealing halt in front of her curb. The boys would be fascinated by that process today. It'd give them something to do while she cleaned up after whatever the techs had left and worked on the upstairs bathroom's moldy tile.

She turned in her seat. "Boys, you can watch the cement truck from the living room window. Don't go near it, and don't get in the workers' way. Okay?"

They both nodded and ran inside, leaving the front door wide open. She gathered their bags and started to follow when Jonas's truck pulled in behind her. The sight of him did something funny to her stomach. Being in his arms yesterday… She thought she was providing him comfort, but the solid wall of his chest, his arms holding her tight… It was something she wanted to experience again.

He climbed out, Charlie right behind him. Charlie gave her a quick sniff, then beelined through the front door.

She laughed. "Guess I know his priorities. I didn't expect to see you here."

Jonas's gaze was steady on her, and she suddenly felt awkward. He reached for the bags in her hand. "I wanted to help you guys get settled, make sure everything is okay here."

"Thank you." She wanted to say more, but she wasn't sure what. Plus, her yard was now crawling with workers. The small basement window had been removed, and a chute ran from the back of the cement mixer to the window.

She shook her head. "Alex. I don't know how he pulled all this off."

Jonas settled his hand on her lower back. "Let's go inside and see what's up."

They headed toward the back of the house, avoiding the chaos in the front.

Alex stood at the top of the stairs to the basement. "Welcome home. The column is in, the floor is no longer bouncy, and soon it'll all be concreted over."

"You didn't have to do all of this. I don't know how I can ever thank you."

He waved her words away. "I wasn't going to leave you with that mess and reminder. Now it'll be like new. It's not a problem." He jerked a thumb over his shoulder. "I've got Samuel working on running what we need for your washer and dryer. It's good training for him. And," he paused. "It really was great for us—especially Claire and Lizzie—to have you guys at our place. Claire is more tired than she likes to let on, so having your help finishing up the rooms was a godsend. And Lizzie enjoyed the company. Anyhow, once you've settled, take a look at the back slope where I pulled the dirt from. Make sure it's okay. We can always get a bobcat out here to move more of it around if you need to."

She nodded, overwhelmed. And very conscious of Jonas's

hand resting on her back, its warmth seeping through her shirt and making her want to lean into his strength.

His hand moved away when he shook Alex's hand. "Thanks, man. I appreciate all you've done."

"No problem. I'm going to check on Samuel, but let me know if you need anything." He headed past them toward the mudroom.

Carissa was overwhelmed. She'd have to think of something she could do to thank the Wilders. In the meantime, she moved down the hall, Jonas following. He dropped the bags at the foot of the stairs and headed into the living room.

She closed the front door. The sound of the cement mixer dulled slightly. She followed Jonas into the living room. The boys were kneeling on the couch in front of the window, watching what was going on in the front yard. Charlie was up there too.

Jonas was next to them. "Cool, huh?"

"Yeah." Brandon turned but Jayden's gaze stayed fixed out the window.

Jonas reached into his pocket and handed something to Brandon. "Want some bubblegum?"

Brandon reached for it, but his gaze shot to Carissa. "Uh, Mom doesn't like the smell of bubblegum, so we can't chew it around her. But if you're going to be upstairs, can we have it?"

Carissa swallowed. Without even smelling it, memories came flooding back. And not good ones.

But it wasn't the boys' fault. As long as she didn't have to smell it… "It's fine. Say thank you."

"Thanks, Jonas." Brandon took the pack and began opening it. He pulled out a piece and handed it to Jayden.

Carissa started backing out of the room.

Jonas frowned. "I'm sorry. I didn't know."

She waved her hand and took another step back. Was there any Diet Coke in her fridge? She should check. "It's fine. Don't worry about it." She turned and headed toward the kitchen.

As she pulled open the fridge door, Jonas was right next to her, putting his hand on the counter and leaning in. "What's wrong?"

She pasted on a smile as she closed the fridge. "I don't have any Diet Coke, that's what's wrong."

He narrowed his eyes. He wasn't buying it.

She sighed. "Let's go look at where Alex took the dirt from. I have more landscaping ideas after seeing what Alex and Claire did."

He watched her for a moment before stepping back. "Lead the way."

Carissa prayed Gladys would see all the commotion and decide to stay away. Jonas had opened up to Carissa, and now she needed to open up with him. But she didn't need a nosy neighbor overhearing.

As they moved through the backyard to the far corner, she spotted the scooped-out section of her hill. It increased the flat area.

"This was a good choice. It makes the yard larger." And even better, they were far enough away from the workers so she and Jonas could talk privately.

Jonas nodded and took her hand. "Tell me what's really going on. I've seen that look before. It's not simply that you don't like the smell of bubblegum. It brings up memories. Bad memories."

She tilted her head up, grateful for the warmth and strength of his hand. "Yeah, it does. When I was in high school, I had a crush on one of the popular boys. I had no chance with him, I knew that. But this other girl and I were sharing secrets during a study session. Actually, I was tutoring her, and she was prying info out of me to avoid working on her project. I was just happy she was interested in getting to know me, because she was part of the in crowd."

She paced a few steps away and kicked at a pine cone, but Jonas didn't let go of her hand, just followed her. "So at lunch one day, that boy I had a crush on read out loud a note he said was from me. Of course it wasn't. But it said that I liked him and wanted to do"—she swallowed—"inappropriate things with him. Everyone laughed and no one believed me when I said I didn't write it. I complained to the teacher, who also didn't believe me.

"It felt like betrayal upon betrayal. I tried to get the note back and couldn't. But I did get a glimpse of the handwriting. It was the popular girl's who I'd tutored. She just was using me for fun. I was teased the whole day and on the bus home.

"We'd had some special assembly that day where the speaker handed out bubblegum to everyone. So everyone who was laughing at me and teasing me was chewing bubblegum. I can't separate the smell from the memories."

"Smells are powerful like that." Jonas's voice was low, and he tugged her closer.

"When I got home, all I wanted to do was go to my room and cry. But my mom wasn't home, and the door was locked. I didn't have a key. So I had to go around to the backyard and climb in the bathroom window at the back of the house by standing on the outdoor faucet.

"Mom finally got home, and I thought she'd at least be on my side and comfort me. But she was in a bad mood and was pretty dismissive, saying it would all blow over, that I should wash my face, and help her make dinner. I felt alone and abandoned."

She picked at some tree bark. "It's hard for me to trust anyone. I don't share my thoughts and feelings, and I try not to be vulnerable. When I'm at my most cynical, I believe that people only want me for what I can do for them, that they can't really be trusted." Tears sprang to her eyes. "That's why it's so hard to understand why people like Alex and Claire are so nice to me."

He pulled her into his arms. The smell of his freshly laundered T-shirt pressed into her face helped the bad memories fade. For a moment, she just wanted to stay here and not have this end.

"Claire and Alex want to help you because they are good neighbors, the kind the Bible talks about." He held her back from him and dipped his head to look into her eyes. "Carissa, you are worthy of being helped, of people being nice to you. Just because you are you and a part of this community."

She let his words sink into her soul, like rain on the parched desert ground. Maybe it only mattered that Jonas thought she was worthy. Maybe his belief would be enough. Maybe hers would come in time.

Returning his gaze, she wished they didn't have a group of workers crawling over her front lawn. Because she wanted another opportunity for him to kiss her.

A slamming truck door caused both of them to turn. Vince was getting out of his work truck, followed by a young man who looked to be about college age, lanky with light-brown hair tousled on top.

"Great," Jonas muttered under his breath.

She wasn't sure if that was because they were being interrupted or because it was Vince. She started across the lawn, intending to untangle her fingers from Jonas's, but he held on tight. She'd already seen how small-town gossip worked. If folks saw her holding hands with Jonas, they'd come to all sorts of conclusions that they'd share with anyone who'd listen. She'd understand if Jonas didn't want any part of that, which was why she'd tried to pull her hand free.

But apparently he was making a statement.

Vince glanced at their joined hands, his smile dimming. "Came by to see if you needed any help moving back in." He gave Carissa an unreadable look before turning to the young man next to him. "This is Eli Schiller. He graduated from college and is working for me for the summer while he figures out his next move."

Eli was staring up at her house. He pulled his hands out of

his pockets and shook her hand. "Good to meet you." He frowned when he shook Jonas's hand. "I think we've met before."

Jonas gave a short nod. "We have."

Eli looked at the house again. "Well, I'd love to see what you've done with the place. My friends and I used to hang out here in high school, when it was abandoned."

Carissa cast a glance at Jonas, but his face was stoic. "Um, sure. There's a lot left to do, but you can come in and look around."

They headed toward the back deck and inside to the mudroom.

Samuel had his back to them, working on something in the wall. He turned, and his face paled. He stumbled back a bit, bumped into the wall, then with a quick, mumbled "Hi," he went back to work.

Had he been teased by Eli at some point? There was at least a four-year age difference, and Carissa didn't know all of Samuel's story, but he sure acted like someone who didn't want to be around Eli.

She shot a glance at Eli, but he was fixated on the basement. Honestly, some people were so ghoulish. "Don't go down there. Alex and the guys are pouring concrete."

Eli lifted his chin. "Sure. Can I take a look upstairs?"

She turned to Jonas.

"I'll go with you." Jonas squeezed her hand as he let it go, and he and Eli moved down the hall.

Vince stuck his head down the basement stairway and then turned back to Carissa. "So are you okay with the area we cleared? I can bring the bobcat back over and change it if you want. But based on what you said you wanted in landscaping, I thought that was a good space to take fill dirt from for the basement."

"Oh, you're the one Alex got the bobcat from? Thanks so much. It's just fine. I think it works really well. I really appreciate all you guys have done to help me."

"Not a problem." Vince cast a glance at Samuel, who was working away, not paying them any attention. "Hey, Samuel. You still planning on working with me next week when you've finished up with Alex?"

Samuel nodded but didn't turn around.

Vince turned back to her. "So you're sure you don't need any help with anything?"

She shook her head. "We've got it under control. But thanks. You've done a lot already."

He glanced down the hall. "Let's go look at that cleared spot, and I can tell you my thoughts about it."

"Um, okay. I've got a few minutes. Then the moldy tile upstairs is calling my name." She gave a little laugh.

Samuel turned and looked at her but quickly turned back around. She'd talk to him once Vince and Eli were gone to see if she could find anything out. She didn't think so, but maybe just letting him know she was on his side would help to make him feel more comfortable.

They headed outside toward the cleared spot. Carissa was acutely aware she'd just been there with Jonas. Not wanting to disturb those memories, she stopped short of the area and gestured to it. "I haven't had much time to think about it, but a few benches would be nice back there. Maybe string up a hammock from the trees for the boys. Kind of a secret garden reading nook."

"I don't know about reading, but I like the secret idea." Vince gave her a wide grin.

She resisted the urge to roll her eyes and ignored his comment. "Anyhow, like I've said, it's bottom of the list. And tile is the top of the list today." She kept her tone light, but she did need to get to work. "Thanks again. I really appreciate it."

"Sure. No problem. Let me know if you need anything else." He stepped onto the back porch and stuck his head inside. "Eli! We've got to go."

CHAPTER
TWENTY-THREE

Jonas followed Eli up the stairs, letting the kid lead, seeing how much he'd reveal of his knowledge of this house. He'd been here before; his prints proved that. But something more than mere curiosity was driving Eli. He was looking for something. Evidence?

Eli's gaze was everywhere. The walls, the staircase, the banister. He entered every room, taking in the walls and doors. When he came to the one with the secret room, he seemed genuinely surprised.

"Whoa, I didn't know this was here. There's a room back here." He stuck his head around the propped open panel. "Not much of a room. But still." After a long moment, he came back out and turned to Jonas. "Did you guys find anything in here?"

"Nothing of any real value."

Eli seemed to deflate a minute then shook it off.

"Did you come here a lot?" Since Eli had opened the door about being here, Jonas was going to walk through it and see what the kid would say.

Eli shrugged. "Some."

"Did you know Tyler Cohen? Hang out with him?"

Eli gave a harsh laugh. "Of course I knew him. We were in the same class. The high school is so small we all knew each other, even the freshmen." He brushed past Jonas and left the room, heading into the hall again.

"Were you here the night he went missing?"

"Nah."

"Where were you?"

Eli turned. "What's with the inquisition? That was a long time ago. And now he's not missing. Case solved." He glanced around before heading downstairs. "Your crime scene folks didn't find anything, did they? Other than evidence of kids just hanging out in an abandoned house?"

Jonas didn't answer, just followed him down.

Halfway down, Eli stopped and turned to look at him. "Any secret stash of money?" His serious expression turned to a grin.

"You don't believe those internet rumors, do you?" Jonas countered.

Eli descended the rest of the way.

Vince yelled from the back that it was time to go.

Eli pulled open the front door. "Thanks for the tour." He gave a mock salute and left.

Jonas peeked in the living room. The boys were still enthralled with the cement mixer. He headed back to the mudroom. Samuel had an adverse reaction to Eli. Time to figure out what that was all about.

Samuel was connecting pex tubing through a washing machine outlet box and shutoff valves.

Jonas rapped on the doorframe as he came through so as not to startle Samuel. The boy jumped anyway as he turned.

"Good job on that." Jonas lifted his chin toward the valves. "That's a handy skill to have. I bet Alex is teaching you a lot of useful things."

"Yeah. And I like helping Carissa."

"I like helping her too." He waited a beat. "Did you know Eli before he left for college?" He kept his voice casual.

Samuel shrugged. "I saw him around."

"Did you ever see him here, when it was abandoned?" If Samuel had been squatting in the Cope House last winter, it wasn't out of the realm of possibility that he'd squatted here, too, when he'd been on the run from various foster homes.

Samuel shrugged again. He went back to work on the valves.

Jonas didn't want to push and scare Samuel off, but he knew more than he was saying. He waited, watching the kid work.

After a moment, Samuel stopped. "Do you think Carissa's in danger?"

Jonas wasn't expecting that. "Do you mean by the person who killed Tyler? I don't think so. Why?"

Again with the shrug. "If they thought Carissa might find something in the house that would say they were guilty."

"The crime scene techs did a good job going over everything in the house. If they didn't find anything, it's not very likely Carissa will. Did you have something in mind?" He thought about the money rumor. Maybe that's what Samuel was referring to. Money could seem very attractive to a kid in his circumstances.

Samuel seemed to think about that for a moment. "Is anyone going to get in trouble?"

"I don't know. If Tyler's death was an accident, someone still buried him. It's a crime to interfere in an investigation." Jonas watched Samuel as he struggled to come to some sort of a decision. The kid knew something. But what?

Samuel didn't say anything more. He went back to work. Whatever he knew, he'd kept it to himself for four years now.

Jonas slipped one of his cards out of his wallet and handed it to Samuel. "You call me if you think of anything you want to tell me or if you see anything or you need any help. Okay?" He waited until the kid made eye contact with him, briefly, before releasing his hold on the card.

Samuel stuck it in his pocket.

Jonas thanked Samuel for his work and went out to find

Carissa. He had to leave for his shift soon. And he hoped Samuel would reach out and tell what he knew.

THE LIGHT IN THE BATHROOM WAS GROWING DIMMER BY the minute. Dusk was settling while the day was ending. Carissa straightened, easing the kinks out of her back. But she had to admit, the tile was looking good. She'd been able to scrub a lot of the mold off, and the tiles themselves were in good condition. She'd cut out the grout and replace it, and the bathroom would look great when she was done. It was a ray of hope in her budget that she didn't have to replace the bathroom tile.

She stripped off her rubber gloves and headed downstairs. The boys had made a fort out of the couch pillows after the cement truck had left. Brandon was inside it reading by flashlight. Jayden had made an elaborate Lego structure on top of it.

"Hey guys. Hungry?" She flipped the lamp on in the darkened room.

Brandon lowered his book. "Yeah. Can we have pizza?"

They'd had more pizza than any family should. But she had some chicken thighs thawing in the fridge to roast on a sheet pan with some veggies the boys liked. "We're having chicken tonight. Why are you reading with a flashlight instead of turning on the lamp?"

Brandon grinned. "It's more fun to read that way in a fort."

"Good point." Movement outside the front window caught her eye. With the lamp on, there was a reflection, and she couldn't see well. She went to the front door and looked out.

George lumbered by, pulling his cart behind him.

She trotted out to the road, as best as her stitched toe would let her. It was getting less sore each day, but it reminded her if she made a misstep. "Hey, George. Get a good haul today?" His cart was full of cans and bottles, as well as wire, metal scraps, and other unidentifiable junk.

"Pretty good. Can't complain. You let me know if you have anything I can take off your hands, won't you?"

"I will. Alex said he'd help me get a Bagster when we get into the demo, and I'll let you go through it to take anything you'd like."

"I'd appreciate that. Well, I'd best get on home before dark. You have a good evening, young lady."

She smiled at that. "I will. You do the same." She waved and headed back inside.

She got the veggies and chicken in the oven and set the timer. "Brandon, come feed Charlie, please."

He clattered into the mudroom and poured kibble into Charlie's bowl.

Carissa admired her washer and dryer, finally all hooked up. Samuel had finished up everything, and Alex had checked his work, complimenting him on a good job. Samuel beamed. Carissa figured the kid hadn't gotten much appreciation in his life. Alex was good for him. She wasn't as convinced that working with Vince and Eli would be so great.

The door to the basement remained closed and locked while the concrete cured. Alex would be by tomorrow to check on it. He'd also recommended she order a new basement window that was more insulated and could be better secured. They screwed her old one back in to keep it in place, but it would be nice to have one that could open for ventilation. She'd check on that while dinner was cooking. She had the measurements in her phone.

Charlie whined at the back door.

"You need to go out?" She glanced at his bowl and frowned. "You didn't finish your dinner. What's wrong with you? You never do that." Usually he was like a vacuum sucking down anything in his bowl. Weird.

She opened the door for him, but he didn't go out. A low rumble emanated from his throat and his hackles rose.

What in the world? Was there a raccoon or some other

animal? A bobcat or mountain lion? She'd have to ask Jonas if they came into town. She supposed they might, since their houses were so close to the national forest.

She grabbed Charlie's collar so he didn't dart out. The last thing she needed was for him to tangle with a wild animal. She peered out but couldn't see anything or hear any rustling. She glanced at her flip-flops and stitched toe. She wasn't in the condition to go chasing off any wild animals. Charlie would just have to stay inside until it was all clear.

He gave a sharp bark then ran back into the house.

She shut and bolted the back door then followed him.

He growled and pawed at the front door.

Something was definitely out there. She shut off the living room lamp and peered out. Something darted past the window.

And it was a human form.

AFTER GETTING CARISSA'S CALL, JONAS FLEW THROUGH town to her house. He pulled up in front of her house and jumped out of his unit, hand on his gun, flashlight in his other hand. He'd told her to stay inside with the doors locked until he came to her. Listening, he didn't hear anything, but he slowly made his way around the front of her house, shining the beam into the bushes and around the trees. He made his way carefully around her house. Since there had been so many people around, there were a lot of footprints.

None of the windows looked like they'd been tampered with. Neither had the front or back doors.

The garage was another story. The lock had been cut. It lay on the ground, the hasp neatly sliced through. Likely Charlie's barking had scared the guy off because the garage door hadn't been opened. He'd have to bring Charlie a bone as a reward.

He went around to the front door, but before he could knock, it opened.

Carissa stood there, one arm wrapped around her middle, the other holding Charlie's collar, her face contorted with worry. "Did you find anything?"

"The lock on the garage has been cut. But Charlie must have scared him off. They didn't get into the garage."

Brandon appeared next to Carissa. "Did you catch the bad guy?"

"Not yet. But don't worry, you guys are safe."

"I'm glad Mom didn't chase after him."

Jonas gave her a steady look. "Me too." Yeah, they'd need to talk. He gestured toward the garage with a tilt of his head. "Want to come see?"

Charlie was a wiggling mass she struggled to control. "Can I let him loose?"

"Sure. Might be interesting to see what he does."

She let go of his collar, and after a quick, friendly sniff of Jonas, Charlie took off down the front porch steps and straight to the garage, his nose on the ground.

Carissa shut the door behind her and followed.

"What did you see?" Jonas shone his flashlight across the yard.

She told him about Charlie's behavior and the figure she spotted. "He was young, moving quickly. It definitely wasn't George."

"Did you leave any tools or anything outside?"

"I don't think so. A few weeks ago my shovel was missing. But I found it on the side of the house where it looked like someone had been digging. Charlie was interested in the area, so I chalked it up to him going after an animal and the shovel getting misplaced somehow. But ever since then, I keep everything in the garage or the mudroom."

Charlie sniffed all around the garage and the back deck then returned to them.

They arrived at the garage, and he pointed his light at the broken lock. "You need some lights out here."

She nodded. "It's on the list."

"I'll pick some up tomorrow and install them in the morning."

"You don't have to do that. I can get to it."

"I know. But I'm going to do it. You don't need to be climbing a ladder in flip-flops, and I don't want it to wait until you're able to do it." He opened the garage. "I don't think he got in here, but check to make sure." He flipped on the bare bulb.

She took a step in and glanced around. "Everything is where it should be, best I can tell. But how am I going to secure it tonight? For that matter, if they're just going to cut the lock, what's going to keep them from coming back?"

"There are locks that are much harder to cut. I'll grab one when I get the lights. As for tonight, I have some ideas, though they know they were spotted, so I don't think they'll be back." He reached for her hand and squeezed it. "It's going to be okay." He really wanted to pull her in his arms and hold her until she felt safe. But he was on duty, and he didn't want his mind clouded. "I'm going to go over and talk to Gladys, see if she saw anything. Pull up your Explorer so the nose hits the garage door. That'll keep it from swinging open. Then I'll zip tie the latch as well."

The worry eased from her face, and she nodded and headed back inside, Charlie at her heels. He was grateful she had that dog.

He strode through the gate in the fence that separated her property from Gladys's and knocked on Gladys's door. He could see her living room light on and hear the TV. After a moment, Gladys's face appeared at the curtains. He gave a small wave.

The lock flipped, and she pulled open the front door. "Jonas, what brings you here so late?"

"Someone tried to break into Carissa's garage. Did you see anything?"

"Oh, that's terrible! No, I don't think so. I've been watching TV. Are Carissa and the boys okay?"

"They're fine. The intruder didn't try to get into the house, and Charlie scared him off. Carissa said she saw someone running away, so I thought I'd see if you saw anything."

"No, I'm sorry that I didn't."

"Okay, thank you. You have a good night." He waved and stepped off her porch, listening for the lock to slide home before he retraced his steps back to Carissa's.

She was exiting her car. "Would you like something to drink? I was in the process of starting dinner when all this came up, but I think at this point it'll be frozen pizza again. The boys will be thrilled." Her voice suggested she felt just the opposite.

"Sure. Let me secure the garage latch, and I'll be right in." A moment later, he had zip tied the latch shut and entered through the front door. Charlie greeted him. He ruffled the dog's ears. "You're a good boy."

Brandon and Jayden appeared, wide-eyed and reticent.

It was the uniform. He thought back. Every time they'd seen him in uniform, something bad was happening: Carissa's cut toe, the discovery of the body. He squatted down. "Mom says you guys are having pizza after all. How does that sound?"

Brandon smiled. "Good!"

Jayden stared at his duty belt. Lots of stuff there to look at.

Carissa called from the kitchen, "Jonas, what would you like to drink?"

He straightened. "Better go see what your mom wants." He ruffled Brandon's hair, but Jayden backed up out of reach. His heart squeezed a bit. He'd hoped Jayden had gotten comfortable with him. But the uniform was imposing. That was the point of it. He just hoped they didn't associate him showing up in uniform with bad news.

He headed into the kitchen.

"Do you want coffee, Diet Coke, or water?" She smiled. "And if you can wait twenty minutes, you can have a slice of frozen pizza."

"Coffee is great. Though the pizza is tempting."

She started the Keurig then leaned against the counter. "Thanks for getting here so quickly. Do you think it was someone checking out the ghost rumors?" She lowered her voice.

"Probably."

She handed him his coffee. He took a sip then asked, "When are you getting your internet installed? It would be good to get some Wi-Fi cameras up, too, so you can see what's going on without going outside."

"Next Monday. If nothing else causes me to reschedule it again."

He nodded. "The lights should help." He chuckled. "And Charlie."

"Yeah, when something distracted him from eating, I knew it was serious." She blew out a breath. "I just hope the boys won't be too scared. We went through a season of night terrors with Jayden. I don't want to do that again."

"I'll be outside your house for most of my shift in between patrolling. I've got some reports to write and research to do. I can do that from my unit. Then I'll get Roberto to do the same thing." He drained his cup. "Thanks for this. I'd best get going. Let you guys get to your pizza."

She smirked. "Thanks. We lead such an exciting life. Maybe more exciting than I'd like."

He reached for her hand again. "It's going to be okay."

She nodded but didn't speak.

With a final squeeze, he released her and headed to the foyer, peeking in on the boys in the living room. "Hey guys, I'm heading out. But I want you to know that I'll be parked outside for most of my shift. Then my buddy Roberto will be there for his shift, okay? You guys will be safe."

"Okay." Brandon seemed to take it in stride.

Jayden didn't say anything, just stared.

With a final wink at Carissa and a wave to the boys, he left the house. He heard the lock click home behind him. As he sat in his unit, he thought about who it could have been. He didn't want to scare Carissa, but maybe it was time to pay a visit to the Schillers.

CHAPTER
TWENTY-FOUR

Jonas was at the hardware store the next morning looking at different motion-sensor lights when his phone buzzed with a text. It was from Alex.

> Any chance you've seen Samuel anywhere?
> He didn't show up today and he's not at the
> Markeys'.

He thought about Samuel's reaction to Eli yesterday. He hadn't had a chance to talk to Samuel, though he had swung by the Schillers' last night. Eli was out with friends, conveniently. He called Alex.

"Hey, I haven't seen him since yesterday, but I wonder if he and Eli Schiller have a history. Eli showed up with Vince at Carissa's yesterday, and Samuel started acting weird. Maybe Eli had bullied him when they were in school. So he might be avoiding Eli, which is going to be hard since they both will be working for Vince. But that doesn't explain why he didn't show up to help you today."

"I wondered if he was at Carissa's, since he seems to have taken a liking to her and enjoys helping her. But she said he wasn't there." The concern in Alex's voice came through the phone.

"Did the Markeys say if Samuel had been home?"

"Yeah, he was there yesterday and gone early this morning. They assumed he'd left early to come work with me. Since he's moving out at the end of the month when he ages out of the system, they don't keep too close of tabs on him."

Jonas thought about the prowler at Carissa's. Could it have been Samuel? Didn't make much sense, and he'd never been one to cut locks or break into an occupied house. "Have you talked to Vince?"

"Yeah, he hasn't seen him either, but Samuel's not supposed to start work there until next week. It's not a big deal on my end. I can get done what I need to without him. I'm just worried about him."

"I'll talk to the rest of the shift, and we'll keep an eye out for him. Let me know if you hear from him."

"Thanks, Jonas. I appreciate it."

Jonas pocketed his phone, grabbed two of the sensor lights, a cut-proof lock, and checked out. His mind was thinking through places Samuel might be. If he was afraid of Eli, what would he do? What would he be thinking?

He'd let the deputies know to keep a lookout for Samuel, and he'd swing by the park and the library before heading over to Carissa's. He didn't think Samuel was in any danger. But he wanted Samuel to feel safe in this town. He thought that they'd accomplished that when everyone celebrated Samuel's graduation and had found him work and a place to stay.

But trauma and bad experiences ran deep. He let out a sigh. Yeah, he knew something about that.

CARISSA WAS TORN BETWEEN WAITING FOR JONAS TO SHOW up or digging into the rest of the bathroom. She'd made a batch of blueberry muffins this morning. Normally they were a weekend treat for the boys, and they were from a mix, but she figured it was something she could offer Jonas for all of his help.

She'd actually been able to sleep last night knowing either he or Roberto were outside keeping watch.

A knock at the front door made the decision for her. But when she pulled it open, Samuel was standing there.

"Hey, Samuel. I wasn't expecting you. How are you?"

"Good. Just wanted to make sure everything was okay here." He scuffed his toe on her porch.

Something was on his mind. "I just made some blueberry muffins. Want to come in and have some?"

"Sure." He entered and headed for the kitchen, head and shoulders scrunched over in his typical posture. That kid did everything he could to be invisible.

He plopped into a chair at the kitchen table, and she put a few muffins on a plate for him. "Do you drink coffee?"

He nodded around a bite.

She snapped a pod in the Keurig and stuck a mug underneath. "So, what are you up to today?"

He glanced up and stopped chewing, then shrugged.

"What do you take in your coffee? Cream? Sugar?"

He nodded, and she put both in front of him, hoping the routine motions of hospitality would cause him to relax, let down his guard, and tell her what was on his mind.

He dumped a good portion of cream and sugar in his mug. She imagined it tasted more like candy than actual coffee.

"You and Alex must be nearly done. The graduation party is going to be held at the B-and-B next weekend."

Samuel nodded but didn't say anything.

What else could she talk about? "You did a great job on the washer and dryer. I'm enjoying being able to use it finally." Then it dawned on her. "Is Alex coming over to check on the concrete in the basement? Are you meeting him here?" With all the drama of last night, she'd forgotten.

He got wide-eyed with a bit of a panic crossing his face. "I've got something to do first." He pushed back from the table, taking a gulp of coffee and the last bite of muffin. "Thanks. Glad you're okay. I'll see you later." He dashed into the mudroom and out the back door.

Carissa followed, watching as he ran down the street. Something odd was going on there. It was like he came to check on her, make sure she was okay. But why would he be worried about her? Did he hear about the prowler last night? Could it have been him?

She thought back. She'd caught a quick glimpse, but the intruder was taller and thinner. Samuel was stocky and average height. Plus, it didn't seem like him. Why would he cut the lock to her garage?

But maybe he knew who did.

THE SHERIFF CAME AROUND AND STUCK HER HEAD INTO Jonas's cubicle. "Gotta minute?"

"Sure. What's up?"

"I just got off the phone with a reporter for the *Mountain Monitor* asking for information on Tyler Cohen's case. Nothing unusual there. They often call for updates on cases. But she mentioned two things of interest. One, the high school will be honoring Tyler during Alumni Days as part of ArtFest, and his name and picture would be added to the In Memoriam wall. Unfortunately, he has no surviving family, but I'm hoping some of his friends will show up."

She lowered herself into the chair next to his desk. "Two, she also mentioned that Kayla Mills was being honored as a Soaring Eagle alumni for her work at a prestigious nonprofit during college. One of her programs has made a big difference for poverty-stricken kids in the Chicago area. She's been offered a permanent position there."

Jonas glanced at his watch. Dinner time in Chicago. "Let's call her now." He picked up the phone and dialed the number out of the case file open on his computer.

Kayla answered. She'd heard about the award but wasn't planning to come back to accept it in person. She hadn't heard about Tyler being honored, but it didn't change her decision.

"Do you remember Samuel Kinsey? He would have been in eighth grade when you were a senior. He was in and out of foster homes. He might have hung out in the Delamar Place from time to time."

She was silent a moment. "Maybe. Barely. If he was around, he didn't hang with us, and I never talked to him."

He thanked her for her time and hung up, looking at the sheriff.

"Why did you ask about Samuel?" She leaned back in the chair.

He told her about Samuel's reaction to Eli, about him being missing today. "And when I showed up at Carissa's this morning to install motion-detector lights and a new lock, she told me Samuel had dropped by to see how she was. She was sure there was something else on his mind, but he didn't spill what it was." She'd also insisted on sending muffins with Jonas, which he was saving for an after-dinner boost.

"Do you think he knows something?"

"Yes, and he's afraid. I think of Eli. I went by the Schillers' last night."

The sheriff straightened. "Zach was there with Isaiah."

"Yeah, I saw him. I didn't see Eli though. I talked to his folks. They were worried that he was getting in trouble again. I told them I was talking to everyone who knew Tyler. His mom seemed relieved by that."

"Amber's really hoping he's changed for good, that he's on the right track."

Jonas twirled a pen on his desk. "It could be that Eli and Samuel had crossed paths in the past, and Samuel's still afraid of him. I found Vince and Eli working on a job for one of those luxury houses on the lake. Neither of them had seen Samuel, and Eli barely remembered him from high school, just like Kayla. I will say that Eli seemed inordinately interested in Carissa's house the other day. Maybe it was just curiosity to see how it had changed from the abandoned building they used to hang out in. Or maybe it was something else. But it sure seemed like he was looking for something. I just don't know what."

"So did you find Samuel?"

"He did finally show up back at Alex's later in the day. But he didn't offer any explanation to anyone as to why he had disappeared or where he was."

He and the sheriff sat in silence for a moment before she rose to her feet. "Let's hope Alumni Day will give us a chance to talk to kids who might have known Tyler, maybe ones we don't know about."

He nodded. Tyler's case was generating more threads, which currently were resembling more of a knot than leads to a conclusion. Which one did he pull on to reveal the truth?

CARISSA HAD SHUT THE WATER OFF TO THE HOUSE AND WAS disconnecting the water supply connections to the claw-foot tub when she heard footsteps on the stairs that were heavier than her boys'. She poked her head out of the upstairs bathroom door.

Jonas was coming up the stairs. He spotted her and grinned. "Brandon let me in."

"Huh. He's not supposed to answer the door."

"He looked out the living room window and saw it was me." He stepped over to her and pulled her into a hug.

She wanted to melt into his arms. They were a safe refuge that was rare to find in her world, and for a moment, she could just lean on someone else. His hand trailed through her hair, and she didn't want to move.

"What are you working on today?" His voice echoed in her ear pressed against his chest.

Reluctantly, she leaned back. "This claw-foot tub is in good shape but it needs to be re-enameled. I found a place down in Redlands that will do it. They can either come get the tub, or they'll charge less if I figure out how to get it down to them."

Jonas moved past her and examined the tub. "Are they open on Saturdays?"

"Yep."

"Let's take it down tomorrow. I can get Alex and Samuel to help wrestle this downstairs and into my truck. We can take the boys and then find something fun to do after. Think you can spare the time?" His gray eyes were steady on her, making her want to forget everything on her list and just spend time with him.

She gave him a saucy smile. "Are you suggesting a date?"

He reached for her and tugged her close again. "What if I am? What would you say?"

"I'd say you're a brave man taking all three of us on. But if you're willing, so am I."

He slid his hands up her back, pulling her closer. His gaze dipped to her lips before glancing back up to her eyes.

She tilted closer to him.

"Mom!"

Carissa stepped back at Brandon's voice. "Uh, what is it?" She ran a hand through her hair and shot a look at Jonas, who gave her a wink and a grin before turning to face Brandon.

"We're hungry. What's for lunch?"

She nudged Jonas with her shoulder. "Want a sandwich?"

He turned a gaze on her smoldering with promise to finish what had been interrupted. "Absolutely."

AFTER LUNCH, WHERE THE BOYS REGALED JONAS WITH A play-by-play of the *Lego Batman* movie, she walked him out to his truck. She wanted a few minutes alone with him. If he was going to be involved with them, he might as well get used to those precious minutes being few and far between.

"So do you have an idea of what we can do Saturday after we drop off the tub?" She walked out the gate in the picket fence.

"Ever take the boys hiking?"

She smiled. "Yes, it's one of our favorite things to do. I have great memories of doing that with my sister as a kid."

"I didn't know you had a sister." He leaned against his truck.

"Christina. She's older and lives in Orange County. I obviously haven't had time to get away to see her, and she hasn't had time to get up here. Plus, I don't exactly have a place to put her yet. Maybe she'll come up once the B-and-B is open."

She leaned against his truck next to him. "We had this wonderful, unstructured day one time when we were on vacation with my parents. They had stayed back at the cabin, and as long as we were back in time for dinner, we could wander by ourselves."

She smiled at the memory. "There was this stream nearby. The water was cool, but the sun was warm, so it felt good. We splashed each other, tried skipping rocks. Someone had started building a dam at one spot, so we waded over there and fooled around with adding rocks to the dam and floating sticks. When we were tired of that, we sat on the sandy shore to eat peaches and Cheez-its and that pineapple-orange soda, Cactus Cooler."

He laughed, his shoulders brushing hers. "I haven't had Cactus Cooler in forever."

"A few other kids showed up. These boys had dragged a log into the dammed up area and were trying to do log rolling, and then they had a cannonball contest."

"Boys showing off, as we do."

"Right. But it was like this world of kids with no parents around. For an afternoon, I could pretend it was just Christina and me exploring the forest and stream on our own. I want something like that for my boys. Less structure, more fun in nature. No agenda. Too much of our lives are run by my to-do list."

He turned to her, tucking a strand of her hair behind her ear. "I think we can make that happen."

"Good."

His hand slipped down to the back of her neck, but after a moment, he removed it. "I'm going to hit the basketball court before work. Call you later?"

"Sure."

He climbed in his truck and she stood, watching him drive away. She was getting too comfortable with him and his help. She knew it and felt powerless to stop it. She didn't want to stop it.

But what if it didn't work out? What if he wasn't ready for another relationship? She couldn't risk her boys having any more heartache. Let alone herself. Why did everything worth having involve risk?

But was it risk if God was in control? Could he be orchestrating all of this?

CHAPTER
TWENTY-FIVE

Tony dribbled the basketball on the community center court while he waited to see who would show up. Marco and Reese were already here. If Jonas showed up, they could play two-on-two. He considered walking down to the sheriff's department to see if he was there. Though, if he was honest with himself, he just wanted a chance to talk to Shannon.

They'd been doing this dance with their regular public coffee dates where they talked about town things. But by the end, they'd transitioned to the personal. Still, it never failed that someone stopped by their table to complain about something, ask a question, or just to chat. He thought perhaps their coffee dates were getting known in the town as a place to reach the sheriff and the pastor at one time. Like public office hours.

There was no way they could go deep in that kind of environment. With Zach's graduation party and ArtFest coming up, he knew she wouldn't be able to get away. But he longed to find a time where they wouldn't be interrupted or overheard. There was a clock ticking; he could feel it.

Marco trotted over, hands up. Tony passed him the ball. He dribbled it a bit. "Think anyone else will show up?"

Before Tony could answer, Zach and Isaiah came through

the gym doors. Tony raised a hand. "Hey guys, want to play with us old folks?"

Zach shrugged. "Sure."

Marco tucked the ball under his arm. "Two-on-two, with someone rotating in?" He passed the ball to Reese.

"Sounds good to me." Reese dribbled. "Who wants to sit out first?"

The gym doors opened again, and Jonas strode through. "Cool. I'm not late."

They divided up into Tony, Jonas, and Zach against Reese, Marco, and Isaiah for a friendly but competitive game of three-on-three. The score was close, but Marco's team hit twenty-one first.

Tony plopped into a chair next to Jonas, swigging water from his bottle. "Next time, you and I need to be on different teams. No fair putting the two old guys together against those younguns."

Jonas laughed and snapped a towel at him. "Who you calling old?"

"Actually, I'm glad you showed up. I was afraid you weren't. You aren't usually late."

"I stopped by Carissa's house. Had lunch with her and the boys."

Tony nodded. "You're spending a lot of time with her."

"Yeah."

The gym had emptied out. He and Jonas had talked on their runs, but Tony was always careful not to push too much. But letting Carissa into his life was a big change for Jonas, and Tony was glad to see it. They could be good for each other. "How's that going?"

"I'm taking her and the boys hiking around Holcomb Creek tomorrow. Give her a break from all the house stuff."

"Sounds like a great way to spend a Saturday." He leaned back and sighed. "Shannon and I need to do that. Too many eyes and ears in this town. But with Zach's graduation party and

ArtFest, I'm not going to be able to pry her out of town until later."

Jonas looked at him. "Are you guys getting…"

Tony shrugged. "I think we'd both like to be more than colleagues. Just not quite sure how to make that happen. As you know, the stakes are higher the second time around. And she and I have the whole town watching us."

"Anything worth having takes risk."

"And prayer." Tony smiled.

The gym door slammed open, and Eli strode through it. "Dude, you might be a cop and all, but this isn't funny."

Jonas rose to his feet. "What are you talking about, Eli?"

Eli shoved his phone at Jonas. It took a moment for the social media private message to register.

I know what you did. Be at Alumni Days or else everyone will know it too.

Jonas tapped the avatar of the sender. The Avenger. The photo was some sort of logo of a sword. The profile was private. He handed the phone back to Eli. "Do you know what this person is talking about?"

"You tell me. You did it."

Jonas raised his eyebrows. "Not our style. We'd just bring you in for questioning. I'll ask you again, what's this about?"

"Forget it, man. You cops are all alike. Busting us for having fun but not there when we need you. I'll handle it myself." Eli turned and stalked across the gym.

"Eli." Jonas raised his voice. "I'd caution you against trying to take anything into your own hands. Let us handle it. But you have to give me more information."

Tony stepped forward. "If you have something private to talk about, Eli, Jonas is a good listener and fair. Why don't you give him a chance?"

But Eli waved his words away and slammed the gym doors behind him.

Tony turned to Jonas. "Do you know what that was about?"

"Maybe." Jonas crossed his arms over his chest. "Samuel trusts you, right?"

"As much as he trusts anyone, I guess."

"Did he ever mention Eli bullying him?"

Tony thought a moment. "I know Samuel was bullied. But if he ever named names, I don't recall. I haven't been here quite a year, so I wasn't here when Eli was in high school."

"Does Samuel have any tech skills that you know of?"

"Probably more than you and me, like every teenager. But he hasn't grown up with access to a lot of computers."

Jonas nodded then smacked Tony on the shoulder. "Thanks for the game."

"Sure."

Jonas picked up his bag and left the gym. Tony wasn't sure what had happened, but he had a feeling things were going to heat up around town.

Jonas hung up the phone in his cubicle. So far Kayla Mills, Anthony Smithton, and Madison Gonzales all admitted to getting the strange blackmail message on social media. He had asked each of them if they knew what it was referring to, and they each denied any knowledge of it. They also didn't know anyone else who had received the message. Apparently, the three of them weren't in touch anymore. Fairly common for friends to grow apart after high school. They all lived in different areas of the country now.

Maybe it was a random prank, and there were more kids who had received the message who he wasn't aware of. But there was one common event that tied these three together, and that was Tyler Cohen's disappearance. And if Eli had gotten the message, that meant he was involved some way too. But who had sent the message? One of them? To what purpose?

Kayla Mills said something interesting to him. She'd changed her mind and was coming to Alumni Days. She swore it had nothing to do with the blackmail message. She'd already decided to come. The organization she worked for heard about the award and thought it would be good publicity.

He tapped his pen on his desk. Which thread to pull? Eli wasn't going to talk to him.

But Samuel might.

A few minutes later, he was pulling up in front of Cope House. Alex and Samuel were working in the garage they had converted into a storage area for chairs, tables, outdoor heaters, and extra equipment.

"Hey, guys. Looks like you're making a lot of progress." Jonas walked up to the garage entrance.

Alex came over and shook his hand. "Yeah, we're getting there. We'll be ready for the graduation party next week. Claire can't wait to show the house off to the town."

"I have a feeling that will be a big draw. Can you spare Samuel for a few minutes? I'd like to talk to him."

Samuel hunched down even lower, as if he could hide within his T-shirt.

"It's fine with me." Alex turned. "Samuel? Sergeant McCann would like to speak with you."

"You're not in trouble. I just want to ask you about something."

Samuel glanced at Alex then made his way out to where Jonas was standing.

"There are a couple of benches over there that might be comfortable." Alex pointed across the yard.

Jonas tilted his head that way and followed Samuel over. Once the kid was perched on the edge of the teak bench, Jonas leaned back and laid his arm across the bench, keeping his body language relaxed and casual.

"Carissa said you came over the other day. She thought you might have had something on your mind." He worked to keep his tone light. "Did you think she might be in danger?"

Samuel was quiet a moment, then he nodded.

"What made you think that?"

The silence stretched out so long, Jonas didn't think Samuel was going to answer. But finally he said, "Eli's a bully. He was looking around Miss Carissa's house that day. I was afraid he might hurt her. So I tried to follow him that night to see where he went. To keep him from doing anything bad. But I couldn't find him."

"Is that why you were missing that night?"

Samuel nodded.

"And the next day?"

He paused, then gave a short nod.

"Any particular reason he might hurt Carissa? Does it have something to do with the house?"

Samuel looked at the ground between his feet. "The night Tyler Cohen went missing, I was at the Delamar Place."

Jonas kept his face impassive, hoping Samuel would tell everything he knew.

"I had been inside, staying there a lot during the day and leaving at night when the popular kids would come. They didn't want me there. I could hide out in the garage and watch them come and go."

He glanced up at Jonas and then back down again. "I kinda had a crush on Kayla. Everyone did. She was pretty and popular and smart. So when she was over at the house, I tried to keep an eye on her, keep her safe. That night, she came in carrying Tyler's letterman jacket. She looked upset. Tyler came in a few minutes after. I heard them arguing upstairs. She yelled at him. He yelled back. I was thinking about how I could sneak in and help her, since her so-called friends weren't."

He let out a deep breath. "But she came running out of the house and drove away. Tyler didn't come after her. I waited, but once I figured she was safely away from him, I left."

"So you never saw Tyler leave the house."

Samuel shook his head.

"How long did you wait?"

He shrugged. "Probably half an hour. But then Eli and Anthony left, and I was cold, so I took off. I figured Kayla was safe at home by then."

"Eli was there?"

"Yeah, his Ford Escape was parked out front before anyone else got there." Samuel squeezed his hands together. "Please don't tell Eli that I said he was there. He'd kill me if he thought I ratted him out."

"I won't. But promise me something." Jonas waited until the kid looked him in the eye for a moment before looking away. "Don't take off again without telling someone, okay? Lots of people around here care about you. You can tell me, Alex, Pastor Tony, or even Carissa if you feel like you need a safe place or someone to talk to, okay? People were worried about you." He reached over and squeezed Samuel's shoulder. "Thanks for telling me."

Samuel nodded then headed back to the garage.

Jonas sat there a moment, thinking about what Samuel said. Now he had to figure out what to do with this information.

JONAS DROVE OUT TO THE LUXURY HOME ON THE LAKE where Eli and Vince had been working, hoping they hadn't finished early. It was a good of a place to start as any. His mind drifted back to this morning. He was drawn to Carissa in a way that nearly took his breath away. He'd wanted nothing more than to kiss her but forced himself to slow down. There were kids involved. And the last thing he wanted to do was hurt her or the boys.

But he couldn't help but admire her strength and resilience. The more he got to know her, the more he saw the layers of her character and personality underneath. He didn't know too many people who would have stuck through all that she'd been through. But she was determined to make a new home for her boys, a place where they could flourish. He wanted so badly for that to be Holcomb Springs for her.

And part of making that a safe place for them meant putting Tyler Cohen's death to rest. As a cold case, it was hard to find leads, and there hadn't been much physical evidence. Even his Jeep just had the expected fingerprints of him and his friends. The car had been put in neutral, with only the ignition key in the on position. Clearly it had been deliberately pushed over the edge of the road. But by whom? And why?

He didn't think Eli would give him any answers, given his hostility earlier, but it was the last place he had to go.

The three-story luxury cabin Jonas pulled up in front of had a wrap-around deck and a wall of windows overlooking Holcomb Lake. As beautiful as it was, anyone on the lake could see inside the house fairly easily. Like living in a fishbowl. Jonas preferred his little cabin tucked away in the woods.

The place wasn't too far from Beckett Lorde's place, where Reese and Ella had ended up last March after being chased through the woods by illegal pot growers. Jonas and Marco had been on the SAR team looking for them, along with a mole working for Lorde who'd nearly gotten them all killed. Lorde came out of it with nothing sticking to him, as usual. Jonas and the sheriff had taken to calling him the Teflon Man because of that. But someday, he'd slip up.

He got out and found Vince and Eli working around back. Vince spotted him first. "Hey, Jonas. What brings you here?"

Eli glanced up, shook his head, and went back to shoveling mulch.

Jonas turned to Vince. "I wanted to have a word with Eli. Can you spare him a minute?"

"Sure."

Jonas walked toward the dock that led down to the lake.

After a minute, Eli threw down his shovel and sauntered over. "What? Come to apologize?"

Jonas leveled a stare at him and let the silence drag out. "You were at the Delamar House the night Tyler Cohen disappeared."

Eli crossed his arms and cocked a leg out toward the lake. "Never said I wasn't."

Jonas waited another beat, but Eli didn't add anything. "Someone said you and Anthony left together that night. Where was Tyler?"

Eli looked off to the lake before turning back. "Dunno. Probably with Kayla."

"Kayla had already left. Why did none of them mention you were there when we questioned them after Tyler's disappearance?"

"Maybe they forgot. A lot of people came and went from that place. No one was taking attendance."

"But Anthony left with you. You'd think he'd remember that."

Eli shrugged. "You'll have to ask him." He glanced over to where Vince was watching them. "Can I get back to work now? I don't want to lose my job."

"Sure. Let me know if you remember anything."

Eli huffed and stalked off.

The kid had an attitude problem for sure. The question was, did it come from the case or something else?

Jonas waved at Vince and headed back to his car. Cold cases were frustrating. You had to follow where the evidence led and then see what happened. Right now, he needed to call Anthony Smithton. Cell service was spotty out here with all the of the mountain ridges blocking signals, so he'd wait until he got back to the office.

As he drove through town, he had a strong urge to swing by Carissa's just to see how she and the boys were doing. But he resisted turning down Gold Mine Road. He was at work and needed to keep his focus there.

Back in the office, he called Anthony and asked him about Eli's presence.

Hesitation laced his voice. "Maybe. All of the nights run together, and it was so long ago."

"But the statement you gave two days later when Tyler was reported missing said that only you, Kayla, and Madison were there." Jonas had the report pulled up and was looking at Anthony's words. "Two days wasn't that long after your best friend went missing."

"I don't know what to tell you. I'll keep thinking about it. I'll be back in town for the Alumni Days, so if I remember anything, I'll let you know then."

Interesting. First Kayla and now Anthony. Maybe the blackmailer was on to something. Jonas hoped so, because right now the case was at a standstill, and unless someone came up with more information, there was no evidence to tie any of them to Tyler's death or burial.

CHAPTER
TWENTY-SIX

Carissa sat on her back deck with a cup of coffee, enjoying the morning sun and a bit of peace and quiet before the boys woke up. And perhaps before Gladys appeared. Today was going to be a great day. The internet was going to be installed, and she'd get her stitches out. So for a Monday, it was looking pretty good.

In fact, it was the latest in a string of good days. Saturday, Jonas had taken her and the boys—and her massive claw-foot tub—down to Redlands to be re-enameled. She had her eye on a chandelier similar to but smaller than the one in Claire's family suite. She wanted to create a small oasis of tranquility in the upstairs bath. She couldn't wait to see how her tub turned out. Between salvaging the tiles and getting the tub spruced up, this bathroom that she thought might be a total gut ended up being a hidden gem.

Thank you, Lord.

After they'd dropped off the tub, Jonas had taken them up the mountains the back way, as he called it. Much less traffic with a slightly terrifying, sharply curving two-lane highway. But the views were spectacular. They headed down some dirt roads until they reached a pullout among the trees. With a little walking, they reached Holcomb Creek; the only sound was the wind rushing through the pine trees and the creek burbling along with its snow melt.

They spent the afternoon playing with sticks and rocks, much like she and Christina had that one memorable vacation. Carissa had packed a lunch for them, and as they found a flat rock to sit on and eat, she marveled at Jonas's knowledge of the area that he shared with the boys. He pointed out safety concerns and good stewardship of the land. He took time to speak with them and listen to them. The thing they craved most was that personal attention; the thing she was so often unable to fully give them, consumed by the house as she was.

On the way home—dirty, tired, a little sunburned, and completely content—she reached over and took Jonas's hand. "Thank you for giving us such a great day."

He held her gaze. "You're welcome."

Hopefully, it was the first of many.

Now, leaning back on her porch, she drained the dregs of her coffee, debating a second cup in the quiet but not quite wanting to move to break the stillness. She sat a moment, listening to two blue jays argue over something.

With a sigh, she heaved herself out of her camp chair, wishing once again she had a lovely porch set like Claire's. Someday.

She'd just returned to the kitchen when the boys came downstairs. She fed them breakfast, thinking about what she could do that wouldn't be too difficult to extricate herself from when the internet installers came. The four-hour window was much better than an all-day one, yet it still limited what she could get into.

But she was pleasantly surprised when her phone rang and the installer informed her he was on his way. She was pulling the Wi-Fi cameras out of their boxes when he pulled up.

And a couple of hours later, the boys were having fun

watching each other on the front and back door cameras on her phone.

Finally, she could access the internet and her email from her computer without using her phone as an unreliable hotspot. She pulled up the email from Greg. She was in a good mood, so it was time to make a decision about this. She hadn't made any headway in trying to talk to anyone at the courthouse who could help her. Time to bite the bullet and call her attorney. And then she could go to the clinic and get her stitches out.

Wearing real shoes never sounded so good.

ON THE WAY HOME FROM THE CLINIC, STITCHES FRESHLY removed, Carissa stopped by Claire's house. The big graduation party was Saturday, and she wanted to see if there was anything she could do. Plus, every few minutes she was tempted to text Jonas, and talking with Claire would help her avoid doing that.

Alex was in the yard when they pulled up. "Hey, guys. Good to see you."

"Just thought I'd show off my stitch-less foot and ask Claire if she needed any help for Saturday."

"Go on in. I think she and GigiMa are in the kitchen. Boys, Lizzie is in her room. You can join her."

The boys ran up the front porch steps and inside.

Alex laughed. "Oh to have that kind of energy again."

"Right?" Carissa followed them at a slower pace. "Where's Samuel?"

"He's working with Vince now. His job started today." Alex's face became impassive.

He didn't have a bad word to say about anybody, which was what Carissa thought had him holding his tongue. "Not a good fit for Samuel?"

"Vince is an okay guy. I just think Samuel has had some run-ins with Eli in the past. I don't want him to be bullied."

"I don't either. If I had enough money, I'd hire him myself. He's a good worker. I certainly have plenty of work."

Alex opened the front door for her. "I know the feeling. Once we get this place booked consistently, I could see using his help around here. But that's a ways off."

Carissa entered and wound her way back through the public parlor into the kitchen.

Claire was bent over the marble island, studying a piece of paper. She looked up. "Carissa! What a nice surprise." She came over and gave Carissa a hug. "What brings you by?"

She lifted up her foot and rotated her ankle. "See, no stitches. Now I can wear real shoes." She laughed.

Claire joined her. "Just in time for Saturday's big bash. Jonas can twirl you around the dance floor."

Carissa's face heated. "That's a picture. I can see Jonas out in the wilderness, but I can't quite picture him on the dance floor."

"You never know. The quiet ones are the most surprising."

For a moment, Carissa let the idea of being in Jonas's arms, swaying to music, play through her mind before she wiped it away. "I didn't just stop by to show you my lack of stitches; I wanted to see if you needed any help for Saturday."

Claire protested at first, but Carissa insisted. The two of them went over the plans. Claire had hosted many weddings and parties at her B-and-B in Michigan, so she had a system. Carissa was impressed, and together they worked out how Carissa could help.

After making their plans, Claire poured them both iced teas and plated some snickerdoodle cookies Erma had made. "Let's sit on the back deck. These barstools are killing my back." Claire grabbed the plate of cookies while Carissa grabbed the drinks.

Once they were settled on the cushioned wicker, Claire said, "So, catch me up. You and Jonas looked rather cozy at church yesterday."

Jonas had sat with her and even helped her keep Jayden occupied during the service. His arm resting across the back of her chair had made it difficult to keep her mind on Pastor Tony's sermon. "We had a nice time Saturday." She told Claire about the trip down the hill and to Holcomb Creek. "And I got my internet installed today, so all in all, it's been a nice run of a few days."

"Well deserved after the string of bad ones."

"Yeah. Also, one more potential bit of good news. My ex-husband, Greg, had sent me an email saying he wanted to take me back to court to ask for a reduction in child support. Things were already going to be tight paying for Jayden's therapy, which I didn't ask Greg to help with. I finally called my attorney today. I didn't want to have to pay for her to help me fight this, because that could be expensive. But she told me she thought Greg didn't have a leg to stand on, and she would reach out to his attorney and get it straightened out. I only have to pay for her to write a letter, which is hundreds instead of thousands of dollars."

Carissa leaned back against the cushions and giggled. "But that's still not the best thing."

"What is?" Claire stretched a bit and rubbed her barely showing belly.

"I get to take a real shower tonight!"

CHAPTER
TWENTY-SEVEN

Jonas was up early and ready to run with Tony this morning, stepping outside as the moon was rising in the east. The new moon would be visible during the day, but it would set early enough to be a good night to look at the stars through his telescope. But likely they'd be tied up with the graduation party.

Strangely enough, he missed running with Charlie and considered stopping by Carissa's house even earlier to take the dog with him on a run. But he wanted to go slow with her, and the idea of seeing her first thing in the morning nearly every day wasn't going slow.

He hadn't run with the guys last Saturday because he'd spent the day with Carissa and her boys. And later today was the graduation party for Zach, Isaiah, and Samuel. It'd have to be a quick run because Jonas was helping Alex get the tables and chairs set up.

But he needed Tony's advice and didn't want to wait.

Jonas had fallen into the habit of stopping by Carissa's before work. Often she'd fix him lunch, and the sense of family—sitting at the kitchen table with her and the boys—smoothed over something rough in his soul. The pull toward them was something he felt nearly powerless to resist. And wasn't sure he wanted to.

But could he trust himself to make a wise decision? Were his emotions clouding his judgment?

He spotted Tony across the community park field. Unfortunately, Marco and Reese were already with him. Dang it. Well, it would keep.

The men ran their loop through the fields, the conversation ranging from what stupid thing a tourist had done lately to the graduation party to the lack of rain and the potential for a dangerous fire season again this year.

There were a few questions about the Tyler Cohen case. Marco and Reese were curious, having found Tyler's Jeep. But there wasn't much to share. The cold case had once again gone cold. It was frustrating. But perhaps not as frustrating as it would have been before Carissa. She balanced him out, kept him from obsessing about work, and gave him something else to think about and look forward to.

She was making him a better man. He liked who he was around her and the boys.

The men slowed near some picnic tables and began cooling down at the end of their run. Jonas lingered, hoping maybe Tony would have a few minutes after the others left. Marco took off with a promise to see them later at the party.

But Reese put a hand on Tony's shoulder. "I need a few minutes of your time this week. Can I get on your schedule?"

Jonas moved away to give them some privacy, finding a picnic table to stretch against.

"Sure. Is it something you want to talk about now?"

"Nope, it can wait. Nothing urgent."

Tony pulled out his phone, and they set something up. A minute later, Reese was jogging away toward the garage apartment he lived in at his brother's house. As a former Army Ranger, Reese ran circles around all of them. Literally.

In the uncanny way he had, Tony seemed to sense Jonas

wanted to talk. "Something on your mind?" He pulled one arm across his chest, stretching.

Jonas shrugged. Now that he had the opportunity, he wasn't sure he could put it into words. "It's been a good week. I've spent a lot of time with Carissa and the boys. We're getting to know each other, and I think we're heading in the direction of having a serious relationship. The thought is equal parts exciting and terrifying." He pulled his ankle behind him to stretch his quads. "More than anything, I don't want to hurt her boys. They've been through enough." He switched legs. "I guess what I'm asking is, how do I avoid that? I know there are no guarantees, but I don't want to screw this up."

Tony laid a hand on Jonas's shoulder. "Relationships are messy. People don't fit into neat, predictable boxes. You know that. The best we can do is to be honest with ourselves and other people. Be humble. Seek to see their perspective. You and Carissa have lived a lot of life, have formed your own opinions about things. Probably different opinions." He laughed. "I'm working through that now. You can either let it be a source of frustration or a source of adventure and curiosity. You can always choose your attitude and perspective."

Jonas let that sit for a moment. "Thanks, that helps." He paused. "I think." He slapped Tony's back. "See you at the party later."

"Absolutely. I'm the wannabe boyfriend of the mom of one of the kids. So I can't miss it."

Jonas was still chuckling when he got home. He was grateful for a man like Tony in his life. Their previous pastor had been an older man who'd retired, wanting to move someplace with less snow. Tony had been a surprise, a former contractor who loved small-town life and wanted to help everyone, including tourists who came up to vacation. It was a different attitude, and one some of their congregation struggled with. But Jonas appreciated Tony's partnership with their department to make the town better.

Now if he only had the skills to help him solve Tyler Cohen's case.

———

PERCHED ON A STEPLADDER, CARISSA USED THE BACK OF her hand to push her hair out of her eyes while she helped Claire drape a CONGRATULATIONS "banner over the front porch. It was a perfect day, warm with a hint of a breeze, but she would definitely need a shower before tonight's party. She was still enjoying the pleasure of a shower after getting her stitches out. She just needed to make sure she got home in time to get ready.

Jonas had picked them up this morning and brought them to the Cope House. The kids had been relegated to watch a movie in Lizzie's room so they'd stay out of the way. And in Jayden's case, keep him from getting dirty and needing a bath. There wasn't time for that on today's schedule.

"How's it look?" Carissa asked. "Is it even?"

Claire studied their handiwork from the safety of the front walk. No way was anyone going to let the pregnant woman get on a ladder. "Looks good to me."

Carissa turned to step down when she felt a hand at her waist. Jonas.

"Let me help."

He held her secure while she climbed down, his hands being more of a distraction than was safe, if she was honest. "Thanks," she said as her sneakers hit the porch.

His hand lingered a bit longer than strictly necessary at her waist. "You good?"

Oh, yeah. She nodded, her mouth suddenly dry. His gray eyes were deepened by the black T-shirt he wore. Very well, she might add.

Claire's barely stifled giggle brought her back to what she should be doing. The yard was dotted with tables, and Alex was rolling more out.

"You'd better go help Alex. Claire and I have this under control." She gestured to the porch.

He hopped off the porch then tossed her a wink over his shoulder.

Yeah, she had to get back to work, but that man was a distraction. She turned to find Claire grinning.

"So, uh, let's get these streamers hung." Carissa dragged the ladder to the next spot. She and Claire worked to get them draped all around the porch. By the time they were done, the guys had the tables and chairs out, along with outdoor heaters in case it got chilly tonight.

With the tables up, the women set out tablecloths and centerpieces while the guys set up the dance floor. Carnival lights crisscrossed the area above it, which normally served as a seating area. It would make for a lovely atmosphere once the sun went down.

"I love how you have all of this space to host this outside. But you know the townspeople are going to want to see what you did with the inside."

Claire tied a clutch of red-and-white balloons, the school colors, to the centerpiece. "I'm counting on it. I figure it'll be good publicity. I'm going to lead tours every thirty minutes or so."

Carissa laughed. "I should have known you'd have a plan. Let me know if you need help. I know this place almost as well as you do by now."

"Feel free to jump in."

Once the outside was ready, the women headed inside to check on the food. Claire had everything prepared in advance in trays and dishes just needing to be set out on ice or Sterno-warmed chafing dishes when it was time.

"Let's get the drink buckets filled with ice and get the drinks cooling in them." Claire stood over their industrial ice maker. "Oh, no! There's not nearly enough ice. What's wrong with this thing?"

Carissa peered in the open chest. Only a scattering of ice cubes lay across the bottom. Definitely not enough. "Is it not on?"

Claire peered at some switches. "I don't know. I'll have Alex take a look. But even if we got it working right now, it wouldn't make enough ice in time." She called outside for Alex.

He came in a moment later, followed by Jonas.

Claire explained the problem.

"We'll go get ice," Jonas laid a hand on Carissa's low back. "Okay with you?"

She grinned, liking the idea that he immediately included her and wanted to spend time alone with her. "Yeah, sounds great. I think we might clean out Marty's and the gas station to get enough, but it's a mission we can handle."

Jonas smiled. "Let's get going."

"Let me tell the boys what's going on." She raced upstairs and leaned in Lizzie's doorway.

The three of them were engrossed in a movie, one they'd seen before but loved. "Hey, Jonas and I are headed out to get more ice. We'll be back shortly, okay?"

Brandon glanced up. "Okay." He went back to the movie.

Jayden was transfixed by the scene. "The dragon can fly, Mom."

"I know. That's pretty cool. I'll see you in a bit, okay?"

He nodded but didn't look at her. Good enough. As long as he knew where she was, he was okay. If she ever went anywhere thinking he wouldn't notice, he would. And it always resulted in an absolute meltdown in terror. It was a simple enough thing to let him know what was going on.

Back downstairs, she snagged her purse off the kitchen counter. "Ready if you are."

Jonas reached for her hand. "I am." He tugged her out to his truck and helped her in. At Marty's, he grabbed a cart and loaded it up with ice, leaving only two bags.

Carissa wasn't necessary on this trip, but she was glad he included her. "Nice of you to leave some for others."

He shrugged and grinned. "I try. We'll still need more, but the gas station should have it."

He was loading the ice in the back of his truck when his phone rang. "Hey, Alex."

What now? It was brave hosting a big event for the town with a newly renovated house. But Alex and Claire knew what they were doing.

"We'll grab some. Be there soon." Jonas hung up and put his phone in his pocket. "When the DJ showed up, they realized they didn't have enough electrical outlets. Let's swing by the hardware store and buy some power strips. Hopefully it'll be enough, and we won't have any problems. I'll ask Marco to look at whatever we set up. Make sure we don't end up burning the place down."

At the hardware store, Jonas helped her out of his truck and then reached for her hand. She thought about the symbolism of that statement. As soon as they walked inside and Stan and Wally spotted them, the gossip would be all over town. And it was late enough in the day that they'd likely be here instead of the Jitter Bug Too.

She glanced up at Jonas.

He gave her that wry grin of his as he pulled the door open.

Yeah, he knew what he was doing. He was thoughtful and deliberate in his actions, and this was no exception.

While they looked at power strips, Carissa imagined for a moment that this was any ordinary Saturday, the two of them working together.

And it was an image she liked.

CHAPTER
TWENTY-EIGHT

Showered, shaved, and wearing dress pants and a deep-blue button-down shirt, Jonas pulled up to Carissa's house for the second time today. The boys came out the front door, Carissa behind him. While the boys looked smart in their khakis and polo shirts, Carissa was stunning.

She pulled the door shut and locked it, and when she turned around, he almost couldn't breathe. She wore a strappy floral dress with heeled sandals, and her hair curled just above her shoulders.

He slowly climbed the porch steps, realizing his hands were sweaty. This felt like a real date, and he hadn't been on one of those in years.

After swiping his hands across his pants, he reached for her to help her down the stairs. Not like she needed his help, but he had an overwhelming urge to physically connect with her. "You look amazing."

"Thank you." Her smile lit up her face. "I love that color of your shirt on you. Makes your eyes deep and mysterious." Her smile turned saucy and flirty.

Tonight was going to be fun.

They drove the few blocks to the Cope House. They could

have walked, but he liked to have his truck handy in case of an emergency, since he and the sheriff both would be at the party. Plus, given Carissa's shoes, driving was the better option.

A number of people were already there—the boys being celebrated along with their families, of course. And the place looked great. Given the mishaps, he'd wondered. But they'd pulled it off.

Taking Carissa's hand, he helped her across the yard as the boys took off. Music created a party atmosphere, and the plethora of balloons danced in the breeze. They said hi to Zach, Shannon, and Tony; Isaiah and his folks, the Schillers; and Samuel with the Markeys. Jonas noticed Eli wasn't here yet. Surely he'd show up to celebrate his brother.

Claire had a nice gift table set up on the porch with each of the boys' names on it, with baskets for gift cards. He was gratified to see Samuel had as many things as Zach and Isaiah did. He and Carissa dropped off their cards for the boys and admired their hard work from the perspective of the porch.

Erma and Gladys had staked out their seats in the comfortable porch furniture and were settled with plates of food and drinks.

"You guys got the best seats. Smart thinking." He smiled at the women.

"The privilege of age, my dear," Gladys said. "You all did a great job. It's a lovely party."

"And we're going to sit up here and enjoy it," said Erma.

"It really did turn out great." Carissa squeezed his hand.

"I had my doubts for a moment there. Let's hope the rest of the evening goes smoothly." All he wanted to do was spend the evening in her company.

"Let's get the boys settled with some food so they'll be free to run around and not complain about being hungry." She waved to the older women then stepped off the porch and called to the boys, who had started exploring the yard. It had been off-limits while they were decorating today, and the boys had already gravitated toward the yard games with the other kids. There was corn hole, a giant Jenga stack of blocks, an oversized connect four game, and a ring toss.

After filling their plates, the four of them snagged a table. He didn't miss the glances they were getting. He knew—probably more so than Carissa—that he'd made a public statement about their relationship. He'd thought carefully about it, but it was where he thought they were headed. He wanted Carissa to have a fun time tonight, and then maybe they'd find some time for a serious discussion.

He watched the folks mingling, his instinct was always to scan for danger or potential problems, even in a group like this where he knew everyone. But the party seemed to be a relaxed and fun one. Even Samuel had loosened up and was enjoying himself, despite the attention seeming to embarrass him.

But then Samuel stiffened, stared across the yard, then dropped his gaze.

Jonas followed the source of it. Eli had shown up. He'd come with Vince. He hoped Eli didn't ruin Samuel's day for him.

"I'll be right back," Jonas said to Carissa as he stood and headed toward Samuel. "Hey, have you had something to eat? Why don't you fill a plate and join us at our table?"

"Okay, thanks." Samuel immediately headed to the food line.

Jonas positioned himself between Samuel and Eli, watching how the dynamic played out. But Eli soon joined the Schillers and didn't seem to notice Samuel.

Once Samuel's plate was full, Jonas escorted him to their table.

They made a bit of small talk while everyone finished their food.

"Can we go play now?" Brandon asked. "There's a beanbag game that looks like fun." He pointed to the corn hole game where Lizzie, in a sundress, stood tossing beanbags into a slanted piece of wood with a hole in it.

"Sure." Carissa touched Brandon's arm. "Please make sure you know where your brother is. There's a lot going on here."

He nodded and they ran off.

Jonas thought about the burden Brandon carried of being an extra set of eyes for Carissa. It wasn't safe to let Jayden roam unattended, and he didn't want to be tied to Carissa all the time. Jonas wondered how he could help. If he could.

Samuel picked up his plate and stood. "Thanks for letting me sit with you guys."

"Happy to have you join us, especially since you're one of the honored guests." Carissa smiled at him.

His face turned pink, and he scampered off.

Jonas laughed and leaned close to Carissa. "Let's go join the boys. Ever played corn hole?"

"Can't say that I have."

He stood and held her chair. "Then let me teach you."

They made their way to the back of the yard where the games were. The oversized games added to the festive feeling.

It took a bit of convincing, especially of Jayden, that there was an actual game to be played. But eventually they broke into teams, kids against adults.

When it was Carissa's turn, she missed the board completely. She broke into laughter as the beanbag landed off to the side. "That was terrible."

Jonas turned to her in mock horror. "Where did you learn to throw, woman? You're going to make us lose."

That made her laugh harder, and she leaned into Jonas for balance.

It didn't help that Jayden, Brandon, and Lizzie all got their beanbags on the board, and Jayden even got his in the hole. If it involved precision and concentration, that kid could beat them all.

On Carissa's next turn, she lined up. "Okay, I'll do better this time."

"You couldn't do much worse."

That started her laughing again. "You're not helping, Jonas."

"Oh, you need help? You should have asked." He lined up behind her, taking her hand that held the beanbag in his, holding her close to him. This might not have been a good idea. Her perfume washed over him, and her hair tickled his nose. He had no desire to let her go.

"Is that allowed?" Brandon asked. "Are you allowed to help someone throw when it's not your turn?"

Carissa turned to Jonas and giggled, not letting Brandon see. She bit her lip. "Um, I think maybe just once, so I can learn. Obviously I'm not very good at this."

Jonas held her gaze a moment. He needed to focus on the game—they had an audience—but all he wanted to do was kiss her. He turned back to the game and swung her hand in his. "Okay, just get the feel of it. And when you're at the top of the arc, let go. Got it?"

"Um hmm." She bit her lip, trying not to laugh.

Together they swung, and she let go of the beanbag. It hit the board this time.

"Whoo hoo!" she whooped. "I did it."

Brandon and Lizzie exchanged a glance. "We still beat you," Brandon said. "For grown-ups, you're not very good at this game."

"No, we're not. Good thing you didn't have me on your team. You guys want to play among yourselves?" Carissa picked up a beanbag and tossed it to Jayden.

"Yeah, we'll have more fun," Jayden said as he caught the bag.

"He always tells it like it is." Carissa reached for Jonas's hand. "I want to show you something. Have you seen the maze?"

"No, I have not, though I heard about it." Jonas was up for anything with Carissa.

They continued farther back into the yard as the music and voices faded. The sun was setting, and the pine tree shadows were deepening. A lattice arch appeared flanked by bushes, and Carissa led him through it.

"It's more obvious once you get inside, and it'll get better as the plants get bigger." She tugged him through the path between the hedges, back and forth and around until they reached a fountain in the middle flanked by two teak benches.

"We could have stepped over the bushes and gotten here faster." He pulled her closer, sliding his hands around her waist.

She smiled. "And what would be the fun in that?"

"Are you having fun?" He studied her blue eyes, looking for the truth there. Did she want this?

Her gaze was steady, her hands slid up his arms. "I am."

"I want you to be happy, Carissa. You're a wonderful mom, strong and determined. But you are also a woman with gifts and dreams to share." He thought of the words she'd written about herself on the dining room wall. He wanted to help her believe them. "I'd like to share them with you, to explore what that might look like." He pushed a strand of hair back from her face, cupping her cheek with his hand.

"I'd like that too." Her voice was soft and breathy.

He slid his hand around the back of her neck as he dipped his head, feeling her lean into him as he touched his lips to hers. Emotions flooded through him, and she was the anchor holding him fast. He explored her lips, the corner of her mouth, the spot beneath her ear. The world had melted away just leaving the two of them together, full of promises of the future.

When he dragged himself away from her tempting mouth, he saw the same roiling emotions in her eyes as swirled in his chest.

What had just happened between them?

SHANNON TOOK A STEP CLOSER TO TONY AS THEY STOOD looking across all the people gathered to celebrate her son, his best friend, and the kid the town had adopted. The parents and kids had created a bit of an informal receiving line, greeting guests as they arrived. She refused to let herself get emotional about the ending and beginning this party represented. Tony had asked if he could escort her, and she'd gratefully accepted. He'd picked up her and Zach, and it was comforting to have his steadying presence nearby.

She slid her hand around his biceps, and he covered her hand with his own. "Having a good time, Mom?" he asked with a grin.

She nodded, not trusting herself to speak until she took a deep breath. "Yeah. This is just perfect. All our friends here, great weather, a lovely venue. Alex and Claire have done something wonderful for our little town."

"We've had a few nice additions recently. If Carissa can weather all the challenges with her house, this could be a good place for her and her boys to have a fresh start."

"Especially if my sergeant has anything to say about it." Shannon had noticed how proprietary Jonas had been with Carissa and the boys and was glad for it. "She's good for him."

"I agree."

Shannon let out a breath. "Well, since it appears most of the people have arrived, should we get some food? It looks fantastic."

"We should." He motioned for her to go ahead of him.

They had filled their plates and were settled at a table when she spotted Dan arriving. He wore a sports coat and expensive loafers. She wasn't sure if he would show up. He had been noncommittal about the whole thing. Over the years, Zach had learned not to count on his dad showing up to anything important. It made her sad for his sake—and Dan's, honestly. He had no idea what he was missing out on.

She slid her chair back. "Dan's here."

Tony joined her.

They walked over to him. "Hi, Dan. Thanks for coming." Shannon turned, scanning for Zach then seeing him talking with his friends. "Zach's over by the food table."

Dan shook Tony's hand. "Good to see you. Nice place here."

Zach had noticed them and started in their direction.

"Yeah, they've been rehabbing it. This is their first event," Shannon said as the awkwardness descended on them. She and Dan were always cordial, but it wasn't a warm relationship. And while she was grateful for Tony's presence, Dan seemed to bristle at it. Not that she cared, but she wanted Zach to have as little friction between his parents as possible.

"Hey, Dad. Thanks for coming." Zach stuck out his hand.

Dan took it and pulled him into a man hug, slapping Zach on the back. "Congratulations, son. I'm proud of you."

"Thanks." Zach shoved his hands in his pockets. "There's a lot of food over there. It's really good."

"Yeah, I'll check it out in a minute. I wanted to give you this." He reached inside his jacket and pulled out an envelope.

"Oh, there's a basket for those on the porch." Zach pointed.

Dan pushed it toward him. "Open it now."

Zach glanced at Shannon, who nodded. Might as well give Dan what he wanted. He'd keep pushing until he got it, and this would make less of a scene for Zach.

Zach tore open the envelope and pulled out a generic graduation card, holding on to a slip of paper inside while he read the card. Then he glanced at the paper. "Oh, wow. Thanks, Dad. I'll give it some thought." He leaned over and hugged Dan.

Dan grinned. "It's a trip anywhere he wants to go. What do you think? Cliff diving in Mexico or rock climbing in Moab? Let's have some adventure." He cuffed Zach on the shoulder.

"Yeah, thanks. I'll have to see. I need to look up the dates I need for orientation and move-in and all that college stuff." Zach put the card back in the envelope and awkwardly held it.

"Don't wait too long. We're already mostly through June, and we don't have much time to make good reservations. If you can pick a place, I can start looking to see what's available."

"Sure. I'll let you know."

"Well, what are you thinking? I mean, does rock climbing sound good? If we go to Moab, there are also other places nearby for off-roading and even some river rafting. I can start making plans."

"I'm not sure. I'll have to think about it." Zach glanced over his shoulder.

"Dan, I'm sure Zach is more focused on his party right now." Shannon touched Zach's shoulder. "There's a lot going on. I'm sure he'll have an answer for you once he has a chance to think about it." She generally avoided stepping in between Dan and Zach, but she wanted Zach to enjoy his party without a cloud of conflict with his dad over it.

"Well, he can't wait too long, or we'll miss some good opportunities."

Oh, the irony. If he really wanted this trip with Zach, he should have brought it up much earlier. But she bit the words back.

"I'm sure you guys will still have a great trip. Sounds like a lot of fun, whatever you decide." Tony's words were light and agreeable, but she could hear the thread of resolve underneath closing the subject. "You should go fill a plate. There's a lot of great food. I'm sure Zach can point out his favorites for you."

Dan leveled a look at Tony then at Shannon. A tight smile crossed his face. "Is he your boyfriend?" He gave a short laugh. "Never thought I'd see that."

Shannon knew without looking that Zach wanted to crawl in a hole. She needed to end this the most expedient way possible. Slipping her arm through Tony's, she said, "Yes, he is. Go grab some food and let Zach show you around." She tugged on Tony's arm, and they moved off, her face hot.

She kept walking until they got to the far side of the house where no one else was. She let go of his arm. "Sorry about that. I just wanted to—"

"Shh. It's fine." He reached for her hand. "Actually, I wanted to ask you something along those lines." His brown eyes were dark and deep, his hand large and calloused enveloping hers. "It's a bit like living in a fishbowl here, especially for the two of

us. I was thinking after ArtFest we could go out of town somewhere and really talk without worrying about anyone over-
hearing us or gossiping. I think there's some things we could talk
about. About our future." He gave a small laugh. "I'd been
trying to find a time to ask you about it but didn't think it
would be today."

"I love the idea." Her voice was soft, and she was amazed
that'd he'd been thinking of this. "Yes."

The squeal of the DJ's mic as he began talking interrupted
anything else they were going to say.

"Guess we'd better get back to the party." He squeezed her
hand and tugged her slightly closer. "But we definitely have
more to discuss on the subject." He let go but stayed close to her
as they returned to where the DJ stood on the dance floor,
asking if anyone wanted to come forward and say anything.

Time to switch to Mom mode, to congratulate the graduates, and hopefully not cry and make a fool out of herself.

CHAPTER
TWENTY-NINE

The lights around the house and the yard were more noticeable to Carissa as the twilight deepened. She and Jonas made their way back to the dance floor as the sheriff was at the microphone, congratulating the graduates for all their hard work and celebrating their futures. She thanked everyone for coming, then handed the microphone off to Isaiah and Eli's dad, Arthur.

Carissa only half listened. Her lips and face still felt hot and branded from Jonas's kisses. His hand was at her back, but all she wanted was to be in his arms again, just the two of them. She glanced over to where the kids were building a tower of Jenga blocks. They were having fun, and Lizzie was as careful and concerned about Jayden as Brandon was, giving him support and a break from always being Carissa's other eyes. They had been so blessed by how this community had welcomed them, house troubles notwithstanding.

The speeches ended, and as the DJ moved into music the kids had selected, they poured onto the dance floor. It looked like a high school dance.

"Want some cake?" Jonas's voice tickled her ear.

She suppressed a shiver and nodded. They grabbed their cake and stood off to the side, watching the kids dance, laugh, and have fun. Plus, the cake was fantastic—chocolate with a raspberry filling and a whipped cream frosting. Yum.

"I'm hoping my brother, Jonathan, and his family will come up for ArtFest and you can meet them," Jonas said. "I'll have to work for most of it, but I'm scheduled to be off the last day."

"I'd like that. I know the boys are looking forward to it." She nudged him with her shoulder. "And I wonder what kind of secrets your brother has to share about you."

He chuckled. "I'll have to warn him."

They finished their cake, and Jonas took their plates to the trash.

Vince was watching them from the other side of the dance floor. He raised his drink to her.

She gave him a tight grin and turned to look for Jonas. He was talking to a few of the kids by the food tables, his arms crossed over his chest. What was that all about?

She headed over, mostly to get the feel of Vince's eyes off her.

"There was no money at the house," Jonas was saying. "That's just an internet rumor. People always want to think there's hidden treasure somewhere."

"Aw, man. That would be awesome if it was true," one of the kids said. He was tall in that gangly way where he hadn't quite grown into his body yet.

"Awesome for Carissa because it would belong to her," Jonas pointed out. "But if any of you think of anything that you heard or knew about Tyler or anyone hanging out at the Delamar Place, let me know. Even if it seems insignificant. I know most of you were in middle school then."

The gangly kid spoke up. "Yeah, those high schoolers wouldn't talk to us."

"Just like we don't talk to middle schoolers now," another kid wearing braces said, laughing.

The kids moved off, and Carissa stepped next to Jonas.

"What was that about money in my house? Just the same old rumor or anything new?"

"Just kids bringing up the same old rumor." He slid his arm around her shoulders. "Don't worry about it. Enjoy tonight."

She glanced back at Vince, who was staring at them. What was with that guy?

The song ended and the DJ spoke. "Time to get all the older folks out on the dance floor with this oldie but goodie." The opening notes of "True" by Spandau Ballet came over the speakers.

Jonas slid his hand down her arm and took her hand. "Dance with me?"

She smiled up at him. "I'd love to."

He led her to the dance floor, and took her in his arms, swaying to the 80s classic. Reese and Ella were already there, along with Amanda and Ryan. Tony and Shannon also joined them, and soon the floor was full of couples dancing under the carnival lights and a sprinkling of stars in the sky. It was a perfect night, and she wanted to keep the memory of it tucked in her heart.

As Jonas moved her around, she spotted Gladys and Erma in their spot on the porch, looking on approvingly. Marco and Vince stood on the porch steps watching, perhaps not so approvingly.

As the song drew to an end, Jonas kissed her forehead. The tempo picked up, and the younger kids flooded the space, including Brandon, Jayden, and Lizzie. Brandon and Lizzie were trying out dance moves they had likely seen on YouTube, and Jayden was either copying them or just jumping around.

She laughed at their antics. Claire had pulled off a celebration that everyone was enjoying. Not an easy feat.

Jonas squeezed her hand and let go. "I'll be right back."

She watched where he headed. Eli was rounding the back of the house like he was on a mission.

And Jonas was right behind him.

THIS COULDN'T BE GOOD. JONAS SPOTTED SAMUEL GOING behind the house, unaware that Eli was hot on his tail. Eli was not going to ruin this party for Samuel.

When Jonas rounded the corner, Eli was up in Samuel's face, backing him up against the house. "You little freak. You still spying on us? I know it was you who ratted us out. You were always creeping around. You'll be sorry—"

"Hey, that's enough." Jonas grabbed Eli's arm, pulling him back.

Eli shrugged him off and shot him a wicked grin. "It's cool, man. Just congratulating the boy here. Who knew he'd ever graduate?"

"Eli, knock it off."

Tony joined them, stepping in front of Eli. He must have seen the same thing Jonas had. Tony started walking, his hand firmly on Eli's shoulder, forcing him back. "Time to go. Party's almost over anyway." He glanced back at Jonas. "I've got this one."

Jonas nodded. "Thanks." He tilted his chin to Samuel. "Let's take a walk."

Samuel wouldn't look at him, but he stepped away from the house, and they walked around it, the party sounds ebbing. "You okay? He didn't hit you, did he?"

Samuel shook his head. "I'm okay." His voice was low.

Jonas's heart squeezed. This kid was so used to being bullied. But he should have been able to enjoy tonight. And if Jonas said anything to the Schillers about Eli, it would ruin the night for them. People were messy and complicated.

"Did you get some cake?"

Samuel nodded.

"Good. You okay to head back?"

He nodded again.

"Samuel. Listen to what I'm saying."

Again with the nod.

"If Eli or anyone else bugs you like that, you let me or Pastor Tony know. We'll take care of it. No one has the right to treat you like that."

"Okay."

Words. Good. Jonas clapped him on the shoulder. "Go on and enjoy the rest of your party, okay?"

Samuel took off. Jonas followed him at a more measured pace. Had Eli figured out that Samuel was the person who'd named him as being present the night Tyler went missing? Or was he just being a jerk?

Eli was gone when Jonas got back. And so was Vince. The DJ was announcing the last song. Claire, Carissa, Gladys, and Erma were packing up the food. The crowd started dispersing.

As Carissa cleared the tablecloth and centerpieces from the tables, he and Alex started folding up chairs and tables. Brandon and Lizzie helped too. Tony and Shannon hung around, but Jonas was glad to see the Schillers and the Markeys had left.

By the time everything was cleaned up and put away, he found Carissa in the kitchen. He slipped a hand around her waist and kissed her temple. "Tired?"

"Very. But in a good way."

"Ready to go home?" His chest twisted at the words. *Home.* That was a loaded word, one he was too tired to think about tonight. But it felt good.

"Yes, I need to gather up the boys. I think they're in the parlor."

They left the kitchen and walked into the parlor. Lizzie and Brandon were playing a game on their Switches. But Jayden was fast asleep curled up in one of the chairs.

"Let's head home, Brandon. Night, Lizzie," Carissa said.

"Night. See you at church tomorrow, Brandon." Lizzie slid off the couch then headed upstairs.

Jonas scooped Jayden into his arms. The boy stirred but didn't wake. The unexpected memory of the weight of a child in his arms took him by surprise. How many times had he carried Ava to bed like this? Tears pricked his eyes.

Carissa opened the house and truck doors for him, and Jonas got Jayden strapped in. He felt the emptiness of his arms as he climbed into his truck. The short drive to Carissa's house was quiet.

"I'll carry him to his bed," Jonas said as he exited the truck.

He relished the weight and the soft breaths against his chest.

Carissa got Jayden's booster seat then unlocked the front door. "Brandon, can you feed Charlie and let him out?"

The boy nodded, but his dragging feet showed how tired he was.

Jonas followed Carissa upstairs to the boys' room and laid Jayden down. She pulled off his shoes and laid a blanket over him. "He's a heavy sleeper. He'll sleep through the night. Guess he can go without brushing his teeth for once. It's nearly impossible to wake him, and when you do, he's crabby."

Once they were back downstairs, Jonas took Carissa's hand. "Thanks for being my date tonight."

"You're welcome. It was a great evening." She gazed up at him, a smile tugging on those beautiful lips, temping him.

"It was." He pulled her in for a tight hug, not wanting to let her go but knowing he needed to. He kissed the top of her head and stepped back. "Good night. Lock the door behind me."

"I will."

Once he heard the deadbolt slip home, he jogged down the steps and to his truck. It still smelled faintly of her perfume. When he got home, he headed to the photos on the fireplace mantel. He picked up the photo of Autumn and Ava. He had wonderful memories of Autumn, but that season of his life was over. He had a deep love for her, but through his grief, his love for her had mellowed from a romantic one to something more familial, like a soft, comfortable blanket, full of good memories, but something he felt he could move beyond.

He left the photo of Ava by herself above the fireplace next to the one of Jon and his family. He went to the hall closet and pulled down a box where he'd stored some things of Autumn's he hadn't been ready to get rid of yet. He placed the photo in there and put it back on the shelf.

CHAPTER
THIRTY

Jonas skipped shooting baskets with the guys and headed early into work Monday, eager to check out something that had been bugging him.

Sunday after the graduation party had been a low-key day, with everyone pretty wiped out from the celebration. He'd had lunch after church with Carissa and the boys, but they both had laundry and things to do before the work week started. Plus, he was conscious of the fact that his emotions were swirling, and until he had a chance to talk with Tony about it, he was taking it slow and easy. Well, maybe not easy, considering it was hard to resist the temptation to kiss Carissa senseless.

He knew they were having a shift meeting about ArtFest, but ever since he'd seen Eli and Vince together, something had been bothering him about that connection. He pulled up Eli's record. Petty theft taken care of by community service and probation. Just a stupid kid stunt. Nothing new there.

But why was Eli working for Vince? He'd gone away to college—San Diego State, if Jonas recalled correctly—but he didn't know what Eli had majored in.

Vince was Anthony's uncle. Anthony and Eli were friends, apparently. They both hung out at the Delamar Place and had some sort of loyalty to cover up Eli's presence there. Maybe because they knew something bad had happened and didn't want Eli to be in trouble for potentially violating his probation?

So did Vince hire Eli as a favor to his nephew? Or was there something more? Someone had to dig that hole in Carissa's basement to bury Tyler's body. And it would have been a lot easier with something like an augur instead of just shovels.

Equipment Vince had in his landscaping company.

Jonas ran a search on Vince. When he got to his employment history, he found something interesting. Vince used to work for Belle Lumber, Beckett Lorde's company. It was after the time he worked for his brother and before he started his own landscaping business.

And where did he get the money to start his own business? He didn't have a business loan, and landscaping equipment wasn't cheap. His brother, Anthony's father, could have set him up or given him a private loan.

It seemed like Lorde had his hand in everything evil in this town. Now he showed up with a connection, tenuous as it was, to Tyler Cohen's death. Could he have had a part in it? It would explain why a case ostensibly perpetrated by high schoolers was stubbornly cold.

He headed back out to the lake house, hoping Vince and Eli would still be working there. He wanted to catch them off guard and not alert them with a phone call. If Vince thought he was in the clear, he wouldn't have time to make something up.

Jonas caught them packing up the trailer. Finally, something went his way. He exited his unit.

Eli spotted him and shook his head. "Hey, man. Is there something about police harassment? I told you I don't know anything."

Jonas gave Eli a piercing gaze then turned to Vince. "I'd like a word with you."

Vince raised an eyebrow but stepped away from the trailer. "Sure. What do you need? Does Carissa need any help?"

Jonas took a few steps down the road, away from Eli's hearing. Vince followed.

"I wanted to ask you about the night Tyler Cohen went missing."

Vince tilted his head back, eyes wide with surprise. "Tyler Cohen? That was like four years ago. I don't think I can remember anything helpful. All I know is that a few days later folks said he was missing."

"Was Eli working for you then?"

"Sometimes on weekends or when there was a big job that needed some muscle." Vince tucked his hands into his front pants pocket.

"What about Anthony?"

"Sure. Same deal." Vince's gaze narrowed. "What's this about?"

"Did you ever have any tools go missing or were misplaced around the time Tyler Cohen disappeared?"

Vince shrugged. "Tools go missing all the time. Kids leave them at job sites or don't put them back in their place. I can't think of anything specific."

"Like an auger?"

The color drained from Vince's face. Jonas saw the moment he made the connection between his questions and Tyler's death. "Jonas, I know you're just doing your job, and I respect that. I really do. But I don't think I want to say anything more without my attorney present. Am I free to go?"

Jonas gave a short nod. "You are." He didn't move.

Vince motioned to Eli and climbed in his truck, Eli shooting daggers at Jonas as they drove away.

———

CARISSA TOOK A BREAK WHILE LETTING COATS OF PAINT IN the bathroom dry. The boys had made progress on their summer reading program and would get free ice cream for their accomplishments. She texted Claire to ask if she could pick up Lizzie to go with them.

The string of smiley face emojis in response made Carissa laugh.

This time they walked. It was warm; the sun heated the pine needles on the ground, releasing a fresh and earthy scent. The boys kicked pinecones along the way while they covered the few blocks to Cope House.

Carissa was delighted to twist the Victorian doorbell—a new, last minute touch that contrasted with the Wi-Fi doorbell and electronic keypad on the door.

Claire's voice came over the modern doorbell. "Hey, guys, come on in. I'm in the kitchen."

She and Erma were baking cookies, and Lizzie was perched on a stool, a stack of library books next to her. It smelled like warm cinnamon and butter.

Claire held out a plate. "Want some samples?"

The boys eagerly grabbed the cookies to a chorus of thank yous.

Carissa was pleased they had remembered their manners without prompting. She leaned against the counter. "Ready for your guests?"

Stretching her back, Claire let out a sigh. "As ready as we can be. Alex fixed the ice machine. It was on the wrong setting. And we've got an electrician coming to add more outlets outside. So the graduation party was good for revealing the final things we needed."

"Are you sure you can spare him Saturday?" Her tub was ready, and Alex was going to help Jonas haul it upstairs and install it as well as help her with some demo in the room with the secret space.

"Absolutely. Once he carries the guests' luggage upstairs, it's all me." She grinned and tapped the counter. "You'll keep him from hovering over me. He means well, but women have been having babies for thousands of years. And, in other good news, we are officially sold out for ArtFest weekend."

"That's fantastic. You guys will get rave reviews."

"We've already got some up on Yelp from the graduation party. This town can be pretty supportive, even if they gossip about you behind your back."

They laughed, and Carissa touched Jayden's shoulder. "Should we head out to the library? And then I was thinking some ice cream as a reward for you all being such good readers."

A cheer went up, and Claire smiled. "Sounds great. I'll see you when you get back."

Carissa led her little troop into town and the library. Jonas was probably working in the office, but she could hope that they'd spot him patrolling while they were walking, which was why she'd timed their walk for the afternoon. The kids checked in at the summer reading program and got tickets for each book they read. Then they could put the tickets with their name on them into jars in front of the prizes they wanted. The more tickets, the better the chance of winning. Plus, they each had read enough to earn a coupon for a free ice cream cone.

While the kids were discussing prizes and picking out new books, Carissa wandered over to the historical society area. She slid into the wooden booth with the phone. It was pretty irresistible. She picked up the receiver and held it to her ear, wondering if perhaps there was a recording or something. There wasn't, but that would be a fun idea. It could talk about the history of the area.

The wooden box for messages had a piece of paper sticking out of it. Tempted for a moment to pull it out and read it, she shoved it further in so no one else would be tempted to do that either. If she were to write a message, who would it be to? And what about? Maybe to her younger self. Then again, she wouldn't be who she was if she hadn't been on this particular journey. And as painful as her relationship with Greg had been, she had her two beautiful boys from it.

Maybe everything had turned out exactly the way it was supposed to.

The kids came over, interrupting her thoughts. They played with the phone for a bit, talking to various people and trying out voices.

Jayden was quite serious with his conversation, however. "Mom, it's for you." He handed her the receiver.

"Who is it?"

He shrugged then smiled. "Batman!"

She laughed. She loved it when he figured out how to make a joke. "Well, Batman," she said into the receiver. "I can't talk right now. I've got to get these big readers some ice cream."

The kids started to cheer, and she shushed them. "Inside voices. This is a library."

Brandon made a whispered cheering sound.

They checked out their books and headed into town to get ice cream. As they rounded the corner on to Holcomb Springs Road, she saw a sheriff's deputy unit. And it was Jonas, writing a ticket for a car she didn't recognize. Probably a tourist.

When he glanced her way, she gave a slight wave, a butterfly coming to life in her stomach. He always looked so handsome whether in his work uniform, a T-shirt and jeans, or dressed up like he had been at the party.

He nodded with a small grin and went back to work.

She ushered the kids into the ice cream shop and let them order, redeeming their coupons. She was taking a bite of her mint chip when a voice behind her said, "Want to share that?"

She turned to see Jonas. She smiled and held it out. "Since it's you and you asked so nicely."

He winked at her and leaned forward for a bite, holding her gaze.

She rolled her eyes at him, then the kids came over, calling his name. He listened to them tell him about the books they picked up and the prizes they wanted to win. He was patient and asked them questions, listening intently to their responses.

And her heart melted a little bit more.

Jonas watched Carissa and the kids head down the street. At the corner, she turned and waved at him. He waved back, wishing he could spend the rest of the day with them instead of at work. The thought struck him hard. He loved his job. It'd been a long time since he'd wanted to spend his time doing something else.

He and Carissa seemed to have a mutual, unspoken agreement. He'd stopped by her house a few times this week for lunch, but he was always careful to have somewhere else to go, like work, so he wouldn't be tempted to stay overly long. Until they could have a more serious talk about where this was going and what the future might look like, he wanted to protect her boys.

Once they disappeared out of sight, he climbed back into his unit. He'd gone running with Tony a few times this week. Tony's listening ear and encouragement helped ease some of the knot in Jonas's chest. On the occasions when he glanced up at the mantel, he didn't feel the pain he expected to at not seeing Autumn's photo there.

Tony did tell him that Shannon had agreed to his idea to go out of town. Even though the sheriff was Jonas's boss, they were also friends. He hoped she and Tony could make it work. If they couldn't, there wasn't much hope for him.

He steered his unit through the twisting mountain roads, looking for illegally parked cars. During the busy season, it was all hands on deck. They were a small department and often hired off-duty cops and deputies to help out, like for ArtFest. But he'd made some time to put in a formal request to see Vince and his attorney for questioning. Jonas had asked about tools and about Anthony's and Eli's roles working for Vince, but between the time since the crime and Vince's attorney's refusal to allow him to answer many of the questions, Jonas didn't get very far. He hadn't expected to. But he was pulling on the threads he had.

Hopefully Alumni Days would be more illuminating. Or he might have to come to terms with the fact that Tyler Cohen's death and burial might remain a mystery.

CHAPTER
THIRTY-ONE

After a week of only seeing Jonas in small bits of time, Carissa was looking forward to having him with her all weekend. They were picking up her tub and doing some demo, with Alex and Samuel helping, so she'd told Jonas to come early for breakfast. The least she could do was feed him.

He arrived as she was flipping pancakes, and soon they were all around the table eating pancakes and bacon, with Charlie politely begging for his own portion.

She carefully watched her boys' interaction with Jonas. They treated him like a fun, new friend, telling him about the shows they were watching and the books they were reading. Jayden even shared some of his made-up adventures. But how would Jonas react when Jayden had a meltdown?

They made the trip down the hill, picked up the tub—which looked better than anything Carissa could have imagined—and headed back up. This time they had two days of work in front of them, but she was just as excited. Getting the bathroom done and the demo started put her giant steps forward on her schedule. And they were things she was certain she would have to hire out, things she needed muscle for.

She had spent the week painting the bathroom, installing the wainscoting, and getting all the wall and floor tile sparkling. It was all ready for the tub to be slid into place as the finishing touch.

When they pulled up in front of her house, Alex and Samuel were there waiting. While Carissa scooted the kids and dog out of the way and opened doors, the guys hauled the tub out of the truck, up the stairs, and into its home. A few more moments to make the water supply connections and it was done.

Carissa surveyed the room. "It looks perfect. Just how I envisioned it. Thanks, guys."

Jonas squeezed her shoulder. "Happy to help. It really does look great."

Alex hefted a sledge hammer. "Just show me where I can start breaking things." He grinned.

Even Samuel kinda smiled at that.

Alex had brought over a Bagster, this packaged, tarp-looking thing that opened up into a giant, industrial trash bag that resembled a kiddie pool on steroids. They laid it outside under the window where they were working, so they could toss bigger pieces out the window. When they were done with it, Carissa could call the number printed on the side and the company would come pick it up and dispose of it.

Of course Charlie thought the whole thing was for him and kept removing pieces of wood he thought made good sticks. Carissa tasked Brandon and Jayden with keeping Charlie occupied and safely away from their work zone.

Inside the room, Carissa had a giant trash can for the smaller items and the plaster. The key would be not to get the can so heavy they couldn't easily get it downstairs. Though given the muscles on these guys and how they'd just wrangled the tub into place, that likely wouldn't be a problem.

Earlier in the week, she'd sorted through the debris in the room, determining if any of the pieces were salvageable or might be useful in the future. And she'd marked where the plaster was damaged beyond repair and needed to come down. It was messy work, and she was grateful for the help.

They had just agreed on a plan of attack when the doorbell rang. She looked at the app on her phone to see who it was. "Pastor Tony's here."

Jonas nodded. "He said he'd stop by if he could get free."

She headed downstairs and let him in.

He hefted his toolbox. "Thought you could use some help."

"I'm learning not to say no to that. Come on up."

With enough guys working on the demo, Carissa was able to turn her attention to the secret room. She'd been terrified the boys would get playing around with it and get locked inside. She grabbed some small tools, a can of WD-40, and got to work on the mechanism, scraping and prying and spraying until it moved freely.

"Jonas, I want to test this from the inside. Make sure I don't get stuck."

He came over to examine the lock. "It looks good from here."

She slipped inside the secret room and pulled the panel shut. From the inside, the latch was easily workable. The light from the dirty window was muted. She'd have to get around to cleaning that. But it kept the space from feeling too claustrophobic. She pushed at the latch, and the panel slid open.

"Whew, that worked." The toe of her tennis shoe hit the raised edge of a board inside the room. One more thing she'd have to deal with later.

"I'm glad," Jonas said. "But I'd have no compunction about taking this wall down to get to you." His gray eyes found hers.

She was acutely aware they weren't alone. "I believe you," she whispered. She cleared her throat. "Now I don't have to worry about the boys locking themselves or each other inside."

"What are you going to do with this room?" Alex asked, wiping his forehead.

"I was thinking it would make a great office or library, with the whole hidden room thing. Nothing as elaborate as what you all did with your guest library. But I think Claire's idea of making a reading nook in the secret room is a great one. Put in some pillows and lighting. The boys will love it."

Alex nodded. "Once we have some guests check it out, it'll be fun to see their reaction."

"It definitely needs some work in there. A good cleaning, and one of the boards is loose, but at least I won't be having nightmares about the boys getting trapped in there."

The demo was done faster than she would have expected. The plaster was swept up and disposed of, and the room was ready to be put back in shape.

Carissa insisted on feeding her helpers for their labor. She'd put some sloppy joes in the crockpot that morning, and they sat around her dining room table, casual conversation flowing among people who were comfortable with each other.

"Thanks so much for this, guys," Carissa said. "I know it was the only available weekend before ArtFest and you all are busy. I appreciate it."

Jonas raised his soda can to Jayden and Brandon. "You boys will love ArtFest. Lizzie too." He nodded to Alex. "Lots of rides and food trucks taking over the park. Artists from all over the country show their work here, including some amazing outdoor installations. You'll see them going up around town this week. Every shop on Holcomb Springs Road will host some exhibits. It's really something."

He let out a sigh. "It's also crowded and a lot of work for us. But it is good for the town." He nudged Brandon. "You'll like it." He turned to Samuel. "What do you think?"

The kid shrugged. "It's okay, I guess."

Carissa laughed. "A ringing endorsement. Perfect."

The little party broke up with Carissa stating her thanks again. And soon, she and Jonas found themselves on the back deck sitting in camp chairs, the first moment alone they'd had in a week, and she was nearly too tired to enjoy it.

He reached over to take her hand. "Your house is really coming along."

"It is. Thanks in no small part to you." She loved the feeling that, just for a moment, her problems were shared by someone else and not borne by her alone.

His thumb ran over the back of her hand. "I'm looking forward to you meeting my brother and his family next weekend. I've told him a bit about you."

That put a quiver in her belly, but if she looked at it logically, it made sense for her to meet his family. They weren't young adults. They were older with lots of history. They couldn't just follow their feelings, because other people were involved.

But just for a moment, she longed to do just that—follow her feelings and repeat that magical kiss. To see that deep look in his eyes of wonder and admiration.

Instead she said, "I'm looking forward to meeting him. And I know the kids are looking forward to rides and junk food. The key is to keep Jayden from getting too overstimulated. He has no sense of his own limits."

"I'll help you. I want to learn more about his autism, about both boys." His gaze on her was soft in the deepening shadows at the end of the day. He shifted his weight in the chair to lean closer to her.

The back door flew open. "Hey, Mom. Is the secret room fixed? Can we play in it?" Brandon asked, Jayden in tow.

She smiled at Jonas. "You sure about that?"

CHAPTER
THIRTY-TWO

I t was the first day of ArtFest, and Jonas was running the command center near what would normally be the baseball field but instead was full of booths, food trucks, and games. A band was playing at one end, and the whole atmosphere was festive.

It made his skin itchy, keeping alert for all the potential things that could go wrong or bad actors who might want to ruin everyone's day. But so far, things were going smoothly. He wanted them to stay that way.

Carissa had planned to bring the boys for a bit, hoping that enjoying ArtFest in smaller doses would keep it from being too overwhelming. He hadn't seen her much this week. Sunday after church they'd hung drywall to replace the damaged plaster. She was going to be mudding and taping it up this week while he worked overtime as the art was installed, booths set up, and tourists swelled their little town to five times its size.

He felt bad he wouldn't be able to spend time having fun here with her and the boys until late Saturday and Sunday when his brother and family came up. But she had reassured him that she was fine, that she was used to doing things by herself, and they all understood the demands of his work. But he couldn't help but feel the shade of the trouble his job had caused Autumn and him sneaking up on his relationship with Carissa.

He pushed the thoughts aside. Tonight was Alumni Night, and he'd be over at the award ceremony and alumni tent to talk to those kids and see if he could get anything moving on Tyler Cohen's case.

"Hey there, stranger."

He looked up at the voice he hoped he wasn't imagining to see Carissa standing across the table at the front of the command center with Jayden, Brandon, and Lizzie. And Vince. Why was he here? With them?

But Jonas's smile was genuine. "Hey, good to see you guys. What have you done so far?"

The kids gestured to some rides behind them and rattled off some names.

Carissa gave Jonas a tight smile. "Vince was kind enough to buy the kids unlimited ride wristbands, so they've been trying a few things out." She shuddered. "Once you get past the kiddie rides, it's out of my league."

Vince stood a little behind the kids, a smile playing around his mouth.

Jonas was glad for the kids' sake that the guy had done something nice for them. He just wished he'd thought of it first. He smiled at Carissa. "Not a roller coaster fan, huh?"

"No thanks."

"Good thing there's lots of other things to see here. And eat. Have you guys had anything fun to eat yet?"

"Mom said after the rides so we don't puke," Brandon said.

Jonas laughed. "Good advice."

"We're headed to the art booths now. They have an area where the kids can make their own art. But I wanted to stop by and say hi." Carissa's eyes said a lot more than her words did.

"I'm glad you did. I was hoping you would." He reached for her hand and gave it a quick squeeze, wishing once again it wasn't Vince escorting them around. "Have fun."

"Oh, we will," Vince finally said, but his gaze skittered past Jonas's before he began to move off.

"Bye!" the kids chorused.

Carissa looked back over her shoulder and gave him a small wave before disappearing behind booths.

He felt strangely sad after their visit; a mix of emotions he couldn't really name swirled through him. And he didn't have time to dissect any of it. He'd spend time with them on Sunday. That would have to do.

IN THE PAST TWO WEEKS, SHANNON HADN'T BEEN ABLE TO get the idea out of her head since Tony had mentioned the possibility of them going out of town somewhere to discuss what their future might look like. At their two coffee dates since then, they'd had so many people stop by to talk, they hadn't been able to discuss it beyond a few texts.

She was in her sheriff's unit, staying mobile and available during ArtFest. It was early for dinner, but it was a good time for her to take a break. Maybe Tony would be free. She swung by the church. His truck was there, along with a few other cars. And then she spotted him talking with a group of guys.

All eyes were on her as she pulled in next to his truck. Tony raised a hand in greeting but went back to talking.

Must be important. She didn't want to interrupt. She thought for a moment, then grinned. She could have some fun with this. Grabbing her notepad, she scribbled a note inviting him to meet her in the town center parking lot for dinner.

Slipping out of her vehicle, she made a show of slipping it under his windshield wiper like it was a ticket, waved, and drove off. Tony and the group of guys noticed but didn't stop talking.

And these kids thought texting was fun. They had no idea how fun a good, old-fashioned note could be.

Jonas was grateful to have Brett Chang relieve him so he could grab some food and head over to the stage for the Soaring Eagle award ceremony. The school had a tent set up for alumni where they were hosting a dinner, and he hoped between the two he'd be able to shake loose some information.

He grabbed a hotdog from a food truck and ate it as he walked over. The sights, sounds, and smells of the festival reminded him that Carissa and the boys were having fun—he hoped—while he was working.

Chairs had been set up in front of the stage, and the alumni tent was off to the side. He situated himself between the two, scanning the crowd, looking for who was around that he could talk to.

The ceremony started. The principal gave a speech highlighting all that Holcomb Springs High alumni had accomplished, and he acknowledged the death of Tyler Cohen and that his name would be added to the In Memorium wall at the school. Then he announced the Soaring Eagle award and read off Kayla Mill's accomplishments before presenting her with the award.

She was poised, more so than the high school girl he had remembered interviewing four years ago. As she spoke, Jonas spotted Samuel in the crowd, staring after Kayla. The poor kid. Crushes died hard.

Then Eli crossed his vision, heading into the alumni tent with Anthony. Jonas made his way through the crowd, following them. As he entered the tent, they were in the back corner, arguing heatedly.

"I already tried once, man," Anthony said as Jonas walked up. He went quiet as soon as he noticed Jonas. "Sergeant."

"Good to see you back in town. Have you remembered anything else about the night Tyler went missing?"

Eli scowled at him but said nothing.

Anthony shook his head. "Not really."

"Let me know if you do."

"Sure."

Kayla entered the tent, and Jonas went over to her. "Nice speech. Congratulations on your award."

"Thanks." She lifted her shoulders and looked around. "It's weird being back."

"I bet. There are a few questions I'd like to ask you about things that came up from Tyler's autopsy. I don't want to take away from tonight's festivities. Could you meet me at the department offices tomorrow morning at ten?"

People were beginning to crowd around and ask for her attention, but Jonas stuck by her side. He wasn't going to leave without her agreement.

"Okay, sure. I'll see you then."

He nodded and moved away. After having a similarly unproductive conversation with Madison Gonzales, Jonas called it a night.

But he couldn't help but wonder where Carissa and the boys were. Hopefully safe at home.

———

SHANNON HAD MEATBALL SANDWICHES GETTING COLD sitting next to her in her unit parked behind the town center. No word from Tony. He had seen her leave the note, so what was the problem? Had it somehow blown away? It was way past her dinner break. Even if he did show up now, it would be too late. But it wasn't like him not to show up. Maybe there'd been an emergency. But she couldn't think of a scenario where he wouldn't at least send her a text.

Putting her unit in gear, she headed back through the traffic over to the church.

Tony's truck was gone. That was weird.

Only one car was left. Marcia's, the church's secretary. And she was coming out the door, locking up.

Shannon pulled over to her. "Hey, Marcia. Where's the pastor? He was just here. He was supposed to meet me."

"He left a little bit ago. He didn't say anything about meeting you. Are you sure he didn't get the time mixed up? You know that tends to happen with him. Especially if you texted him."

"I left him a note."

"Well, you know how it is with his dyslexia. Handwriting especially is hard for him. He probably just mixed things up. Give him a call."

Shannon went cold. Only her years of professional experience allowed her to keep her reaction under wraps. "Yeah. I'll check with him. Thanks."

"Sure." Marcia waved and got in her car.

Shannon headed back to the town center, but her appetite was gone. Tony had dyslexia. Wow. She was amazed that he'd accomplished everything he had and kept it a secret. Obviously Marcia knew. He'd have to confide in someone to help him. And she assumed Shannon knew, probably because she knew they were close and thought Tony would have confided in her.

And that's what upset her the most. Why hadn't he told her himself?

Her radio squawked, demanding her attention. Her break was over, and she was needed. She'd have to deal with Tony later.

CHAPTER
THIRTY-THREE

Jonas drank his coffee in his kitchen the next morning. Jon and his family would be coming up later today. The guest room was ready. He had tomorrow off, and they'd spend it with Carissa and the boys at ArtFest. Then they'd watch the fireworks over Holcomb Lake. He was a little nervous about combining two different areas of his life.

He pulled down the box of Autumn's things from the closet and set it on the kitchen table. If he remembered correctly, there were some pictures of all of them together—Jon and Alison and their two girls with him and Autumn and Ava. They might like to have those. He started pulling things out, digging around until he found a stack of photos. It had been a day at the beach. They'd lived close enough in Laguna Vista that it was their go-to place.

Flipping through the photos, he smiled at the memories, fondness filling his heart with a touch of sadness, like for an old friend. But not overwhelming grief. He set the photos aside. Hopefully, they would bring back good memories for Jon and Alison as well.

He glanced at the clock on the wall. He had to get going to meet Kayla Mills at the station.

AND SHE WAS RIGHT ON TIME. JONAS USHERED KAYLA Mills into an interview room.

"Can I get you coffee? Soda?"

She shook her head. "No, thanks."

He sat across from her. "We've uncovered a few things since discovering Tyler's body, and I'm hoping you can help us shed some light on what might have happened that night. We know Eli Schiller was there that night, but none of you mentioned it in your statements. Why is that?"

She studied her hands on the table. "I should have mentioned it at the time, but I guess I didn't think it mattered. He was going up the stairs as I was going down them, leaving the house."

"Did you and Tyler have some sort of altercation? We found some blouse buttons, and Tyler had a wound on the back of his head consistent with a stair spindle we found. It wasn't enough to do more than cause him to bleed and maybe give him a headache. It didn't kill him."

She buried her face in her hands. After a minute, she looked up. "He— He wanted more from me, physically. When I said no, he grabbed at me, ripped my shirt. I snatched up whatever I could find. There was a bunch of junk in that room, and I swung at him to keep him away from me. It gave me time to get away. I ran downstairs. Eli came up. I was relieved, thinking he'd talk to Tyler, give me time to get away from him. I just wanted to get out of there."

That was consistent with their theory. "Why didn't you say anything at the time?"

"I should have, but Tyler had gone missing, and his parents had always been very sweet to me. They already had so much on their plates with his mom's dementia. I didn't want to add to their pain by saying their son had been a jerk to me. I figured that since he was gone, it didn't matter anyway. I was the only one he'd hurt, and I was fine." Her shoulders hunched forward, and she looked more like the high school girl he remembered than the poised woman who'd accepted her award last night.

"Why do you think Eli went up the stairs as you were going down? Did he know what Tyler had tried with you?"

She thought for a moment. "I don't see how. We were in a room away from everyone else. I was trying to break up with him in private. But"—she bit her lip— "Eli was always a loud-mouthed hothead. Tyler was tutoring him and other kids. He was making money at it, good money. So maybe they were arguing over that."

More things that pointed to Eli, but nothing they could make stick. He asked her a few more questions and went back over the same questions in different ways, but nothing new turned up.

Jonas got to his feet. "Thanks for your help. I think that's it for now, but let me know if you think of anything."

She stood and headed for the door then turned back. "I drove by the Delamar Place yesterday when I got into town. Someone is living there and is fixing it up. Is that how Tyler's body was discovered?"

He nodded.

"Have you seen the house? How does it look?"

"It's really nice. A lady with two young boys is rehabbing it and doing a good job."

"Good. I always loved the beauty of that old place. It's nice to see someone taking care of it and fixing it up."

"If you'd like to see inside, I think I could arrange that."

Kayla hesitated. "I'll think about it. Thank you." She turned and left the station.

Jonas considered her words for a moment. He headed by the sheriff's office, but Shannon wasn't in. It was time for him to head out to the fairgrounds.

TONY SIPPED ON HIS COFFEE WHILE HE PACED HIS LIVING room and tried to decide what to do. He hadn't slept much, and his prayers seemed to be hitting the ceiling. He pulled out Shannon's note from last night. It meant a lot to him that she'd made the effort, even if it was a source of frustration.

He knew this was a busy time for Shannon, and he didn't want to distract her. But he did owe her an explanation. And the longer he waited, the worse it got.

He sent her a text.

> I know we need to talk. And I know you are busy. But if you have any time, let me know.

Getting her note yesterday had been equal parts thrilling and frustrating. Thrilling, because she'd left him a note. And frustrating because he struggled to read her handwriting—a sharp, blocky printing. And because it was a private note, he didn't want to show it to Marcia, who often did his decoding for him. And because he was prideful and hadn't admitted to Shannon yet that he had dyslexia, he couldn't bring himself to text her to find out the place and time she wanted to meet. At least, he thought she wanted to meet.

So he'd driven around to the likely places, but the town was so crowded with ArtFest it was impossible to really see anything. So he'd come home.

Why hadn't he made time to tell her before now? He knew why. He had all the excuses. But none of that was helping now.

His phone dinged with a text. It was a voice message from Shannon. He played it.

"I have a few minutes. Meet me in the parking lot behind the town center in fifteen minutes."

It wasn't much time, but it was all he was going to get. As he was heading out the door, one other thing became clear. Shannon not only knew about his dyslexia, she'd purposely sent him a message in a format—a voice message—he couldn't misunderstand.

Not wanting to deal with the growing traffic, he left his car at home and headed out on foot. Maybe walking would help sort out some of the swirling emotions running through him.

He arrived at the town center without coming to any resolution or clear thoughts. Shannon's sheriff's SUV was parked in the back, and she was inside. She spotted him, and he climbed in the passenger side.

"Hey, I'm really sorry about last night." He needed to apologize, so might as well start with that. "I wish I could have spent some time with you, even if it was just for a few minutes."

Shannon nodded, but she didn't say anything.

He knew they didn't have much time, but he still struggled getting the words out. *Just walk her through what happened.* "When you pulled up at the church yesterday, I was talking to a few people who were upset about ArtFest. It's the same old people who get upset about the tourists invading their town. There's always a group that never want anything to change. They teased me a bit about getting a ticket in my own church parking lot, but I was curious to see what you left under my windshield wiper. When I was done talking with them, I walked over."

He let out a breath. "I couldn't decipher your handwriting. I have dyslexia, which I think you might have figured out. Because I'm prideful, I didn't just pick up the phone and call you. I tried to figure it out on my own."

"Who else knows?" Shannon asked.

"Marcia." Tony stared out the window. "Janelle, when she was alive, was a huge help to me. I couldn't have gone through seminary without her. She helped me set up the systems that I use today. I just kept thinking that once I was here longer and people knew and trusted me as their pastor, then the dyslexia wouldn't be a big deal to them. I just didn't want anyone to lose trust in me or my abilities because of my disability."

Shannon turned in her seat. "Tony, I'm not upset that you

have dyslexia. It actually makes me admire you all the more, knowing what you've had to overcome. What I hate—" Emotion clogged her voice, and she swallowed. "What I hate is that I had to find out from Marcia instead of from you. And she only said something because she assumed you had already told me. Did you think I would judge you? Did you think so little of me?"

"No, Shannon. I—" He couldn't quite put it into words. "I wanted to tell you. I planned to tell you whenever we got out of this town and got some time alone without prying eyes and ears. There's a lot I want to tell you, more than I know you have time for today. But I never planned on withholding it from you."

"Dan used to tell me whatever he thought I wanted to hear, but he kept important information from me. He thought very little of me and my abilities. I know you and Dan aren't the same at all, but this smacks of that. It brings up a lot of negative emotions. You and I have been working together for months. I find it hard to believe there was no time where you couldn't be honest with me about this."

He couldn't argue with her. He should have done it before now.

Her radio went off, and she answered it. "I've got to go. I know there's probably more to say, but I'm going to need some time. This was not what I would have expected of you, and I'm not sure what to do about it."

Tony opened the door and slipped out. "I know. And I'm more sorry than I can say."

She nodded, and he closed the door, watching as she drove off. Had he just messed up the best thing in his life?

CHAPTER
THIRTY-FOUR

Carissa was burning off nervous energy working around the house. She was meeting Jonas's brother and family today, once Jonas got off work. The boys had had a fun but exhausting time at ArtFest yesterday. Their art creations were hanging on the fridge. She was glad Lizzie had come to go on rides with Brandon, rides Carissa didn't want to go on.

And she was also glad to use the boys as an excuse to head home early. Vince was sweet to buy the kids the ride bracelets, but she couldn't help but feel it came with strings attached. And she didn't like that feeling at all.

She had a hard time keeping the boys occupied today. They wanted to go back to ArtFest and kept asking when they could go. Charlie kept running to the various windows as new cars drove by and people parked and walked through their neighborhood.

She fed the boys grilled cheese sandwiches and tomato soup as a late lunch. Tonight's plans were vague, depending on when Jonas got off and when Jon and his family arrived. And that was something Jayden just couldn't understand. But having good food in his belly would help stave off any sugar-induced meltdowns.

And they could walk around downtown and study some of the oversized art installations they'd seen going in this week. Keeping Jayden within arm's reach was a challenge due to the crowds, and it meant she kept her eyes on him more than she did the art. But it got them out of the house, and they were able to appreciate the wide variety of creativity people brought to their projects.

Her phone rang. Jonas. She stopped both boys, and they stepped off to the side before she answered the phone.

Jonas jumped right in. "I've got a favor to ask. I'm caught up in a traffic accident, and Jon's almost here. Can you walk over here and get my house key then head over to my place to let him in? You'll get both places faster on foot than he would get trying to drive through this mess."

"Sure, I'm happy to. We're actually downtown right now."

"Good. I'm at the end of the main drag where Holcomb Springs Road curves into Polique Canyon Road."

"I know right where that is. We'll be there in about five minutes." She hung up and explained to the boys what they were doing. Now that they had a mission, they picked up their pace a bit.

Soon she spotted Jonas near two recently dented cars pulled off to the side of the road. He was talking to the drivers. Another officer was directing traffic around the accident. It didn't look like anyone was hurt.

Jonas noticed them and jogged over. "Thanks for doing this." He handed her the keys, giving her hand a quick squeeze in the process. "Sorry I won't be there to do the introductions. The tow truck is having a hard time making it through all the traffic. But I'll be along as soon as I can."

She dropped his keys in her crossbody bag. "We'll see you soon."

Jayden was fascinated by the goings-on. "Can we stay and watch?"

"No, we don't want to be in the way. Plus, we've got to let

Jonas's brother into Jonas's house." She ushered the boys back the way they had come. Once they left downtown proper, the crowds thinned out, though people were parking all through the neighborhoods.

It got quieter toward Jonas's street, and his long driveway made a peaceful transition away from ArtFest, though they could still hear faint strains from the band. No car was here, so they'd beaten Jon. She unlocked the door and entered. It was odd being in Jonas's house without him. It smelled faintly of coffee and laundry soap.

The boys headed through the house. "Can we go in the backyard?" Brandon asked.

She nodded. But her eyes landed on the box sitting on Jonas's kitchen table. It was open, and laying on top was the photo of Autumn and Ava that she had seen on the mantel. Emotion shot through her, weakening her legs.

Next to the box was a stack of photos. The first one looked like it could be Jonas's brother and wife, along with Autumn and Ava.

This was Jonas's private life, and she wasn't going to pry. Yet, he'd left it out. Had he been reminiscing? Was he not ready for a relationship with her? Was he missing Autumn? Thoughts and feelings chased themselves through her head and chest, making it difficult for her to make sense of any of it.

On shaky legs, she walked to the back door and watched the boys. All she wanted to do was get out of here, to protect her boys... And herself. What if Jonas spent the weekend reliving old memories with his brother, noticing how she wasn't Autumn. Jon and his wife couldn't help but make comparisons.

She thought back to how she and Jonas met. The second time. He started talking to her because he needed to be rescued from Mariah. What if she was the rebound girl, the one that got him back in the market? Did he have genuine feelings for her? Or was he just trying to replace the family he lost?

She didn't want to be humiliated, and she didn't want her boys to get hurt.

A knock at the front door broke into her thoughts. She took a deep breath and headed to the door and pulled it open. A lighter-haired, slightly shorter version of Jonas stood there next to a woman with blonde hair and a warm smile. Two girls about Brandon's age stood off to the side.

"Hi, I'm Carissa. Jonas got stuck at a traffic collision and asked me to let you in."

"I'm Jon." He shook her hand. "This is my wife, Alison, and our girls, Liane and Lily."

"It's nice to meet you." She stood aside so they could all come in. "My boys are in the backyard. Come in and make yourself at home. I'm sure Jonas will be here any minute." She gathered up her purse and went to the back door. "Boys, come on." She turned back to Jon and Alison. "I'm sorry. I forgot to feed our dog."

"I don't wanna go." Jayden threw himself through the back door. "I want to go on rides."

She bent down next to his ear. "Later."

She gave them a tight smile. "It was nice meeting you."

"Noooo!" Jayden threw himself on the ground.

Carissa squatted down next to him, pushing out of her mind what Jon and his family must think of her. "Jayden, we'll do rides later, I promise. You don't want Charlie to starve, do you?"

Jayden looked up at her with watery eyes. "No."

She helped him get to his feet and ushered the boys out the front door and headed at a brisk pace down Jonas's driveway. She had to get out of that house.

The boys kept asking what they were going to do and when they were going to go to ArtFest. Carissa put them off; she didn't have answers either. Soon they were home, and Brandon obediently fed Charlie. She collapsed in a camp chair on the back deck and buried her head in her hands and let the tears fall. She didn't even know why she was crying, other than it seemed to release everything pent up inside.

"Now, dear, just let it all out. We all need a good cry now and then." Gladys's voice came from beside her.

Carissa looked up and wiped her eyes. "I guess you're right." She wasn't even questioning why or how her neighbor seemed to just appear.

Gladys lowered herself into the camp chair Jonas had occupied previously. Today her tube top was a blue tropical print. "Anyone hurt?"

Carissa shook her head.

"Any new house disasters?"

Carissa laughed at that. "No more than usual."

Gladys patted Carissa's knee. "God is still on his throne, and he still loves you more than you can possibly imagine."

"Thanks for reminding me. I needed to hear that."

"That's what neighbors are for, dear."

The boys came out the back door. "Mom, when are we going to ArtFest? Where's Jonas?" Brandon asked.

Jayden bounced up and down. "I want to go on rides."

"I'm not sure guys. I don't think we're going to go tonight." She knew it was the wrong thing to say, but she was out of ideas and emotional bandwidth.

"No!" Jayden threw himself on the deck, sinking into full meltdown mode.

Gladys got to her feet. "I'll let you deal with this. I'll be praying."

JONAS PULLED INTO HIS DRIVEWAY. HE HATED RESPONDING to car wrecks because of the memories it brought up, but no one was hurt in the fender bender, which helped. He spotted Jon's car. Good. He hoped they were all getting along and deciding what to do this evening. He was nervous about this weekend, introducing Carissa to his family and that whole dynamic. But he was also excited about this next step with Carissa and him. He was hoping it would bring healing and closure.

He walked in the door. Quiet voices came from the living room. He spotted the box still sitting on the kitchen table. Had he left that out? What had Carissa thought?

In the living room, Jon and Alison sat on the couch, the girls in chairs. They turned at the sound of his footsteps.

Where was Carissa? And the boys?

"Hey, guys. Glad you made it up." Jonas went around and gave hugs to his family, who stood to greet him. "Where's Carissa? She let you in, right?"

"Yeah." Jon shoved his hands in his pockets. "She said she had to go home to feed the dog." Concern filled his eyes.

Jonas closed his eyes. She had seen the box. And drew who knew what conclusions. "Let me change and then we can talk about what we want to do for dinner. There's water and soda in the fridge. Help yourselves."

He went into his bedroom and closed the door. Pulling out his phone, he called Carissa.

"Hey, Jonas." Her voice was subdued.

At least she answered. He was afraid she wouldn't. "You saw the box. I'm sorry."

"It's fine. You don't owe me an explanation."

"I do. I want you to know." He let out a breath. "There's a lot to talk about, but can we still stick with our plans? I really want you to spend some time with my brother and his family."

She let out a breath. "I can't. Jayden is in full meltdown mode, and I don't want to reward that behavior. I think we just need a night at home."

Jonas was quiet for a moment. Disappointment washed over him as his evening plans crumbled. "I understand. You take care of Jayden. But we will talk, Carissa."

"We will. I just can't tonight."

Jonas hung up. How to explain all of this to his brother?

At least Liane and Lily were having fun, Jonas thought as they walked around ArtFest. The girls went on rides, and the rest of them ate funnel cake, barbecue beef sandwiches, and fried pickles. Jon and Alison didn't say much—what could they say? But what Jonas had hoped would be a weekend of fun and fresh starts had become anything but. All he really wanted to do was talk to Carissa. But he was giving her space. Still, he didn't think she could process everything about Autumn without talking with him. But that wouldn't happen with his family around. He could understand her not wanting an audience.

And Jayden obviously was sensing the tension if he was having a meltdown. He wanted to help Carissa with that, but there was so much he didn't know.

It would all take time.

They stood near the stage and listened to the band for a bit while the girls went on some upside-down ride. It was playing 80s covers, and he couldn't help but think of how he and Carissa had danced at the graduation party.

A tap on his shoulder almost made him think Carissa had changed her mind and decided to join them.

Mariah stood there with a grin on her face. "Hey, stranger. Dance with me?"

He glanced back at Jon and Alison. Jon raised his eyebrows. Man, he was going to have some explaining to do.

"Uh, no thanks."

She reached for his hand and tugged. "Come on. I don't see you here with anyone else."

He disengaged his hand. "Sorry, Mariah. I'm just not interested in you in that way. I'm sure you'll find a more willing partner elsewhere." His irritation made him shorter with her than he would have liked, but at least he'd finally told her.

She started to say something else, but Samuel came up to

him, slightly out of breath. He had hardly seen Samuel race anywhere. The kid tried to stay invisible.

"What's going on, Samuel?" Jonas turned his back on Mariah.

"I think Eli's up to something. Somehow he learned about the secret rooms. Maybe he overheard me and Zach talking about it, or maybe Isaiah told him. I don't know."

"Okay. Why is it a big deal if Eli knows about the secret rooms?"

"He and Anthony were arguing about money. I don't know, but maybe Eli thinks there's money in Carissa's secret room."

Jonas shook his head. "I've been in that room. There's no money there."

"But if Eli thinks there is, he'll try to get in there." Samuel studied his shoes. "Sorry. This is my fault. I blackmailed them all to get them here. I thought if they all came, you could figure out what happened with Tyler and Carissa would be safe."

Jonas's brain spun trying to keep up with Samuel's words. "You sent them the social media message? To Kayla, Anthony, Madison, and Eli?"

Samuel nodded.

"Have you seen Eli tonight?"

"He and Anthony were arguing over by the rides earlier. That's where I heard them talking about the money and the secret room. Then I came looking for you."

Jonas had a weird feeling in his gut, one he didn't like to ignore. He needed to get over to Carissa's right away.

CHAPTER
THIRTY-FIVE

Carissa had bribed the boys with pizza and ice cream and had finally settled them down with a movie. She sat in the dining room with a cup of decaf and a bowl of rapidly melting ice cream. Sometimes it was so hard to figure out what was going through Jayden's mind. And even Brandon was whiny with disappointment. But tonight she was out of energy.

She needed some time alone to examine her feelings about Jonas and what the future might hold. It wasn't as if Autumn was a secret, but knowing that he was sorting through their memories and reliving his time with her… It felt like a betrayal, which was ridiculous because Autumn was dead, and Carissa didn't have a committed relationship with Jonas.

Though her heart begged to differ.

She wanted to climb into her claw-foot tub and listen to an audiobook. And she was debating doing just that when her doorbell camera triggered. Picking up her phone, she waited for the image to resolve. When it did, it looked like the same gangly kid as before. Eli?

She thought about calling Jonas but didn't want to interrupt his night. He deserved to have a good time out with his brother, even if she and her kids had blown up his plans. Maybe it was good that he learned this about them now.

Grabbing her phone, she peered out the window, but the reflection made it difficult to see anything. She flipped the front porch light on and stepped outside. She didn't see anything. She was tempted to let Charlie out and see what he discovered, but he was happily ensconced with the boys, and he seemed to help keep Jayden calm. Right now, that was a top priority.

She didn't see anything at first. But then she heard some rustling in the bushes. She switched on the light on her phone and shone it toward the sound. What kind of animal was it?

A human, apparently. Eli appeared, stepping out of the foliage. He gave her a sheepish grin. "Hey, there."

"What are you doing in my bushes, Eli?"

"Oh, I just was curious as to the work you've been doing around here. It looks great. So much better than the last time I was here." Lit by the porch light, Eli scuffed his toe in the ground. "Any chance I could get a look at the inside?" He gave her a grin he clearly thought would win her over.

"No. That won't be possible."

"Really?" He continued with the grin. "I'll be quick."

She shook her head, unnerved by his request. "No. And don't be sneaking around my bushes. It's not cool. Next time, I'll call the sheriff."

The grin dropped off his face. "Fine. Have a good night." He gave her a mock salute then headed down the street.

The rumble of George's cart sounded down the street. Carissa waited for him to show up into her pool of light, hoping Eli wouldn't harass the old man. "Evening, George."

He paused and looked up. "Well, hello there, Carissa."

"Did you have a good day?"

He glanced back at his cart. "I did. These tourists throw a lot of stuff out."

"That turns out to be good for you, then." She smiled at him. "Oh! I have some cans for you. Let me get them." She hurried into the house and grabbed the garbage bag of Diet Coke cans she'd been saving for him. She carried it out to him. "Are you headed home now?"

"Yep. Thanks for these." He started down the road again and waved. "See you later."

"Good night." As she looked around, she thought she smelled smoke. Was someone having a bonfire? Those weren't allowed up here because of the high fire danger, but with all the tourists in town, it was possible someone had started one. It smelled awfully close.

"Do you smell that, George?"

He stopped and turned. "Nope, but my smeller doesn't work as good as it used to." He waved and headed down the road into the dark shadows.

She started toward the back of the house. The smell was stronger. And then she saw the flames. The back of the garage was on fire. Darting back inside, she tried to punch in 911 with shaking fingers. Once she relayed the emergency, she ran through the house. She needed the boys, the dog—he would need his leash—her purse.

Brandon was in the living room watching a movie on the computer. Alone.

"Grab your shoes. The garage is on fire."

"What?" Brandon jumped up and ran for the front door where his shoes resided.

"Where's Jayden? And Charlie?" Barely controlled panic laced her words. She didn't want to scare Brandon.

He scanned the room. "I don't know. He was here."

"Wait by the front door." She punched in Jonas's number. Smoke began filling the house. How long before a stray ember caught the house on fire?

He picked up immediately.

"The garage is on fire. And I can't find Jayden." She grabbed Charlie's leash from its hook next to the door.

"I'm almost there. Hang on."

She didn't stop to think about the logic of his words. She was just grateful he was close by as she ran upstairs. "Jayden!"

He wasn't in the boys' room or her room. She grabbed her purse. Sirens sounded in the distance. The front door opened. She heard Brandon then Jonas's voice.

His steps pounding up the stairs was the sweetest thing she'd heard. "Carissa!"

"I'm here." She ran into the hall. "I can't find him." The smoke was thicker up here.

"Get downstairs. The fire department is on its way. Take Brandon and get out. I'll get Jayden."

Tears streamed down Carissa's face. "I can't leave Jayden."

Jonas took her shoulders. "I'll find him. Now go."

She shoved Charlie's leash into his hand then headed downstairs, the hardest thing she'd ever done. *Lord, please.* She had no other words.

Brandon was nowhere in sight. She darted out the front door.

He was across the way with Gladys's arms around him. Dear, sweet Gladys. Carissa hoped Gladys didn't lose her house too.

JONAS CALLED JAYDEN'S NAME AS HE DOVE TO THE FLOOR to check under Carissa's bed. Nothing. Then her closet, the boys' room under their beds. Kids often hid during fires. Plus, the air was better down here.

He was not going to lose someone else he loved. *He was not.* He might not have been able to save Autumn and Ava, but he could save Jayden.

"Charlie!" Maybe the dog would respond. His natural fear of fire should help.

A slightly muffled *woof,* but from where?

The room Carissa was rehabbing. The one with the secret room. Jonas hunched over as he ran to the room. "Charlie!

Jayden!" The *woof* was louder this time. And the panel to the secret room was shut.

He ran over and pushed on it. "Jayden, it's Jonas. We've got to go. It's not safe here."

Charlie was digging on the other side while Jonas frantically pushed on the panel, trying to find the right spot. "Help me out here, buddy."

The panel popped open, and Charlie leaped out, licking Jonas. Jonas snapped the leash on his collar and reached inside the space. Jayden was huddled in a ball in the corner. As he grabbed Jayden, it looked like a small strongbox and a lifted wood plank sat to the side. No time to think about it now and not enough hands to grab it. He lifted Jayden into his arms, and they hurried down the stairs.

Thank you, Jesus.

Outside, the fresh air was a balm to his achy lungs. The fire engine pulled up as he descended the stairs. It took a second, but he spotted Carissa across the way with Brandon and Gladys. He hurried over.

Carissa's arms opened, and he set Jayden on his feet inside her embrace. Just as he started to check in with her, movement caught his eye. Someone was darting into the house.

Samuel!

Jonas took off, running back up the front steps and inside, smoke burning his eyes and lungs. "Samuel!"

The kid stopped a few steps up. "It's Eli. He's inside. He's after the money."

Sure enough, Eli was headed toward the top of the stairs.

Jonas took them two at a time. Eli paused at the top, as if trying to orient himself. Jonas tackled him, pulling Eli's arm behind his back in a submission hold.

Before Jonas could even wrangle Eli to his feet, heavy boots climbed the stairs as the firefighters approached.

"You guys gotta get out of here. Anyone hurt?"

It took Jonas a moment to recognize Marco in full gear.

Jonas hauled Eli to his feet. His eyes were streaming, his lungs burning. "On our way."

Outside, Brett Chang had arrived, and Jonas turned Eli over to him to be cuffed and Mirandized, then he went to check on Carissa and the boys.

Brandon sat on the side of the road, tears running down his face, hugging Charlie. Samuel and Gladys stood behind him.

Carissa had both arms wrapped around Jayden, who was struggling to break free.

Jonas knelt next to them, enfolding both of them in his arms, and putting his mouth next to Jayden's ear. "Hey, buddy. It's okay. It's gonna be okay."

"My Legos!" Jayden wailed, throwing himself against Jonas's chest. "They'll get burned up."

"We can buy you new ones, I promise. But we have to keep you safe. See all the gear those firefighters are wearing? They need that to protect them. Fire is very dangerous."

Jayden stopped thrashing about and studied the firefighters, momentarily mesmerized by all the activity as they lugged hoses across the yard.

Carissa eased her hold, and Jonas pulled Jayden onto his lap as they both sat on the ground, watching the firefighters work. Jonas pointed out everything he could think of—from the truck to the hoses to the turnout gear, trying to keep Jayden engaged and occupied.

Carissa's hand landed on Jonas's shoulder, squeezing.

He glanced up.

"Thank you," she whispered.

He nodded. He needed to interview Eli, but he also wanted to make sure Jayden was calm enough before he left.

Carissa sank to the ground next to them, and he transferred Jayden to her lap. "I've got to take care of a few things, but I'll be back soon, okay? I'm just going over there." He pointed to Chang's unit. Once Jayden nodded, Jonas got to his feet.

Eli was sitting in the back of the unit when Jonas

approached. He bent down and peered in. "What were you doing in Carissa's house?"

Eli didn't say anything, just stared straight ahead.

"You come for the money?"

That got Eli's attention. His head whipped around. "Where was it?"

"Is that why you killed Tyler? For the money?"

Anger flashed across Eli's face. "We didn't kill him. He fell through the railing. He was stumbling around upstairs. I tried to stop him from going after Kayla. She whacked him good with a piece of wood. But he leaned over the railing, calling after her, and it broke. He fell and landed weird, on his head." His eyes widened as anger morphed to panic. "You've got to believe me. It was an accident. But I was on probation and didn't want to get in trouble. So Anthony and I borrowed some equipment from Vince and buried Tyler in the basement and told everyone he said he was heading out on a road trip. We didn't know what else to do. The moon rumors were Anthony's idea." Eli sagged against the back of the seat.

Jonas would interview Anthony again to corroborate Eli's story, but it fit with the coroner's findings on Tyler's death and Kayla's testimony. He straightened and looked at Chang.

"I'll take him in and get him booked." Chang glanced back toward the side of the road where everyone had gathered. "Looks like you have your hands full."

Jonas nodded. The fire was knocked down. He needed to find Marco. "Thanks, Brett." He tapped the unit and moved off, searching the turnout coats for one that said VALDEZ on the back of it. Spotting him, Jonas jogged over. "Hey, how's it look?"

Marco turned. "Fire's out. We'll spend the rest of the night on overhaul, pulling down walls, making sure fire isn't lingering anywhere inside. The garage is a total loss. So is her SUV. The back porch, mudroom, and kitchen all have significant damage. The rest of the house will have smoke and water damage."

All that hard work up in flames. Carissa's burden settled on

Jonas's shoulders. But there was one thing he could do. "I need you to find something for me."

JONAS STEPPED ASIDE TO SPEAK WITH THE OWNER OF THE Belleville Flats Diner while everyone else got settled at the table. It was nearly closing time, but he knew the owner would be okay with staying open late if he knew the circumstances. And he was.

He hoped the Old West theme, complete with cowhide upholstery, farming and ranching implements mounted on the walls, and even hay embedded in the plaster would serve as an entertaining distraction. Jonas seated himself next to Carissa. Brandon and Jayden sat across from them, and Jonathan, Alison, Liane, and Lily filled out the rest of the table. Jonas had jogged home to get his truck and called Jonathan on the way to explain what happened and to ask them to meet up at the diner. Jonas knew he needed to get Carissa and the boys away from the scene, and comfort food seemed like a good choice.

The scent of smoke still lingered as they placed their orders. The mood was somber and subdued, but once Jonas started asking the girls about the rides they went on, the discussion got lively as Brandon piped in about the rides he liked. By the time their food came, they were talking about what they wanted to do at ArtFest tomorrow.

Carissa leaned over to Jonas. "I don't even know where to begin."

"One step at a time. I'll get you over to Sleepy Bear Lodge tonight. Tomorrow will be soon enough to begin making plans. Letting the kids go to ArtFest seems like a good one."

The door to the diner opened, and Pastor Tony stepped in.

Jonas wasn't too surprised. News traveled fast, and Tony would want to offer his help. Jonas waved him over. "Come join us. We can pull up another chair."

"Thanks, I can't stay long."

Jonas introduced Tony to his brother and family. Tony shook everyone's hands, asked the girls about the fair, then squatted down next to Carissa. "I'm so sorry about your house." He handed her a gift card. "This is to help you replace some necessities while you're waiting for everything to get sorted out. If you need anything, just let me know. We'll get you taken care of."

Tears welled up in Carissa's eyes, and Jonas watched her struggle to keep her emotions under control. "Thank you so much."

"We're a family." Tony stood and patted Carissa's shoulder. "Jonas, can I speak to you for a moment?"

"Sure." He pushed his chair back and bent down close to Carissa. "I won't be long."

She nodded, and he and Tony headed to the front. "Thanks for doing that for her. I know she's overwhelmed."

"Hopefully, I can help with that. I have an idea I wanted to run by you." Tony's shoulders slumped, and he looked like he was carrying the weight of the world, which was unusual for him.

"Shoot."

"If you wanted, you could let Carissa and the boys stay at your house. You have a fenced yard for Charlie."

Tony hadn't finished talking before alarm bells started going off in Jonas's head. No way could he live in the same house as Carissa without compromising their morals. He actually couldn't believe Tony was suggesting it.

"And you could stay with me." Tony finished.

Jonas's brain caught up with Tony's words. "Wait. What?"

Tony shifted his stance. "I really screwed up with Shannon. And I could use some support. I won't bore you with all the details right now; you've got enough on your plate. But I wanted to make the offer so you guys could start making arrangements. I talked to Marco—who's on his way over—and the rehab is going to take some time. I don't want Carissa to have to spend money for housing if she doesn't have to."

"Tony, I don't know what to say. That's a generous offer. Thank you. I think that could be the perfect solution." He was certain this would take a load off Carissa's mind, and he'd do anything to make that happen.

Before he could say anything else, the restaurant door opened again. Marco entered still wearing his turnout pants and boots but not his coat. The smell of smoke was even stronger on him. His hands were full of bags. Jonas didn't even ask how Marco knew where they were.

"Hey, guys. We grabbed some clothes and toiletries for Carissa and the boys to tide them over until it's safe to get in their house." Marco set the bags down and pulled a metal box out of one. "And I found this for you. It was right where you said." He handed it to Jonas.

It was the strongbox. Jonas popped it open. A Lego guy sat on top of a pile of cash. He smiled. Jayden clearly had found this earlier.

"Thanks, Marco. For all of it."

"Sure thing. Tell Carissa we'll be in touch tomorrow about her house." Marco left.

Tony turned to him. "I'll be going too. But let me know what you decide."

"I will." Jonas shook Tony's hand, meeting the man's gaze. Soon Jonas would have to learn what burdened Tony. He couldn't imagine that he'd screwed up bad enough to end things with Shannon. It didn't seem possible. "Thank you."

Tony nodded and left.

Jonas took a deep breath then gathered up the bags, tucking the strongbox back inside one of them. He'd take it to the department after getting everything settled tonight. When he returned to the table, the conversation flowed as if he'd never left. Carissa and Alison were deep in conversation, and Jonathan and the kids were discussing a movie they'd all seen. His heart warmed.

"Marco brought you guys some things from your house to tide you over until you can get back in safely." He tucked the bags under the table next to Carissa.

Carissa's eyes welled again. "That was so kind." She looked through the bags and lifted a small, plastic bin. She shook it, and Jayden's gaze darted to her.

"My Legos! They didn't all get burned up." He grabbed the case from Carissa and burst into tears.

Jonas picked him up and tucked his head into his chest. "It's okay, bud."

Jayden sobbed, his little shoulders shaking.

Poor little guy. It'd been a rough day. He glanced at Carissa.

She was holding back tears. "Thank you," she mouthed.

He needed to get them to the lodge so they could get to bed. And maybe Carissa could get in the shower and let out all those tears she'd been suppressing. Tomorrow would be here soon enough. "What do you say about getting out of here?"

Carissa nodded, and Jonathan, Alison, and the other kids gathered their things and left the restaurant. Jonas carried Jayden —who was clinging to his neck—out to his truck. Carissa and Brandon lugged the bags Marco had dropped off.

Charlie, who had been left in the truck, whined at their approach.

Jonathan held Carissa's door for her. "Let's plan on us picking you guys up for breakfast and then heading to ArtFest."

Jonas was buckling Jayden into his booster seat. "Great. Then I can meet you all when I get free. I have a few things to take care of first." He slipped Charlie a hamburger patty he'd gotten for him. The dog inhaled it in two gulps.

Carissa agreed, but she was clearly exhausted. A few minutes later, they were pulling up to the Sleepy Bear Lodge. She checked in, and Jonas helped her get the boys and their bags to their room.

Mariah wasn't around, a small mercy he was grateful for. He hoped she'd found someone to dance with. It seemed nearly impossible that his encounter with her had happened just earlier tonight.

Once their bags were deposited in their room, Carissa pulled the boys and Jonas into her arms, wrapping all of them together. Her tears wet his neck.

Right now, everything that mattered to him was right here.

CHAPTER
THIRTY-SIX

Carissa eased out of the hotel bed and started some coffee. The boys slept like the dead, so she didn't worry about waking them. Even though she'd showered last night, the boys had been asleep when she'd gotten out. The faint smell of smoke lingered, probably on them. Maybe it was permanently imprinted on her.

She didn't really want to go to Artfest today. But it was a Sunday, so she wasn't going to get anywhere with the insurance company. The boys deserved some fun, and Jon and Alison were very sweet. Under different circumstances, she'd enjoy getting to know Jonas's family.

The coffee sputtered out of the drip basket into the foam cup, and she added a little plastic cup of cream. Leaning against the desk, she watched the boys sleep. She'd need to wake them soon, but for now… Jonas had been good with Jayden last night, giving him the security and distraction he needed. Previously she had wondered what it would be like the first time Jonas saw one of Jayden's meltdowns, but he'd taken it in stride. It did funny things to her heart, things she didn't have the brain space to dissect.

She sipped her coffee and peered out the curtains at the

lovely sunny day. They should go to church. It was within walking distance. But she wasn't sure she was ready to face everyone and their condolences yet. The pain was too raw, and she hated crying in front of people. She'd done enough of that last night, thank you very much.

So breakfast and ArtFest with Jon and Alison and the girls sounded like the ticket.

Time to get ready. She rummaged through the bags Marco had brought them. He'd been great. It was a little weird to think of him in her underwear drawer, but clearly he'd just grabbed handfuls of things. He was probably more embarrassed, even though she was sure he did it all the time. And she was grateful for clean undies and clothes. Plus, bringing Jayden's Legos had been a godsend. He clearly knew what would bring comfort to a family who had just lost their home.

She was still in a daze last night when he'd told her about her house. But it sounded like the upstairs rooms were okay except for the smoke. However, until the house was deemed stable enough to enter, they couldn't retrieve anything. And Gladys's house had been fine. The wind off the lake pushed the fire from the garage into the house.

There was much to be thankful for. Her brain started spinning, wanted to make lists of what needed to be done. But it could wait.

She slid a finger across her phone, opening the photos app. The pictures she'd taken of the work she'd done on the house would come in handy for the insurance. She came across the photo she'd take of the words she'd slapped up on the dining room wall before she'd painted over them. She stared at them a moment and thought about what Jonas had said about them being true. Something she'd only barely hoped to believe in he already saw as fact.

And he'd backed up those words with his actions—last night and many other times before. The bud of hope in her heart began to blossom into something she was sure was going to be beautiful. She could finally see it.

Carissa took one last look at the boys' sleeping faces. So peaceful. Then she shook their feet to wake them. "Ready for some pancakes?"

Jonas left the interview room and headed into Shannon's office. She was in, which was weird for a Sunday. But perhaps, given what Tony had told him, she didn't want to hear him preach today. And given the closed-off look on her face, she wasn't open to discussing it.

"Interviews done?" She had a bag of peanut M&Ms open on her desk, jumbo size.

"Yes. Anthony's and Kayla's accounts corroborate what Eli said. Anthony was charged with a number of misdemeanors for tampering with evidence and interfering with human remains. He'll be out on bail soon. If he and Eli hadn't panicked four years ago, they wouldn't have been in trouble. The investigation would have cleared them. But Eli has just made things worse for himself. Arson is a felony, and so is attempted murder, since Carissa and the boys were inside her house when he set the fire."

"I'm glad the case is finally wrapped up." She popped a handful of M&Ms in her mouth.

"Me too. I ran prints on the strongbox and recorded the amount of money in the report, but I'll return it to Carissa since it has no bearing on the case. Less than a thousand dollars. Such a small amount for the trouble Eli ended up in." Jonas sat for a moment, waiting to see if she'd say anything further.

The sheriff let out a sigh. "Thanks. Now get out of here and go enjoy ArtFest."

He kept his gaze on her another beat, then did as she ordered. He climbed in his unit and swung by Carissa's house on his way home. He wanted to see what progress was being made and when it could be released. Caution tape ringed her picket fence, but the fire department had left.

However, someone stood across the street staring at the house. Kayla Mills.

Jonas parked, climbed out of his unit, and headed over to her.

Kayla didn't turn as he walked up. Her arms wrapped across her middle. "It's so sad that it burned. I was always afraid we would burn it down with all those stupid candles we lit as kids." She finally turned to Jonas. "Is she going to rebuild it?"

"I don't know. I haven't talked to her about it yet."

"I hope she does." Her voice was wistful. "Thank you for finding out the truth about Tyler. I did care about him at one time. It's good to know what really happened."

Jonas nodded. "Closure is usually helpful."

"I need to go so I can catch my flight. I don't anticipate ever returning here, but I'd like to see pictures if she does decide to restore the house."

"I'll make a note of that."

Kayla climbed in her rental car and drove off.

Jonas studied the blackened shell. The front didn't look too bad. He could picture himself helping Carissa rebuild. He was sure Tony and Alex would help too. The only question was did she want to?

After another long look, he got into his unit and wove his way to the fairgrounds, parking in the sheriff department's reserved spaces. He wasn't on duty, but he'd be available if they needed help. Which he hoped they wouldn't.

He texted Carissa.

Where are you guys?

Near the Tilt-a-Whirl by the giant slide.

Be there in a few.

Once he got to the rides, the giant slide was easily visible. After a bit of searching, he found Carissa next to Jon and Alison. He pulled her into a hug and kissed the top of her head. "Where are the kids?"

She nodded toward the Amazing Maze of Mirrors. "Hopefully, they'll find their way out eventually. Have you eaten?"

"Nope. I wanted to find you first."

"If you and Jon want to go get food, Alison and I can wait here for the kids."

"Anything in particular you want?"

Carissa grinned. "It's fair food. Fried and sugared. What could be bad about that?"

He intertwined his fingers with hers, not quite wanting to let her go, but Jon was clearly eager. Jonas squeezed her hand before releasing it. "We'll be quick."

Jon led the way, and they headed toward the food stands. "Get everything wrapped up?" Jon asked.

"Yeah, finally. Thanks for taking care of Carissa and the boys this morning. I knew they'd need the distraction."

"Happy to. I really like her, Jonas. Her boys too." Jon stopped in front of a stand that had potatoes fried every which way. A tornado potato, deep-fried potato salad, loaded potato skins. "Last night." Jon blinked away moisture that gathered in his eyes. "You were great with Jayden. I've missed seeing you in dad mode. You did good."

Jonas's own eyes grew wet. He cleared his throat. "Thanks, man. That means a lot." It was like a blessing he didn't know he was hungry for was being conferred on him. Because Jon was talking about more than last night. He was telling Jonas he could have a good future with Carissa and the boys. Jon could see it.

And so could Jonas.

CARISSA WONDERED WHAT THE NEXT TWENTY-FOUR HOURS would bring; the last twenty-four had been a doozy. Jonas was taking them someplace special, but he wouldn't say where. Carissa didn't really care. All she knew was they were driving around the lake.

Jon, Alison, and the girls had left a few hours ago to head home after a fun-but-exhausting day at ArtFest. Brandon and Jayden were pleasantly worn out, Charlie between them on the back seat.

Jonas turned off the main road onto a barely visible stretch of dirt that wound among the trees. He stopped in front of a chain that blocked them.

She raised her eyebrows, but he just grinned and hopped out, unlocking the chain and driving through. After a few minutes, the road opened to a clearing. He pulled to the side. "We're here."

And once she slipped out of his truck, she realized where they were: a lookout over the lake with a fantastic view of the west, where the sun would soon slip away. "This is fantastic. I had no idea it was here."

He grinned as he slid his arm around her waist, his other hand holding Charlie's leash. "I know. It's for locals only. It's called Little Bear Lookout. We gather here to watch the sunset. Since it's the last night of ArtFest, we might not get as many people, which is fine with me. But we should have a good view of the fireworks."

Benches hewn out of logs ringed a firepit that looked like it had been unused for some time.

Jonas stopped the boys. "Don't run off. I'm going to show you how to get down safely to the lake." He turned to Carissa. "Wait for me?"

"Absolutely." She grinned.

He winked at her then directed the boys down a trail where they disappeared.

She needed a minute anyway, and this was a beautiful place to take it. She sat on one of the benches, letting the peace soak into her soul.

Jonas was back shortly, this time alone. "It's safe, I promise." He slid onto the bench next to her, draping his arm over her shoulders.

"Okay." After last night, she was still shaken by the thought of losing her boys. She hadn't slept much. At least the house was insured. But there was a lot of damage. She'd wondered deep into the night if maybe she shouldn't just pack it up and... Do what? Where would they go? This town had become their family. And as crazy as that house had been, it had become their home.

"The fireworks will start once it gets dark. And there's going to be a full moon. The blue moon." Jonas's fingers trailed along her shoulder.

"So the crazies showed up at my house a day early?"

"I think that was just a coincidence. Eli wasn't thinking about the moon. He was thinking about money. Jayden found the lockbox when he was playing in the secret room. It was under a loose board. Marco brought it to me last night. It's in evidence right now, but you'll get it back soon. It's just under a thousand dollars. A lot of money for a kid doing tutoring but not enough to really help you with the house." He told her what he'd learned from Eli, Anthony, and Kayla about how Tyler's death had been an accident.

"They started the moon rumors and stuff like that to keep people from buying your house. Anthony had been digging around your bushes when you moved in, looking for the money. He figured Tyler's body would be found soon, and he wanted a chance at getting the cash."

Carissa shuddered. "I'm just glad that mystery is solved."

"Me too." Jonas shifted on the bench until he was facing her.

He took her hand in his. "I need to tell you about the box of Autumn's things you discovered."

"You don't have to. I overreacted."

"I want to. I had the box out because, when I was putting her picture away the other day, I realized there were pictures of us together with Jon and Alison. I thought they might want them. So I'd pulled them out, intending to give the photos to them. But I had to hurry off to work and forgot to put the box back. I know how it must have looked to you." He ran his thumb over the back of her hand.

"You had a happy marriage before. I had an unhappy one." She let out a sigh. "I guess I was worried that I'd come up short in comparison to her, of what the two of you had together. But I also see how you have treated me and the boys, especially the last twenty-four hours. Maybe the concern will always be there in some form, but it's faded."

He lifted her hand to his lips and kissed it. "You and Autumn are very different. She and I didn't have a perfect marriage. I don't think anyone does. But my feelings for her have mellowed into something more like a fondness for an old friend. My feelings for you are quite different than that." His slid his hand up the back of Carissa's neck. "I'm never going to leave you, Carissa. I love you. And the boys." He grinned. "And that silly dog."

She smiled. "I love you too."

He leaned forward and kissed her, gently at first, and then more intently with all the hope and promise the future held for them.

When he broke the kiss, she leaned back, warm and content.

"Before the boys get back, I have something I want you to consider." He gazed at her fully. "I want you and the boys to move out of Sleepy Bear Lodge and into my cabin. I'll stay with Tony until your house is ready."

It took a minute for his words to sink in. "And Pastor Tony is okay with this?"

"He is. Things are rocky with him and Shannon right now, and I think he'd like the company."

"That's amazing, Jonas. I was wondering how we were going to continue to pay for Sleepy Bear Lodge. Cope House is completely booked, though I know the Wilders would put us up if they could."

"So you've decided to continue working on it?"

She nodded. "It's our home." And it was.

The boys came running up the path, Charlie on their heels. The full moon tipped over the trees behind them as dusk settled in fully.

Jonas pointed out to the boys where the fireworks would take place. They settled on the bench with the best view. Carissa was happy they would be far enough away. Jayden wasn't a fan of the loudness of fireworks.

"That full moon is awfully bright. It'll compete with the fireworks." Jonas slipped his arm around her shoulders as the first fireworks lit the sky. Luckily, the sound was a small *pop* and not a *bang*.

She snuggled into him. "I think we need to rethink the legend around these full moons. First, I suggest calling it something other than a blue moon. That's such a vague term for blue. I'm voting for indigo, a moody dark blue that matches the evening sky."

He laughed. "Okay, I'm with you. But what should the legend be?"

She pretended to think for a moment. "We must always visit the lake under the full moon. And if we can't do that, then you must kiss me under it."

"That's a legend I can get behind. Kissing under an indigo moon." Jonas kissed her cheek, and they watched the rest of the display.

After the grand finale, Jonas and Carissa got to their feet as the boys ran over.

"That was awesome," Brandon said.

"Those kind weren't scary," Jayden said.

Carissa slipped her arm around Jonas's waist as she hugged her boys. Soon they were in one big group hug. Everything that was important to her—and her future—was right here.

They were home.

AFTERWORD

Hey, this is Anne Cartwright, the librarian. If you want to know something about this town, ask me. I know. Believe me, I know.

Do you want to know if Shannon and Tony can figure things out?

And what about Alex and Claire? What's their story? It's told in the novella, *The Inn at Cherry Blossom Lane*, and you can get it for free by going here: https://bookhip.com/RRCKMX

And Samuel? He originally met Alex and Claire in the short story, "An Evening to Remember." You can get it too by going here: https://bookhip.com/GBWDCXL

Finally, someone's getting married! If you read the In the Shadow series book 1 *Off the Map*, you'll be happy to know that Allie and Collins are finally tying the knot in our lovely town. Read about it here: https://BookHip.com/KJGKMZX

These bonuses will make you my guests of Insider Updates. Some of your favorite characters (that might possibly be me) will make an appearance on occasion, and JL has specials that only her Insiders have access to. It's totally worth it.

You'll also get the prequel novella to the Hometown Heroes series, *Promise Me*— Grayson and Cait's story. It's adorable. I haven't met them yet in person, but I hope they'll come up to Holcomb Springs soon.

I promise I won't share your email address with anyone but JL, and you can unsubscribe at any time, but why would you want to miss out?

Do you know how I spend most of my day? As a librarian, I recommend books to people. You can do that too. If you enjoyed this book, please leave a review. It's simply telling other readers what you loved about this book. It can be as simple as "I couldn't put it down. I can't wait for the next one." It helps raise the author's visibility and lets other readers find her. Because I can't talk to everyone. But I'm trying!

—Anne Cartwright, librarian and historian, Holcomb Springs

ACKNOWLEDGMENTS

This book would not be possible without the patience and willingness to read early drafts by Jennifer Lynn Cary. Jenny gets an extra dose of thanks for helping me brainstorm when I got stuck. Many thanks to my early readers!

My team at Tandem Services—Brooke, Colleen, and Morgan—are the best editors anyone could hope for. They made this book better.

Much thanks and love to my children, Caitlyn Elizabeth and Joshua Alexander, for supporting my dream for many years and giving me time to write.

And most of all to my Lord Jesus, who makes all things possible and directs my paths.

AUTHOR'S NOTE

This might have been one of my hardest books to write. Mostly it had to do with life getting in the way. But I also caught the dreaded virus while I still had 25,000 words left to write. I don't remember writing most of that part of the book, but I do remember feeling like I had rushed the ending and had no more energy to fix it. I was up against a pre-order deadline, so the book had to get finished.

Because I have an amazing team of editors, I knew they'd tell me what I was missing, and I hoped to have enough energy to write what was needed at that point. They did, and I did.

I've played around with the idea for this book for a long time. As per usual, my story ideas often end up being quite different in reality from how I envisioned them. This book was originally supposed to be a women's fiction book. But when I started plotting the Holcomb Springs Small Town Romantic Suspense series, I knew I wanted to include the story. Which meant it needed to become a romance and a mystery.

Ultimately, I was happy with Carissa and Jonas's story. I've enjoyed crafting the town of Holcomb Springs and its quirky characters. While the town of Holcomb Springs doesn't exist, there is a Holcomb Valley that was the site of a gold rush in the

1860s. I took the liberty of imagining what would have happened if that boomtown—known as Belleville—had continued on to become a resort town similar to Big Bear or Lake Arrowhead. I liked the idea of having a small town on the edge of the wilderness with all of the problems and possibilities it can bring. And it was within driving distance of Laguna Vista, so all of our old friends could come up and visit. I hope you enjoy what's to come.

ABOUT THE AUTHOR

My favorite thing is discovering how much there is to love about America the Beautiful and the great outdoors. I'm an Amazon bestselling author, a mom to two navigating the young adult years while battling my daughter's juvenile arthritis, exploring the delights of my son's autism, and keeping gluten free.

A California native who's spent significant time in the Midwest, I'm thrilled to be back in the Golden State. Follow me on social media to see all my adventures and how I get inspired for my books!

JLCrosswhite.com

Buy books directly from me here: JCrosswhiteBooks.myshopify.com

Twitter: @jenlcross

Facebook: Author Jennifer Crosswhite

Instagram: jencrosswhite

Pinterest: Tandem Services

facebook.com/authorjennifercrosswhite

x.com/jenlcross

instagram.com/jencrosswhite

pinterest.com/tandemservices

BOOKS BY JL CROSSWHITE

Romantic Suspense

The Hometown Heroes Series

Promise Me

Cait can't catch a break. What she witnessed could cost her job and her beloved farmhouse. Will Greyson help her or only make things worse?

Protective Custody

She's a key witness in a crime shaking the roots of the town's power brokers. He's protecting a woman he'll risk everything for. Doing the right thing may cost her everything. Including her life.

Flash Point

She's a directionally-challenged architect who stumbled on a crime that could destroy her life's work. He's a firefighter protecting his hometown… and the woman he loves.

Special Assignment

A brain-injured Navy pilot must work with the woman in charge of the program he blames for his injury. As they both grasp to save their careers, will their growing attraction hinder them as they attempt solve the mystery of who's really at fault before someone else dies?

In the Shadow Series

Off the Map

For her, it's a road trip adventure. For him, it's his best shot to win her back. But for the stalker after her, it's revenge.

Out of Range

It's her chance to prove she's good enough. It's his chance to prove he's more than just a fun guy. Is it their time to find love, or is her secret admirer his deadly competition?

Over Her Head

On a church singles' camping trip that no one wants to be on, a weekend away to renew and refresh becomes anything but. A group of friends trying to find their footing do a good deed and get much more than they bargained for.

Holcomb Springs Small Town Romantic Suspense

Beneath a Star-Lit Sky

When Reese and Ella are thrown together on the overnighter, what starts as a simple trek ends up being filled with danger when they stumble across something they weren't supposed to see.

Under an Indigo Moon

A single mom starting over has dropped all her savings into vacant Victorian she bought at an online auction, hoping to flipping and build a better life. But when things go missing, her house is vandalized, and the basement contains a grizzly surprise, she wonders what she's really gotten them into. Is this one more bad decision or something truly dangerous?

BOOKS BY JENNIFER CROSSWHITE

Contemporary Romance

The Inn at Cherry Blossom Lane

Can the summer magic of Lake Michigan bring first loves back together? Or will the secret they discover threaten everything they love?

Historical Romance

The Route Home Series

Be Mine

A woman searching for independence. A man searching for education. Can a simple thank you note turn into something more?

Coming Home

He was why she left. Now she's falling for him. Can a woman who turned her back on her hometown come home to find justice for her brother without falling in love with his best friend?

The Road Home

He is a stagecoach driver just trying to do his job. She is returning to her suitor only to find he has died. When a stack of stolen money shows up in her bag, she thinks the past she has desperately tried to hide has come back to haunt her.

Finally Home

The son of a wealthy banker, Hank Paulson poses as a lumberjack to carve out his own identity. But in a stagecoach robbery gone wrong, he meets Amelia Martin, a a soon-to-be schoolteacher with a vivid imagination, a gift for making things grow, and an obsession with dime novels. As the town is threatened by a past enemy, Hank might just be the hero they all need. Can he help without revealing who he is? And will Amelia love him when she learns the truth?